A CYCLIST'S GUIDE to VILLAINS & VINES

ANN CLAIRE

Kensington Publishing Corp.
kensingtonbooks.com

KENSINGTON BOOKS are published by

Kensington Publishing Corp.
900 Third Avenue
New York, NY 10022

ISBN: 978-1-4967-4572-9
ISBN: 978-1-4967-4573-6 (ebook)

First Kensington Hardcover Edition: June 2025
First Kensington Trade Edition: May 2026

10 9 8 7 6 5 4 3 2 1

Printed in the United States of America

The authorized representative in the EU for product safety and compliance is eucomply OU, Parnu mnt 139b-14, Apt 123
Tallinn, Berlin 11317, hello@eucompliancepartner.com

Praise for *A Cyclist's Guide to Crime & Croissants*

"Fasten your bike helmets and prepare for a thrilling ride through the French countryside with a plucky heroine, a group of cycling tourists, and a murderer." —Ellery Adams, *New York Times* bestselling author

"A delicious, fast-paced mystery across the French countryside with a spirited amateur sleuth, a vibrant cast of characters, and a mélange of memorable suspects. Grab this one tout de suite!" —Cleo Coyle, *New York Times* bestselling author

"Aside from the rain and the murders, a good time is had by all." —*Kirkus Reviews*

"Buttery, layered, and dangerous. . . . This oddly soothing, picturesque adventure through the South of France somewhat incidentally involves a little murder." —*Rocky Mountain Reader*

"Hits all the right notes with scents, scenery, the people, and the fantastic food. . . . Warning: you'll want to stock up on French cheeses and croissants!" —Krista Davis, *New York Times* bestselling author

"I thoroughly enjoyed this cycling tour through the French countryside. Descriptions of the scenery were vivid enough to make me feel like part of the group, and the food was *superbe*! Tour owner Sadie Greene was both savvy and relatable as she wrangled a diverse set of cyclist suspects with aplomb. I'd be happy to follow her anywhere." —Laurien Berenson, author of *Peg and Rose Stir Up Trouble* and the Melanie Travis Canine mysteries

"A fun, fast-paced ride through France, and readers will be left eager for a return trip to Sans-Souci-sur-Mer." —*BookPage*

"Claire's novel is a lighthearted whodunit with a touch of continental flair." —*Boulder Weekly*

The *Cyclist's Guide* Mysteries by Ann Claire

A Cyclist's Guide to Crime & Croissants

A Cyclist's Guide to Villains & Vines

A Cyclist's Guide to Poppies & Predicaments

Dedication: To Laura, your brilliant story ended too soon.

A note about places: The towns and villages visited on this Oui Cycle tour are real, although the main village of Riquewihr has been modified for the sake of sleuthing. L'Auberge des Trois Cigognes and its surroundings are purely fictional.

STAGE 1: Pedal Back in Time

CHAPTER 1

Saturday:
The village of Riquewihr, just after midnight.

KEEP PEDALING AND LEAVE YOUR REGRETS IN THE DUST. So said a mug I once spotted in a thrift store back in my hometown of Elm Park, Illinois. I still think of that mug. Not because it was a rare find. The base had a chip, and all-cap italics dubbed it the property of *STEVE*.

I'm Sadie. Sadie Greene, proud proprietress of Oui Cycle, the best little bicycling-tour company in southern France. But pedal away regrets? There's a message I can embrace.

I urge my sleep-soggy legs to pedal faster. My wheels and bones chatter over ancient cobblestones as I aim for the flickering halo of my headlamp. Too far ahead, another lamp bobbles into the darkness. A darker darkness, I note. Overhead, clouds as gnarled as witches' fingers grasp at a plump moon. *Run!* I want to yell to the unsuspecting celestial body. *Look out behind you!*

For a moment, the moon appears to hear. With a triumphant glow, it slips free, etching the skyline like a page from a pop-up storybook. Steeply pitched roofs glimmer in dragon-scale tiles. Stork nests as big as king-sized beds perch atop chimneys, and a tower of stone and timbers watches over the slumbering village.

A surreal feeling grips me. *My bike and I have ridden back in time!* I imagine the sights and sounds. Women in rustling gowns, come down from the castle on the hill. The scrape and creak of wooden-wheeled carts, the clop of hooves. Minstrels and knights, bakers and archers and—

My front wheel slams into a gap-toothed pit in the cobblestones. Reality shoots back with pain from my wrists to my molars. My lamp stutters.

All the while, regret spins merrily along at my side.

Leave your regrets in the dust? That mug was a liar!

Do I regret sinking my life savings into a bike touring company I purchased sight unseen? Never! Do I wish I was still toiling in my suburban Chicago accounting cubicle instead of leading cycling tours around glorious France? Double, triple, infinite times nope! However, while I may be a former accountant, I'm a forever enumerator. I shake aches from my wrists and launch a mental tally of remorse.

For one, I should have bought that mug. The message was inspiring, and for $1.99, I could have overlooked the chip. As for Steve, well . . . I could have launched a Steveware collection worthy of an ironic coffeehouse. Plus, the vessel was technically a vat, capable of holding a good four cups of coffee, the minimum I'll need in the morning.

Correction, later this morning. My eardrums still reverberate from riding under church bells announcing the time in sixteen clangs: four for the top of the hour, twelve for the time.

There's a bigger regret: it's after midnight. I should be back in my bed. And what a luxurious bed it is, fit for a princess and the posh inn my tour group will call home for the next week. The pillows are perfectly plump, the sheets soft as silken filigree, and the eiderdown duvet just right for the dew-cooled night.

Which rolls into my prime regret: not only did I abandon my bed, but I also let Keiko Andersson drag me out into the dark. Ye olde fallacy, "The client is always right," requires serious questioning at all hours but especially around midnight.

A bang slices the inky silence. A door? A shutter? Jousting knights? A dog barks, a single sharp note bouncing off tile and stone. My rationalizations tap out their own tally.

I am out here because Keiko Andersson—a guest—begged me for help. Because she was ashen-cheeked and insistent. Because of what she saw.

Said she saw, I amend. *Thought she saw.*

I shift to rational explanations: Keiko saw a shadow, a trick of the dueling moon and clouds. Things look different at night. We've proven that by circling the village of Riquewihr at least three times, searching for the spot where Keiko—

Nope! I won't even think the words. There are so many more probable possibilities. A nasty prank. An honest misunderstanding. A medical emergency, happily resolved.

That's really why I'm out here. I am here to politely prove my tour guest wrong. Keiko will thank me later. We'll laugh about it in the morning. Better yet, we'll never mention it again.

I stomp on my pedals. Farther ahead, Keiko zips around a corner, a sixty-eight-year-old leaving me in her dust. In my defense, she's on an e-bike from my new battery-assisted fleet. If my wheels and teeth stopped clattering, I could follow the bike's breathy acceleration through the quiet lanes.

I've never seen Riquewihr so deserted. Granted, I haven't

ridden its streets after midnight. I've only been here a week. I arrived early to plan for this tour. More correctly, to cram like a student who's forgotten to attend class all semester, the night before the final.

There's another regret: I need sleep if I'm going to bring my guiding A-game to this group. Sure, they seem like six pleasant seniors, a cycling club with a cute name, the Silver Spinners. They are pleasant and enthusiastic. They're also intimidating and know everything about, well . . . everything.

I want to wow the Silver Spinners. They want to be wowed. They said so on their pre-tour questionnaire. *Stun us! Thrill us! Show us something to die for!*

No dying! Death is *not* on our itinerary!

As for wowing, I'd feel more confident back in my home base of Sans-Souci-sur-Mer, a village with "no worries" right in its name, nestled between the Mediterranean Sea and the high Pyrénées. The Silver Spinners requested a tour in Alsace in the northeast of France, my farthest tour from home yet. Don't get me wrong, I'm thrilled to be here. Alsace is glorious, an idyllic wonderland of fairy-tale half-timbered houses and rolling vineyards, perfect for cycling.

This, however, is not my idea of idyllic. I round a corner too fast. My back wheel skids. An age-buckled wall juts into my path, pale as bone. I do what I warn my guests against. I squeeze my brakes and propel toward the handlebars.

Accidents can happen faster than a blink on a bike, the stuff of a cycle guide's nightmares. I wrestle my bike back into balance and face a personal guiding fear: I've lost my rider.

"Keiko?" I stage-whisper into the inky silence.

Narrow lanes spoke in three directions, gobbled by shadows. The clouds have caught the moon, and moths muffle the wan glow of an antique streetlamp. Reading the mood, my handlebar lamp flickers, dims, and dies.

Great. Just great. Cue another regret. I failed to charge my lamp. A year into professional tour guiding and I'm still making rookie mistakes.

I try again. "Ms. Andersson?"

High on a third floor, lace curtains waft, as if softly snoring. A rhythmic *whoosh* brushes overhead. I look up in time to spot a stork glide by. Storks are considered good luck here, yet the sight seems so prehistoric that I grip my handlebars tighter, lest my bike and I tumble down, down, down through the eons.

Where is Keiko? I can't flee this time warp until I find her.

I listen, hard. Soft clacks come from above. Clicks and scrapes. I hope it's only those good-luck storks. I'm searching for the flashlight app on my phone when more human sounds reach me—a low, muttering grumble. At first, I think my feelings have taken flight. That mutter sounds frustrated. *That would be me!* Except my jaw remains clenched shut and the sound comes from the lane to my left.

Of course it's that lane, the darkest of the three, no wider than my arms outstretched. In a scary movie, that's where danger would lurk. A psychotic mime, ready to overact strangulation. A charcuterie maniac, armed with cleaver, hook, and curing salts.

Given what Keiko *said* she saw, that just might be true.

I wheel my bike down the inky tunnel, calculating an escape. *A bicycle can act as a shield. Gears can be a weapon. I can leap to my saddle and—*

A dogleg corner opens into a small courtyard shaped

like a wobbly triangle. Ancient buildings press shoulder to shoulder, nodding in sleep. Keiko stands at the center, her bike lamp aimed at a hip-high wine barrel.

She wrenches the handlebars, turning her lamp into a color wand flashing over rosy plaster, golden roses, and shutters in periwinkle, emerald, sea blue, and red.

"This is the place," Keiko says, frowning all around.

I wrench my expression into what I hope is professional concern and care. A polite fib. My true feelings combine giddy relief with *You dragged me from my princess bed and scared me half to death for nothing?* But that's okay. It's okay!

"It's not right," Keiko scrapes a hand through her hair, mostly dark with silver highlights. A daisy print decorates her cycling shorts. Pink earbuds dangle from the pocket of her peachy windbreaker. She's all of five-foot-nothing with a towering confidence I attribute to her profession. Keiko is an orchestra conductor, semi-retired. Our cycling tour had to work around her schedule. She had a classical music festival in Stockholm in July. Later in the fall, she's co-organizing a Wagner "extravaganza," fifteen hours of opera to be staged in a grand converted chicken barn near her home in the Cotswolds. I'll cycle all day, but that much opera in a barn sounds like way too much endurance for me.

Keiko points to the barrel as if directing it to change its tune. "I recognize that barrel."

I do too. I came by this courtyard the other day on a dining reconnaissance mission. The barrel held handwritten menus for a *winstüb*, a rustic bistro serving local favorites, heavy on German influences. Think ham hocks and sausages, pretzels, chicken braised in white wine instead of red, and sauerkraut. Lots and lots of sauerkraut. I have pickled cabbages on my itinerary.

On my prior visit, I snapped photos of the menu and the scene. The wineshop next door is picture perfect, its second story decorated in old-timey vineyard equipment: baskets, hammers, and the spigot-tapped tops of wine casks. A vintage handcart stood out front, filled with geraniums color-matched to blood-red shutters. The cart must be tucked inside for the night, like the suits of armor that guarded the antiques gallery next door and the statue of a beret-wearing pizza chef at the restaurant on the corner. At the pizzeria, I photographed my first encounter with *tarte flambée*, a crispy flatbread topped with crème fraîche, onions, and smoky lardons. What a revelation! Continued taste-testing research is needed.

Keiko's lamp flashes over metal. The pizzeria's aluminum tables and chairs are stacked against their restaurant for the night. Come lunchtime, they'll extend into the courtyard and bordering lane—a lane that leads downhill before a short quarter-mile spin to our inn. We could be back in our beds in a flash. I inch my bike that way.

Keiko whips her handlebars back toward me.

I blink against the light. "Well, then!" I announce. Tour guides everywhere would recognize my tone, taut but firm, a tone that says *Okay! We've enjoyed just about enough of this trainwreck of a stop!* "We can return to the inn down that lane," I add, gesturing hopefully.

Keiko wheels her bike in the opposite direction. She stops at the wine barrel and wobbles it, ear cocked toward its hollow, empty *clonk*.

"I wasn't even going to turn," she muses, her hand on the barrel. "A cat ran across my path, coming from this direction. I had to swerve and ended up here. It was a calico. You know how calicos are."

I don't. I nod along anyway. When confused, I have a bad habit of bobbing my head as if I understand. This automatic reaction—like my semi-obsession with croissants—was cemented on my first trip to France. Then, just out of high school, my *A* grades meant I could formally announce my name, ask directions to libraries and swimming pools, and talk exhaustively about luggage.

But I *wanted* to understand. I felt like I should. Thus, I nodded along to whatever French speakers might be saying. You have a dire disease? *Why, yes, sounds wonderful!* You want to sell me a large household appliance? *Oui, oui, merci!*

"Calicos are bossy," Keiko says. "They have 'tortitude.' You can look it up."

My head agrees. Fine, my priority is to herd Keiko back to the inn. Tomorrow, I'll redeem the sweet reputations of calicos.

"So I come this way and that's when I see it." Keiko scowls back at the cobblestones.

My head switches course to *no, no, non*!

"A man." Keiko lowers her voice. "A *dead* man!"

Chills skitter up my arm. I stare at stones worn smooth by the centuries. They're clean. Clear of any bodies, that's for sure. Even stray geranium petals have been brushed into a neat row by the antiques shop.

Too clean? No! Ridiculous! Riquewihr is among the officially designated Most Beautiful Villages of France. Les Plus Beaux Villages de France are tidy and safe. They're filled with flowers. They are most definitely *not* scattered with bodies.

"I didn't hit him." Keiko's eyes shift from mine. "I swerved just in time."

Is she protesting too much? But there's no body to hit. I clasp my hands in a prayer disguised as a rallying clap. "Well!" I announce again. "He's gone, so . . ." *So, let's get out of here!*

Shutters creak shut somewhere above us. Keiko is a statue, melded to the stone.

What does she want me to do? I remind myself that tour

guests crave new understandings of the world. I wave an open palm over the corpse-free cobblestones and offer fresh perspectives. "Perhaps the gentleman was drunk? A local who enjoys the wine too much? A tourist? People on vacation let go."

There's a thought. I inch closer to Keiko and take a discreet (I hope) sniff. I detect delicate jasmine perfume and a scowl equivalent to a slap.

"I know what I saw," Keiko says. "He was right there. Right where you're standing."

My feet lurch back before I can stop them. They, along with my twisting stomach, believe Keiko.

"Did you . . . ah . . . check his pulse?" My mind spins more rationalizations. He fainted. He swooned from the Most Beautiful Village beauty of it all, recovered his senses, and stumbled home to dream of half-timbers and pickled cabbages.

Keiko's lip curls in revulsion. "I don't go around *touching* strange men."

Then—just as I'd feared—there's miming.

"He lay like this." Keiko splays an arm and twists her head, chin up, mouth and eyes wide.

"Oh, don't give me that look!" she huffs, when I apparently fail to hide my horror. "He was dead. Even if he hadn't been lying like that, he had the *aura*. The death aura. You, of all people, should understand, Sadie Greene."

Me, of all people? I could feign incomprehension or offense, but I know what she means. I also know that literally and metaphorically, lightning can strike the same place twice. So, too, could crimes zap a small cycle-touring company centered on joy, discovery, and stops for croissants.

But come on! What are the odds of such cosmic injustice?

I will myself to shake off the thought, for my head to issue a firm no, no, *non*! Fear has frozen me solid.

I had followed Keiko into the darkness to prove her wrong. The empty courtyard suggests I did just that. I should be delighted—skipping, cheering, and spinning wheelies. Why, then, am I even more terrified that Keiko is right?

CHAPTER 2

Saturday:
Good morning! I hope you enjoyed your first night at L'Auberge des Trois Cigognes. The Inn of the Three Storks will be our home base for this tour. After enjoying a gourmet breakfast, we'll strike out for a full day of cycling adventures.

Who came up with counting sheep as a route to sleep? Common wisdom credits an ancient shepherd, tucking in her flock. As a tour guide, I doubt that. Oh, I get the obsessive accounting. But don't the sheep leap over a fence? A fence they could hurtle back over as soon as the shepherd drifts off? And what about predators slipping under the rails?

When I fell into bed at 1:42 a.m., luxury linens and leaping lambs failed to lull me. If I closed my lids, I imagined dead eyes and Keiko cycling defiantly back into the night as a shadow watched from the vines.

Other numerical distractions also flopped. I ranked recently enjoyed croissants. I counted the steps from the sea to my cottage back in Sans-Souci and the ticktocks of the antique wall clock.

I didn't sleep. *Couldn't* sleep. Or so I thought.

My counting resumes with a shock. Three shocks, actually.

One: I'm suddenly awake, meaning I must have drifted off.

Two: eaves. As in, my attic bed is tucked under a steeply pitched roof. Levitating from my pillow like the possessed protagonist of a horror film means I slam my forehead into fifteenth-century Alsatian oak.

Three: light. Not the pale periwinkle of pre-dawn. Not the golden hues of first sunrise. Not even the dancing sparkles of a near concussion. Bright, clear daylight streams through lace curtains.

I didn't just sleep. I overslept!

I toss off the abused duvet and tug on work attire, once again giving thanks for spandex, with no time wasted buttoning, zipping, or heaven forbid, ironing.

The wall clock reads 8:40. Up in the village, a bell clangs once for the quarter hour. I'm so late that minutes matter. By my carefully calibrated schedule, we will depart for a full day of cycling at precisely nine.

I hurry down the back stairs, flip-flops slapping wood. I'm usually the hotel guest who tiptoes and whispers. Desperate times! Plus, this home-turned-inn is exclusively ours for the week. The innkeeper and her family live in a separate cottage just across the exquisite back garden. I hope my riders will be out in that garden, strolling among the blooms. Better yet, I hope they're in their rooms getting ready for the day. I don't want them to see me, frazzled and late. Early impressions matter in tour guiding.

I collected the Silver Spinners from the Strasbourg train station yesterday morning. I arrived early, clutching a sign with their name. Then I almost missed them because I was ogling the station, the historical façade encased in a modern glass shell, like standing in a Christmas ornament.

The Spinners were blasé about the station and my memorized lines extolling its historicist architecture of the Wilhelminian period. They'd seen it before. They'd explored Strasbourg in all seasons, too, including its magical Christmas markets, a treat that's still on my wish list.

So, I piled them into the Oui Cycle van, and we came straight here. After a leg-stretching ride and picnic at a vineyard, they relaxed at the inn before gathering for a first-night feast. I'd then accompanied Keiko on her midnight body search.

In the bright morning light, that nightmare is fizzling away. *A body? A disappearing corpse? Please! How did I believe that?*

But I know how. Those witchy clouds and dark alleys. The night sounds and my too-fresh crime PTSD. Keiko, as well, so adamant in her urgency.

The back stairs steepen before shooting me into a between-spaces corridor. I think I hear footsteps shuffling away and a door creaking. My imagination again? Ghosts? If I believed in spirits, I'd picture them haunting this ancient, rambling home. Portraits of the innkeeper's ancestors watch from a forest of exposed beams as I make my way down the main hallway. I interpret their unblinking stares as disapproving. Who am I to flip-flop through their family home? Who do I think I am, leading tours in Alsace? Anywhere in France? On a bike, no less!

My cottage back in Sans-Souci feels like home now. A dream home, despite some leaky roof tiles and blackbirds nesting in my chimney. My colleagues are like family. I've made friends and maybe, possibly, a budding romantic connection. I am known to innkeepers, museum docents, market vendors, and bakers in a wide swath of the glorious Pyrénées-Orientales.

I'm known for my past troubles, yes. However, I'm also increasingly greeted with a *bonjour, Madame Greene* and chitchat about the weather, baked goods, bikes, or *fromage*. I adore those hold-up-the-line chats!

Yet sometimes, doubts crash in, hissing in my ear like a leaky tire. *You're an imposter, an interloper, a fraud.*

I hustle on, toward voices burbling from the breakfast room. At the threshold, I pause. The room is a newer addition, more air and light than heavy beams. Glass doors open to the flower-filled patio. Cups clink, newspapers softly ruffle, and Scarlett Crabtree-Thorne holds forth at the head of the table.

Scarlett is the matriarch of the group, the queen. She even has a touch of royalty, being married to an honorary knight, Sir Rupert. Rupert isn't on the tour.

"Rupy never enjoyed cycling," Scarlett told me yesterday on the way down from Strasbourg.

That's understandable—except for never enjoying cycling, but to each their own. Other aspects of the absent Sir Rupert are less clear.

Scarlett waggles a butter knife at Keiko, who wears a sunny yellow blouse and a sour-lemons expression. Is she still mad that I refused to call the police last night? And report what? An overly tidy courtyard?

"So, I said to my Rupy—" Scarlett is saying.

Scarlett's drawl hails from Charleston, South Carolina, where she was born, raised, and married the first of her several husbands.

"I said, 'Rupy, darlin', if you don't join your ancestors soon, I won't be responsible for what I—' "

Join his ancestors? So, this is what I really don't get about Sir Rupert. Scarlett has mentioned things such as *darling Rupert resting in peace* and *dear, dear Rupy, gone beyond.* Is he dead? I can't very well ask. I keep meaning to google him. A "Sir" must be easy enough to find, especially if there's an obituary attached.

Scarlett is rolling her head dramatically when she spots me. "Sadie, darlin'! There you are! We worried we'd lost you too!"

Maybe she talks about everyone like that? I press up a smile.

"You poor lamb." Scarlett pats under her eyes. Her skin is taut and smooth. She's closing in on eighty and spends her days in the sun. Either she's cycled to the fountain of youth or a tasteful plastic surgeon. Her hand flutters to her flawless forehead, needlessly pinpointing the location of my blossoming goose egg, a gift from my bedroom ceiling beam.

I know, I know . . . I don't look my best.

"Just look at her," Scarlett orders the table. "Our Sadie is exhausted!"

Maurice Guidry and Benjamin "Benji" Patel—partners in love and a shared passion for art and antiques—lower matching newspapers and assess me. Two heads shake. They add a chorus of tuts.

Scarlett turns back to Keiko. "Kei-Kei, apologize. This dear girl is *spent*, and we haven't even started. We can't have her flatlining like that unfortunate Tunisian guide we had to leave behind." Her razor-sharp bob is flashy silver, dyed with a shimmery swatch of ruby red.

"That was a *tiresome* tour," murmurs Maurice, crossing spindle-thin legs, ropey with cycling muscles.

"No, no! I'm fine," I assure them. "Great! Grand." I hope I'm not tiresome. A guide must never be tiresome, or boring, or bossy, or prone to crime, getting lost, or running late. "I just need—." Coffee. I *need* coffee.

The table is decorated in red-and-white Alsatian linen. There are pretty porcelain cups, wicker baskets, and cut-glass carafes. There's also destruction. Desolation. Crumbs and pulp and beautiful buttery shards of croissants now gone. A flock of ravenous ravens might have descended on the inn's "complete and gourmet breakfast."

It's fine, I assure myself. I have snacks in my pack, and my tours include stops for fortification at least every fifteen kilometers. By fortification, I prefer croissants, but when in Alsace, a soft pretzel or apple strudel will certainly do.

But coffee . . . I count four French presses—*cafetières*, I should say—plunged to their desiccated grounds.

"Apologize?" Keiko huffs. "Why would I apologize to Sadie?"

"I'm the one who should be apologizing," I say to Keiko's hearty agreement. "I overslept. It's these lovely beds. I must have slept like the—" My hasty fib is careening toward a verbal hazard. I try to reverse. "I mean, I slept—"

"Like the dead?" Keiko interjects, tone as dry as a week-old baguette. When I wince, she turns to her friends. "See? I told you. Sadie believed me. I found a dead man." She raises a spoon in triumph. The sleeve of her blouse slips up, revealing a bandage across her elbow. She sees me looking and tugs the fabric down.

Maurice neatly folds his paper. The front page announces that a llama, known to munch on pinot noir vines, is on the loose.

"You *believe*, Sadie?" Maurice asks. Maurice is a fellow American but has lived in England for enough decades to acquire crisp consonants. To my ears, the accent adds to his scholarly air. So does his rumpled Einstein-in-cycling-gear look of wildly fluffy hair and gold-framed spectacles perched at the end of a crooked nose.

I wonder about his crooked nose. Maurice is an avid cyclist. Has he taken some tumbles? Do brainy antiquarians get into fights? Brawls at estate sales? Rumbles at *Antiques Roadshows*?

"But where did the body go, ladies?" Maurice taps a philosophical finger above his upper lip. "Did the deceased gentleman rise and walk away? Do we have a zombie in Alsace?"

Benji drops his newspaper in a rumple. "Wouldn't that be thrilling?" A flatcap in mauve covers his bald crown. Thick eyebrows pinch in delight. "Finally, something *new* and exciting on one of these trips."

My head shakes no. My palms open upward, suggesting there's wiggle room between dead and undead, between a corpse and a man who walked away. I'm being polite for Keiko's sake.

She's disemboweling a grapefruit. She slams her spoon down with porcelain-threatening force. "*I* saw the body. That should be good enough."

"Hush now, you all." Scarlett nods pointedly down the table. "No talk of *missing bodies*. We promised the young ones a *fun* adventure! Remember, we want them to become devoted members. The Silver Spinners need young blood."

"We're like vampires," Benji whispers to me. "Roving the midnight streets in search of youth."

Their "young bloods" are the fifty-something first-timers of the group, Rosemary Perch and Lionel Lloyd. Rosemary is Scarlett's goddaughter. She runs her family's third-generation bakery, Rose Petal Shortbreads. Lionel is the cookie factory manager and chief financial officer. They study a Michelin road map, foreheads touching like teens in first love rather than a long-time widow and longer-time bachelor.

Rosemary looks up, fingers twined in the loose blond braid looped over her left shoulder. "We're *fine*, Scarlett. Keiko, that must have been very distressing, I'm sure."

"Thank you, Rosemary," Keiko says with prickly primness. "I'm sure as well."

Lionel studies the map as if it might whisk him away. Far away. His finger is pressed over the border in Switzerland.

I want all my groups to have relaxing, joyful, transformative tours. Secretly, selfishly, I want this group to have all those experiences and more. The Silver Spinners hail from Lower Thornbury, a village in the English Cotswolds known for golden-stone cottages, scenically grazing sheep, and an award-winning garden club.

I know Lower Thornbury as the English hometown of my mentor in all things cycling and expat living, Bea, who split her childhood between there and Bermuda. Later, Bea fell in love with France, cycling, and her Provençal honey, Bernard. Decades later, when ready to retire, those two marvelous people changed my life by choosing me to take over their cycle-tour business.

Bea's sister still lives in Lower Thornbury. So does her son, Bea's adored "baby" nephew—that would be Lionel, the fifty-seven-year-old man aggressively staring into a road map. Despite his family connections, Lionel has never taken a Oui Cycle tour. The elder Silver Spinners have done several. At dinner last night, they raved about what delightful guides Bea and Bernard were. Informed, spontaneous, fun, fit, and fabulous. No surprises there! No pressure for me, right? *Yeah, right!*

I want to show the Spinners that I'm a worthy new leader of Oui Cycle, more than an outsider who almost crashed the business. I'd love to earn a line or two in their future stories. *Remember that glorious tour with Sadie? Wasn't that the best trip ever? The food, the sights, the spreadsheets!*

As long as I'm fantasizing, I also dream of glowing reports sailing off to Bea and Bernard, who are on a Caribbean cruise with Lionel's mother. Talk of bodies won't make for the sort of wish-you-were-here postcards I desire. I scramble for a more positive topic.

"We have lovely weather." I wave toward bright blue skies and talk up our first stop, the tiny village of Hunawihr, home to winegrowers and a notable fountain.

Benji breaks in. "We *adore* fountains! Remember bathing with the macaques in those luscious Japanese hot springs? Divine!"

Safe to say, today's fountain will lack macaques. It's small but historic, a must-see for fans of seventh-century saints of washerwomen. I've memorized details of Saint Hune. I can also talk about the Church of Saint James the Greater (pink sandstone, unique staircase, notable sixteenth-century frescos) and the *maisons de vignerons* (houses of the winegrowers, distinguishable by the presence of gates).

Saint Hune reportedly turned the fountain's water into wine. That's a big deal. A miracle!

Still . . . no macaques.

The elder Spinners, minus grapefruit-stabbing Keiko, have moved on to other fountain adventures. *Remember when our Scarlett skinny dipped in Trocadero! Ohhh . . . mooning the Eiffel Tower under a full moon.*

"Hot flashes." Scarlett demurely fans herself. "I needed those twenty jets of cool water."

Keiko gives the grapefruit a vicious jab. "*I* found a dead man, and all you lot yammer on about is Scarlett's international nudism?"

Benji stifles a giggle. Looks shoot across the table, dense with meanings I can't translate. This is the thing about guiding groups of old friends. You can ride alongside them, but you can never catch up.

"Go on," Keiko demands. "Say what you're thinking."

Maurice dips his head in an obliging bow. "Aristotle would not burden us with proving a negative. However, perhaps there was no body? Remember Namibia, when we saw the same mirage?"

"Not the *same* mirage," Scarlett says. "You all saw generic men. I saw Peter O'Toole." She pats her heart. "*Young* O'Toole. Lawrence of Arabia. Ah! I swooned!"

"You swooned over O'Toole in Morocco," Maurice

corrects. "After the dodgy tagine but before those customs officials and the . . . mmmm?" He mimes peeling off bills and smiles at me. "We tend to get lost in deserts. Good you've managed to leave those off our busy, busy itinerary, Sadie."

Was that a dig? I have put a *lot* on my daily itinerary printouts, partly as a cheat sheet for myself. I can't worry about that now. More concerning: What's this about getting lost in deserts? Deserts, with all those wide-open sight lines?

"I didn't imagine an actor," Keiko huffs. "A real man was on the pavement. I ran over his—" She stops herself and my breathing. "He was dead. Then he was gone. Poof!"

"Real bodies do disappear," Rosemary says, a tremor in her voice.

Lionel clasps her hand. He's finally looked up, but it's to scowl around the table. Some people have well-practiced frown lines, deep as tourism-worthy erosional features. Lionel's discontent looks like it's cracking new ground.

Great. One guest insists on a corpse. Another is learning to frown.

Even before this, Lionel didn't seem overly enthusiastic about the tour. He arrived with a bundle of tourism brochures he'd ordered away for. That might seem like he's eager, but yesterday afternoon, he sat in the garden, flipping through glossy brochures with the look of a man reading the side-effects literature of a prescription medication.

Why did he come on this tour? Love? Arm twisting? Bea confessed that if her beloved nephew had any faults, they were these: Lionel was too serious about work. He was also "still on his way to discovering the joys of cycling." Translation: He's not an avid cyclist.

I understand the workaholic rut. That was me, spinning

my wheels in my office cubicle. And not all guests are keen cyclists. I've had riders tugged along by spouses or friends. Others haven't cycled since they were kids, if ever. Usually, but not always, they come away as cycling converts.

That will be Lionel. I'll make his auntie proud of both of us!

Scarlett slaps the table. "Kei-Kei, please, you know our Rosemary can't tolerate such talk. Disappearing bodies! Heavens, why bring that up?"

Rosemary's cheeks flare. "I'm fine, Scarlett. Completely fine."

That's not a "fine" fine.

Scarlett points to me. "You've upset Sadie too. Poor girl, fresh from *all* those bodies."

I want to lodge a mathematical protest. "*All* those bodies" implies a group-size measurement like a flock or herd or . . . A murder of crows flies to mind. I keep quiet.

Scarlett rolls on, ignoring Keiko's building-storm expression. "Here's what happened: You were sleep-cycling again, Kei-Kei. I know, you stopped taking those insomnia pills, but who's to say they caused the past episodes? You might sleepwalk and sleep-cycle all on your own. You did borrow my melatonin last night."

"Melatonin gives me unsettled dreams," says Rosemary. "Have you tried chamomile tea, Keiko? Back home, I'd suggest a warm Horlicks malted milk. I wonder if they have Horlicks here?"

Scarlett praises her goddaughter's suggestions. "Also, Kei-Kei, you had white wine last night. *Two* glasses. You know what chardonnay does to me."

Shivers ripple through the group.

"Makes her *venomous*," Benji whisper-hisses my way, lifting a forearm dotted with actual goosebumps.

"Opera," Maurice intones. "That's the troublemaker. All that Wagner lately. I heard *The Ring* leaking from your earbuds, Keiko. Wagner can be unsettling in any locale, but especially this close to the Rhine."

Benji leans in again. "Golden apples and immortality and Valkyries and funeral pyres. You wouldn't want to meet any of them in a dark alley."

I'm completely baffled and thus nodding with enthusiasm.

"There it is," Scarlett declares. "A hallucinogenic cocktail. Melatonin, white wine, and Wagner. You were sleep-cycling again, Keiko."

"Don't worry, Keiko," Benji says. "We stand ready to collect you from any errant barges." He laughs. "Just don't reach international waters again. What an adventure that was! Certainly corrected my romantic notions of pirates."

My fears don't know whether to retreat or muster. On the one hand, here are explanations that don't involve a corpse. On the other hand, Keiko cycles in her sleep? Onto barges? I have waterways on my itinerary. And what's up with chardonnay and possible bribery of customs officials and no talk of missing bodies around Rosemary?

This is exactly why shepherds and tour guides can never let down their guard, not even in their sleep.

CHAPTER 3

Saturday:
Our first stop of the day is tiny Hunawihr, home to just over five hundred residents but a big name in beauty. We're off to another Most Beautiful Village of France.

Twenty minutes later, I am ten glorious minutes early. Scarlett decreed a 9:45 departure. While I don't want Scarlett to think she's in charge (well, not *totally* in charge), I was happy to oblige. I slurp down more sugary, bitter sludge, the best worst coffee I've ever tasted.

"Thank you!" I exclaim to Nadiya and hold out the thermos cap for seconds. "But only if you truly don't want any more."

My co-guide grimaces. "No! I only took it to, how do you say? To laugh at Jordi? With Jordi? You know, make humor."

"Humor Jordi," I say.

Nadiya is Ukrainian and speaks multiple languages. She repeats "humor Jordi" to commit the phrase to memory and frowns toward a sweet scene. The Oui Cycle van is parked by the inn's outbuilding, a stone-and-timber structure peaked like a witch's hat. Our bikes stand in a line on the shady side. Nadiya's and mine look dainty next to six substantial e-bikes, purchased with a generous donation from a grateful former guest.

Jordi Vollant—my bike mechanic, tech wizard, van driver, and Nadiya's now-official boyfriend—polishes gleaming frames and whistles like a cartoon songbird.

"You want to know a man?" Nadiya says darkly. "Go camping with him."

She rolls her gray-blue eyes and sighs heavily. A breeze flutters her hair, gold with blue at the tips, the color of her country's flag. She doesn't fool me. Anyone who foregoes a room at a luxury inn to camp at a goat farm owned by her boyfriend's former rugby pal is seriously in love.

Nadiya continues. "Jordi, he can chop wood, make fire, give me all his blankets so I can sleep comfortably on the ground. He cannot cook. Nothing. Not coffee. Not water. He burns water! He does not notice or care. This means something . . ."

It means he's smitten to the point of distraction, I suspect. Either that or he simply can't cook.

"Your Detective Laurent, he camps?" Nadiya asks.

I could protest that Detective Jacques Laurent is not *mine*. We're just friends. Friends who cycle together, who spent a glorious July exploring new restaurants and bakeries, who occasionally stroll by the Mediterranean at sunset, sit on the pebbled beach, listen to the waves whisper their history. I could say that, but my cheeks are flaring at the memory of a first—and a farewell—kiss Laurent dropped on my lips when he saw me off at the train station last week.

"He's actually kind of camping now," I say. "He's at a gendarme wilderness training camp at a military outpost in the Alps."

"Ah-ha! It is unfortunate you cannot witness this. A man in the wilderness, that would show you all."

"I know a lot about him," I say. Okay, that's a stretch. I

know Jacques Laurent as a man who irons his linen jackets, who enjoys long lunches, and who prefers Côtes de Roussillon reds, in which he can taste the terroir of their vineyards. He's meticulous, fastidious, a gourmand. However, he's also a man who careens over boulder-strewn trails on his mountain bike and chases killers.

I know Laurent prefers to be called by his last name, that he lives in the now, à la Proust. Cherry-picking his Proust, he has no time for remembrances of things past. Laurent can be as mysterious as his case files. I haven't heard much from him since he left, but I didn't expect to. The barracks have no Wi-Fi and spotty cell reception, he warned me. He's not big on texts on any occasion.

So far, I've heard from him twice. Two texts, both food photos with only-the-facts descriptors. The first, a stunning tart shaped like a fig, coated in smooth green marzipan. Caption: La figue, afternoon off in Chamonix. The second: a plate of beige meat and potatoes captioned with a single sad-faced emoji. Yes, Jacques Laurent sent an emoji. I interpreted that as a cry for help.

I reciprocated with photos of wood-fired *tarte flambée*, the picture-perfect wineshop, and a pretzel as big as my bike wheel. I'm happy to continue with food flirtations if that's what this is. They're a lot easier to interpret than emojis or those text acronyms I always forget.

However, some personal updates might be nice. Maybe I *should* propose camping when we both get back home. Except, I enjoy a comfortable bed and hot coffee and a croissant in the morning. We could camp in a cozy loft above a café.

I return the thermos cap. "You saved me. I can't believe how late I slept."

"I believe," Nadiya says. "I heard. You lost a dead man. Is this true?"

"No," I say, my optimism emboldened by the sugary caffeine sludge. "No dead man. It's all good."

"*Pfft.* Nothing is ever *all good*," says Nadiya, dark as the day is sunny. "In fact, Gabi, the innkeeper, she must talk with you. She lost our money, she says." Nadiya shrugs. "Missing money, missing bodies. Already, too many troubles."

"What?" The accountant in me wants to fly into numerical action. The small business owner in me fights back anxiety.

We paid a hefty deposit, more than I'd usually allot for lodging, but my group chose the inn. I built our itinerary around it. "Our check was deposited. How can it be lost?"

"You must ask her." Nadiya nods across the garden. Our innkeeper, Gabi Morel, lives in the back cottage with her grandfather and English husband. I won't have to seek her out. Gabi is hurrying our way in a swirl of red. Her copper-red curls spring from a chaotic bun. Her shades-of-sunrise dress has more ruffly layers than mille-feuille.

Bonjours fly among us before Gabi's expression darkens. "I have done something awful."

"Did a person die?" Nadiya asks. When Gabi gawps in wide-eyed horror, Nadiya shrugs. "Then it is not so horrible, *non*?"

Nadiya has survived the horrific war in her homeland, not to mention our June tour of murder. She offers a good perspective, albeit a tad too bluntly.

"Nadiya said our deposit is, ah . . ." I prompt.

"Missing." Gabi looks almost relieved now. "Yes, I am to blame. Eddie, my husband, left for a hoteliers' conference the other day. In Lyon, lucky him. Before he left, he must have moved your deposit to another account. I received notice of an overdue bill. I must pay it, but I cannot recall the banking passwords." She puffs her cheeks and exhales heavily. "This is my problem, not yours."

I hold back my puff of relief. *Not my problem.* But I still wish I could help. "Your husband might know the passwords? Can you call him?"

Gabi rolls her eyes. "*Mais oui.* Yes, certainly, I *can* call. I can message and WhatsApp and email. Will he respond?" She puffs her cheeks again and blows a quintessential French raspberry of resigned exasperation. "When Eddie is away on trips, he is like the neighbor dog, Chou Chou." She gestures toward the inn's nearest neighbor.

We're on the fringe of Riquewihr, far in both distance and atmosphere from the suburbs of my childhood. Gabi's family home sits a short distance outside the medieval walls that ring the village. Aside from vineyards, her nearest neighbor is a compact château of creamy yellow plaster and stone turrets capped in red tiles. Its owner operates a small but well-regarded winery. Pollard-pruned trees—poodle-pruned, I always think—mark the property boundary. Through their line of trunks, I spot a black dog the size of a bear. He has small, pointed ears and a stubby tail and is zigzagging between flowers, as flighty, it seems, as Gabi's husband.

"Travel," Nadiya intones darkly. "It is like camping. It shows you who people are."

"My Eddie," Gabi says fondly. "He is a boy at heart. Ah, voilà! This is an idea: A boy and his dog! Eddie adores Chou Chou. He would own Chou Chou if not for my allergies and the fact that Chou Chou is a mammoth who eats everything. Perhaps that is the password. Chou Chou? Chou Chou's birthday?" She trots back toward her home, waving to the Silver Spinners on the way.

My group walks their bikes over to us. Keiko's sourness looks like it's fermenting. The headphones wedged in her ears connect to a phone strapped to her arm like a blood-pressure cuff. I detect a faint but dramatic crescendo.

Do I dare ask her to remove at least one earbud? We'll start on peaceful lanes before turning onto dirt tracks through the vineyards. The route is generally safe from speeding traffic. Still . . . cyclists should be aware of their surroundings, for safety and enjoyment. Why not soak in a symphony of nature? Wrens, blackbirds, and goldfinches; cicadas, crickets, and frogs?

She catches me looking and presses the buds in more firmly. Fine, she's an adult. Maybe my pre-departure talk will lure her out.

Since we're already late, I hurry through safety reminders and the route. "We'll take a scenic, looping route to Hunawihr," I say. "There are some lovely stops for photos in between." I aim this last part to Lionel, hoping I've spotted a true interest. He has a camera the size of a newborn strapped to his chest and his cell phone clipped to his handlebars. He removes the phone and snaps shots all around.

"Be ready to photograph any runaway corpses, Lionel, old son." Maurice chuckles.

Keiko's scowl could frost the wine crop. Under the influence of Jordi's magic coffee sludge, I take this as a positive. Keiko can hear through the earbuds and orchestral chaos.

I raise my voice and sing out the best words in tour guiding. "Let's ride!"

"Tallyho," cries Scarlett.

"Away!" chimes Benji. "Let the ride begin!"

I take the lead. When we reach pavement, I pick up speed, confident my e-bike riders can keep pace. We pass the neighboring château with its founding year, 1715, written out in faded red calligraphy across four massive wine barrels, each standing taller than me.

Joy powers my pedals. We're off! We're outpacing trouble! The sky is a perfect robin's egg blue. Sun warms my cheeks. Frogs serenade from verdant ditches lining the narrow lane. Beyond, vines stretch as far as the eye can see, dotted with the spires and rooftops of ancient villages, which seem to float like mirages. Bike bells ring behind me. My group is as thrilled as I am. I can't wait to show them the—

More ringing. Strident *bring-brings*. A voice, yelling . . .

"Sadie, stop! *Arret!*" Nadiya speeds to my side. "I have been ringing and calling your name! Did you not hear?"

So much for keeping my ears open. I'd muffled them in daydreams.

"There is trouble." Nadiya points behind us.

I twist in my saddle and my stomach and balance lurch. The road is empty. No cars. That's good. No dogs nipping at our wheels. No loose livestock or flat tires. Always good.

No cyclists. Not good.

We've gone barely a few hundred meters, and they're already lost? All of them?

Nadiya swings into a U-turn. I follow, almost bumping off the narrow road.

"Madame Scarlett," Nadiya explains when I catch up. "She sees the gentleman from the beautiful château. He is handsome and riding an old bike. The kind with the large front wheel? What is it called?"

"A penny farthing?" I suggest.

"Yes, yes, that is it. Madame Scarlett must see. The others, they follow her. You were far ahead. I tried to yell but not sound like I'm yelling, so they don't think I'm upset that they throw our day off course. You know what I mean?"

Oh, I do. Frustration powers my legs now. Frustration at Scarlett for hijacking my itinerary but mostly at myself for not watching them more closely.

Chou Chou bounds down the château's long, curving drive to welcome us. He issues two bass woofs to Nadiya and then the same to me. With our furry guide leading the way, Nadiya and I ride into a scene from a vintage travel poster, the kind composed of blocks of color. The lane circles a burbling fountain in front of the château. A spoke to the right leads to an attached stone structure—the winery and tasting room.

The Silver Spinners have dismounted to watch a dapper man circle the fountain on a penny farthing, a dinosaur of a bike. The front wheel is my height, the back wheel barely larger than a salad plate.

Once again, I get that spinning feeling that I've ridden back in time.

I glance at my watch, not for the era but for my shattered schedule. I'm a stickler for details, a holdover from my prior life in numbers. I plot my itineraries down to the meter and minute. I like to be on time, if not early. I get great satisfaction from making a list and checking off completed items.

I could be *that* guide, the guide who insists on the schedule no matter what. We have a fountain to view, a village to admire, and a three-course lunch on a bijou patio that was extremely difficult to book in the high summer season.

But even I recognize that life's detours can be better than anything planned. This could be one of those happy chances. For goodness' sake, we're at a château with turrets and a smiling vintner doffing an imaginary cap. This could be a marvelous stop.

Jordi's sugar-sludge optimism surges through my veins. Why not? What could go wrong?

CHAPTER 4

Tour-guide tidbit: Alsace produces some 150 million bottles of wine per year. Almost 90 percent are whites, including elegant Rieslings and aromatic Gewürztraminers.

Our host introduces himself as Pierre-Luc Bauman, but I already know that. I've studied every brochure and booklet the Office de Tourisme has on offer, and I've seen him in the glossiest publications. Raising glasses of pale-gold Rieslings at wine-soaked benefits. Smiling with other well-dressed attendees of gallery openings. Posing amidst his vines. The things I imagine château denizens doing, rolling in different circles than bicycle guides.

Yet, a vintner is a grape farmer at heart, attuned to season, sun, and soil, and Pierre-Luc seems like a down-to-earth guy. His smile is bright, his hair sun-bleached, and his tan deepened by a life lived outdoors. I'd guess he's around the age of Rosemary and Lionel, upper fifties, more or less? I'm bad with ages between infancy and centenarian.

Almost-octogenarian Scarlett might be confused by his age too. She's either batting her eyelashes flirtatiously or under attack by invisible gnats. "Gorgeous," she drawls, leaving a long pause before adding, "*Quel beau vélo.*"

"That is a gorgeous bike," agrees Maurice, his eyes on the penny farthing. "Is that an 1880s model?"

I start to translate into French but am overridden by Scarlett, over-pronouncing like a romantic stage actor. We needn't have bothered. Pierre-Luc answers in English.

"*Oui*, she is my new old baby." Pierre-Luc extends a leg back. His foot lands on the tiny single step that allows riders to mount and dismount the beast.

Pierre-Luc steps off with a bouncy hop. "You are Gabi and Eddie's guests? The world-famous cycling tour?"

"We are known for our *adventures*," Scarlett says suggestively.

"We were featured on BBC Cotswolds," Benji says.

"He means Oui Cycle." Keiko removes an earbud. "He's talking about Sadie and her murders. Didn't you make *BBC World*, Sadie? All the tabloids?"

Headlines spin through my head. NO, NO, OUI WON'T CYCLE! CYCLE OF MURDER! TWO-WHEELING DEATH SPREE!

Our host is agreeing that yes, he was thinking of my "incidents."

That's a nice way of putting it.

"You are all brave to keep cycling," he says.

"Those incidents are in the past," I say firmly. "Nothing like that will happen again."

Recently, I picked up a French women's magazine at the supermarket. The cover article ordered me to start each day by voicing my aspirations with confidence. Not just little things like doing the laundry or waxing bike chains. Big, self-betterment goals. I try some out now. *Today, I will bring enthusiasm and flexibility to my guiding. Today, I will appreciate beauty in people and châteaux. Today, I will find no corpses!*

The same magazine also forbade athleisure wear outside the home, so I can't count on its relevance to my life.

Keiko removes her other earbud. "Except it *did* happen again. I found a dead body in the village last night."

"A *dead* body, Madame?" Pierre-Luc's distaste is palpable, like a fashion editor witnessing me enter a Michelin-starred bistro in padded bike shorts. "How horrible! Whose body?"

"There's no body," Scarlett says, eyelashes throbbing. "Our darling Keiko bicycles in her sleep. She gets disoriented." She pats her friend's arm, heedless of Keiko's venomous look.

Time for a conversational detour. "Your bike," I proclaim, so forcefully Pierre-Luc blinks. "Can you tell us more about it? Are you a collector?"

Ah, the joys of bikes, the bike-obsessed, and collectors of all sorts. Pierre-Luc brightens and details the bike's vitals: age, height, weight, and wheel sizes.

"I am a collector of this and that," he says with a modest shrug. "Vintage bikes, art, whatever strikes my fancy. Would you like to see? But you surely do not have time. You are touring."

Maurice and Benji have time. They look like kids offered the run of a chocolate shop. Gratifyingly, they turn to me for permission.

Scarlett is about to beat me to it.

"We'd be delighted," I say, raising my volume over Scarlett's gushing acceptance. Then, because I will forever be bound to my mother's rules for not being a bother, I add, "But only if we're not interrupting."

In Mom's world, invitations should be questioned and resisted, assuming the inviter can't possibly mean it.

Pierre-Luc laughs. "Friends of Eddie and Gabi are friends of mine. Come, come. Unless I will bore you with my talk of art and bicycles. And wine? You like wine? You should stay for lunch."

Pierre-Luc parks the penny farthing in a bike rack forged from an artistic mix of metal and bike chains. A faux-antique sign designates the area for bike parking only. We arrange our rides, and Pierre-Luc leads us into the cool cavern of his tasting room. The stone walls are decorated in art.

"We have lunch reservations," I say, and ignore a gusty sigh of disappointment from behind me. Probably Benji. Maybe Maurice. All of them?

"You should join us for lunch, Monsieur," says Scarlett in more of a command than an offer. "My goddaughter is also a culinary entrepreneur. You'd have oodles to talk about."

She tugs Rosemary forward. "Rosemary operates a third-generation shortbread bakery. Rose Petal Shortbreads. You've heard of them?"

"I have more than heard," Pierre-Luc says, dipping his head toward Rosemary. "I have enjoyed your delicate shortbreads, Madame Rosemary. You sent a gift of sample packages to the inn when you made your booking, *non?* Gabi generously shared one of these culinary treasures with me. I had been awaiting your arrival to compliment you." He pinches his fingers and makes a kissing gesture.

I have a blush-pink rose back in my garden that's blooming in the exact shade of Rosemary's cheeks.

Scarlett beams. "How lovely to hear, Monsieur! We brought Gabi a new tin to replenish her supply. She was absolutely thrilled. We brought extra, too, in case we meet special new friends." Her lashes flutter more than a migrating swarm of monarchs.

With a dismissive hand flick over her shoulder, Scarlett adds, "Lionel back there will bring you a deluxe tin. He works for Rosemary."

As the CFO and factory manager, I could note. He's hardly the stock boy. But Lionel is happily oblivious to Scarlett's snub. He's yards behind the rest of us, photographing wine barrels.

Rosemary takes a deep breath, as if summoning patience. When she releases it, she changes the subject. "Tell us about your wine, Monsieur. It's award winning, Gabi told us?"

We pass a bar with tall stools and bottles lined up for sampling. Pierre-Luc continues through a doorway fringed in an old-school curtain of beaded threads like I've seen in rural homes around Sans-Souci.

He makes a dismissive *pfft* sound. "Award-*nominated*, yes, but winning? How do you say in English? I am forever the brides man?"

"Groomsman?" suggests Nadiya.

"Forever the bridesmaid," I say, and sadness prickles. Over a year out and sorrow still crashes in unexpectedly, like hail on a sunny day. The death of my best friend Gemma prompted my very-unlike-me move to France. I'm living our shared dream of cycle touring, but Gem and I had other dreams too. I would have been Gem's bridesmaid. She would have been mine. Unless, of course, we turned out to be happy singletons rolling through France. The hit-and-run killed all those dreams too.

"Bridesmaid," Pierre-Luc repeats. "That is me. Never the most celebrated."

I'd say he's doing okay. We enter a space I thought only existed in design magazines and Instagram.

"My salon," Pierre-Luc says with the nonchalance of introducing a broom closet. The Silver Spinners—a group who have seen it all and more—give admiring *ooohhs*.

"I host small gatherings of friends," Pierre-Luc says.

Lucky friends. I take in the artfully mismatched chairs and age-darkened wine barrels holding lamps and books with well-worn covers. Watercolors of the village and vineyards float against stone walls, suspended by silver threads attached to the ceiling beams.

"A local artist," Pierre-Luc says, waving to the watercolors that Maurice and Benji are admiring. "I host an informal gallery. If my customers enjoy my wine samples, they become more inclined to purchase beautiful art." He moves a guitar from a love seat and a book of poetry from a wingback, urging us to sit.

I pick a seat with a view plucked from a classic film. At any moment, Audrey Hepburn might drive up the cobbled lane in a vintage roadster. Chou Chou lies by the fountain, front legs crossed like a statue—if statues gnawed on grape vines. I hope he hasn't uprooted future wine.

Pierre-Luc shrugs. "I may not win, but I enjoy myself here. That is most important in life, *non*?"

"Handsome and modest," Scarlett titters.

"A veritable twin of your Rupert," chuckles Benji.

"Dear, dear Rupy, lounging in the heat below." She and Benji laugh. I remain in the dark about Sir Rupert, but an hour later, I am certain we aren't bothering Pierre-Luc. He's offered up wine, coffee, and gourmet nibbles and shown off barrels, bottles, and bikes, along with fascinating cycling memorabilia from his family, including an uncle who cycled in the Tour de France and won a King of the Mountains polka-dot jersey in the nearby Vosges Mountains.

Pierre-Luc issues a standing invite for us to visit anytime. The Silver Spinners are delighted. So am I, but I have a problem. How am I going to pry them away?

This is the château version of the cool-kids space, and what could be cooler than that? Now, to compound my dilemma, Maurice wants to try out the penny farthing.

"Darling, please, you're *old*." Benji pleads. "I haven't had the heart to tell you before, but it must be said. You're an ancient man with bones of chalk. If you break everything, I'll have to say I told you so and push you around in a wheelbarrow."

"*Pish*," declares Maurice. "If the Marines didn't break me, a bicycle older than even you certainly won't."

Maurice was a Marine? I'd like to ask, but there are more immediate concerns. Like Maurice breaking all his bones!

"There is much danger in any *velo*," Pierre-Luc agrees amiably. "If you go over the front of the penny farthing, you are a missile." He acts out an arching missile, complete with an explosion or the shattering of Maurice's bones. *Not helpful, Pierre-Luc!*

"Here is the secret, my friends," our host says. "You must believe you will not fall. Do not think of what you fear. Never utter the word."

Benji covers his own mouth with both hands.

Maurice practices on the tiny step. He balances, leans, and repeats. Up, down, up . . .

I'm soothed. *Nothing scary in this.*

Then suddenly, he's lurching onto the saddle. He whoops. The big wheel wobbles like a tipsy top.

Benji covers his face with his cap and moans.

"He is a natural," Pierre-Luc says.

Maurice looks fragile and breakable above the massive wheel. He also looks oh-so-pleased.

"I'll take her for a jaunt on the open road, shall I?" he says.

Before I can find a polite way to tell him no, Pierre-Luc encourages him.

"Ride like the wind, *mon ami*! Believe! Be fearless!"

Maurice rolls down the cobbled drive, Chou Chou leaping dangerously at his side.

"Ah, but you must tell him this," Pierre-Luc says, turning to me and belatedly issuing safety instructions in rapid

French. I wish Nadiya were here. She's the faster translator, but she's calling our lunch bistro, letting them know we might be late.

"Sit tall!" I call as Maurice picks up speed.

I jog after him, yelling over Chou Chou's delighted barks. "Keep pedaling! Remember the, *ummmm* . . ." French and English fail me.

"The thingamajig!" Benji zips by on his bike, nearly clipping me. "The step! The step is behind you, Maurice! Brake, but not too hard!"

Maurice barrels toward the road we should have left in our rearview mirrors. Benji, hunched over his handlebars, is catching up with Maurice. More bikes pass me like a madcap scene from a silent film. The Spinners are giving chase. All we need is a soundtrack, I think. Then I hear it.

Electronica pulsates across the vineyards. The beat grows louder. I break stride and squint into the sun. A flash of bumblebee yellow zips around the village, taking the form of a low-slung convertible. Throaty acceleration turns up our road. I don't have to calculate velocities to know with gut-pitching certainty that the sports car, my tour group, my fleet of expensive bikes, and a beloved canine are on a collision course.

I try to sprint, but my bike-honed muscles twinge and cramp. Like in a nightmare, I'm freezing up just when I need to go faster.

A chipper *beep beep* comes from behind me. Pierre-Luc chugs down the drive in a utility vehicle. Vine trimmings and tools bounce in the back bed.

"*Allez*," he says, patting a worn bench seat. "Jump in."

I slide onto the seat and am promptly crushed by a wooly mammoth. Chou Chou pants in my face, giddy with doggy delight.

"Maurice knows how to brake?" I ask, ducking slobbery kisses. "You went over that?"

"He has the natural instinct," Pierre-Luc says. "Monsieur understands how the penny farthing was designed to be ridden—with joy and abandon!"

In theory, joy and abandon form my core philosophy of cycling. In reality? I want my guests encased in Bubble Wrap.

Maurice is extending back a leg but missing the tiny step by a long shot. In a few more zigzagging wobbles, he'll reach the road. Chou Chou's barks mingle with the club music and Benji's frantic cries to *brake, turn, abandon bike*! Pierre-Luc is humming—humming as if he hasn't a worry in the world!

I squeeze my eyes shut, hold Chou Chou's warm doggy body close, and attempt those positive aspirations the women's magazine demanded. *This will be a fun story for the Silver Spinners. Years from now, they'll remember this tour fondly. The time when Maurice rode a runaway penny farthing and our guide was crushed by a wooly mammoth and—*

A horn honks, a polite honk that morphs into an unrelenting blare. I clutch Chou Chou harder, bracing for the crash we won't feel except in my soul. Metal on metal and bone. Pavement scraping away soft tissue and spandex.

There's a sickening thump. The horn lets up with a yelp, replaced by Chou Chou's baritone barks. My stomach pitches until a cheer crashes in.

"*Voilà!*" Pierre-Luc declares, and the weight lifts, figuratively and literally. Chou Chou leaps from my lap, and I gape at a scene I'd usually file as a disaster. The convertible has left the road, forded the roadside ditch, and stopped grill-to-oak against the fourth massive barrel, the 5 in 1715. The music stops. The driver, a leather-tanned man with slicked-back hair is issuing a master class in rude gestures and vivid Italian cursing. I can't say I blame him. He swerved to avoid a rogue penny farthing. His good deed has left his sporty ride wedged against a seven-foot barrel.

I, however, am focused on the positive. Maurice is upright. He's gloriously standing, flicking imaginary dust from his white jersey, as unmarred as the vintage bike. The Spinners surround him. He takes a bow.

He did it! We did it. We dodged a disaster. Pierre-Luc is smoothing things out with the driver and helping him reverse. "Slowly, slowly, Monsieur, so the barrel does not bobble toward you."

Pierre-Luc has that covered, so I join my group. Enveloped in their happy bubble of laughter and chatter, I barely register the first creak. I hear the second, an agonized groan. As the convertible eases back, the barrel rocks on its wooden cradle.

Pierre-Luc and the driver register the situation simultaneously but with opposite reactions. Pierre-Luc yells for the driver to brake. The driver punches the gas. With a wheezy whine, the car surges backward. Pierre-Luc jumps aside. My group scatters as the convertible skids back onto the road. The driver jumps out to inspect his bumper. I don't speak Italian, but between the obvious curses and hand gestures, I intuit that Pierre-Luc will be hearing from insurance adjusters. Which means that Oui Cycle might be too. My stomach flips to the beat of the thumping bass as the luxury car revs, then peels off down the lane.

Meanwhile, the barrel looks like it's waving goodbye. It rocks on its rounded stand. For a moment, I think it's about to wobble safely back to rest. That wouldn't be my luck today, would it? With a groan, the barrel crests the stand's lip and starts to roll.

Scarlett yells. "Save the wine!"

Lionel throws himself in front of Rosemary, although they're uphill of its path.

"The barrel is empty," Pierre-Luc calls. "But stay back, please! It is heavy."

The barrel bounces across the ditch and onto the road. I

imagine it toddling off on a tour of the countryside, visiting family in the forests and vines. My fantasy—and the barrel's tour—end as it gutters in the opposite ditch.

My group gives a collective gasp.

Pierre-Luc laughs. "We survive! Come, my friends, shall we toast our good fortune?"

"A toast to living!" Maurice agrees, grinning like a kid.

"To cycling on," I declare, both relieved and hoping to plant the idea of moving on in my riders' minds. "Thank you, Pierre-Luc. This has been extraordinary. We'll toast your hospitality and then get out of your—"

I'm interrupted by the sounds I dreaded minutes ago. Metal creaks. A rusty stave gives way. Wood buckles. The barrel's top pops off like a bottle cap.

"Oh dear," Maurice says, adjusting his glasses.

Benji tuts in scandalized delight. Lionel hangs his head as if he had predicted such a sorrowful fate.

"I'm sorry!" I exclaim. "Oui Cycle will pay."

The accountant in me trembles. Old French oak barrels are practically worth their weight in gold. Does my insurance cover preventable folly?

Pierre-Luc flicks his hand. "It is nothing. My farmhand will be delighted. He can use the wood to repair other barrels. Now, come, we shall toast."

"A photo first," declares Scarlett. "So we don't forget."

There's laughter—*as if they'd ever forget this!*

A happy story! I'm in their legends.

Lionel perks up. "We must compose the photo just right. Here, stand on the road so the barrel is in the background and we capture the utter shambles and skid marks. Perfect! Pierre-Luc, please, stand in the middle."

I volunteer to take the first shots. Lionel hands me the camera and joins the group. Arms loop over shoulders. Scarlett leans too close to Pierre-Luc's sun-kissed face. Benji squishes his cheek to Maurice's. Keiko rolls her eyes theatrically. Rosemary tickles Lionel's side and makes him giggle.

"Get our good sides, Sadie, dear!" Scarlett commands. "Then we'll set the timer and get you in here."

I aim the camera high, then low. I'm not even sure what caught my eye. Was it the small patch of pale in the age-darkened wood? The shape, like fingers? The gold glint?

Time and my heart seem to stop. I lower the camera and blink, willing the image to change. One by one, my riders turn. The birds and crickets go silent, or maybe the whoosh pounding through my temples drowns them out.

Pierre-Luc reacts first. With a gasped "*mon Dieu*," he dashes for the barrel. We all follow. This time, I pass the Silver Spinners in my sprint, but we stop a few feet away, as if crashing into a wall of horror.

"It's him!" Keiko's voice rises in triumph. "That's the man! I recognize that watch. I told you he was real. I *told you he was dead!*"

CHAPTER 5

Tour-guide tidbit: Large wooden barrels capable of holding thousands of liters are often used to age wine in Alsace. These barrels are called *foudres*, which is also the term for "lightning." Perhaps because both make striking impressions?

Pierre-Luc tugs at a stave. "We must free him! How is this man here, in this ditch, of all the places and times?"

"Hold up there, mate." Maurice bends and peers into the wreckage. "He's not in the ditch. He's in your barrel. Look there. That wrist is lying on old oak. He was already inside when it rolled, wouldn't you say?"

Pierre-Luc steps back as if singed. "Inside? But . . . *Non!* How? How is a man in my barrel?"

Not even Scarlett has an answer.

Rosemary pushes through the little crowd. "I know first aid. We must check for his pulse."

"He's dead," Keiko calls over. She waggles her phone. "*I'm* calling the police now."

I nod vigorously. *Great, wonderful, call away!* Except Keiko doesn't speak French, which is why she didn't call last night. I'm torn between taking over the call and stopping Rosemary. Guests should not have to touch bodies on a Oui Cycle tour.

Rosemary extends a trembling hand.

"Stop!" I exclaim, so sharply that she startles. I put a hand on her shoulder, and she jumps again.

"I'll do it," I say. I'd rather be run over by a barrel, but this seems like an unwritten duty of guiding, a task way beyond such burdens as lugging luggage, navigating the French railway ticket website, or detouring around striking farmworkers blocking major motorways with mountains of manure.

"Sadie knows her death," Scarlett says supportively. "She's our little murder leader."

"Murder?" Rosemary says shakily. "Who said it's murder?"

"No one! Let's not assume that!" I blurt, again forgetting my don't-yell-at-guests rule.

Pierre-Luc scowls but steps away, clearing my view. The man—I assume—wears a thick watch that looks old, gold, and expensive. I kneel beside him. In this too-close view, I can see two lines peeking from underneath the wide watchband. They're blue, angled like waves.

I inhale and jab my hand out, fast. I've barely touched the wax-still skin when my fingers jerk back as if burned. The morning is warm. He is cold. I stumble up and back. I'm in the middle of the road when Scarlett grabs me.

"Sadie!" she chides. "Be careful! We can't lose you too!"

I register a crunch of tires. For a moment, I'm buoyed. Help is here! I can leave this to the professionals. We'll cycle on, letting the wind blow away the tarnish of death and—

The vehicle is boxy and buttercup yellow. It's coming not from the village but the direction of the Inn of the Three Storks.

Gabi pulls up and leans over the passenger seat to the open window. "What is happening?"

Pierre-Luc explains. There are gestures and shocked gasps, and Pierre-Luc announces that he's calling the police. Thank goodness. Keiko is loudly enunciating into her phone. "Dead man. Dead. Mort?"

Fingers touch my arm and I jump.

Nadiya's eyes are as wide as wheels. "I step away to call the restaurant and there is this? A person in the barrel? Who?"

"No one we know," I say and am immediately ashamed at my relief. My group is safe, but someone will know this man. They may be pacing their kitchen right now, worried, texting, waiting for him to come home.

"It's terrible," I add quickly. "A tragedy." Relief clings to me like a sticky, sickly film.

Nadiya crosses herself. "Yes, yes, terrible. But it is not our tragedy. Not this time."

A car door slams. Gabi rounds her sunny hatchback, pushing by a protesting Pierre-Luc. He's right. No good can come of her seeing the man. She can't help.

She frowns down at the body. Then, with a cry, she falls to her knees. Her wail rises in a pained duet with the whoop of a siren.

"Pierre-Luc, *non, non,* look, under that watch, the tattoo! It's my Eddie! Oh, Eddie!"

"Poor Gabi." Benji tuts as more emergency vehicles cram the narrow lane. We've been relegated to wait at the end of Pierre-Luc's drive, the side opposite three wine barrels ringed in crime-scene tape, red and white like candy cane stripes.

"Her husband!" Benji continues. "Dead in a barrel? What are the odds?"

My statistics-loving mind latches onto that question. What *are* the odds? Better than death striking a second Oui Cycle tour? The barrel was close to the victim's residence. Statistically, most deaths occur at home. It only makes sense. You're there a lot, and there are all sorts of hazards: overheated toaster ovens, candles by curtains, stairs to trip down, pets underfoot, invisible gases, and electrical currents, and tornados . . . I could go on. I briefly dabbled in actuarial tables.

On the other hand, it's only August. Tabloids documenting my June tour of murder must still linger at dentists' offices and beauty salons. What are those odds?

Maurice sighs, interrupting my impossible calculation. He consults his watch once again.

I do the same. Forty-three minutes ago, Annette Dubois, chief of police, promised she'd be right with us. I could tell Maurice that forty-three minutes is a minor wait time at scenes of suspicious deaths, but this is expertise I don't want to flaunt.

"Poor darling," Scarlett echoes Benji. She's fussing at the chipped edge of a nail.

We've been repeating versions of *poor Gabi, poor dear, poor thing*. What else can we say? Really, the poor woman! How shocking! How tragic! *How very odd . . .*

I've kept that last thought to myself because it seems rude, but it is strange, isn't it? Wasn't her husband supposed to be at a conference? Enjoying foodie Lyon, talking up the inn, mingling? Just this morning, Gabi thought she was texting Eddie there. Did he return early? Never leave? How did he end up in the courtyard, then in a barrel? I have so many questions!

"At least she knows," says Rosemary. "That's a blessing." She's sitting in the grass, legs crossed, a daisy in hand. She beheads the flower with a flick of her thumb.

"Yes!" agrees Scarlett. "Good point, Rosemary, dear.

Maurice, you're a hero. That man could have gone mummified in that big old barrel. Poor Gabi might never have known."

Benji declares his partner selfless. "That's what your reckless endangerment is, *mon petit chou*. Selfish and selfless." He loops his arm around Maurice's waist and pulls him close.

Mon petit chou? I imagine myself calling Detective Jacques Laurent *my little cabbage*. Ha!

Levity fizzles when a gendarme hatchback completes an eleven-point turn on the narrow lane, opening our view of poor Gabi. There's another tragedy. Her name will be double-barreled, *Poor-Gabi Morel*. My mother had an auntie like that. Forever Poor Marie.

Poor Gabi sits slumped in the back of the ambulance, feet hanging limply off the end. Pierre-Luc stands beside her, hand on her shoulder. Both look shattered. Chief Dubois is speaking with them. She's apparently in charge for now, although a specialized gendarme investigator will likely be sent in. I know this stuff now. Murder is how I met Laurent—not exactly the meet-cute of a romance novel.

I think about texting Laurent, then reconsider. This could still be a freak accident. Laurent will be busy with whatever he's training for in the forest. Wilderness survival? Tracking? Endurance of unsavory buffets? And, okay . . . There's another reason too: I don't want Laurent dwelling on my statistically high association with suspicious death.

Benji tuts again. "If Gabi did it, she's utterly devastated now, poor lamb."

"Did it?" Rosemary's head jerks up.

Lionel—a teddy bear of a man, according to his doting auntie—balls his fists.

"Not every dead husband has been killed by his wife," Rosemary says tartly.

"Oh, now, Rosie Petal," Benji tuts. "I didn't mean you!"

What? Bea filled me in on her beloved nephew's new romantic relationship. Rosemary is a sweet woman, Bea had said. Quiet, efficient, a devoted mother and businesswoman, tragically, a widow too young. Rosemary and Lionel have known each other for years, but only recently had bereaved Rosemary been ready to date again.

"It is a reasonable supposition." Maurice strikes a pensive pose, a finger tapping his upper lip. "Even if we like Gabi and anecdotally know wives who *likely* didn't murder their husbands."

"Likely?" Rosemary splutters.

Maurice addresses me. "Sadie, you know crime. Is the spouse always a prime suspect?" He tilts his head, as if innocently querulous. He clearly thinks he's right.

"We don't know it's a crime yet," I say.

Nadiya, lying on her back in the grass, snorts.

"*They* think it's a crime." Benji nods toward the emergency vehicles across the street. "The lights are as flashy as a nightclub over there. Sadie, you were here before us. Did you meet the husband? Was he the type to be murdered?"

Offended huffs from Rosemary and Lionel.

"I didn't meet him," I say. "I was in the area but stayed near Colmar." To save money, I stayed in a chain hotel in the nearest city. Every morning, I'd cycle over here and fine-tune my itineraries. The day before the Spinners arrived, I stopped to double-check our booking. I spoke with Gabi. Eddie would have been in Lyon. At least, that's where he was supposed to be.

"No matter," Benji says. "We're already way ahead of the police. Keiko saw the body first."

"So now you believe me," Keiko says, distractedly rubbing her bandaged elbow.

I wonder how—and when—she scraped it.

"A pity," Maurice says. "If you hadn't seen the body, Keiko, we could simply explain the barrel accident and be on our way."

"Excuse me!" Keiko huffs. "You and your bicycle handling are what have us waiting here."

I interrupt. Tensions are clearly high and frayed. "We'll do all we can to help, then cycle on."

"Exactly so," says Maurice. "All right, troops, here is the plan."

I feel my shoulders squaring to attention. In this moment, I can see Maurice as a Marine commander.

Maurice pushes back his glasses. "We give that policewoman just the facts. No chitchat. No speculation. No dishing out information unless she specifically asks for it."

"But darling . . ." Benji says, pouting. "We can help solve this. You know I've always wanted to solve a murder mystery. Keiko, we need you to awake from your sleep-cycling fog and produce a clue."

Keiko presses fingers to her temples.

Benji rolls on. "Besides, we have Sadie, our super-sleuth. Wouldn't it be a feather in our helmets if we solved this? We could! Think of our combined experience."

Nope! No more crime solving! "Maurice is right," I say firmly. "We'll be most helpful by keeping out of the way and out of trouble."

Benji sighs.

Nadiya sits up. "Too late for that. Trouble comes for us."

CHAPTER 6

Tour-guide tidbit: Storks are considered good luck in Alsace, but they needed more than luck to rebound from population losses. Stork conservation efforts include the construction of nesting platforms on rooftops, chimneys, and poles. These platforms must be strong: stork nests can weigh up to five hundred pounds!

"You're *that* bike tour company?" It's a question, but not a question. Chief Annette Dubois is around my age. My age, and she holds a top title in her field. Mom would brag about that. She'd tell strangers—grocery clerks, pedestrians stuck at crosswalks, clients of the real estate company where she works as the office manager. I doubt she brags that her single, thirty-year-old daughter ditched a good job with benefits to ride a bike. Although, I am chief cycling officer of *that* bike company.

"We're Oui Cycle," I say. "From Sans-Souci-sur-Mer. That's south of—"

"I know where it is," Chief Dubois snaps, stern as her hairstyle, a bun pulled so tight it's giving her a facelift. At least she has a light-hearted sidekick. Chou Chou has come along, likely hoping for more fun chaos. His ears perk. His pollen-dusted nose twitches. With the thrust of a pointer, he jabs his snout at Lionel's salmon-colored capris.

Lionel gasps and steps away.

The chief snatches Chou Chou's collar, leaning back to keep him in check.

"Why are you *here*?" the chief asks, as Chou Chou pants enthusiastically. "What are you doing in our *beau village*?"

Didn't she just answer her own question with *beau village*? I muster a smile and a line from my recently renovated website. "Oui Cycle offers personalized and customized tours throughout France." I wave a palm at the obvious. "This is a beautiful region, lovely for cycling and—"

"It's my fault, I'm afraid," Rosemary interjects.

"Never!" blurts Lionel, stepping up to grip Rosemary's hand.

"Nonsense!" Scarlett agrees. "No one on our tour is to blame."

"Yet who among us is truly blameless?" Benji muses.

"Script!" Maurice barks. "Hold the line, troops!"

Good luck with that.

Chief Dubois cocks her head as if innocently interested. "Madame Perch, why do you say this is your fault?"

"I selected this destination," Rosemary says.

"And quite right that you did," says Scarlett. "Dame Scarlett Crabtree-Thorne," she says to the chief. "I am Rosemary's godmother. I *insisted* that Rosemary choose. Picking the location is part of the adventure. Take life by the handlebars, that's what I say!"

Rosemary offers a rueful smile. "Yes, well, I was at a bit of a loss. I'm not as well-traveled as the Silver Spinners. I've been busy raising two boys and running a business, but now my sons are grown and have their own families and—"

"Time to live a little!" Scarlett says a touch too heartily given our proximity to death.

"Quite," Rosemary agrees grimly. "I decided I needed a fresh start all around. I did a good clear-out of my wardrobes and my spare room—my box room full of this and that. You know . . ."

Jacques Laurent would be happy to let an interviewee gabble on, knowing they might say something interesting, something unintended, something incriminating. Chief Dubois apparently lacks such patience. She spins an index finger in a wrap-it-up gesture. "Your point, Madame?"

"My apologies!" Rosemary flushes. "That's when I found it, you see. At the back of my closet. It seemed like such a good sign and—."

"Found what?" I ask lest the chief explode. Her lip had been twitching.

"A brochure." Rosemary shakes her head as if still marveling. "It was wedged behind a box I hadn't touched in ages, the prettiest brochure of this lovely village with an inn listed on the back. Lionel agreed it looked lovely. We did some research—well, Lionel did the bulk of the research—"

"I merely sent away for literature," Lionel says. "You had the inspiration, Rosemary."

Rosemary draws a deep breath. "It seemed perfect, so here we are."

"*D'accord,*" the chief says through a sigh. *Agreed.* "That explains why you chose Riquewihr. But why did you choose *this* cycling company? A company from so far away? A company with a dubious reputation?"

Dubious? I decide I'm not in a good position to argue that insult.

"Dubious?" Scarlett huffs on my behalf. "Our cycling club has used Oui Cycle for several outstanding tours."

She pats her silver helmet of hair. "The former owners are dear friends. They sold the business to young Sadie here, and what with Sadie's recent *adventures*, we thought we should show our support."

"Her *adventures* with multiple crimes?" the chief says mildly. "That was a deciding point for you?"

"Absolutely!" says Benji. "We're chuffed to have such a famous guide! Of course, we never imagined we'd get our *own* murder." He bites his lower lip, probably trying not to look thrilled.

Maurice hangs his head.

"You think it is murder, then?" the chief asks. "You know so?"

"No!" I practically shout. I lower my tone to somber. "All we know is that we feel awful for poor Gabi. She's a lovely woman. This is tragic."

"Tragic," Benji repeats. "But we do wonder . . . The spouse is a prime suspect, no?"

The chief directs her reply to Chou Chou. "Hear that, Chou Chou? The tourists offer us a suspect. What would we do without them?" Chou Chou pants up at her, then betrays their moment of camaraderie to lunge free and again jab his snout at Lionel.

"I say!" Lionel blurts. "Cheeky dog, isn't he?"

"He's after the cookies in your pockets." Rosemary laughs, then covers her mouth. "I'm sorry. It's no time to laugh."

Benji chuckles, unabashed. "Anytime is a good time to laugh. That's a motto of the Silver Spinners. Guard your cookies, Lionel. You've become quite the man of desire these days."

"Here now," Lionel huffs, stepping back and drawing out a travel-sized packet of shortbread. He rips open the packet and offers a thick, fluted shortbread to Chou

Chou, who inhales it like he's starving. Fibber. Back in the salon, we'd treated him to gourmet cured meats and dog biscuits from a specialty bakery in Strasbourg.

Lionel rubs his fingers on his pants. "These are Rose Petal Shortbreads from Rosemary's family bakery. Chou Chou has refined tastes."

The chief scoffs. "Chou Chou eats everything, anything. Shoes, plaster, one of the finest pinot noir vines in the department. He is *un chien criminel*, a repeat offender."

The dog criminal shoots her a toothy grin before resuming his aim on Lionel. Lionel gives up and tosses the remaining shortbread.

I'm not surprised Chou Chou is an eater of shoes. I'm also unsurprised that the chief knows the village down to its canines. Everyone knows everyone and everything in a village.

Back in Sans-Souci, my neighbor two doors down recently asked me how I enjoyed the *pain au chocolat* from a bakery three villages to the north. "*Très sucré?*" she'd said with a wink and a twinkle. *Very sweet.* I'd been on a bakery scouting mission with Laurent. We'd cycled there over serene back roads. I hadn't noticed anyone from Sans-Souci, but I wouldn't need to. Someone must have recognized Laurent or me and mentioned the sighting to my neighbor. Or to the butcher who spoke to the neighbor's cousin's hairdresser. Such is the superpower of village gossip and observation.

Hope rolls in. That's how this case will be solved. Someone will have seen or heard something.

The chief pats her pockets. "I will show you a photograph of the deceased," she announces. "You will tell me if you have seen him previously."

Do we have to? I recall the chilly wrist and recoil.

Keiko steps forward. "I'll look. Did Pierre-Luc tell you

that I found the dead man last night? You'll wonder why we didn't call you."

The chief's smile is that of an alligator anticipating a juicy body part. "Pierre-Luc did tell me, and it is true, I wonder many things."

"Don't we all," says Maurice with a heavy sigh.

I take a deep breath and let my apologies out in a whoosh. "That's my fault. Keiko came to me for help. When we returned to the spot, he was gone."

"The body walked away?" the chief says.

"Zombies . . ." Benji whispers. "Ow!" He's been elbowed by Maurice.

At the chief's request, I describe the location: the courtyard with the *winstüb* and wineshop, the antiques, and the pizzeria with twelve varieties of *tarte flambée*.

"The *winstüb* with the good sauerkraut?" the chief asks, handing her phone casually to Keiko.

Maybe? Before I can answer, Keiko is pointing at the screen.

"That's him! I'll never forget those eyes. That birthmark too—I could see a fragment of it, under his collar. I *told* everyone I'd seen a dead man. No one believed me." Keiko frowns at us all.

"Keiko, darling, you're our hero!" Benji bubbles. He turns to the chief. "You'll want your forensics people up to that courtyard. Shame it's so late in the game. The place will be absolutely overrun with tourists." He tuts, as if we're above tourism.

In the middle distance, a tour bus pulls into the parking lot outside the village's medieval walls. It looks like a cruise ship floating above the vines.

"I'm sorry," I apologize once again. "I wish I'd called the police. When the gentleman wasn't there, I reasoned that he'd been drunk or passed out. I thought he walked away on his own."

"*Like a zombie*," Benji whispers again.

"Walked away? A dead man?" The chief asks, scorn dripping.

I'm afraid Benji is about to elaborate on zombies.

Maybe Maurice is too. "We don't know he was dead," Maurice says firmly, as Keiko gestures in frustration toward the scene across the street.

Maurice taps his upper lip thoughtfully. "Keiko, you say you saw the prone gentleman. As Sadie suggests, he might not have been dead. Perhaps he took a tumble? Suffered a bump on the head like our Sadie?"

The chief stares at my goose egg so hard I swear it throbs like a telltale heart.

"When did you get that?" she asks.

I explain beams and an abrupt morning wake-up. Her eyes narrow, as if her region isn't rife with forehead-threatening timbers.

Maurice keeps spinning his story. "The fated gentleman arises. He stumbles downhill. His home is not far, but he is weary. His injury makes him confused. In the true tragedy of the evening, he decides to rest, to curl up for a nap somewhere private. Natural causes take their effect and then . . ." Maurice dips his head in a little bow toward the scene across the street. "Voilà."

Voilà, indeed! Of course, there are massive holes in the theory, like the gaping crevice between a nap and sudden death in a sealed barrel beside the road when his comfortable house and his buddy's hip hangout are mere meters away. But I won't argue. I'd had the same hopeful thought myself.

My group is nodding as one. Chou Chou grins as if he's in too.

Chief Dubois looks less convinced. "So . . . an adult man with no known medical condition crawls into a barrel and dies?" She lets that thought hang among us before shrugging. "*Peut-être.*"

"Yes, perhaps," says Maurice, looking pleased.

The chief puffs her cheeks, then exhales like a pufferfish deflated by disdain. "But then, how do we explain the blunt force wound to the back of his head and the mark of what appears to be a bicycle wheel on his clothing?"

Keiko pales and slaps a protective hand over her elbow. "No, I swerved! He was dead. Already dead!" She thrusts the phone away. Maurice grabs it.

Maurice says crisply, "Dead or alive, we don't know this gentleman, so we can help no further." He taps the phone screen to life.

I'm expecting him to hand it straight back, stranger confirmed.

He stares. He holds the screen out, then close. He pushes back his glasses, then pulls them down and looks over them.

"Darling? Are you ill?" Benji touches his partner's arm. "Too much sun? Your brush with that Italian death convertible!"

"It's the death aura," Keiko declares. "He's seen it. You have to look straight at the eyes."

Benji is staring at the phone now too. He and Maurice are huddled over the small screen.

"Now they've both seen it," Keiko says, but a frown etches her forehead. She senses it too, clear as the blue sky above. Something's wrong. Correction: something else is wrong. Unease doesn't just tap on my shoulder; it rams it like a jousting knight.

"Scarlett!" Benji whisper-hisses, waving a cupped hand, urging her to join them.

She ignores him. She's borrowed a multitool from well-prepared Lionel and is filing her chipped nail.

Benji breaks away and tugs her over to the phone.

Scarlett grumbles about her nail. Then her scowl deepens. Like Maurice before her, she cycles through gape-mouthed incomprehension to shocked denial. "Good glory in the morning! No! No, it can't be! Why, look at the next photo, the wrist detail. A tattoo? Never! That's not him."

"You do recognize him?" the chief asks, unable to hide her surprise.

"That birthmark," Benji whispers. "The ears, too little for that massive hunk of a skull. *It's him!* We *have* to show her. Give me the phone, Scarlett. Give it!"

Scarlett holds the phone high and away. Chou Chou perks up. He could get in on this game.

"It's coincidence," declares Maurice. He steps back and smooths an impossible-to-wrinkle cycling jersey. His glasses remain askew. "I admit, I was initially surprised. The unfortunate man was cursed with a resemblance. You're correct, Scarlett. Our boy would never have a tattoo. Especially one so . . . so trite."

"Basic," Benji says. "But that birthmark. You saw it. It's shaped exactly like, oh, what did you always call it, Scarlett? A flattened flounder? *That's him!*"

"What's happening?" Rosemary approaches, face pinched in concern. "Scarlett? What's upset you?"

"Show her," Benji begs. "Madame Chief will if we don't."

"*Oui, certainement*," the chief agrees. "I will." She and Chou Chou sport the same look of eager intensity. *Things are about to get fun.*

I want to leap in, block my group, toss the phone in the nearest ditch, take to our bikes, and ride away as fast as we can. Beside me, Nadiya bristles. I know what she's thinking. This has nothing to do with us. It can't. None of us are from here. We're tourists, far from home.

"What has gotten into you people?" Keiko demands.

"This was largely before your time in Lower Thornbury, Kei-Kei," Scarlett says. "You didn't know him as well, so you wouldn't see the resemblance. In any case, it's a false alarm. All's well. Carry on, as we half-English say, right, Maurice?"

Quick as Chou Chou stealing a cookie, Rosemary snags the phone from her godmother's hand.

I'm not big on sports analogies, but Jordi plays rugby and I've been to some of his matches. The players clump up in scrums. That's what I'm seeing now. A protective, silver-haired scrum has closed around Rosemary.

Lionel tries to get in, but the three elders jostle him away.

Rosemary is as unmoving as marble. I worry she's not breathing until she gulps air. Her friends inch closer, cooing, patting, murmuring sympathetic words. She shoves them aside.

"He's been alive? Alive all this time?" Her voice shakes before turning as low and chilly as a grave. "Here in this beautiful place while I . . . Oh! Oh, I could kill him!" She lets the phone drop and takes off toward the stricken barrel and body.

"Twice too late for that, petal blossom," calls out Benji, jogging to keep up with Rosemary. "But fine sentiment. We all agree, I'm sure."

Scarlett and Maurice join the pack storming a likely crime scene.

"Rosemary?" Lionel tags behind them like a worried puppy. When Rosemary doesn't stop, he backtracks and grabs up the phone. His face goes ashen. His knees buckle, but there's no cluster of friends to catch him.

I rush to Lionel and help him up. His palms are chilly and clammy.

The chief looks torn about who to follow. Chou Chou lopes off after a butterfly, leaping and missing. I want to go with him.

"Who is he?" I ask Lionel instead. "Who did you see in the photo?"

The chief hovers at my side, muttering urgent commands into her radio. I sense movement in the periphery of my vision, EMTs who'd previously had nothing to do are rushing our way.

"Edwin," Lionel says. His warm brown skin has acquired a sickly gray tinge. "It's Edwin Perch. It's impossible but unmistakable. That birthmark. Those ears. That's *Rosemary's* husband."

The dead man is Rosemary's husband *and* Gabi's husband? That makes no sense. Clearly, I need to improve my listening skills. "But—but I thought Rosemary was a widow?"

Lionel puddles onto a clump of clover, still gripping my hand like a life raft. "She thought she was a widow too. For the last fifteen years, we all did."

CHAPTER 7

Saturday lunch:
I hope you've worked up an appetite: We'll enjoy a three-course menu at a delightful bistro in Ribeauvillé. Get ready to make some tough decisions, though. The bistro offers four choices each for appetizer and main plate, plus the option of cheese course or dessert.

Revised Saturday lunch:
Sandwiches?

Rosemary is lying down, upstairs in the room with the four-poster bed and a view of Riquewihr framed in diamond-paned windows. She wanted to be alone.

Lionel is also lying down. Since Rosemary claimed the room they share, he's in the library, a downstairs room stuffed with beams and books and upholstered armchairs flanking tall windows. I yearned to test each chair, rating its squashy comfort while escaping into a nice fictional mystery. Previous guests left vacation reads behind, paperbacks by Dan Brown and Stieg Larsson, Ann Cleeves and Patricia Cornwall, and an entire shelf of Agatha Christies in a world of languages.

Instead, I opened each window, reached out—once

again marveling at rural France's aversion to window screens—and drew the shutters closed. A wasp and a swarm of dust motes rushed in before I could do up the latches. The wasp required a shooing eviction with a *Cuisine et Vins* magazine. The dust suggested it had been a long time since anyone wished to banish the daylight. I closed the door and left Lionel prone on a green velvet love seat, ankles over the armrest, a damp towel over his eyes.

This was nearly an hour ago. I should probably check on Lionel, but I don't dare leave the elder Spinners unattended.

A wine cork pops. We're lunching in the breakfast room with a guest who makes me more nervous than the wasp. Chief Dubois assigned a young deputy to sit with us. Presumably, he's here as a grief counselor. From his extensive notetaking, I suspect he's really here to record anything suspicious we might say.

"Ah, very nice, 2010 pinot gris, Fronholz," Maurice says, squinting at the fine print on a long, elegantly necked bottle. "Biodynamic, bracing acidity, grown in quartz, hints of stone."

"Sounds like you, *mon cheri.*" Benji holds out his glass.

Jordi went on a wine run earlier with a pocketful of Euros and instructions to "hurry, before they close off that nice wineshop by Keiko's crime scene" and to "get something good." By good, the Silver Spinners meant aged because "everything is better with age!"

Also, because "age comes with a price," Jordi was given permission to go up to seventy Euros per bottle.

The pinot makes its rounds. When the bottle reaches me, I admire the label and automatically translate the sticker price. Sixty-eight dollars, rounding up. We're pairing the expensive (to me) wine with baguette sandwiches Nadiya foraged from a picnic caterer in the village. She and Jordi are dining in the van and decompressing.

I pour myself some wine, just enough to admire the floral aroma and savor a taste or two. I want to keep my wits about me. I wish the Spinners felt the same, but I get their reaction too. Someone they knew has died. Again.

"Sure you wouldn't like a splash, son?" Maurice asks Deputy Allard. The deputy looks up from his notebook. He's surely past the drinking age of eighteen—he is a deputy, after all—but he could pass as a young teenager. He's tall, fresh-faced, and eager. Way too eager.

"*Non, merci, Monsieur*," Deputy Allard says politely, stretching the fingers of his writing hand. He must be cramping from recording so many suspicions.

"I resent Edwin now," Benji declares, reaching for a hunk of baguette with butter and ham. "Living here when we all thought he'd been taken by the waves and sharks and whatnot." He shudders, although we can be pretty sure none of that happened.

"*Resent?*" Scarlett snorts. "I can whip up stronger emotions than resentment. That man took his lovely wife and sons on vacation and then up and disappeared for fifteen years?" She reaches for a tomato, Munster, and basil sandwich. The catering shop offered Nadiya what they called their "party" sampler, the baguette equivalent of finger sandwiches. Nadiya thinks they had a last-minute party cancellation. The sandwiches came packed in lidded plastic platters decorated with inappropriately festive balloon stickers. I recast the balloons as a regional thing, which is true. The nearby rounded Vosges Mountains are called "balloons."

"I, personally, could throttle him," Scarlett continues. She waves her wine glass at Deputy Allard. "Write that down, young man. I am sorry he's dead because I would like to throttle him."

Deputy Allard mouths out "throttle" and nods rapidly. I can relate. The young deputy was likely chosen for his

English abilities, but he's out of his depth with the Spinners' reeling conversation. I resist the urge to helpfully define and spell *throttle*.

Maurice clears his throat pointedly. "Remember the plan."

That would be the plan to volunteer no information? We've seriously detoured from that practical path.

"Remember the weekend Edwin went missing?" Benji counters with a burdened sigh. "Talk about ruining *everyone's* plans. Maurice and I were supposed to attend an estate sale in Chipping Norton. Instead, we hauled off to Cornwall and stabbed hiking sticks at the dunes, hoping to unearth Edwin's bloated body. My skull got burned. I didn't want to complain at the time because, well . . . moldering Edwin, tossed out to sea and all." He pats the flatcap that seems a permanent fixture unless he's wearing his bike helmet.

"A wake-up call," Maurice says. "You were in denial of your hair situation." He smiles fondly. "Or lack of it, and that was fifteen years ago."

"Among the many miseries of that blighted weekend." Benji groans, then turns to me. "There were so many volunteer searchers, they gobbled up every decent hotel. We had to get a hostel. A hostel!"

He raises his glass to Scarlett. "I'm with you, darling. I want him alive to give him a good telling off." He whips his other hand back and forth to suggest the telling off would include a firm slapping.

"*Oui, oui,*" Deputy Allard murmurs. "Very good."

None of this is good. I'm relieved when Keiko shifts to less violent memories.

"Pink ribbons," Keiko says. "That's what I remember. I was out of the country when Edwin went missing. When I returned, all of Lower Thornbury was wrapped up in pink. I donated to a breast cancer benefit before I realized the bows were for Edwin. Edwin, of all people!"

"Those were Rose Petal Ribbons of Hope," Scarlett says, refilling her glass. "Lionel's idea. I told him the ribbon color was confusing. I wanted flyers: STUFFY DO-NOTHING, MISSING. WIFE BETTER OFF WITHOUT HIM."

Maurice tuts. "You were right all along, Scarlett."

"Of course I was," says Scarlett. "Rosemary has been better off."

"Quite," agrees Maurice. "Although, as I recall, you also told Rosemary there was hope he remained alive."

"I was right about that too," Scarlett says, patting her hair in a preen. "Except I was lying through my teeth at the time. Heavens, I thought he'd float up in Ireland eventually. Poor Rosemary, waiting and wondering all these years. And now for him to appear here? Oh, I could—" She puts down her glass and mimes strangulation.

"*Ah-ha!*" Deputy Allard says. "*Étrangler?* Strangle?"

I nod in confirmation. I get that language learning is a challenge.

"So unlike our Edwin," Benji says. He turns to me. "Just between us friends, Edwin was all talk. He never actually *did* much."

"The man couldn't complete a round of golf," Maurice says. "Especially if he was having a bad round. He'd walk off the course with some excuse. The weather, his work, the kids . . ."

Scarlett refills her glass. "I warned Rosemary not to marry him. I said, 'He won't go anywhere.' "

At that, she looks around, taking in the sunny room and lush gardens.

"How on earth did he end up here?" Maurice asks. "Here, with a nice woman like Gabi and this fine property?" All heads shake in bafflement, the deputy's included.

"And with the name Eddie Ainsworth," marvels Benji. "Ainsworth sounds posher than Perch, but then anything would. And *Eddie*. That's oodles more fun than stodgy old Edwin."

Baffled silence falls.

I break it with a question. "Was Edwin a Francophile?"

Scarlett, Maurice, and Benji repeat "Francophile" and "Edwin" with rising pitches of incredulity until Keiko holds her ears.

"Must have been," Maurice concludes.

"He and Rosemary went to Provence once," Scarlett recalls. "That was before the children. But when it came to going abroad, he usually had excuses: the language, the cost, the weather, the travel time, the dining hours, the *bother* of going to the fuss. Used to drive me wild with frustration! They'd end up vacationing at that choppy beach in Cornwall where his parents used to go. The man was the embodiment of stuck in a rut. I simply cannot believe he'd run off, let alone to France."

"I can't believe he'd succeed," Maurice says, swirling his wine. "At anything."

"Not at anything so *thrilling*," Benji amends. "Rest his soul and all that, but our Edwin was rather a bore, don't you think? Worst kind—the sort who thinks he's not."

"All hat, no cattle, as my second husband used to say," Scarlett drawls.

Deputy Allard bobs in vigorous agreement, but of course none of this makes any sense.

As a pre-teen, I mooned over France like other girls swooned over pop stars. I pinned posters of the Eiffel Tower and lavender fields over my bed and covertly practiced my guttural *r*'s. Yet, no one would have predicted that sensible adult me would upend my stuck-in-a-rut life and move here. When I did, though, I told people. I forwarded my mail and never would have left friends and family searching for me, mourning me.

I nibble a baguette crust and ponder motives beyond a love of France. Was Edwin running from something or someone? A bill collector, threatening his life or kneecaps? A crime? Did he witness a crime? Is there a move-to-France witness protection program? I decide I shouldn't ask about anything criminal in front of the deputy.

"Cornwall," Benji muses. "It's lovely, to be sure, but if I went missing on purpose, I'd go bigger than Cornwall in April. I'd want a splash!"

"Oh?" Scarlett says, egging him on. "Where would *you* go missing, then?"

I can't stop them, so I console myself with fromage-flavored potato chips. Deputy Allard takes a chip too, raising it briefly my way in a toast.

Benji taps his fingers, twists his lips, and makes *mmmm* sounds that suggest serious thought. "The Amazon!" he declares, slapping the table. "I'd fling myself from an air-boat with some chum so it looked like I was mangled by propellers and piranhas and whatnot."

He moves on to our dessert course, a selection of chocolate bars. He snaps off a square of dark chocolate with sea salt. "Oh! Even better—I'd make it look like I was kidnapped by someone horrid like drug lords or human traffickers or a rebel army. Maybe I'd get some ransom money in addition to the insurance payout? Or a GoFundMe? Would that be tacky?"

"Yes," Keiko says.

Benji helps himself to a square of praline and milk chocolate. "Speaking of insurance . . . Will Rosemary have to pay back the death benefit? He's definitely dead now. Ow!"

Maurice is re-crossing the leg that I assumed just kicked his beloved under the table.

"And then what would happen in your plan?" Maurice asks. "You'd leave me to pick up the chummed pieces?" He's eyeing a third bottle of wine. I want to swipe it away. I'm not their mother, but I am their guide and should stop them from careening into yet more trouble.

"Coffee?" I ask brightly. "The chief will probably be by to question us soon." *Hint hint . . .*

Maurice sighs. "Fine."

A Nespresso machine and a basket of pods sit on a sideboard by the windows. How did I miss that in my coffee desperation this morning? Maybe they set it out after breakfast? In any case, I'm delighted to see it. I retrieve the basket and hold it out to Maurice as if I'm offering a raffle draw. He picks a winner, an extra-dark espresso.

"You'd be in on it, darling," Benji says. "Obviously! You'd pretend to weep. You took that theater class. When the life insurance paid up, you'd send it to an offshore account and we'd live it up in, *mmmm* . . . Where should we go? Ibiza? Too young for us these days. Always was, if I'm honest. Southern Thailand? No, northern Thailand. I prefer their noodles. Or somewhere with oodles of expats pretending to be someone else? The Dordogne! All of Britain's there. Someone would recognize us for sure, but it is a temptation. This French living is nice."

"It's cowardly," Keiko declares. "Running away, if that's what he did. I barely recall Edwin. Was he a coward?"

The others share shrugs.

"He could be petulant," Scarlett says. "Petulance shows weak will."

I feed the coffee machine a pod and let my thoughts sputter along with its gurgles and hisses. I can imagine spouses colluding on insurance fraud. Didn't I even read about that, a real case of an Englishman and his wife faking his alleged kayaking death? But not Rosemary! The woman deals in cookies! Call me pastry-biased, but I don't believe someone so sweet could do that.

The coffee machine splutters to silence. I feed it more pods and distribute little espresso cups on tiny clinking saucers.

"Well, it worked out well for Edwin," Maurice says. "This is a nice place."

"Lower Thornbury is awfully nice," Scarlett counters. "So is my Rosemary. She and the boys were far too good for him. The way I see it, he finally got what he deserved."

Silence falls over the table, save for the clink of spoons and Deputy Allard's speeding pen.

Cyclist's Log

Saturday, 11:18 p.m., L'Auberge des Trois Cigognes

I just heard a stork up in the village, beak clacking like a rattle. It dragged me up from a Google deep dive. Thank you, stork. I was drowning in everything Edwin Perch. I've now plugged my phone in far across the room. I should recharge myself too, but I'll update you, Diary, before I go to bed.

Where to start? How about some nice, known numbers?

Fifteen years ago, on April 15th, Edwin Arthur Perch (age 42), his wife, Rosemary (41), and their sons Artie (13) and Alf (11) went on vacation to Cornwall. They rented a three-bedroom cottage near the sea. Pretty place—the cottage is still up on Holiday Lettings, so I toured the photos. Nice light. Fenced garden. Sea and dune views across the street.

I got onto Google Street View and wandered the road. Yes, I got a teensy bit obsessed. I mucked around in tabloid stories too. I wasn't going to—not after what they *wrote about me—but tabloid reporters do get all the sordid details.*

And not so sordid details too. The Perch family had bonfires by the sea. The boys kayaked. Rosemary read. They enjoyed drinks with neighbors whom they knew from previous years. Edwin swam. That's the important bit.

Edwin was on a diet, a "regime" of health food and bracing morning swims. Here, the tabloids and I agree: There are two broad reasons a married, middle-aged man takes up intense exercise: 1. To get in shape—for himself, his wife, to outrun the reaper. 2. To get in shape for another love interest. Is there a third? For an excuse to go missing at sea? TBD.

On the third day, a storm churned off the coast. Edwin went for his sunrise swim, nonetheless. Rosemary cooked a full English breakfast because Sunday was Edwin's "cheat day" from his diet. They had plans for happy hour drinks with the neighbors later.

When Edwin failed to return by 10 a.m., Rosemary assumed he got caught up chatting with the neighbors. Eventually, she went to check. They hadn't seen him. She ran to the beach, "in a right panic," the neighbors reported. Edwin's towel lay on the beach, held down with rocks. Edwin was gone.

I'll only say this here, Diary, but what shocks me is how Edwin Perch became the hot news that April. Let's be honest, if you go missing, you need a certain something to catch the public's fascination. You're an adorable toddler, say, or an influencer traveling the world in a van or yacht. You're a royal, a movie star, a Disney child actor.

Edwin Arthur Perch, 42 and battling a paunch, wasn't any of those. His surname was a fish, and he worked in a shortbread factory. Maybe that's what it was: Edwin's incredible ordinariness. If this man can disappear, so can you!

Shortbread fundraisers flourished. The cookie factory added extra production. In the years to come, tabloids and locals regurgitated the story. There were spottings of widowed Rosemary bravely going on living, shopping for groceries, tending her flower garden, volunteering with ocean-awareness programs.

Of course, there was some nasty speculation that Edwin had run off on purpose. Also, that Rosemary might be in on that very, very long con. Such talk was mostly confined to the tabloids, Reddit forums, and a "resident of Lower Thornbury wishing to remain anonymous." There were discredited Edwin sightings in Costa Rica, the Isle of Man, and a Russian prison. An oceanographer supplied the most likely scenario. Edwin was swept away by a rip current and/or a rogue wave.

Exactly ten years later, Rosemary finally, quietly, had her husband legally declared dead. "For the sake of the boys," she was quoted as saying. "For closure."

For the insurance? A tabloid photograph showed Rosemary smiling in the vicinity of an insurance office but she could have just been walking by.

Then, five years and four months later—on my tour—Edwin Perch reappeared, recently dead. But the corpse wasn't just Edwin Perch: It was also Eddie Ainsworth.

One body, two names, two widows.

I certainly can't explain it, as I told Chief Dubois over and over.

As the chief promised (threatened), she arrived to interview (interrogate) us after lunch. She brought a translator and a recorder and set up in the library. Scarlett roused Lionel and strong-armed him to the breakfast room for coffee.

I volunteered to go first. I wanted the Silver Spinners to have time to wake up and sober up. Full disclosure: I wanted to get the interview over with. The chief makes me nervous in the way Laurent's mother does, as if she's looking for fault but won't approve of me no matter what. She spent a lot of time eyeing the bump on my forehead like I had blood staining my hands.

I may have been first, but she still made me wait, taking a phone call, then making another. I flipped through the Cuisine et Vins magazine I'd used to oust the wasp, pretending I was fascinated by gratins and not at all worried about what she might ask. I took bets with myself on what she'd ask first: Why was Keiko cycling at night? Why I didn't call the police? Where were each of your riders?

You'll never guess her initial question. I sure didn't.

"How is Jacques?" she asked, before I realized she was off the phone.

Jacques? Of course, I thought of "my" Jacques. Not that he's mine, obviously. It's a common name—Jack, John, Juan, Jacques . . .

"Jacques Laurent," she clarified. "You still call him Laurent?"

She smiled then. A real smile. "My information regarding your close relationship is incorrect. Sometimes, I am glad to be wrong."

What?! She knows Laurent? She knows him by his first name and heard we were in a "close relationship"?

Of course, I asked how she knew him. Of course, she changed the subject and interrogated me about my riders, my staff, and our innkeeper.

She must have known that the Jacques thing was bugging me. And, yes, I know, I know . . . I should simply text Laurent. I could send him a photo of the baguette party platter. I bet he'd intuit trouble from lunch in a plastic container. But I don't want to explain the death. I can't explain it. I'll sleep on it.

If I can sleep.

I fear I'll be up all night counting suspects, too many connected to my tour.

CHAPTER 8

Sunday:
Good morning, Silver Spinners! If you're up early and exploring Riquewihr, you can't miss the Dolder Tower, twenty-five meters tall, made of stone and timbers. This medieval fortification is now a museum, offering a glimpse into history. If we have time this afternoon, let's stop by.

I am foggily aware I'm dreaming. A happy dream. I float and bob on its currents. *I'm in Sans-Souci. I can hear the whisper of the sea, the chuckle of the gulls. I know it's my favorite time, right before dawn, when the village seems like my private secret. I'll pour my coffee into a travel mug, stroll down the hill, sit on the pebble beach until the sun peeks over the curve of the horizon. An illusion, that curve.*

I nestle deeper into my pillow, clutching at the dream. *I'll stop at my favorite bakery on my way home and pick up a croissant for my* petit déjeuner. *No, two croissants. Maybe Laurent will drop by and we'll—*

My legs register the soft sheets, the plush bed. My ears detect the chime of bells that aren't quite right. With a slap, reality hits like a cold wave. My eyes pop open. No sea. No croissants. A lot of worries.

The room is dark. So is the world beyond the slatted shutters. I groan, tug up the covers, and squeeze my eyes shut, willing the dream to return. Edwin's cold wrist flashes by. Nope! No way I'm risking sleep if that's in the picture! I reluctantly slide from bed, tug on civilian attire (by which I mean an outfit *sans*-spandex), and tiptoe downstairs.

The inn is quiet aside from the creaks and groans of an old building shifting in sleep. Gabi's ancestors eye me from their portraits. This time, I frown back.

"You could have warned Gabi that her husband wasn't who he said he was," I whisper as I pass. "Some ghosts you are."

The breakfast room is dark, as I knew it would be at barely five-thirty. I'm after the Nespresso machine. I switch on the light, already anticipating the caffeine jolt. Except . . . the sideboard is polished and bare.

Who hides the coffee? Resident ghosts, occupying their eternity with pranks and unnecessary tidiness? Ghosts, as I imagine them, wouldn't carry a small appliance far. I make my way to the sideboard.

Maurice and Benji would know the sideboard's era. I recognize it as old and pretty, the wood burled with swirling knots. The door sticks, then wobbles on its hinges when I tug it open. I catch my breath. *I don't want to break anything!*

Too late for that, I think ruefully. So far, my tour has crashed into a dead man, broken two widows' hearts, shattered a barrel, and cracked open secrets. Edwin Perch's secret, for one. Also, his killer's. Whoever stashed Edwin's—Eddie's—body surely didn't expect that barrel to be smashed open mere hours later. The barrel was convenient to the road. I wonder if the killer planned to return once they located a better hiding place.

My stomach twists on unsavory questions. Meanwhile, my caffeine-dependent brain cheers: I've found the coffee machine! I set it on the counter and am going back for the basket of coffee pods when other goodies catch my eye.

The cabinet contains a Christmas tin featuring dancing gingerbread men, a box of German "cat's tongue" cookies decorated in smiling felines, and a package of Swedish licorice fish, the salty kind. Then there are two tins decorated with the pink floral abundance of an English garden and a name that stops me cold: Rose Petal Shortbreads.

No surprise, I tell myself, recalling Scarlett talking up Rosemary's family business to Pierre-Luc. Rosemary—or probably Lionel—had sent a gift box of shortbreads when we booked the rooms. The Spinners presented Gabi with a tin when they arrived. Cookies make a fabulous present, but now I wonder how they were received by the recently deceased host.

The tins are stacked one atop the other. I pull out the top one and find it mostly filled with shortbreads. Is this the new gift? I slide it back inside the cabinet, open the other, and frown at the contents. This tin is filled to the brim, but with tea bags, the sort of miscellaneous mix that accumulates at vacation residences, forgotten or left behind when suitcases won't fit another ounce.

That tin must have been here a while.

I down two high-octane espressos while I ponder a dead man with two lives. Edwin Perch abandoned his family and shortbread company to become Eddie Ainsworth. Did he bring the older tin with him? Purchase it later as a reminder? If so, what sort of reminder? Fond nostalgia? Guilt? A private prompt to remain vigilant with his lies?

Maybe he didn't even know it was here. When I dropped

by to meet Gabi the day before the tour, she said she handled everything to do with the guests and the house, her old family home. Her husband took care of the "important" business side. The money side, I assumed, though to my mind, tending to guests is the most essential part of any hospitality enterprise.

Finding no answers in the shortbreads, I decide to take a walk. I'm too jittery to return to bed, and fresh air might clear my head. I wash my cup in the attached butler's kitchen—no need to upset the tidy ghosts—but leave the coffee service out in case any riders are also up early. I let myself out a back door with an ornate antique knob and modern keypad entry lock. Through the leafy garden, a light glows in an upper window of Gabi's home.

Poor Gabi. I'm half-tempted to knock on her door and see if she wants to talk. And scare her half to death and pester her with my nosy questions? No. Even at a decent visiting hour, I wonder if she'll want to see any of us. She and Rosemary are mourning the same man. Furious at the same man? I recall Rosemary's initial reaction. *I could kill him!*

Gravel crunches under my sandals as I make my way around a garden path. The sound reminds me of home—my home in Sans-Souci, with its rocky vineyards. Here, the vineyards are draped in fog, long and low like slumbering ghosts. Dew weighs down the air, the grass, and the candy-cane crime tape. The moon and stars have the sky to themselves. I don't need a flashlight. In fact, the view is almost too clear. When I reach the road, I pick up my pace and keep my gaze at my feet to avoid the sight of the shattered barrel.

When I look up again, my insides jolt. A figure approaches through the mist, tall and stretched, a walking shadow. Back in Sans-Souci, my pre-dawn jaunts seem as safe as snuggling into my pillow. But there's a killer in Riquewihr, and I'm guilty of a classic tourist wrong move: letting down my guard in a pretty place. I'm so focused on the figure that I fail to watch my sides.

Oof! A hundred pounds of damp dog leaps from the vines. Chou Chou plants muddy paws on my chest. I laugh in relief while failing to dodge his slobbery greetings.

"Chou Chou!" Pierre-Luc calls.

Chou Chou ignores his human as fervently as he disregards my suggestion to sit.

"My apologies." Pierre-Luc jogs up and catches his dog's collar. "Chou Chou is too enthusiastic in the morning."

"And during other hours of the day?" I ask.

"During every other moment, he is perfectly behaved and obeys all commands and never, ever smothers pedestrians or the mailman or cats or goats or other dogs with kisses."

He raises a smile that I'm glad to see.

"You're out early," I say, thinking it better not to start with the tragedy.

"I could not sleep," Pierre-Luc admits.

I murmur sympathies. I slept surprisingly well until reality shocked me awake.

"I cannot comprehend," Pierre-Luc says. "I dropped Eddie at the train station in Colmar on Wednesday. He was looking forward to the trip, to exploring Lyon. I recommended restaurants to try. Why would he be back here and without telling me or Gabi?"

"You saw him get on the train?" I ask.

A shrug. "No, but why go to a train station if not to get on?"

Why go missing off Cornwall when he had a family and a cookie factory?

Pierre-Luc's sigh mingles with the fog. We fall silent and a chorus starts up around us. Crickets and frogs, the earliest warbles of blackbirds, and Chou Chou panting happily.

I feel awful for Pierre-Luc—and awful for asking—but my guests and I are entwined in this tragedy too. "Did you hear that Eddie had a, ah . . . connection to one of my guests?" I ask.

Nadiya would roll her eyes at my indirect approach. Then she'd translate to direct interrogation: *Did you know Eddie was named Edwin and was already married and declared dead in England? Did he mention the search parties and pink ribbons and a grieving widow and two sons?*

Muttered curses suggest Pierre-Luc knows. "Annette informed me. Chief Dubois, I should say. More than his death, this I cannot comprehend. He was missing? He was married to an English woman?"

I nod. "His disappearance was all over the British news when it happened. Do you remember?" I was a teenager in Elm Park, Illinois. It hadn't registered to me.

Nor to Pierre-Luc, who says he has no time for French news, let alone that of the English. He shrugs. "I admit, I know of people—men, mostly—who pretend they are single when they are not, but for a night, at the bar in Amsterdam or Paris or Lisbon. But to keep up the lie? How? It would be exhausting. Too exhausting."

It would be. Plus, he was an expat. In my experience, expats get a *lot* of questions, although maybe that's just me. My mentor, Bea, says I broadcast my American-ness by my open smiley expression. Expats, tourists, and locals see that look as an invitation to ask my life story. I'm happy to give it, but it would be just as easy to spin a fib, to be someone else. Is that what Eddie did?

"What did Eddie tell you about his past?" I ask.

Pierre-Luc gives a full-body shrug. "He said he was English. Obviously. He could not hide his accent, his manner, his delight in jellied eels." Pierre-Luc gives a mock shudder at the eels, but his smile dips. "Eddie said he preferred life in France. He said, oftentimes, that he could 'be himself' here."

Even Chou Chou seems to ponder that. His faked self was his real self? His real self was a fraud? I sure wish I could ask him.

Pierre-Luc gazes out over his vineyards. "Eddie enjoyed his life, and why not? He had a beautiful partner, a beautiful home, a happy—"

"Partner?" I interrupt. "Were he and Gabi officially married?"

"They were official between themselves," Pierre-Luc answers, somewhat testily on his friends' behalf. "Many years ago, Gabi divorced. It did not go well. She did not want that again. And Eddie . . . What is a piece of paper and notaries, he would say. He complained of the bureaucracy of France, of the European Union, of Britain, all of it. As a vintner, I understand."

I do too. As soon as I get home, I need to file forms for my *visa de long séjour*. A long *séjour*, a long stay—the very name fills me with joy. As always, anxiety sneaks into the party. I'm here as long as I don't mess up a bit of paperwork. Or get wrapped up in too many murder investigations? There's probably a form for that . . .

"I feel responsible," Pierre-Luc is saying.

"What?" I fear I've missed vital words. "For what?"

Pierre-Luc rocks on the soles of his canvas shoes. He's in well-worn jeans and a linen shirt which makes me think of Laurent. One, because I wish linen-loving Laurent was here. Two, because Pierre-Luc's shirt is as rumpled as his wooly dog. Laurent would be dashing for the nearest ironing board.

"I introduced them," Pierre-Luc says, running a hand through already mussed hair. "Gabi and Eddie."

He stares out into the mist as if seeing into the past. "I met Eddie at a wine tasting. When was it? Ten years ago? No, twelve years? Gabi would know. *Le temps file.*"

Time flies. It sure does.

Pierre-Luc gestures toward his home.

"Eddie had been traveling, he said. Working here and there for resorts. I have seen the type. You work a little. You get to stay in beautiful places."

There are a lot of beautiful places. I press for some names.

More shrugs from Pierre-Luc. This conversation is exercising his shoulders. "Spain, perhaps? Somewhere in the south of Spain with lots of sun? I recall he talked of Amsterdam too. But he was ready to settle. He said Alsace was as beautiful as in his dreams. I assured him that he'd found the best place. I invited him to one of my gatherings. He met Gabi and that was that. I considered myself the great matchmaker. Maybe I am not so good."

He gives a rueful smile. "I must not be. I myself remain single."

Chou Chou moans, either in sympathy or because Pierre-Luc has forgotten his canine companion.

Pierre-Luc sinks into thought. I watch as headlights trace the road around the village and weave out into the vineyards. The light reminds me of circling the village with Keiko. Where was the killer as we rode around, searching for a corpse? For that matter, where was Eddie's body? A car couldn't squeeze up the narrow lanes leading to the courtyard. I picture a faceless shadow hiding in the dark. Watching Keiko and me? Ready to silence us too?

Pierre-Luc shifts from foot to foot, a sign he's preparing to leave. I squeeze in a few more questions. "Did you hear anything the other night? Were you home?"

He smiles. "I see, yes . . . You are the murder expert, as your guests say. You ask the same questions as Annette. She will worry you're coming for her job."

I'm glad he can't see me blush in the dark. "I want to help Rosemary," I say. "And Gabi."

I want to help Oui Cycle too. If—when—the news gets out, the tabloids will go wild. I don't know the number of murders a small business can weather, but I'm thinking I'm at my limit.

"I wish I could help," Pierre-Luc says. "You and I, we could solve the case. And Chou Chou too. Actually, he tried to tell me. You are wise, Chou Chou."

Chou Chou is curled like a pretzel, attempting to bite his own stubby tail.

Pierre-Luc is saying that he had an early night. He was in bed by eleven. I'd consider that late, but I nod, urging him on.

"I was woken around . . . *mmmm* . . . 11:45, perhaps? Maybe later? Chou Chou jumped off the bed and barked at the window. If I had gotten up and looked out, would I have seen the killer? That is what kept me up last night." He pats his dog, who's given up on his tail. "Chou Chou, you would have run to save Eddie?"

I can relieve his guilt about this, at least. "Around midnight? You'd have seen Keiko and me cycling to the village." And by that time, no one could have helped, at least according to Keiko. Is it terribly wrong that I hope she's correct? I want to believe that there was nothing we could have done if only we'd cycled faster, or looked out the window, or called the police.

"Keiko . . ." Pierre-Luc muses. "Her friends said she was asleep? Sleeping on her bike? I do not understand that either."

I'm right there with him. I admit my doubts about the sleep-cycling. "She seemed awake enough to me." *Especially when she was chewing me out for not calling the police. Rightfully so, in retrospect.*

"Apparently, she's gone bicycling in her sleep in the past," I tell Pierre-Luc. "So that's what her friends believed. In any case, she found Eddie and sped back to the inn to get me."

Me, her guide. I hang my head. Chou Chou leans supportively on my thigh. I rub his ears but find little comfort. I was worse than no help—I refused to believe my guest.

CHAPTER 9

Tour-guide tidbit: Looking for a pre-breakfast snack? A favorite of the region is *brioche tressée*, braided brioche. This buttery treat is light, airy, and sweet and sometimes flavored with citrus or filled with chocolate, fruits, or almond paste.

The sensible solo woman would return to her inn. She'd read, write in her diary, or drink more coffee—anything besides traipsing out into the dark.

Pierre-Luc suggests such a sensible course. "Chou Chou and I shall escort you to your door," he says. Chou Chou's ears perk. Gallantry would surely earn him treats.

I consider their offer. I do. But the sky is brightening in ombré increments. Lights are popping on in windows. Storks are clacking in their nests. And unless it's wishful dreaming, I detect sweet buttery scents.

I decline with thanks. "I need to stretch my legs."

Pierre-Luc frowns. He doesn't have to say it: There's a killer in town. A killer who might have stood at this spot, sizing up his barrels for body storage.

I wait for Pierre-Luc to issue a version of *a single woman shouldn't be out here alone, in France alone, running a cy-*

cling company alone, alone anywhere, or she'll be responsible for anything bad that happens to her.

He surprises me. "A walk? But won't your legs be tired? You will cycle today, or have you canceled your tour?"

I appreciate that he's considering my job and my quadriceps. I wish I knew the answer to his other questions. "A walk will do me good," I assure him. "But I'll need to ask my riders about today." I pause, wondering how to describe the senior Spinners. The stubborn elders? The bold and the reckless? But, then, I'm not one to talk. I'm about to recklessly stroll off into the dark.

"The Silver Spinners take pride in riding through any problem," I say diplomatically.

Pierre-Luc smiles. "They are passionate, especially Madame Scarlett."

So he's noticed her blatant flirtations? "Yes, and I hope they will ride on. Cycling does wonders to heal grief."

"That, I understand," Pierre-Luc says, nodding seriously.

"You can come with us," I offer.

He smiles. "Alas, I must work. Work will occupy my mind. I wish you the same for your walk."

Questions occupy my mind, but an hour later I'm glad I kept walking. I have not been murdered. I've strolled serene streets and enjoyed a delicious braided brioche fresh from the oven. I'm making my way back to the inn, admiring grape leaves turned translucent as stained glass by the morning sun, when a gravelly voice shatters my peace.

"*Eh! Vous là!*"

You there? Where is he? I scan all the wrong places: The broken barrel ringed with caution tape, the empty road, ripples in a murky puddle.

"*Bonjour?*" I call out, head spinning.

A chuckle comes from behind the three upright barrels.

I step back. Here I'd been feeling so pleased with my stroll through the dark, but villains are harder to spot in the daylight, going about their business.

A face emerges from behind the first barrel. An ancient face, like a gnome who's spent the last few centuries guarding the château gates. White hair wisps out the sides of a gray beret. Olive-green overalls softly sag over a hunched frame. He waggles a carved wooden walking stick the size of a sapling.

"You there!" he repeats. "You're the bicycle guide." His French is so laced with age and accent that I have to replay the words several times.

Wrinkles crinkle around narrowed eyes. "I've seen you and your bikes. All day, all night, riding and riding. *Pah!*"

Unease has me smiling brighter than the sunrise. "*Oui*, I am with Oui Cycle. *Bonjour, Monsieur.* It is a beautiful morning."

This earns me a devious grin. "It is, it is, Madame! *Magnifique!* I got rid of him, didn't I? A fine day!"

Is that an Arctic breeze blowing in with the sunrise? Goosebumps rise on my arms.

He chuckles, whaps down a strip of police tape with his stick, and steps over it with surprising agility. "I must be moving before I get caught."

"Caught, Monsieur?" I ask as he stumps off toward the inn. Have *I* just caught the killer? No, surely not. He's ancient, for one. And two, I haven't caught anyone. He's leaving me behind.

"*Ma petite-fille,*" he calls back. "Gabi forbids me to poke around in the police business. Tend your own onions, she says. I tell her, you've been told salads, my girl. Ha!" He chuckles—cackles more like it—and picks up his pace.

His granddaughter. I know who he is now. Gabi's grandfather. But onions? Salads? Did I hear that correctly? More importantly, did I misinterpret that gleeful chuckle when he said, "I got rid of him"?

I jog to catch up. "I'm sorry for your family's loss, Monsieur."

He keeps going. "What did I lose, Madame? My mind? Not again!"

"I doubt that," I say, a polite fib. "Eddie. I'm so sorry about his death."

"*Ooh là là,* I imagine you must be very sorry. I expect you wish you'd stayed somewhere else, *non*? Cycled your Frankenstein bikes and their *whir, whir* noises to the museum of textiles, to the cemetery of the war dead? Always remember your history!"

"We'll visit the textile museum. It's on my itinerary." This is far from the most important point, but, hey, I want him to know that I appreciate regional plaid fabrics.

He picks up his pace. "Good, good! Eddie is not history I wish to remember."

Ouch! Poor Eddie! On the other hand, here's someone who'll speak his mind about the deceased, if I can make sense of him. "I didn't know Eddie. What sort of man was he?"

Another cackle. "*Et bien*, who was he? I know this: the cow who moos loudest doesn't necessarily produce the most milk. You understand? Yes, of course, you do. You are very sensible, I can tell."

What? Of course I don't understand! I'm about to ask when the old man curses. "Caught! *Zut alors!*"

"Pépère!" Gabi wears a baggy tracksuit in shades of gray. She latches onto her grandfather's elbow. "What are you doing here, Pépère? Are you telling wild tales to Sadie?"

He twinkles. "Telling her the truth. There's treasure in these lands. Treasure from the castles and the battles. I'll find it." He turns to me. "Found myself a gold coin. Napoleonic. When there's one, there'll be a hoard. I resume my explorations today!"

"Oh, no. No, no, no," Gabi tuts. "There will be no digging of my garden, and leave the château alone too. Pierre-Luc's had enough trouble." Gabi's tone is chiding but a smile flickers.

I bet they've had this little tussle before, that it's as comfortable as a fluffy blanket. I'm glad she has her grandfather. I just wish I knew what he was telling me about cows, salads, and onions. I suspect he's like my late grandfather, a fan of idioms, the more old-timey and obscure the better. French idioms trip me up. They're also a reminder that there's more to understanding France than memorizing facts and vocabulary.

"Nice meeting you, Monsieur," I say when we reach the inn. "Gabi, if I can be of any help . . ." I let the trite phrase roll away into the dawn. How could I possibly help?

"You can," she says. "Please, join us at our house? I need to talk with you."

My stomach flips. *We need to talk* rarely ends well. Is she going to kick us out? I wouldn't blame her.

"We have a guest for coffee," she's telling her grandfather, speaking loudly toward his ear.

He splutters that he's had enough of guests. "Trouble. Nothing but trouble."

"I'm sorry, Monsieur," I offer, already wondering where I'll find same-day accommodations in the high season.

Gabi tuts. "No, *we're* sorry, Sadie. Our guest is one of yours, in fact. Please, do come."

Who will it be? Keiko, out at odd hours again? Caught sleepwalking toward the small garden fountain?

"It's Rosemary," Gabi says, a tremor in her voice. "Poor, poor Rosemary."

"Oh!" I can't hide my surprise. Accidentally sharing the same spouse would be socially fraught at the best of times.

Sharing the same murdered spouse who seemingly deceived you both? Gabi is an above-and-beyond hostess.

Gabi is saying, "Rosemary was out in the garden. She looked awfully lost. I understood." Her voice breaks. "We have had tears and talking, but we need answers. We have many, many questions."

So do I. But if the two widows don't have the answers, who will?

Gabi's "cottage" is a renovated barn. I had admired the exterior and hoped for an invitation to see inside, although not under such sad circumstances.

"The oldest foundation is from the fifteenth century," she's saying. "It was an outbuilding of the château estate next door."

"It's a barn," Pépère grumbles, stepping out of green rubber boots. "She has her old grandfather in a barn while strangers live in our home."

His granddaughter makes soothing sounds. "Hospitality is our business. We must be hospitable."

"Pah!" Pépère shoots me an impish wink.

I take in the nicest barn I've ever seen. Rough-hewn beams soar in the open living space. Wooden stairs lead up to a loft-like second floor. The furniture looks soft and cozy. Family photos decorate the walls. Is Eddie among the faces? I'd love to linger, but Gabi is leading us toward a scent that would draw me anywhere: fresh coffee.

We enter a kitchen of my cozy cottage fantasies. Not a designer kitchen, all matching and sparse, but a happy explosion of potted plants, ceramic bakeware, copper pans, and a royal-blue enameled oven with silver-handled doors.

Rosemary sits at a long wooden table, hands wrapped around a mug.

When I say her name, she jumps.

"How are you?" I ask.

She manages a tight smile. "How am I? I warned Gabi. Everyone will ask that today. For me, it's an awful déjà vu."

"I'm so sorry!" I kick myself. For goodness' sake, how did I expect she'd feel?

"Oh, I'm sorry!" Rosemary says. "That was rude of me."

"I'm not sorry," Pépère interrupts. "That man was a liar. I knew it. I'd like to—"

"You'd like to have your breakfast," Gabi says, turning him back toward the door. "I set it out in the garden so you can watch for the storks."

"Banished again. Evicted from my own barn!" He slips back into his boots and shuffles out.

At Gabi's urging, I take a seat and gratefully accept a large mug of coffee.

"I'm sorry I was terse, Sadie," Rosemary says again. "It's the shock, I expect."

If anyone deserves to be terse, it's Rosemary. Gabi too. "You've both had horrible shocks," I say, continuing my trite streak.

Gabi sinks into a seat. "We were going through the timeline. Eddie"—she looks to Rosemary and revises—"Edwin came into my life about eleven years ago. He had memory troubles. He thought he'd had some concussions, playing cricket and maybe swimming."

"He was hit by a cricket bat," Rosemary says. "Our boys were playing, and a bat slipped and flew into Edwin's forehead. It was Alf. Or was it Artie? I'll never tell them. They'd feel so terribly guilty."

I wonder about that. Lionel told me last night that "the boys" had been informed of their father's much-delayed death but were too terribly busy to come over to France. "Better for Rosemary this way," Lionel had rationalized. "She wouldn't want to see them sad."

I question Edwin's memory-loss story even more. A concussion led to him going missing at sea, evading a massive search party, and reaching France?

Gabi is saying, "Only one moment is important, he would say. *Now. I live for now. Live it up.*"

Rosemary clutches her coffee mug. "My Edwin would never say that. We got on with our days, of course. We did what needed doing. Breakfast and chores, work, the boys . . . But he wasn't 'living it up.' " The words seem sour on her tongue.

"Most people aren't," Gabi says supportively. "They are happy with mundane life. I am."

Rosemary agrees but twines her fingers anxiously. "Maybe Edwin wasn't happy. He would sometimes joke that when we met, he was under the impression I lived a cocktail-party life. I was living at Scarlett's home then, at her third husband's estate. It was very posh. They'd throw grand parties. That wasn't me. I had the shortbread factory my parents left me. It's a lot of work, but never seems so because I love it, if you understand."

We all understand that.

"Did Edwin yearn to travel?" I ask gently.

Rosemary frowns into her coffee. "He enjoyed traveling to trade shows. I stayed home with the boys. He'd treat himself to nice meals and hotels. Those trade shows cost us more than they brought in, but they were important to him."

Gabi rises and clatters around—putting on the kettle, thumping used coffee grounds from the press. "My Eddie enjoyed hoteliers' conferences. That is where he was supposed to be. He had booked a nice room in Lyon. The police called there. He never checked in."

Room bookings, now there's something I know. "Did he book well in advance?" I ask.

Gabi's exaggerated pout suggests she's unsure. "I think perhaps a month ago? No, maybe less?"

Not long, then, but also not a panicked few days before the Silver Spinners arrived.

I'd called to reserve L'Auberge des Trois Cigognes as soon as Scarlett had booked a tour and informed me that they wanted to stay here. That was back in December. I'd felt beyond lucky to snag the entire inn for a week in the Silver Spinners' tight window of available dates. I'd spoken directly with Gabi.

"Did Eddie deal with the bookings?" I ask.

"Did he know we were coming?" Rosemary translates my indirect query.

The teakettle whistles. Gabi gets up to refill the *cafetière* with fresh coffee and steaming water. "Eddie didn't deal with the bookings. He handled the parts I don't enjoy—the money, the promotion, the trade-show events. I believe I told him a group of English cyclists were visiting us."

"What about the gift shortbreads?" I ask gently.

"The shortbreads we sent?" Rosemary's voice is barely a whisper. "I'm afraid Lionel probably sent you a burdensome number of samplers, Gabi. He was so delighted we were able to book your inn, you see."

Gabi has both hands on the *cafetière*'s plunger. She murmurs distractedly about the generous gift, her brow wrinkled in thought. "I don't know if Eddie had any cookies," she says. "I kept several packages here for Pépère. My grandfather has a sweet tooth. The rest I took over to the inn to share with guests. Eddie was on a diet. He was trying to avoid sugar, but he has—had—an even sweeter tooth than Pépère. I tried not to tempt him." She plunges the coffee grounds, leaning on the *cafetière* as if it's the only thing holding her up.

"His memory," Rosemary blurts. "That *must* be it. Amnesia. He wouldn't leave his boys or forget all about us, about his life and work and our shortbreads."

Gabi is steadying herself on the coffee press. "Nor would he lie to me."

Rosemary sits up straighter. "I've read about such things. Why, didn't Agatha Christie go missing under a stress-induced fugue? Edwin was under stress before our holiday. Lionel had discovered money problems at the factory. Edwin almost stayed home to work. I insisted he take a vacation."

Rosemary closes her eyes. "For all these years, I regretted that. I could understand the sea taking him away, but surfacing here?" She looks out to the garden, where Chou Chou has joined Pépère. The old man appears to be lecturing the dog. Chou Chou is rapt, surely because Pépère is gesticulating with a slice of ham.

Rosemary thumps down her mug. Coffee sloshes. "Was he happy?"

Gabi's eyes are glassy. "He was happy. Everyone loved him! Eddie was *la vie de la fête*, the life of every party. He lived for the parties." She sniffles.

Rosemary looks dazed. "Edwin? Life of a party? But if everyone loved him, who would hurt him?"

They turn to each other, and I swear, their thoughts are as clear as closed-captioning. *Was it someone you know? Was it you?*

Their camaraderie, forged in grief, cracks. They pull back, expressions wary.

Just as quickly, their synchronicity returns. Two voices, one in French, one in plummy English, speak over one another. *We must know the truth.*

"We must," Rosemary repeats. "I cannot drown in questions forever. Sadie, Lionel's Aunt Bea told me about you. You helped solve the crimes on your tour earlier this summer?"

If by helping, she means almost getting myself killed, yep, that was me.

Rosemary reaches across the table and grabs my hands. "I believe I'm on this tour for a reason. Sadie, you can guide us to the truth!"

CHAPTER 10

Tour-guide tidbit: Riquewihr has around 1,200 residents but a lot more visitors: some two million people visit this beautiful village annually.

Since moving to a village, I've become hyper-aware of watchful eyes. I feel eyes, sticky as honey, as Rosemary and I cross the garden back toward the inn. Or maybe I'm feeling my own unease. I stressed to the widows, politely but firmly, that I am just a bike guide, not a detective.

"Not *just*," Rosemary said with an assertiveness that reminded me of Scarlett. "Never say *just* about your passions, Sadie."

I'll admit, I basked momentarily in that affirmation. Correction: I let down my guard while Rosemary and Gabi agreed that an outsider's eye would be best.

"We each see the man we knew," Rosemary said. "Sadie, you didn't know Edwin or Eddie. You're a neutral party."

I'm not really. I have a bike business and my guests' best interests at heart.

"You have a chief of police on the case," I'd said. "She seems very . . ." I'd settled on the word *rigorous*.

That, according to Gabi, was the problem.

Chief Dubois's "rigor" had gotten her in trouble recently. "She had a big case. She was eager—too eager—to make an arrest, but she was blatantly incorrect. She was embarrassed when her mistakes came to light."

According to Gabi, the chief has been eager for another big case, a chance to prove herself.

"She will catch someone," Gabi said darkly. "Of that, I am certain. But will it be the true criminal?" She'd stared into the distance. I'd watched Chou Chou devour a slipper while Pépère spied on the château through a monocular.

He's probably watching us now.

My riders definitely are. I see silver flashes in the inn's window, highlighted in ruby.

"Scarlett," Rosemary sighs, identifying the spy. "She means well. My parents passed away in a sailing accident when I was young. Scarlett stepped in as my legal guardian. It was lovely and generous of her, but she can be pushy. She forgets that other people are not her. That we're okay with pleasant, quiet lives."

I'd happily take pleasant and quiet. As I think this, Chou Chou lopes by, knocking me into Rosemary in his attempt to inhale a bobbing butterfly. Thankfully, he misses. That butterfly surely wanted a nice, quiet morning too.

Five pairs of eyes now stare through three separate windows and a door.

Scarlett ushers us inside. "There you are!" she declares, almost shutting the door on me to keep Chou Chou out. His doggy face droops with betrayal, as if he's a starving orphan instead of a pedigree who lives in a château.

Not just any pedigree, either. Chou Chou is a Bouvier de Flandres, Gabi's grandfather told us as we were leaving. Also from Pépère, as he tossed Chou Chou a hunk of baguette: *That is Alsace for you—We are so beautiful, everyone wants to be here! Flanders!*

"We were about to send out a search party," Scarlett continues, gripping Rosemary into a hug and violently kissing her cheeks. "Lionel declared you missing."

"I only said Rosemary wasn't in our room," Lionel protests. "Did you go for a walk again, darling? You need your sleep."

"I went out," Rosemary says with an airy ambiguity that surprises me.

The Silver Spinners take their places around the table. I claim a seat optimally positioned to reach croissants and coffee. Yes, I've already had two espressos, a full mug of dark roast, and a brioche, but I feel I'll need an extra boost today.

Gabi's kitchen helper, Greta, is putting out the final touches: pots of strawberry jam, Nutella, and butter. Tall, robust, and encased in a full-length ruffled apron, Greta looks like she materialized from the embroidered folk-dancers decorating the tablecloth.

"Eat," she orders, with a touch of German to her accent. "Eat or the monster dog will break down the door. Do not become weak and feed him. He has a home. A good home."

Chou Chou issues a yodeling moan and presses his nose to the closed glass door.

Greta scoffs. "He has words for everything, that dog. Special barks for people, for the mailman, for birds, goats, cats, and other dogs. That is his poor-starving-me sound. Do not believe him. He lies."

Chou Chou's jowls tremble. I have to look away. I must not cave. Greta is wielding a substantial knife. "Fruit knife," she announces, thwacking the knife down beside a bottle of trembling peaches before stomping back into the kitchen.

We all seem to hold our breath until we hear clanging

pots. I expect talk of murder to blossom. Instead, cheery conversation ensues. *What lovely weather! What fine croissants! Delicious coffee! Pass that fruit saber, if you please.*

I'm relieved—even more so when I register that my group is dressed for cycling. Helmets dangle from chairbacks, panniers line the window bench, and the coconut scent of sunblock mingles with the perfume of croissants and coffee. But something else pulses in the air: nervous energy.

The Silver Spinners have cycled every continent on two wheels. They've skinny-dipped in fountains and lost their way in deserts, but rolling into murder . . . This has to be new for them, and it's not how I wanted my tour to stand out in their memories.

I'm down to the last crispy end of croissant when I dare ask, "Do you, ah, want to ride today?" Before they can answer, I speed on. "Chief Dubois said we could go out for the day as long as she can reach us. But if you don't want to, I totally understand. I can arrange for some other activities, or we can stay here and rest or . . ."

I have no idea how I'd occupy them. I cross all the fingers I can under my napkin.

"Do we want to ride?" Scarlett repeats with drawled incredulity. She's seated beside me and slaps a ringed hand on my arm. "Why, we're chomping at the bit for a good ride, aren't we, y'all?"

"Chomping and champing, rearing and raring," says Maurice. "My mother always said the best remedies for an upset are Champagne, brisk exercise, and fresh air."

My mother's remedies include stifling emotions and, in desperate times, an indulgent pint of Jeni's ice cream. Not that I'm knocking Mom's stifling. It means that she hasn't wanted to rehash my prior troubles. *Maybe I can avoid telling her about Edwin!* If she emails, I'll talk about sauerkraut. She'll say that sauerkraut is not for her, and we can both leave the electronic correspondence unscathed and happy.

If only . . . Someone will tell Mom. Thanks to the internet, the world is a village.

Maurice holds up a flask, silver with tarnish highlighting intricate engravings of peacocks and peonies. "To riding on!"

The elder spinners raise their glasses.

"Rosemary should decide," Lionel says, vigorously buttering a slice of baguette. "It is a day of mourning for *some* of us."

Storm clouds flicker over Rosemary's face. "I get to decide again?" she asks. "How fortunate for me."

I cringe on Lionel's behalf. I'm sure he meant to be considerate, but I can guess Rosemary's feelings too. Scarlett made her choose the tour destination, and look where it's gotten her. And all because of a brochure she found in her spare room? Was that a terrible coincidence? Fate? A darker plot? But Rosemary couldn't have known Edwin was here. No one did.

Did they?

Scarlett answers on Rosemary's behalf. "We'll keep pedaling forward! That's the motto of the Silver Spinners."

"I thought it was 'Pedal 'til we're dead,' " says Benji, adding an indignant "What?" when shushing ensues. " 'Pedal 'til we're dead' *is* one of our mottos! We have it printed on Christmas jumpers! Scarlett, you have it in Danish cross-stitch on a throw pillow."

Rosemary squares her shoulders. Her voice is as stiff as her frame. "We shall continue."

"Righto! That's the spirit!" Benji claps. "Moving on!"

Rosemary has flushed crimson. "No, I can't move on. That's the point. I need to see this place Edwin called home. I need to understand what happened to him, to us. Sadie's going to help me."

Benji claps. "*Ohhhh* . . . That killer's in serious trouble now!"

I reach for a croissant. Yep, I need extra fortification today. The person in serious trouble could very well be me.

STAGE 2:
Châteaux in the Sky

CHAPTER 11

Sunday:
Alsace is castle country, with more than five hundred former fortresses. Look to the foothills to find the most ruins. Medieval power players wanted what today's mega-wealthy crave: seclusion, security, and views from high above the common folk who might revere them or one day revolt.

Last week, on a scouting ride, I spotted a tower of time-weathered stones jutting from the pillowy forests and caught myself thinking, *Oh, just another ruined castle, ho-hum.*

Ho-hum? I'd never have said that back in Illinois unless I took myself on a tour de White Castles. Even then, White Castle burger franchises number less than two dozen in the greater Chicago realm. Yes, I looked that up.

We've already spotted several rocky remains on our ride this morning and are now aiming for the most stunning castle around, Château du Haut-Koenigsbourg. I debated whether to include the grand château on our itinerary. For one, the aforementioned stunningness means the castle is as popular as a picnic tart atop an ant mound. The Silver

Spinners requested hidden gems. They also requested something to die for. Sadly, I've given them that.

Second, like any good fortress, Haut-Koenigsbourg perches atop a seriously steep hill. Even with the battery boost of e-bikes, the steep grade is a challenge, especially with motorized tourist traffic clogging the roads.

Nadiya is leading the group this morning. If anyone can stay ahead of cranked-to-the-hilt e-bikes, it's her. She wanted the lead for another reason.

"You can try to stop them," she'd said, referring to the Silver Spinners and their propensity to veer off course. "See if you can."

Oh, I will. I'm on it, I assure myself, gulping air like a fish on a mountaintop. I'm lagging, and we're barely a third of the way there. Maybe Pierre-Luc was right, and I should have preserved my leg energy. Rationalizations spin faster than my pedals. From my back-of-the-pack perspective, I'll be able to spot any runaway riders. I can also see and count the whole group. Sometimes, that is. The road's serpentine twists and turns gobble the views, and twice traffic has forced me onto the berm, treacherous in its leafy forest softness. Once, I had to fully dismount and wait as behemoth buses squeezed past like elephants on a tightrope.

I stomp on my pedals, heaving my body weight from side to side, trying to make up lost ground. Four guys in a Porsche convertible cheer my effort—at least, that's how I choose to interpret their *whoops* and *hey, heys* before they speed past in a poof of exhaust. A petite woman wearing a backpack larger than herself scoots by on a moped. Car after car after bus and camper van pass with centimeters to spare, and my heart thuds from more than effort. Was this a mistake? *The Silver Spinners are experienced cycle tourers. They'll hold their own on the road.*

I spot the red stripe of Maurice's jersey as he disappears into the shade of the thick forest. We're almost there! The road has switched to a one-way loop, and drivers are surging and braking, vying for parking spots. I keep my eye on taillights and the bright patch of sky peeking through the branches. Near the top, I spot Nadiya. She's stopped and is craning her neck and straining on the tiptoes of her high-tops. I pull up beside her, plant my feet, and catch my breath.

Beyond, the elder Spinners have descended on a souvenir pavilion. Rosemary stands at a low rock wall overlooking the vast view of the valley below.

Nadiya and I speak simultaneously. Well, she speaks. My words are more of a pant.

"Where's Lionel?" we ask each other.

In unison, we scan the road.

"He's not with you?" I ask, grasping for time in which Lionel can magically appear.

"No. He is not with you?"

We crane some more, searching for an aerodynamic red helmet bobbing through the traffic jam.

Nadiya says, "I was first here. Scarlett tried to race me. I won. Then, I counted them, one by one until I reach five."

Which means that Lionel got away from me. I groan and stare downhill.

"Okay," I say to Nadiya. "Will you keep everyone else occupied? I don't want Rosemary to worry."

She nods solemnly. "I will lie if necessary. I will say there is a mechanical issue. Ah! I know! I will tell jokes! Ukrainian jokes. Do not worry, I will say them in Ukrainian because they are dark."

I agree to this plan because untranslated Ukrainian sounds way better than telling Rosemary I've lost her boyfriend. "Watch that Lionel doesn't come around the wrong way," I say, walking my bike so I won't get horn-blasted—or, worse, pulled over—for going against one-way traffic. When I reach the two-way road, I get back on but pump my brakes, my head swiveling like a metronome. *I can't lose another rider! I can't lose Bea's beloved baby nephew!*

Then I remember I have Lionel's cell number. I risk a moving violation and dial, counting six rings before the phone goes to voicemail. I try again, prepared to leave a falsely chipper *Where are you?* message, until music slips through between the traffic. Is that . . . ?

I risk the ire of a BMW with Croatian plates, throw out my arm to signal an abrupt left turn, and dart through a gap in the traffic. A picnic table, tipping more precipitously than the mountain, sits among the pines. Lionel perches on the upper bench like he's stuck on the high end of a seesaw.

I could hug him. Or, to steal Scarlett's words, I could throttle him. I redial and watch as he stares at the phone—at my caller ID—as it sings out the theme song to *The Great British Bakeoff.*

I hang up and ring my bike bell. Lionel looks up.

"Ah, Sadie," he says, having the grace to look bashful. "I was just about to get back on my bike." He stands and brushes down his shorts.

I gasp. His shorts are ripped at the hip. "You're hurt!"

"No, no, only my ego," Lionel says. He looks down. "And my attire, I'm afraid. I can wrap a windbreaker around myself."

"What happened?" I ask and quickly text Nadiya that I found him.

He sighs. "I was distracted, stewing on problems. For one, I haven't told Auntie Bea about Edwin. Have you?"

I cringe. "No. I, ah . . ." I try to explain how I don't

want to worry her and ruin her vacation. "It's not like she can fly back and help," I say. *I'm a coward,* I could add. I don't want to disappoint her.

Lionel rubs a hand over his eyes, moving on to his close-cropped curls. "I feel the same," he says. "In any case, I was stewing over that and the various quandaries when a vehicle bumped my back wheel. It was an accident, I'm sure." He frowns.

Is he not sure?

"What sort of vehicle?" I ask.

Lionel waves a hand. "Couldn't tell you, I'm afraid. I pitched forward, overcorrected to avoid a lorry, then found myself off the road and grazing a tree." He fusses at his scuffed shorts. "I suppose I was a touch shaken. I took myself here for a sit and a think."

I feel bad. I'd sympathized with Pierre-Luc over the loss of his friend and neighbor, but has anyone thought to console Lionel? For that matter, has anyone else noticed he's not with the group?

"A rest is a good idea," I say. "Do you want to sit a bit longer?"

Lionel sinks back to the bench. The picnic table wobbles.

If I sit on the lower seat, I'm afraid we'll summersault. I perch on the other end of his bench. "I'm sorry about Edwin," I say. "You were close?"

"We saw each other every day at work," Lionel says with a heavy sigh. "You could have called me his right-hand man."

The forest smells sweet with piney resin and warm earth. Also, less romantically, of diesel exhaust. I watch a small beige bird—a wren?—flit through the branches.

Lionel doesn't speak. Some people need a nudge to share their feelings. I try again.

"I understand," I say. "I lost my best friend. I often wish I had someone to reminisce about her with, to keep her memory alive. I'm here if you ever want to talk."

He makes a sound reminiscent of a cat with a hairball.

I've struck emotion! Now what? I don't have tissues, but I do have emergency toilet paper in my pack. Lionel stands abruptly. My end of the bench dips.

"Edwin Perch was not my *friend*, Ms. Greene. Did you know the police questioned me in Edwin's death?" Lionel glares down at me. "Over his first death?"

I do know that. In my internet deep dive, true-crime discussion boards and tabloid reporters hypothesized that Lionel did away with his professional and possibly romantic rival. Clearly, Lionel did *not* ambush Edwin on his morning swim or run him over or lure him onto a fated rowboat from which he pitched him out to sea all those years ago. *Some people have wild imaginations.* Those people would include me: fear tingles in my fingertips. Lionel—sweet, happy Lionel—is spluttery with anger.

"I've lived under that cloud of gossip ever since," he huffs. "And Rosemary, dear Rosemary . . . It was terribly worse for her and the boys. Edwin Perch never deserved a good woman like that. As awful as discovering his body has been, at least now she might finally move on."

He grabs his bike and pushes it toward the road. I hurry to follow him.

"Did Rosemary send you back for me?" he asks, clicking on his helmet.

Last I'd seen, she was gazing at the view, probably lost in her thoughts.

"She'll be getting very concerned," I say. Surely, by now she'll have noticed. She'll be looking for company in the misery of Nadiya's untranslated jokes.

Lionel seems to take heart in my oblique reply. He wedges

his way into traffic, commands the center of the lane, and powers uphill.

Questions fuel my legs. Was that why Lionel lingered? To test whether Rosemary cared enough to come looking? More importantly, how passionately did he want Edwin Perch gone from his and Rosemary's lives?

CHAPTER 12

Sunday:
Let's tour the Château du Haut-Koenigsbourg! As we do, keep in mind that we're viewing a reconstruction. Destroyed in 1633 during the Thirty Years' War, the castle lay in ruins until undergoing a meticulous restoration by German Emperor Wilhelm II in the early 1900s.

The world streams by us. I tally languages: German, Japanese, Mandarin, Swedish (I think?), Greek, and several English accents. My group is all back together with tickets in hand. Rosemary affectionally fussed over Lionel's scuffs, to his great pleasure. Scarlett tsked that he should have held his ground on the road. Benji slapped him on the back and told him, "Good effort, mate," and Maurice lent him an extra pair of cycling shorts. Keiko acknowledged his return with a tilt of her chin but otherwise hummed to her own soundtrack.

I lead the way to a relatively quiet curve in the stone wall, put on a beaming smile, and launch into my memorized talk. I zip through the twelfth-century origins and a noble German family. I dash across battles, castle owners, and abandonments.

"This place could have its own home improvement show," Benji says. "If only they'd had reality TV in the 1600s."

"Mmmm . . ." Maurice muses. "*The Real Emperors of the Thirty Years' War?*"

I was getting to that war. The Swedes attacked, the castle burned, the—

Maurice is already on it, elaborating in detail worthy of a doctoral dissertation. Keiko wedges her earphones in deeper.

Scarlett interrupts. "Catholics, Protestants, Holy Roman Empire, neither holy nor Roman." She sighs dramatically. "We adore you, Maurice, but spare us that tedious war. We've heard it before."

Maurice pushes up his glasses. "You haven't heard it *here*, at the western helm of the realm."

"Exactly!" I say, as if anyone asked me. "We're about to step into history." I have a smorgasbord of tidbits memorized: battles, crests, symbols on crests, the stairs designed with mismatched treads to throw off one's enemies and tour guides.

I employ my most tour-guide of moves and walk backward. "If we continue on your left, you'll see—"

"Ah, Sadie? Darling?" Scarlett raises her hand like a know-it-all student. "Sweetheart, now please don't be offended, but . . ."

I brace for incoming offense.

"We explore on our own," Scarlett says, with affirming murmurs from the others. "The Silver Spinners don't *do* guided tours. We're *immersion* visitors. Sponges. We soak it all in."

"Right!" I clasp my hands as if this is delightful news. Maybe it is. This way I won't mess up empires and Wilhelms. "Okay, well, ah . . . soak away. Be sure to take in the apothecary garden and the views. How about we meet back at the entrance gate in one and a half hours?"

"Two hours, at least," Maurice says. "There's a bookshop, after all."

"Two and a half," says Scarlett, always with the final directive. "I need to analyze the tapestries and invade that gift shop."

"Wonderful!" I enthuse as they ignore me and scatter.

Nadiya leans back against the stone wall and exhales.

"Over seven hundred meters in elevation," I say, releasing some of my memorized facts. "Awe-inspiring views all the way to the Black Forest. Did you know the Swedes attacked?"

Nadiya snorts. "No. But I am not surprised. People who desire castles never keep to themselves." Then she smiles. "We paid our admission. Let us walk all over their castle."

Nadiya sightsees like she rides. Fast and with vigor. She speeds off toward the highest tower. I linger over the everyday objects. A stove that is as beautiful as a sculpture, extending to the ceiling in green-glazed tiles. The clothing—no comfy spandex in the 1500s! The shoes—also no springy athletic sneakers. I breeze past Kaiser Wilhelm's over-the-top decorative flourishes (so many weapons!) and on to the medieval herb garden, figuring it's a good place to wait to gather my riders.

I haven't seen anyone since passing by Lionel and Rosemary, engrossed in a seemingly serious conversation by the ramparts. My riders are fine, I assure myself. What trouble could they get into in a castle? A castle with massive drop-offs and deadly objects . . .

I staunch dire thoughts and focus on the garden signage. I'm admiring a lovage—a seven-foot herb that smells intensely of celery and is supposedly an aphrodisiac—when I get the first whiff of trouble. Correction, not a whiff, an olfactory wave of cologne more overpowering than the celery. The Eau du Overkill is followed by a throat clearing like a phlegmy bullfrog and breath close enough to brush against my neck.

Great. A space invader, and by the aphrodisiac celery no less. Part of me wants to hold my ground. *I'm admiring this lovage, Monsieur! Cheer your heart with the antidepressant borage until I'm done!*

The cologne is making my eyes water. What would Laurent, an expert wine sniffer, detect? Sandalwood, diesel, pine air freshener, and musk ox? I step away, a casual step, suggesting I'm drawn to a fascinating patch of rue. *Rue, good for indigestion.*

"Madame Greene?" the bullfrog says in brusque French.

I freeze and wonder if rue has disappearing properties.

"Madame. You are the responsible party for the group, the—the Silver Spinners?" In his heavily accented English, the name sounds like a 1930s crime gang.

I reluctantly turn and take in a man wearing a pinched frown, a blue polo shirt decorated with the castle crest, navy pants a touch too tight, and blindingly white trainers. His hair is slicked back with what could be candlewax.

Rosemary and Lionel hover a few yards back at the entrance to the garden. Lionel shakes his head as if disappointed. Rosemary studies a rose with an intensity that suggests she's avoiding my gaze or embarrassed to know me.

I press up a smile. "*Oui*, may I help you, Monsieur?"

"Unfortunately, there is an incident, Madame. A grave trespass. The perpetrators claim that you, a bike guide—an American—will make it right?" He chuckles as if this is the greatest absurdity the castle has seen. A bike guide? An American? Me?

Indignation flares, followed fast by a reality check. If there's a schedule or route to micro-manage, count me in. Minor tire punctures and chain repair? A lunch that needs reserving, a bakery that begs for assessment? I'm on it! But an "incident"? *A grave trespass?* I pray that isn't a euphemism for a serious crime.

He steps closer. I force myself not to back up.

"Two of your bicyclists, Madame, they have made a very serious infraction. A trespass most heinous. Most outrageous. Most outside the bounds of—"

He rambles on. I note that he hasn't mentioned bodily harm or corpses. Good news! But what and whom is he talking about? Rosemary and Lionel? Is that why they won't meet my eye?

I raise a palm, hoping to stop the guard. He's dwindling anyway, down to sputtering huffs of indignation.

"I'm sure this is a misunderstanding," I say, not at all sure. "Some of my group members speak very little French. I should have stayed with them. I am, as you said, responsible."

"*Oui, oui,*" agrees Monsieur Eau-de-Outrage. He stomps back toward the castle, passing by Lionel and Rosemary without a glance. They fall in step a few yards behind. We pass through a stone-wrapped hallway, by that amazing green-glazed stove, and on to a narrow hallway blocked with a satin rope thick as my arm, the sort of rope that screams *Do Not Enter*. In case visitors don't read satin rope, the sentiment is spelled out in French, English, German, Chinese, and Japanese.

The guard unloops the rope and ushers us to a door I half expect to be guarded by knights in armor. Instead, there's a broad woman in historical garb—a white head cap, a red jumper dress, and a leather belt with a dangling pouch that I first take for a weapon. Then I realize it's an invention I hold dear: a pocket.

She grunts and steps aside. The room we enter reminds me of my bike barn back in Sans-Souci, if my lovely stone barn held bits and bobs of armor, crockery, and stew pots large enough for bathing.

Also present: Maurice and Benji. They sit in wooden chairs with backs so upright and ornately carved they could be torture devices. Maurice manages to look as if he's lounging. His legs are crossed, his body tilted, his head at a pensive angle. Benji perches on the edge of his seat, knees bouncing. Not in anxiety, I guess. Not in chagrin. He's having fun!

"Ah," Maurice says when he sees me. "Here she is, our minder. We are like children of advanced age."

"He finally admits it!" Benji says. "Senior discounts, here we come!"

I already got senior discounts and a group rate on our tickets.

"What's going on?" I ask.

The woman in red erupts in French so rapid and outraged, I can't keep up. *Invaders?*

"We experience a *peste,*" she continues. My mind turns to termite problems. Mice, rats? I scan the room until I remember that *peste* can also mean "plague."

"What?" I say, now horrified.

The odiferous guard agrees. "Burglaries of fine art have plagued the Great East Region. The culprit was thought to be caught, but no, the thief remains among us. All places that value art, culture, history, and good taste are warned to be on high alert."

Oh . . . A plague of burglaries.

"There have been art thefts in the area," I translate for Maurice and Benji. "Serious theft."

"Well aware," says Maurice.

"Ghastly," Benji says. "The prettiest places are absolutely filthy with crimes. Criminals everywhere!"

"They think *you're* the criminals," I clarify, in case they haven't gotten that part.

The men nod in unison.

"We were merely exploring," Benji says. "Testing their

limits. Translate that to the perfumed bloke, Sadie. We crashed their limits!"

No way am I saying that. Could I tell the guard they're befuddled seniors? No . . . They both seem to speak a lot more French than they let on, and I doubt the guard would believe me.

Maurice unzips a pocket hidden near the hem of his jersey and draws out a wallet. "Maurice Guidry," he says, selecting a card from several and offering it to the guard and the woman in red. When neither take it, I do. The heavy paper has a creamy surface and embossed text in a subtle silver font.

"You're art security consultants?" I ask. First I've heard of this. On my pre-tour questionnaire, Maurice and Benji listed themselves as "magpies" of art and antiques. Magpies are said to collect pretty and glittery objects. *Collect or steal?* No, no, I tell myself. Maurice and Benji are curious, that's all.

"When we feel our calling is required," Maurice says haughtily, peering down his crooked nose.

Benji *tsks*. "Security is seriously lacking in this castle. Why, we could have walked right out with . . ." He looks around, fingers peaked and tapping. "Crockery. I'm in a crockery mood. Maurice goes for the higher end stuff. He's the same in restaurants. Such a reef and beef man."

Is that surf and turf? That's the least of my concerns. I summon complex French grammar that sounds respectful, formal, and removed from trespassing.

"The gentlemen became regrettably lost," I say. "They're incredibly sorry for their mistake and ask your forgiveness. It won't happen again."

Maurice and Benji snort.

The guard draws himself up taller, rousing the cloud of cologne. "No, it will not happen again. You will all leave."

Can it be that easy? Have I solved this problem? I'll deposit Maurice and Benji safely outside the castle walls, gather the others, and we'll speed downhill. Safely, of course. Obeying all laws for helmets, hand signals, and speeds.

The guard marches us out. The disapproving woman in red follows, her pocket pouch clinking against her thigh. Perhaps it is a weapon, loaded with lead coins.

"It's been a while since we were escorted out of a castle," Benji titters. "Remember Montenegro? I thought our guide would simply *die*."

"So few possess the spirit of exploration," sighs Maurice.

I sympathize with that guide in Montenegro. The present guard is making a show of our expulsion.

"Coming through," he bellows, his voice bouncing off the stones. "Clear the way, *s'il te plait*. These guests are no longer welcome!"

Kids giggle and point. Mothers look disapproving. Fellow guides avert their eyes, as if our condition is catching. Keiko and Scarlett witness our parade of shame as it passes between them and a display of lutes.

"*Ohhh* . . . Have you boys been naughty?" Scarlett drawls. "I'm not leaving this castle until I hit the gift shop. You'll be publicly shamed in the parking lot, I assume? Meet you at the pillories?"

"If they don't dust off the trebuchet and fling us over the walls," Benji calls back cheerily. "Then we'll be first to lunch! I'll order a bucket of bubbly!"

You'd think they were enjoying this.

"Thank you," I say tightly after the guard has marched us through the exit. "Our apologies again for the misunderstanding."

He sniffs dismissively. The woman in red plants fists on her hips, but her gaze hovers over my shoulder, and for the first time since I've met her, she smiles. A happy smile that rounds her cheeks like an apple doll.

Tension seeps from my shoulders. This could have been so much worse. We might have endured hours of explanations and pleadings, fines, banishment from a prime tourism spot, our photos posted on a castle wall of shame . . .

The woman jerks up her chin and addresses someone behind us. "You arrived rapidly, cousin. I knew you would be intrigued."

I spin around and the tension trebuchets back. Chief Annette Dubois strides toward us. Deputy Allard trots at her heel, notebook in hand. Cousins? I search the two women for a family resemblance. I detect nothing in body type, profession, voice, hair, clothes, stance . . . When I reach the eyes, I see it. They're practically twins in their suspicion.

"Looks like we'll have another chat," the chief says to me. "I hope you don't have anywhere you want to be."

CHAPTER 13

Sunday:
After storming a castle, we deserve a hearty lunch. We'll dine in Saint-Hippolyte, a village named for a saint born in the late second century. Saint Hippolytus is known for his writings and honored with a feast day, coming up soon on August 13th.

My schedule didn't include ninety minutes of police questioning. However, we made up some time by speeding to our next stop. I count that as a win. The maître d' at the Michelin-noted restaurant I reserved for our lunch does not. To him, we are inexcusably, insultingly, outrageously late.

"I am terribly sorry," I say once again. I add gestures of dismay. I throw in a pouty-lipped, ruffling exhale, as if the maître d' and I share a similar aggrievement. He is as unmoved as his hair, swept back in a glossy, gel-fixed wave. His pristine apron reminds me of armor. He is the chef's liege, defending the sanctity of the menu.

"We were unavoidably delayed," I say.

"Avoidably detained," corrects Scarlett, over my right shoulder.

"*Pish*," says Benji, my unhelpful left flank. "You had fun, Scar! Don't deny it! We learned juicy clues!"

The maître d' opens a reservation book and studies its oversized pages.

As he runs a haughty finger over each line, I tally what we learned. One, do not violate velvet ropes. But I suspect we already knew that.

Two, there's a plague of art thefts in the area. Maurice and Benji knew all about that. They listed the stolen works to Chief Dubois. This was a case of facts and knowledge not being helpful, at least to their claim of innocence.

Three, the plague of art thefts is the major crime that Chief Dubois has failed to solve. Thus, she sped to the castle when her elated cousin called in a lead. More than a lead. Seemingly, art thieves had been caught red-handed.

Initially, the chief looked disappointed to see us. She quickly rallied and demanded to inspect Benji and Maurice's passports.

"Back at the inn," Benji told her. "Locked in the safe. Thank goodness, with the theft plague going around."

The chief had then asked whether they'd been in France earlier this year.

"France?" Maurice asked, managing to look mystified, as if we weren't standing outside a castle the French had fought for over multiple centuries.

"You popped over to Artcurial," Benji said to Maurice. "That was May?"

Artcurial, they clarified, is an auction house in Paris. Maurice had had his eye on some watercolors.

"Romantic watercolors," Benji said adoringly.

Deputy Allard made many notes.

Maurice and Benji then attended a birthday party in the Dordogne in June, traveling by train, then rental car. "But the Dordogne is like little Britain," Benji said. "I don't think we spoke French once, other than for food and wine. Does that count as *being in France*?"

"Art collecting has provided you much leisure time and

income," the chief observed, with a mirthless smile to me. "In law enforcement and cycling, we are in the wrong businesses."

Not me. Cycle touring may not bring monetary wealth, but the joy is incalculable. Usually.

Four, a brazen burglar is on the loose. What if Eddie had stumbled across a theft in progress? The panicked criminal might have lashed out to hide his crimes. I suggested as much to the chief.

"You'd like that, wouldn't you?" she said.

Yes, actually, I would, very much, so long as the art thief is unconnected to my tour.

Five, and this is another point already known but worth stressing: I must not let this group out of my sight!

I turn and do another quick headcount. The Silver Spinners are all here, not that I'd expect anyone to pass up lunch in this fabulous restaurant. Mouthwatering aromas drift from the kitchen. Copper pots hang like ornaments from hand-hewn beams, and waiters glide between tables like ballet dancers. Far in the back, crowded between a stone wall and a hallway to the restrooms, are two empty tables.

Convenient, cries my bladder. Perfect, rejoices my grumbling stomach.

"Maybe we could have those tables in the back?" I suggest, smiling hopefully toward their open emptiness. "We're happy to split up."

The maître d' puffs his cheeks as if the end of the world is upon us and flips another page.

Scarlett nudges my kidneys. "Assert yourself," she whispers. "Remember: high maintenance equals high quality. That's our motto!"

"I prefer a table by a window," Maurice says. "Facing the door, no direct sun, not too close to the kitchens, no banquettes."

Yep, they're high maintenance.

"No tables!" the maître d' snaps his tome shut.

"My husband is a knight," Scarlett announces in French overenunciated with a tinge of the Queen's English. "I am a lady. We have a reservation."

"You might be a lady, Scarlett, but you're no *lady*," Benji says, giggling.

Keiko snorts.

"*Pah!* Impossible," the maître d' declares. "Your reservation is void. When you did not arrive, we awarded your table to a most appreciative group from Paris. If you wish, you may rebook at your convenience. Our earliest lunchtime seating for a group such as yourselves is . . ."

He returns to the book and savors a dramatic pause. I play guess-the-date-of-never.

"Tuesday," he says. "In two weeks, at 1:55, but do be aware, the kitchen closes at two."

Oh, he's making that up! It doesn't matter. I'm defeated and we both know it.

"*Bon!*" I say with false brightness, and herd my group out, with Scarlett loudly claiming that "the food didn't look that good anyway." There's a lie if I've ever heard one.

Outside, the afternoon sun radiates off the sidewalk and my sizzled brain.

"So, what are we in the mood for?" I ask as if this is a delightful opportunity. "There are sure to be lots of choices."

There aren't. It's Sunday in a small village.

"Seafood?" Keiko suggests.

The village of Saint-Hippolyte is many things. A crossroads of empires, a mingling of cultures, a famed producer of pinot noir. By the sea, it is not.

Benji moans. "My arm! I could eat my own arm, I'm so famished!"

Lionel offers him a shortbread, but Benji says he doesn't want to ruin his appetite.

"Let's wander and see what we discover," I say, hoping to exude carefree calm. Usually, I have a list of backup restaurants. I was so happy to snag the one I had, I didn't look much further.

Lionel has his phone out. I sneak a glance and see he's searching nearby restaurants.

"Spot anything good?" I ask.

He sighs. "The prior restaurant is the best value for the price point and atmosphere."

Preaching to the choir, Lionel. Except for the atmosphere of that maître d'.

We pass another restaurant that looks lovely aside from the sign taped to its gate announcing a staff vacation. In a move that seems designed to toy with tour guides, the start and end dates are unspecified.

"This place is highly rated," says Lionel, wistfully gazing at the posted menu. "They have terrines. I adore a good potted meat."

"A couscous would be nice," Keiko says. "A tagine? A curry? Something different. Less French."

My temples thump. "I'm sure we'll find something. It's fun to explore."

"Exactly what Maurice and I always say," says Benji. "That security guard made such a fuss when all we did was peek into some cupboards. No harm done."

"Except to our reservation," Scarlett points out. "And my nose. I can still smell that guard's cologne. That's a crime."

I pick up my pace. I'm leading by several yards when I round a corner and smack into a group of guys around my age. They're jostling, laughing, and speaking in Australian accents about a fine lunch. Or are those New Zealand accents? Either way, I heard "lunch."

"Pardon," says the lead guy. He's tall, tanned, and grinning, his cheeks red from the sun and probably good wine.

"My fault," I say. With those two words, they peg me as American and issue hardy g'days. We expats and tourists are always interested in origins. Some of us attempt to hide from our homeland, getting huffy if caught out. Others dig in, sticking to their own cultural and culinary bubbles. I try to float in between.

After confirming our home countries, I unleash my lunch desperation on the Aussies. "Did I hear you talking food?"

They all start in, raving about puff-pastry pie, escargot, wine flights, and a delicate chocolate mousse.

Honestly, I hadn't pegged them as delicate mousse kinds of guys. Another lesson, once again learned: never assume.

"And an awesome burger," says the one in plaid Bermuda shorts.

Ah, good, I didn't completely misjudge their culinary characters.

"I asked for beetroot, and the chef didn't blink an eye," plaid shorts says.

That makes me blink. He laughs and informs me that's the Australian way. "You have to add the beetroot. To get 'the lot,' you add pineapple, bacon, fried egg, lettuce, tomato, and cheese. Amazing!"

"Wow" is all I can manage. I'd give it a try.

"Mate, the chef only had to pluck the beetroot off my salad," says the tall and ruddy leader of the pack. He twinkles at me. "Can't stand beetroot."

"Which is why he's nicked off here," another says. "He's an exile. The boys and I have come to redeem his better character." They laugh that he's unredeemable, to which he gives a rakish grin.

My riders have caught up. Another round of "*bonjours*," "hellos," and "g'days" ensues. I break in and ask about the restaurant. "Is it close?"

"Right around the corner and a turn," their spokesperson says, and gives the name, La Cigogne Rouge, the Red Stork. "Yeah, I'll show you. Borrow your phone a sec?"

Call me suspicious. I don't hand over my phone to strangers, especially unknown men. However, they seem like a nice group of foodies. I hold out my phone. He takes it and taps. For a restaurant that's supposedly nearby, he's writing a lot. Does he think I need that many directions to turn a corner? When he hands back the phone, he's grinning.

"My number," he says, flashing a white, toothy grin. "You find yourself in restaurant distress in Strasbourg, shoot me a text, yeah?"

"Oh . . ." He left me his number? I'm sweaty, stressed, road gritty, and windswept. "I'm, ah . . . I live down south."

"First rate!" says burger guy. "Our boy needs to make his way back south."

They laugh. Scarlett drawls into the conversation.

"It'll be worth your while, boys. She's famous. Sadie Greene of Oui Cycle. Look her up."

Please don't look me up!

"Ah-ha!" Lionel holds out his phone. "The Red Stork is a hidden gem, Tripadvisor says. We must move quickly. They close table seating in half an hour."

Thank you, Lionel! "Thanks," I say to the guys. "You saved us."

They depart with calls of "cheerio" and "at your service, m'lady".

Scarlett turns her high-beam look on me—too bright and blinding. "What nice men, especially the tall one with good teeth. Did I hear he's irredeemable? I spent a summer in Australia with an irredeemable man . . ." She fans herself suggestively. My flaring cheeks benefit from the breeze. "You should call him, Sadie."

"No, I have a, ah . . ." A dining companion who texts me pictures of sexy pastries?

Thankfully, Scarlett has moved on, chiding Lionel to get his nose out of his phone. "We'll see the menu when we get there, Lionel. Be spontaneous!" She strides ahead to lead the lunch charge.

"You have a significant someone?" Rosemary falls into step beside me.

"Maybe, kind of, I hope?" I say, not wanting to jinx the prospect with too much confidence. "At least, I'm not looking for anyone else right now."

Rosemary sniffs. "That will not fend off Scarlett. She'll always try to find you someone *she* considers better. She never liked Edwin. I used to think . . ." She brushes her fingers across a soft red rose spilling over a garden wall. Petals fall and she draws back.

"What?" I ask.

We're yards behind the others, but Rosemary still lowers her voice. "The week before I married Edwin, Scarlett attempted to bribe him. She would have paid him a substantial amount to leave me. Scarlett is minted, thanks to her various marriages. She's married upward, at least in terms of money, each time."

Here's my chance to ask after Sir Rupert. I don't dare interrupt.

Rosemary stops in front of a house so pretty it's literally featured on postcards. The ancient building is wedged in the pie-shaped intersection of two lanes. Beams crisscross whimsically, and the plaster is painted a bright sky blue. I wonder what it's like to live inside. Magical, I think, but then remember: Don't assume. You can never know what goes on inside a home or in a relationship.

Rosemary sighs. "When Edwin went missing, I wondered, well . . ."

"What?" I prompt again when Rosemary goes silent. "If Scarlett tried to pay him off again? Were you and Edwin having troubles?"

Rosemary bats away my suggestions like biting flies. "No. No, of course not! Edwin would have told me, like he revealed the bribe before our wedding. We laughed about that." She gives me a rueful smile. "Although, I was upset. I dared to confront Scarlett at my wedding dinner. She claimed she was only testing Edwin's loyalty, ensuring he wasn't merely after my lifestyle and money. As if I had those."

Up the way, the group has stopped. Scarlett is beckoning for us to hurry.

"Wait," I say, before Rosemary can obey. "When Edwin went missing, did you ask Scarlett if she paid him off?"

Rosemary glances warily toward her godmother. "I was frantic. I *did* ask her."

I wait.

"She was offended," Rosemary says. "I should say, she pretended to be. She said she'd do no such thing. She swore on Rupert's life and afterlife, on her grandmother's Bible, and on her favorite horse. She loves that horse. Still, sometimes, I did wonder." She takes a deep breath. "Gabi *has to* be right about Edwin's memory loss. I couldn't live with the thought that anyone I loved—Scarlett or Edwin or any of my friends—could purposefully cause me such pain."

Rosemary trots ahead. I lag behind, adding to my list of lessons.

What am I up to? Lesson six? Don't trust Scarlett.

Lesson seven: Trust Eddie/Edwin even less.

CHAPTER 14

Tour-guide tidbit: Our itineraries include parts of the Véloroute du Vignoble, the Cycling Route Through the Vineyards. The fifty-mile segment through Alsace is part of the much longer EuroVelo 6 route, running from the French Atlantic to the Black Sea in Romania. Who's in for a 2,270-mile tour?

The vines glow in gold, greens, and ripening purple. The dirt track under our wheels is pillowy soft. Birds and frogs serenade us. Keiko has removed her earphones. Maurice and Scarlett are singing an Edith Piaf classic, attempting to mimic her songbird's warble. Benji joins in to sing the refrain that's also the song's title: "Non, Je ne Regrette Rien." "No, I Regret Nothing."

"They should regret some things," says Nadiya, but she smiles. "Like this cabbage." She has a ceramic bowl the shape and size of a giant cabbage strapped to her back.

"At the very least," I agree with a grin.

Lunch reset the day. We lingered over three delicious courses. No one brought up murder. The Spinners laughed over tales of faraway lands. After lunch, we wandered through the village with no particular destination, snapping photos of gorgeous houses and gardens. Back on our bikes, we rambled, detouring to villages beckoning on the horizon. We stopped for gelato and an outdoor antiques market, where Benji and Maurice acquired the cabbage, a most impractical purchase to carry back by bike, but we all laughingly agreed we must. We had fun. It felt like we were playing hooky from the sad reality waiting back at the inn.

And now . . . The vineyard path drops us out above Riquewihr. My stomach tightens as we zip down the hill and turn onto the lane to our inn—to the crime scene. A tractor chugs our way, taking up the pavement even though it's the narrow kind designed to squeeze through vineyard rows.

As we near, I recognize the driver.

Pierre-Luc is in coveralls and a beret. The tractor putters to a stop. He tips his hat. I hope no sportscars will come speeding around the bend. Between our bikes and the tractor, we have the road blocked.

Pierre-Luc leans on his steering wheel with a smile that strains to raise the lines fanning his eyes.

"You look like cyclists who've had a full, fun day," he says.

Guilt twinges. We were lucky. We got to ride away from troubles, at least for a few hours.

"Make hay while the sun shines," says Scarlett.

"You make hay?" Pierre-Luc asks.

Scarlett giggles and switches to gushy French and eyelash flutters.

Rosemary grips her brakes even though we're standing still. "Pierre-Luc, I hope you don't think we're awful," she says. "Myself especially. I need to see where Edwin lived. *How* he lived. I need to understand."

"*Absolument,*" agrees the Frenchman. "You should do

just that, Madame. You should know that Eddie—your Edwin—made a good life here with many friends. I am honored to count myself among them."

Eddie also made a mortal enemy. Either that or he crossed the wrong path. I'm thinking about the art thief when I register that Pierre-Luc is asking about our plans for the evening. Before I can switch gears and respond, Scarlett answers that we're free and "eager for all experiences."

"*Bon!*" Pierre-Luc says. "You must come to my home then. I crave friends and wine and talk of happy times. We will toast Eddie Ainsworth and Edwin . . ." He pauses and frowns. "I am sorry, what is his other name?"

"Perch, like the fish," Benji says. "Good battered and fried."

"Like a bird's roost," Rosemary says. She then sadly adds, "He flew his perch . . ."

Pierre-Luc nods. "We will toast to a good man and the good times. I will tell you of the time Eddie and I danced barefoot in a vat of pinot noir grapes for hours. Many, many hours!"

I'm glad Rosemary is gripping her bike so tightly. Otherwise, she might have toppled in shock. "Edwin? Dancing in grapes? Barefoot?"

Maurice and Benji are to either side of me. Maurice leans across me and whispers to his partner. "Are we absolutely *sure* that was Edwin?"

Benji inhales like a reverse leaky tire. "What if it was his party doppelgänger! Maybe we *all* have one somewhere. Maybe I *am* the *fun* doppelgänger."

How I'd love that to be true. Mistaken identity! We'd all ride off on our way. Except that was something else we learned from the chief back at the castle. There's no doubt: Eddie who stomped on grapes and Edwin who went missing while swimming are one and the same. Fingerprints and dental records matched.

Which means, the chief told us, that "everyone who knew him remains a suspect. Everyone and their guide." That last bit seemed petty to me. But then, she had stormed through tourist traffic to discover minor snooping. Suspicion is her job. Mine too, if I want my riders and business to roll away unscathed.

This is why I join Scarlett in enthusiastically accepting Pierre-Luc's offer. Fun-loving Eddie couldn't have spent *all* his time gleefully stomping on grapes. He'd had to hide his massive secret, his very identity. To do so, he must have had other secrets too. Did one of them get him killed?

An hour later, I'm back on my bike. I've showered, changed, and resisted the temptation of a nap in my princess bed. I have a task, possibly the toughest of the day: What to take as a host gift to a château? Pierre-Luc breezily said to only bring ourselves. *Non, non, your company is more than enough.*

Miss Manners might give me a pass in this case. My mother would not. My guilty conscience wouldn't either. I want to take a little something on behalf of Oui Cycle. An offering that says thanks for inviting us to your home at this difficult time. Sorry for crashing your wine barrel. Apologies for bringing a murder investigation to your door.

What says all that and fits in a gift bag I can carry on a bike? Wine? But Pierre-Luc is a vintner. I wouldn't dare choose, unless it was his wine, and he already has that. Back home in Sans-Souci, my go-to gift is a box of local cookie varieties. Alas, bakeries will be closed by now.

I glance at my watch and pick up my pedaling. I've worn my going-out outfit, a tiered skirt of crinkly fabric in dusky lavender. I've paired the skirt with a dressy white T-shirt and, of course, bike shorts underneath. When cycling in a skirt, you never know when you might experience sudden gusts or the urge to speed downhill. If time is tight, I can ride back straight to the château.

I let that last thought spin along with my wheels.

Look at me, Sadie Greene, voted Most Predictable by my high school class, off to an evening soiree at a château. Riquewihr is adding to the fantasy. Storks dance in their nests, and the peachy sky silhouettes peaked roofs and towers.

I lock my bike by the Office de Tourisme and set out, wishing I had a guide.

Then I realize I do. The little cat is mostly black with orange and buff splotches. Her tail is raised like a flag. Her round belly sways with her purposeful sashay. She meows once before trotting off. I follow, calling to her with a singsong whisper.

"Pretty kitty . . . kitty, kitty . . ." She keeps going. Silly me, she's a French kitty.

"*Minou, minou,*" I sing out. If anything, she ignores me harder. Yep, she's a French cat, all right.

I'm so amused by her sassy disdain that I pay little attention to where we're going.

"Oh!" I stop abruptly at the edge of the courtyard. *The* courtyard with the wineshop and *winstüb*, the antiques, the pizzeria with a dozen kinds of *tarte flambée*, and the bit of crime-scene tape still stuck to a flowerbox.

The shops are as deserted as they were at midnight when Keiko and I stood here looking for a corpse. I shiver despite the evening's warmth. I jump when I hear a woman's voice.

"Kitty, kitty . . . *Mon petit minou.*"

I spot Gabi in the shadow of a tower of café chairs. She

sits in one that's been separated from the stack. The cat gallops toward her.

"Gabi," I say, crossing the cobbles. "I—" I don't know what to say. We're at her husband's death scene.

The cat leaps onto Gabi's lap and leans in for pats. Gabi presses up a weak smile.

"You'll think I'm a ghoul, sitting here in this courtyard," she says, unknowingly echoing Rosemary's earlier fear.

"Of course not," I say. "You'll think *I'm* the ghoul, coming back here. I swear, I followed this cute cat."

Is this the calico who ran in front of Keiko, sparking the first unfortunate detour? If so, I wish she could tell us what she saw. Was she running in fear?

Gabi rubs the kitty's chin. "Eddie liked that *winstüb*. And the wineshop, it was his favorite. He'd join Pierre-Luc here for tastings. But why was he here at midnight, when he should have been in Lyon?"

"If we knew that . . ." I let the thought trail off, hoping Gabi has theories. She only shakes her head.

There's a shorter tower of chairs. I heft one down, tangling with the cable lock that links them together. The only way the chair will sit flat is facing away from Gabi. I perch twisted on its edge. The cat purrs contentedly while Gabi and I stare at the courtyard as if it will whisper back answers.

The pizzeria isn't the only shop with a new sign. The antiques store is advertising a VENTE FLASH!! A flash sale. They've added urns of gaudily striped petunias flanking their doors too. Over at the wineshop, the vintage cart is back, stuffed with potted geraniums. Petals flutter with a warm breath of evening breeze.

Gabi sighs and scratches the cat's chin.

"Has the chief talked to you?" I ask. "Does she have any leads?"

Gabi responds to the cat. "Chief Annette thought she was onto something big this morning, didn't she? She dashed off, but then, no, wrong again."

I bite my lip to hold back the confession. The chief was misguided, yes, but that was the fault of my snooping riders.

"I wonder . . ." Gabi twists to face me. "Your cycling guest, Keiko? Annette tells me that Keiko has an 'intense' personality. That she cycles at night, in her sleep, and is obsessed with dramatic opera. What if she was riding in a trance and struck my Eddie? Marks of a bike's tire were found on his sleeve."

I wince at the image, for Eddie's sake and Keiko's too. But rolling over a sleeve isn't fatal, and Chief Dubois is pretty "intense" herself.

"Keiko is passionate about music," I say, swerving from the sleeve. "She happened on this courtyard by accident. A cat—maybe this cat—ran in front of her and she turned to avoid an accident. She didn't recognize the man she found. She'd have no reason to harm him."

None that I know of, at least.

"Edwin Perch," Gabi muses. "That man sounds nothing like my Eddie, but also oddly similar in some ways. Rosemary said he managed her business finances too."

Mismanaged, I'd say. "Did you get into your other bank account?"

Gabi again addresses the cat. "I failed. I need a computer expert. I need a hacker, I think, to get by the password."

I could help with that. I have a hacker on staff. In addition to fixing bikes and brewing up coffee sludge, Jordi Vollant is—*was*—a hacker. An ethical hacker, he'd specify, a distinction the law doesn't see.

"Maybe the police can help?" I suggest instead.

Gabi snorts. "Believe me, they are trying. They brought warrants to my home. As if I wouldn't let them look anywhere they wanted? They took my laptop and my grandfather's dinosaur of a desktop. Pépère is upset—he thinks they will steal his writings about history and treasure hunts. I will have to buy another laptop for my bookings if they don't return ours soon. More trouble. Trouble follows trouble, doesn't it?"

She gently sets the cat down, rises, and wishes me a good evening.

I watch Gabi go. The cat yawns, raises her tour-guide tail, and sashays off in the opposite direction.

Trouble follows trouble, I think, and follow the cat.

CHAPTER 15

Tour-guide tidbit: Do you feel like you're going in circles? Narrow, spiraling streets are common features in ancient French villages. The layout maximized space while also creating obstacles for potential invaders.

I'm falling behind, both behind my calico guide and in my quest to acquire a gift. Souvenir shops are still open, their wares ranging from trinkets to high-end crafts. Pierre-Luc's family has lived here for generations. He doesn't need a snow globe, a tea towel, a pretzel-shaped keychain, stork-themed placemats, or a glass knickknack.

A hat shop gives me pause, not for a fedora but for the writing on the windows:

STETSON. THE BRAND THAT IS MADE OF AMERICA.

There's also a royal crest, flanked by a beaver and, what is that? A bird? A rooster? A phoenix? The more important question: That can't be the real Stetson's motto, can it? The beaver, maybe. I vaguely recall that beavers were hunted to near extinction for their pelts. Still, I have my doubts. On the other hand, what do I know? Living abroad has made me aware that I don't know my home country as well as I assumed.

The cat stops a few meters up the wide pedestrian avenue to preen in front of a cooing group of adoring Dutch ladies. She trots off again when I come within petting distance. She's either toying with me or trying to save me from my absurd strategy of following a cat. Yet, she leads me down a side street with a *nougaterie*—an entire shop devoted to sweet, chewy nougat! Nougat would make a perfect gift.

The shop is closed. Church bells ring out the half hour, reminding me that more shops will soon shut their doors. Day-trippers have returned to their homes and hotels. Locals and lucky overnighters stroll between outdoor menu boards, like a game of connect the culinary dots. The air smells of savory delights and wood-fired ovens.

I could take baeckeoffe, the regional casserole!

I nix that idea as more absurd than following a cat. *Baeckeoffe* isn't the kind of dish to lug around on a bike or casually hand over at the door. *Here, I brought you this twenty-pound stoneware vat of meat and potatoes simmered in Riesling.*

I *should* buy wine and be done with it. I'm about to backtrack to a souvenir shop with bottles in its window. The selection might be touristy, but locals probably don't shop in such stores. Maybe I'll pick a novelty wine Pierre-Luc has never tasted. Just because it's sold to tourists doesn't mean it's bad.

First, however, I'll thank my guide. I glance ahead just in time to see an orange-splotched tail disappear into a shop. Curiosity kills the tour guide's schedule? Possibly, but I have to see where she's been taking us.

The ancient building sports rosy paint and emerald window trim, highlighted in pink geraniums as flashy as neon lights. A patinaed plaque lists an age that boggles my mind, 1423, and a name of AUBERGE DU PETIT PINOT. "Auberge" can refer to an inn, a hostel, a restaurant, or their combination. In this case, I step into a lobby that might be the home of a garden gnome or an Instagram cottage-core influencer.

Plants drape from the beams like leafy waterfalls. Sepia-toned photos, German cuckoo clocks, and antique wooden clogs line the walls. A woman my age or a little older sits behind a burled oak desk, writing with great concentration. She has dark curls and a leaf-printed blouse that blends in with her surroundings.

The cat announces our arrival with loud meows. The woman looks up, and I see that she's not writing but painting. She plunks her brush into a glass jar of pale blue water.

"*Bonjour!* How may I help you?" She pats the countertop and the cat hops up, purring as the woman pours treats from a canister.

I admit I was led here by her feline friend.

"It happens," the woman says and introduces herself as Céline. "Madame Minou should work as our advertising department."

Céline continues, addressing the cat, telling her she'd gladly hire her. "The boss will not allow it. No pets, she says. She is cruel beyond comprehension." She doles out more treats and holds a finger to her lips. "Our secret. I feed her whenever she visits. She is eating for several, I think." Her hand moves to make a rounded circle over her belly.

Kittens on the way? I hope the cat has a home. I'm about to ask, but Céline is inquiring if I want a room for the night.

"We offer private rooms with a shared hallway bath, a private bath, or dormitory bunks in the back. The private rooms with baths book quickly, but do not feel you are too old for the dormitory. We get all ages. We serve dinner starting at seven-thirty and offer a rustic but affordable menu."

I cut in with apologies, admitting I don't need a room or

dinner. Although, seeing the truly reasonable prices displayed on a wooden board behind her, I'm tempted to come back on my own someday. *Like for Christmas! I could finally see the holiday markets.* I tamp down the urge to book a private room with a bath. Céline's suggestion that I'm "too old" at thirty stung a bit, but let's face it, I *do* want my own space.

I promise her that I'll come back as a guest. "But maybe you can help me tonight? I'm going to a gathering at a château." Does that sound braggy? But then, you can't twirl a bike chain without hitting a wine estate around here. I carry on. "I want to take a small food gift to the host, maybe some—"

To my observational credit, I couldn't see the case behind her until I stepped closer. When I do, I spot edible gold.

"Kugelhopf!" I blurt, clasping my hands in delight. Imagine crown-shaped loaves with golden crusts and soft, buttery interiors. Being me, I did my homework on this regional treat, a culinary cousin of brioche and panettone. My deep research dive revealed contentious debates over the bread's origins, ingredients, and even its spelling. One thing is beyond argument: Kugelhopf is delicious.

Céline beams. "You have been led to the right place. My mother—the wicked boss—bakes the kugelhopfs. We offer savory and sweet. Our guests often take them home as remembrances of Alsace."

I thank her. I thank the cat. I ask for two kugelhopfs—one with smoky lardons and salty Gruyère cheese from neighboring Switzerland, the other scented with spices and plump raisins soaked in sweet wine.

"You're English?" she asks as she wraps up the breads. "Where do you stay?"

I'm reluctant to give the name of our inn, but she's been so nice that it seems wrong to refuse. I clarify that I'm American, then mumble out L'Auberge des Trois Cigognes quickly, shifting swiftly to praise the beauty of Riquewihr, the village, the surroundings, the—

She interrupts. "You stay at the Three Storks? No wonder you wish to be away for the evening. It is shocking. Gabi must be drowning in grief."

"You know Gabi?" I ask, although obviously she does.

She's saying *of course, of course, Gabi is a member of their local innkeepers' association. Very nice, very kind, very hardworking.*

Céline spins off course to complain about the dues of the innkeepers' association. I nod along, moving closer to peek at her watercolor in progress. It's a local scene, a vineyard landscape. I recognize her style.

"Your paintings," I say, when she takes a breath. "They're beautiful. I've seen them at Pierre-Luc Bauman's. That's where I'm going tonight."

Her pleasure at my praise turns quickly to sympathy. "I feel for Pierre-Luc. He must be devastated. He and Eddie were the best of friends. What a shame for such a good man to endure yet more trouble."

"More trouble?" *I'm not the only one who attracts crime?*

Apparently not. Céline reports that Pierre-Luc lost art to the thief. "Not my paintings, regrettably."

When I raise an inquiring eyebrow, she blushes. "To be stolen, you must be highly desired."

I assure her that her paintings are worthy of thievery. Do unto others, right? Maybe someday someone will console me for *not* being involved in crime.

Céline seems pleased.

"But what was stolen from Pierre-Luc?" I ask.

She describes a painting of Saint George slaying a dragon, a 1960s interpretation of a Gothic artist's work. She ends with "few who are not from Alsace would know the artist or the original."

That would include me, although I'm nodding along as if I can picture it.

"Pierre-Luc had only recently acquired the work and then, gone!" Céline puffs her cheeks and exhales. "At the time, it was most upsetting to him, but now he can console himself. At least it was not murder."

That had been my midsummer consolation too. *Four flat tires on a single day? Nowhere close to murder. The train and truckers' strike that stranded an incoming tour group in Barcelona? Still not murder.*

"But you," Céline says, frowning at me. "You say you are staying at the inn? If that is so, you must be . . ." Her eyes widen.

Before I can react, she's holding up a finger and ducking under her desk. Newspaper rustles. My stomach clenches. *No . . . I'd been hoping for a few more days of anonymity.*

Céline reappears and holds a front page forward, gripped between both hands. It's upside-down but in English and such a huge, screaming font that I can easily read the headline: MISSING PERCH MIRACLE ROLLS INTO MURDER.

"A guest left it," Céline says. "I kept it to practice my English, but I cannot believe what I read and hear. Eddie was a missing man? He had an English wife, and she and her friends arrive to kill him and enjoy a vacation too? *Incomprehensible!*"

"No, no!" I splutter, clutching my breads like a shield. "His wife didn't know he was here or even alive. None of them did."

A skeptical snort from Céline. "But then why is she here, if not to kill him?"

"Bicycling!" I force a cheery tone. "They came to take a cycling tour of this lovely region."

Céline looks unconvinced. "Whatever the case, it is sad. Why bother Eddie? He was a fun man. Good for a drink, a laugh. I feel quite guilty."

My feet have been inching backward in a slow-motion reverse flee. I stop. The cat looks up from her meal.

"Why would *you* feel guilty?" I ask. It's unlikely she's about to confess to murder. Unlikely, but not impossible.

"There's nothing to be done now." Céline taps her paintbrush over the water jar, a signal that she's ready to get back to work.

"You could still help," I say encouragingly. "Help Eddie's loved ones understand what happened."

She makes a *what-can-we-do* gesture—a shrug, puffed cheeks, pouting lips. "If I knew, I would tell Gabi. I would tell the English woman too, if you are correct that she did not kill him. And if I could go back in time, I would warn Eddie instead of walking by him. But he was ignoring me too. My good fortune, I thought then."

A cuckoo clock erupts in an operatic cackle. I should be going, but I need to know. "What happened?"

"I saw him the night before he died." Céline shrugs. "He's a chatty man, especially to younger women. You understand?"

At least I'm back in the "younger women" category. I think I understand what she's saying. Eddie was a flirt? There's a possibility. The killer could be a jilted lover? Someone I don't know, unconnected to his nice, jilted wives?

"Eddie liked ladies," Céline confirms. "I was dressed up. I was going to a gallery opening in Colmar. I did not want to be delayed. Eddie would have complimented me—*Ah, Céline, your hair, your legs, your lips*. He would have asked me for a drink, pretended to be injured when I said no." She clucks her tongue sadly. "You see? I was too early to help him, but also too late."

I'm both relieved and disappointed. I didn't get a confession, but I'm also not alone in a leafy den with a killer. Then it strikes me. Eddie was in town the night before he died? Maybe Céline is confused about the days because he was found so close to midnight. "What night was that? Where?"

"Thursday," Céline says. She points out the door, toward the northern gates of the medieval walls. "I saw him by the parking lot." She daubs her brush in paint, a clear hint it's time for me to go.

I hold my ground. "Have you told the police? Chief Dubois will want to know."

"Wouldn't she, though?" Céline looks up with a curl of her lip. "Then she should be nicer to people." She points her brush at me. Her manicure is red with dots of white, like mushroom caps, the poisonous kind. "The newspaper says you solved a murder? Annette will be jealous. Be careful. In fact, if you are smart, you will stay far, far away from her."

Her desk phone rings. She's already answering as she waves goodbye.

Out in the village, I dodge pedestrians on autopilot, my mind on the mystery of Eddie. He could have known the Silver Spinners and his wife were coming to town. Hiding suggests that. But why hide here when he could have been far away and out of sight in Lyon?

At the tourism office, I unlock my bike, tuck the breads gently in my panniers, and let downhill momentum carry me out of town. Fresh regrets dance alongside my wheels.

I'll have to tell Annette Dubois that Céline saw Eddie. Céline won't be happy with me. From the sound of it, Chief Dubois won't be happy with a helpful tip either.

And there's my biggest regret: I wish I could heed Céline's warning and stay far, far away from Annette Dubois and her investigation.

Cyclist's Log

Sunday evening, past my bedtime

I'm back from the soiree. I just wanted to put that in writing. Yes, I'm in late from a night of good food and wine and tales of Eddie Ainsworth. Shocking tales, judging from Rosemary's reaction.

As promised, Pierre-Luc elaborated on the grape stomping. He, Eddie, and dozens of others smushed grapes for hours, raising money for a stork rehabilitation center. A good cause, even if their feet were stained for days afterward.

"Edwin?" asked Rosemary. "But Edwin wouldn't go barefoot in our house, even after I hoovered. He was fussy about debris. Are there seeds in wine grapes?"

"Eddie," said Pierre-Luc, in a gentle but no less shocking correction. And, yes, the grapes contained seeds.

Eddie Ainsworth had a tattoo of waves on his wrist, but that wasn't all. He also had a mermaid inked on the soft cove of his ankle—a mermaid! Even I found that surprising.

Rosemary gawped—the most gawping gawp I've ever seen. Lionel looked disgusted, but I bet that was about Edwin and not the mermaid. The elder Silver Spinners repeated "mermaid" as if it might take on an understandable meaning, like "Eddie wore sensible knee socks."

Scarlett recovered first and demanded the facts: How large was the mermaid? What hairstyle? Did the mermaid overlap with Edwin's leg hair?

She did.

Benji opened another bottle of wine, and I'm glad I didn't buy a souvenir-shop bottle. Benji and Maurice sent Jordi out to buy some seriously good vintages. Pierre-Luc was impressed.

Maurice launched into a dissertation about an ancient Mesopotamian fish god, the likely predecessor of mermaids. If he was trying to shift our attention, it didn't work. I know I kept imagining Eddie's mermaid, which sounded more like a Disney princess than a five-thousand-year-old bearded fish guy.

Benji suggested that Edwin was taken by

a mermaid. She swept him away to her paradise but then realized he was stodgy and fussy, so she tossed him out.

Keiko said that seemed as likely as anything. I had to agree.

Here was another shocker for the Silver Spinners: Eddie's go-to drink was Crémant d'Alsace. Crémant is a sparkling wine similar to Champagne but made outside the Champagne region so you can't legally call it that. Like Vidalia onions, English Stilton, or French Roquefort. I could have served up some info on protected products.

Again, I'm glad I didn't. Maurice and Pierre-Luc got very detailed about Crémant regulations. I won't go into those. It's late and I'm trying to wind down. Actually, maybe that's my sleep aid: dreamy thoughts of secondary fermentation, varietal percentages, and soothing bubbles . . .

Back to Eddie's bubbly: Rosemary said, "My Edwin's favorite wine was beer." Edwin Perch preferred an English ale on the warm side.

One more Eddie story, then I'm done, I promise: Eddie won Chou Chou in a poker game! He was good at cards and awful at cards, Pierre-Luc said. Nothing in between. Isn't that often so? Eddie had accompanied Pierre-Luc to a fellow vintner's estate.

This, by the way, is exactly how I'd imagined château life: popping over to neighboring mansions to toss around money in the afternoon.

Eddie had a good day. He won a thousand Euros. The man with the losing hand, however, had a litter of pedigree Bouvier de Flandres puppies, including a runt offered at a "bargain" price of just two hundred Euros more than Eddie's winnings. Eddie ended up paying the difference to take home the pricey pup. For Eddie, it was love at first sight. For Gabi, not so much. The runt grew to the size of a bear, made Gabi sneeze, and ravaged her beams like a hundred-pound beaver. She was threatening to send Chou Chou back to his original home when Pierre-Luc offered to take him. Eddie visited practically every day.

"We were like two dads." Pierre-Luc laughed. "Like you see in American movies, the kind they show on airplanes."

"Edwin wouldn't let the boys have a pet," Rosemary said. "He said the boys weren't responsible, that pets are messy."

Which made me sad for Rosemary and the kids until Chou Chou bounded in with muddy paws and a spade between his teeth. Gabi's granddad followed moments after, waggling his walking stick and demanding his spade back.

While Pierre-Luc tried to negotiate with Chou Chou—a cured sausage for the spade—Pépère waved his stick at us. "Which one of you killed him?" He grinned and promised not to tell.

Rosemary looked like she wanted to hide under the sofa cushions. I don't blame her. Chou Chou accepted the bribe, and Pépère took his spade and left. We waited, listening to the thump and scrape of his walking stick. Scarlett nudged Keiko, wondering if she'd heard that on her midnight ride. Keiko has a musician's ear, Scarlett pointed out. The percussive beat might be hidden in her subconscious. Keiko closed her eyes and tried, but she couldn't remember.

Pierre-Luc insisted that Pépère is harmless. Just a bit eccentric.

I buy eccentric, but harmless? That walking stick could deal a solid blow. It's pretty clear that Pépère didn't like his unofficial son-in-law.

The subject of Pierre-Luc's stolen painting also came up. Okay, I brought it up. Maurice and Benji offered their services as security consultants. First, they said, they'd need to assess his holdings. This was an obvious ploy to tour the château, but I was happy to get a look and Pierre-Luc seemed delighted to show us his collections. He has some noteworthy paintings, judging by Maurice and Benji's oohs and ahhs.

I was more impressed with his cycling memorabilia. His great-uncle rode in the Tour de France! For a few years, the uncle held a time record for a mountain stage in the Vosges.

Back to the stolen painting. It was plucked off Pierre-Luc's wall last month. Pierre-Luc suspects it happened in daylight, when he was in and out between his wine cellar and the house.

I offered my theory that Eddie might have seen something. Pierre-Luc was skeptical. Eddie was his friend, he said. If Eddie had seen something, he would have told Pierre-Luc.

Maybe, but hadn't we spent the evening talking about Eddie/Edwin's shocking personalities?

On to things I do know. The kugelhopfs were a huge hit! Pierre-Luc recognized them as Céline's mother's. See? Everyone knows everyone and their baked goods in a village.

I didn't want Rosemary to hear, so I cornered Pierre-Luc in the kitchen later and asked if Eddie might have pursued women other than his wife. Women like Céline?

That gave Pierre-Luc a chuckle. Eddie may have tried, safe in the knowledge he'd fail. Céline, he said, has art-patron aspirations. As in, she wants a man wealthy enough to support her art.

Was that a way of telling me that he and Céline are an item? Or maybe he aspires to date such a talented—and younger—woman? I told him Céline had seen Eddie on Thursday evening, hoping he might know more. He didn't.

He went on about how he adored Céline's art. Her works sparkled, resonated, breathed imagination. I admit, I zoned out a bit. I tuned back in when he mentioned that Céline's imagination extended into her life.

"She is fanciful," he said. "Céline adores being part of the action. She places herself there."

She fibs? I had to ask.

She "might now and then exaggerate," Pierre-Luc allowed.

Now I'm even more conflicted about telling the chief. But I have to, right? Odds are Céline saw Eddie. If so, that's important. Besides, I have my own story I want to run by the chief.

It could be the Crémant talking. I had two glasses, and bubbles go straight to my head. I'll also blame the bubbly if I've just woken up Laurent with a late-night text.

I sent Laurent a photo of a fluted glass, sparkling in the lamplit salon. Très atmosphérique. I added words too. Yep, actual words: Met someone you know. Annette Dubois?

Laurent hasn't responded yet, but here's how I imagine our exchange will go. He'll ask how I met her. Then, I'll say . . . What?

Oh, I don't know! There's way too much to explain by text. Maybe I'll simply say, "Wish you were here"? I do wish he was here, but I don't wish this case on him.

He needs a break from murder.

I hope that doesn't mean he'll want a break from me.

CHAPTER 16

Monday:
This morning, we'll wend our way over the hills and through the vineyards to the lovely village of Kaysersberg, offering the perfect blend of history, culture, and scenic beauty.

Cycling is a balancing act between sensible caution and throwing caution to the wind. In this spirit, I wake the next morning and call Chief Dubois before I can chicken out and change my mind.

I get her voicemail and leave two messages. In the first, I tease that I've met a crucial witness. That should anger her—and thus hopefully entice her to call me back. In the second, necessitated by her machine cutting me off, I continue to stumble over the grammar for moving a corpse and the vessel by which I hypothesize said dead body was moved. I should have been more cautious and consulted a translator app before I called.

At 8:45 a.m., I assemble my riders for an early start. We gather under blue skies dotted with puffy white clouds, peaceful as grazing sheep. I watch them for signs of cumulous gatherings.

A mere kilometer out of town, a van cuts off Maurice. He swerves toward a ditch but recovers. I memorize the van's plates—just in case—and drop back to ask Lionel if that was the vehicle that shoved him into the trees yesterday. I try to ask discreetly, but Scarlett is suddenly crowding our wheels.

Lionel can't recall. He doesn't notice cars, he says. He's not into them. I get that. If a croissant were careening down the highway, I'd note every flaky layer, but a vehicle? I might notice the color or if it was a cute vintage model.

Scarlett reels off the make, model, likely year, and number of cylinders of the van that just messed with Maurice.

"Someone tried to run you off, Lionel?" she drawls. "You? Why?"

I think of Scarlett trying to run off Edwin Perch with bribes. Has she tried that with Lionel too?

"An accident, I'm sure," says Lionel dryly. "I carried on."

We all do until kilometer 6.5, when Keiko gets a flat. I whip out my trusty puncture kit and direct my riders to stand safely in a nearby vineyard. At this point, my caution has geared up, and I'm tempted to warn my riders of any and all dangers. I resist listing threats to the vines: powdery mildew, gray rot, and bunch worms. Is that pinot-munching llama still on the lam?

At kilometer 10, we hold our breath and sprint through a chemical cloud puffed from a farmer's sprayer. We're gulping in clean air when a hound bounds from a yard to froth at our pedals. Maurice kicks, wildly missing and providing the hound with a fun moving target for its teeth. Keiko belts out an ear-piercing operatic yodel. The dog is so startled, it turns and runs back home.

"The magic of opera," Keiko declares.

"My feelings about opera exactly," says Maurice, neglecting to specify whether he's referring to the magic or the instinct to flee.

"No one appreciates my high notes," Keiko sighs.

When we roll across the pretty stone bridge into Kaysersberg, a jewel of Alsace, I allow myself to relax. We're here. We'll lock up our bikes and explore this gorgeous—

"Oh, my goodness!" Benji yelps and brakes inches in front of me.

I'd been looking to my left, my eye caught by an elderly lady in a purple housecoat. She leapt from behind a postcard rack and is jaywalking at speed straight toward us.

I slam on my brakes. My front wheel skids, while my back wheel spins out diagonally.

"That's the hotel where Anthony died!" Benji plants his feet on the pavement and points. I stop with inches to spare. Madame in the purple housecoat powers through like the *Queen Mary II* at full steam. She wields a plush toy stork like a cudgel and kicks my wheel, on purpose, I suspect. If looks could curse, hers would be a blue streak.

She's the one crashing into us!

Nonetheless, I murmur a *pardon, Madame*. That earns me a huff and a word spat like an epithet. "*Touristes!*"

I grant her the point. Benji is yelling for the rest of the group to return. One by one, the Spinners make illegal U-turns across the bustling and cobbled Rue du Général de Gaulle. General de Gaulle would probably want to kick our wheels too.

"Anthony Bourdain," says Benji, thumping his chest in sad reverence. "He died in that hotel. Remember the moment we heard, Maurice? I should have brought a candle or a chef's knife or . . . something, anything! A negroni, that's it! That was Tony's favorite cocktail! Sadie, did you know? Is that why we're here?"

I did know. Back in 2018, never guessing I'd be leading

tours here one day, I'd googled the beautiful inn where the traveler, chef, and writer ended his life. What inner torment he must have felt. Such a tragedy! However, that is emphatically *not* why we're here today. I would have rolled by the upscale hotel, foregoing its award-winning *winstüb*.

Believe it or not, I try to avoid tragedy on my tours. Also, I doubt the inn encourages death tourism or that its Michelin-recognized brasserie would welcome us in our present state of spandex, sweat, and sunblock.

"The airport," Maurice says, aligning his bike into the neat line of riders now staring at the unfortunate inn. "We were trapped in the international terminal in Barcelona. There was that child who wouldn't stop banging on the piano. You had to hold me back from physically removing him, Benji."

"Hard to do when you're in full Marine mode," Benji says with a chuckle. "I had to resort to an aggressive public display of affection and hug you back to your seat."

Keiko removes an earbud. "I know that piano. I petitioned the airport to remove it from amateur hands. It's a crime to subject ears and keys to such abuse."

"Princess Diana," Scarlett intones. "Remember where you were then? I was in Paris at the very moment of that car crash. I swear, I felt the city shudder in sorrow."

Why do I bother with upbeat?

"New Orleans for Princess Di," Maurice says. "Benji and I were visiting my cousin. We were in the French Quarter. I lost count of the Sazeracs we downed in her honor. The bar stayed open until dawn."

"Tokyo," says Keiko. "By time of day, I knew before the accident even happened."

"August 31, 1997?" Nadiya murmurs, consulting her phone. "I was not born."

I was a toddler. I'm glad no one has asked us. I already feel inexperienced around this group.

Lionel walks his bike across the street to snap photos of the inn with its striking red plaster, pale stone trim, and flowers cascading a half-story from their window boxes. Rosemary has turned her bike in the direction we should be going, her gaze focused somewhere in the blurry green distance of vineyards and gumdrop mountains.

The purple-clad Madame stomps back through, muttering about clearing the way. Now she's just cursing us for sport, I think, but she still has a point. So does Rosemary. We have other places we should be rather than blocking pedestrians.

Scarlett is talking about someone named Claude. Another husband? A boyfriend? Claude dissed Diana's tragedy as a traffic nightmare and is "gone but sadly never to be forgotten."

"Hear, hear!" agrees Benji. "You slayed that marriage, Scarlett. Slashed and burned!"

He makes Scarlett sound like a serial killer or serial romancer. *I don't need to know!* I clasp my hands in a wasn't-this-a-delightful-stop clap.

"Well!" I declare. "Shall we ride to the end of the street? We'll park our bikes by the Église de l'Invention de la Sainte-Croix. That's the Church of the Discovery of the Holy Cross. The foundations date from the twelfth century, and there's notable stained glass if you'd like to pop in."

They may not want my details, but I'll sneak some in.

I wave a hand at the beautiful avenue of tourist delights, minus the elderly woman, who's glaring from behind a rack of sun hats. *Why pick on us? Maybe she senses we're trouble.* I crank up my smile. "I'll let you explore on your own. Remember the map of highlights in your packs.

You'll want to see Maison Faller-Brief, dating from the fifteenth century."

At least I've gotten them off the subject of celebrity deaths. Plus, to escape my burst of guiding, they're pedaling for the church. When we arrive and they're still a semi-captive audience removing their helmets, I check my watch and say, "Let's meet up back here at eleven?"

I'm prepared to insist on my schedule. Lunch is just over an hour's ride away, and I can't miss another hard-wrought reservation. I remind them that we'll be dining at a *fromagerie*. Then I hold my breath, waiting for someone (Scarlett) to alter the schedule.

My good luck holds. Or rather, I've made my own luck this time by arranging for lunch in a cheese shop. A cheese shop in the cheese-famous town of Munster, no less. No one resists the meeting time. They scatter in pairs, as if late for critical appointments.

Nadiya offers to stay and watch the bikes and bags. She likes her alone time.

I'd like some too. My phone buzzed in my thigh pocket when we were riding. Maybe the chief called me back? Maybe Laurent—*gasp*—used a phone to make telephone calls, not just text? I resist the temptation to check right away. I'm walking toward the bubbling stream, hoping for a shady bench, when I hear my name.

Rosemary jogs to catch up.

Lionel lingers behind, photographing the ruined castle on the hill, framed by colorful half-timbered homes.

"You probably want a break from all of us," Rosemary says apologetically.

"Not at all."

Her smile acknowledges my *petite* fib. "I'm hoping you can help me."

I hope that too. My hand itches to check my phone. The

chief might have called, crowing that my clue solved the case! Right. I'll watch for pigs flying on the thermals with the storks.

Rosemary is saying she's been thinking of Edwin's disappearance. "Honestly, I've been thinking of that for fifteen years. But now I know he wasn't lost to the sea, I'm seeing things differently."

I bet she is. I hold my tongue, hoping she'll keep talking.

"Edwin wanted *more*, I fear. From me, from our life. He would propose ideas, big and small, but rarely follow through." She laughs mirthlessly. "Why, he thought we should modernize our shortbread recipe and flavors. Change Rose Petal Shortbreads? Our recipe is over a century old and beloved, but I told him, go ahead. Develop a recipe, test the flavors, arrange for focus groups, and work up a budget. We have a tight profit margin." She shakes her head. "He blustered that I squelched his ingenuity. I wonder if he wanted to be stopped. He was mortified by any failure."

I know people like that. They'd rather blame others for holding them back than take a risk for something they're passionate about—or *think* they're passionate about. How do they know if they never give it a try?

We've made it to the River Weiss, its water as clear as melted ice. I yearn to climb down the embankment and stick my toes in.

"There I was," Rosemary muses, leaning on a low stone wall. "Back home, mourning like a fool. Here he was, living a dream life."

"Things can seem like a dream on the outside," I say gently. "It doesn't mean they are."

I think of the tormented chef and the gorgeous hotel a few blocks away and gaze at the flowing waters below. A heron stands on the bank, statue still, ready to grab an unsuspecting fish going about its business.

Rosemary continues. "I insisted to everyone that Edwin would never leave his family. That's when the police focused on dear Lionel."

Dear Lionel has been trailing behind us. He's giving us time to talk, I suspect. Or giving himself a moment alone with his camera. He's photographing a landmark from my map: a fortified stone bridge dating from 1540. Notable features: stone arches and defensive towers.

Rosemary is saying, "The police concocted a theory that Lionel had stolen from the Rose Petal accounts and killed Edwin to cover up his crime. Imagine!"

I try not to imagine. Bea would be crushed. *Lionel cannot be a thief and a killer!* I remind myself once again that, obviously, he didn't kill Edwin fifteen years ago. I ask about the money.

"An accounting error, I thought at the time," says Rosemary. "Edwin didn't *enjoy* accounting. Who does?"

I do! Nice, logical numbers, readily sorted and summed.

"Now I wonder if Edwin took that money," Rosemary says. "If he did . . ."

I recall her reaction when she'd seen the photo of his corpse. *I could kill him.*

Rosemary shakes her head briskly. "I am trying to believe Gabi's theory that he lost his memory. It would be better, emotionally, for both of us, but . . ." She bites her lip.

Yeah, I'm having trouble with the memory-loss theory too. "It's possible," I say supportively. "People can lose their recent and long-term memories, sometimes forever." Flying pigs are probably possible too, if some tech mogul wanted to go Dr. Frankenstein.

"Yes," Rosemary says tightly. "Anything is possible. But there's something else. His name, Eddie Ainsworth. The

Eddie is obvious. It's a more fun version of Edwin, isn't it? But Ainsworth. Do you know what that is?" She speeds on before I can admit that I don't. So much for my deep Google explorations.

"Ainsworth is the town where he was born," Rosemary says. "It's in Greater Manchester."

"Oh," I say, my mind spinning with the implications.

Rosemary nods knowingly, like my *oh* confirms her worst suspicions. "I visited Gabi again this morning. She's incredibly kind to host me, given our situation. I told her those names mean that he remembered himself. He *must* have."

Lionel is on the bridge, photographing the ancient stone tower. He sees us, waves, but drops his hand awkwardly when Rosemary doesn't react.

"What did Gabi say about the names?" I ask. My phone vibrates against my thigh. I resist its siren call. This is too important.

Rosemary stares at the water rushing below. "She insists it confirms her theory of memory loss. Edwin—Eddie—had only returned his deepest base memories, she said. Like persons suffering from dementia can recall their younger years but not the present. He recalled his birthplace and the name his mother called him, Gabi said. I said his mother called him Edwin Perch. She remained adamant."

"Mmmm . . ." I try to sound neutral, although I'm with Rosemary. That seems suspicious. She's asking me a question. I realize I've missed some words.

"So," she says, "I hope you might ask her?"

"Her?" I ask. "Gabi?"

"Yes, Gabi might tell you something she wouldn't want to say to me," Rosemary says patiently. "But I was hoping you'd speak to Chief Dubois? I want to know about Eddie's name, how he acquired proper identification. The French are quite strict about documentation, are they not?"

Strict? What is a word beyond strict? Strident, stringent, bordering on impossible? Notaries hold the power of kings here. The paperwork for my work and residency visas is too bulky to stuff under my bed.

Rosemary is right. You need ID for many basic aspects of life in France. An amnesiac Edwin would have had to bumble into France's most helpful and easygoing bureaucrats, or he acquired high-end fakes good enough to get his paperwork trail rolling. The latter would not suggest blameless memory loss.

"I'll ask the chief," I promise. "I left messages with her this morning." I pat my thigh pocket. "I just felt my phone buzz. Maybe she's called me back."

"Wonderful! Smashing! I'll get out of your way so you can check." Rosemary sounds so hopeful, my heart aches.

Lionel meets her at the bridge. He beams and they link elbows. I watch them wander off. They're an adorable couple. He's a sweet guy. No way they're involved in bashing a man over the head and stuffing him in a barrel.

I hope that's true. I know better than to bet on anything.

I find a bench under a linden tree and take out my phone. My heart leaps when I see the first text message, left right after we set out on our ride.

Sender: Laurent

Message: **You met Annette? What's wrong?**

Okay . . . There's a negative assumption. On the other hand, it shows he knows me. Something is very wrong.

Two more recent texts are from an unknown number. I open the first and frown at the words. They're in English so I understand them, yet I don't.

Keep away. REMAIN SILENT!!

The next message sprouts goosebumps on my arms.

I will get to you!

Who sent this? A wrong number? A phisher, hoping I'll reply so they can reel me into a scam?

A wasp buzzes my face, so close I feel its wings. Cool air slides down the river. Overhead, the clouds have gathered to gray and menacing without my noticing. Fear shoves aside caution. I know someone who'd want me to keep far away from this crime, someone I pray isn't coming for me: *the killer*.

CHAPTER 17

Monday:
Welcome to Munster, home of Munster cheese! Shelve any images of American supermarket muenster. French Munster can only be made with milk from this region. Unpasteurized milk is formed into semi-soft rounds, like Brie or Camembert. And that pinkish-orange rind? That's from periodic washings with brine and *Brevibacterium linens*, a type of bacteria. Get ready for some powerful taste!

"Something stinks around here." Maurice stands astride his bike. He raises his nose, closes his eyes, and sniffs as if he's breathing in the finest perfume.

I agree. This stink smells divine.

"That's our smelly reputation." Benji giggles, unclipping his helmet and smoothing his mostly bald crown before covering it with a peachy flatcap. "We promise we won't get kicked out of this town. Can you ever forgive us, Sadie, dearest?"

How can I be mad at them?

Answer: Easily!

Back in Kaysersberg, instead of following my handy map to, say, a fifteenth-century architectural wonder or the childhood home/museum of Nobel Peace Prize laureate Dr. Albert Schweitzer, the elder Spinners hightailed it to Anthony Bourdain's final hotel. I get that. He was an inspiration to many, an everyman's gourmand, a true traveler. Plus, sometimes we tourists focus on ancient history and miss the recent past.

However, they could have toasted Chef Bourdain downstairs at the stately bar. Surely, he once sat there, admiring the beams and gleaming bottles. They could have left massive tips for the kitchen staff in his honor. Large tipping is gauche in France, yes, but would Anthony have cared? No!

Or here's a radical idea: my group could have quietly sipped their drinks, remembered a fellow journeyer, and kept out of trouble.

Instead, while Scarlett distracted the bartender with flirtations—and Keiko apparently endured this embarrassment with a gin and tonic, heavy on the gin—Maurice bribed a maid for a room number. Benji then sneaked up to Bourdain's former suite, intending to leave a negroni as a votive. He ended up scaring the current occupant and getting most of the drink on himself. "She scared me," he claimed. Now, pink splatters of vermouth stain his white cycling top and have attracted a bee.

Benji then informed the room's occupant about its last-breath association. That, more than the sneaking and drink spillage, got him and his co-conspirators kicked out. Unless you're a hotel selling ghost stories or *The Shining* associations, you don't want guests dwelling on deaths at your establishment. The same goes for cycle-tour companies.

I could easily be upset. But who could be mad after such a gorgeous ride? Perspective spun in with each turn of my wheels: No one was hurt. No one was arrested. Their inglorious eviction had a positive side too. We regrouped ahead of schedule and have thus arrived early for our cheese-tasting lunch in Munster. Yes, that Munster! The Munster of the namesake cheese!

Except, not the cheese you're imagining if, like me, you're familiar with American muenster, mild and squidgy, encased in a soft orange rind. This Munster—protected by an Appellation d'Origine Protégée designation—can only be made here. It's aged, slightly oozy, and smells like forest floors and mushrooms with a hint (or smack) of stinky feet. It's glorious!

I'm happy for another reason too. A storm is thrashing its way over the mountains in grumbling rumbles and gusts zinging with chills and ions. *Let it rain!* We'll be safely tucked in La Grande Boutique de la Fromage for our curated lunch. Red awnings flutter, beckoning us in. Below the second-story windows, painted directly on the building like a fresco, are words worthy of a culinary shrine: *fromage*, *charcuterie*, *vin d'Alsace*, *miel de forêt*. Cheese, cured meats, local wines, forest honey.

I scan back down the street, counting heads. I led the ride from Kaysersberg to Munster, our longest leg yet at an hour and a half riding time, with breaks for quaint towns in between. I can easily make out Scarlett. At our last stop, the clouds were spitting pinpricks, and she donned a fashionable belted slicker the color of the ruby flash in her hair. Keiko is beside her. The two are buddies despite their verbal tussles. Maybe because of their little spats. Best friends can be themselves together.

Nadiya will be bringing up the end of our little pack, and Lionel and Rosemary are just rolling up. The younger couple wear matching yellow slickers. Lionel removes his helmet, then the rainproof hood he'd cinched tight underneath. Precautionary, that's Lionel. Fending off problems before they happen. Lionel is a man after my own heart.

A customer exits La Grande Boutique de la Fromage to the clanking of cowbells swinging from the doorknob. A gust of funkiness follows her. I salivate like Pavlov's cheese-obsessed dog.

Lionel's face wrinkles. Every bit of it, chin to forehead, even around his ears. Can ears frown? He's getting too much practice with unpleasant reactions on my tour. Once he's inside, hopefully, a sample or two of honey will sweeten him up. Rosemary has that faraway look again, like she's off in another time and place.

"I wonder if Edwin ever came here?" Rosemary murmurs. "I'll ask Gabi. Perhaps Pierre-Luc knows. Edwin liked a mild cheddar, didn't he? A ploughman without the pickle."

Lionel's scowl turns on me, as if I've chosen this stop specifically to rouse Rosemary's memories.

Mild cheddar sounds like the Edwin Perch I never knew but feel I do. So does a ploughman without pickles. Is it a ploughman then, or just a cheese and bread sandwich?

I bet bon vivant Eddie Ainsworth asked for pickle, chutney, horseradish, and the most odiferous *fromage*. Did his taste buds change with his new personality? That could be evidence of a personality-altering bump on the head. Or did he force the switch to match his new living-it-up persona?

In any case, I bet he visited Munster. We're less than twenty miles from Riquewihr, and this town celebrates some of the most odoriferous cheeses around. It's also a pretty place, with an above-average population of storks perched high on municipal buildings and tall posts erected to hold their massive nests. While cycling into town, I counted seven nests, which has to be good luck.

Scarlett and Keiko roll up as the clouds spit and rumble. Keiko helps Nadiya lock our rides to a rack. Like Maurice, Scarlett closes her eyes and inhales deeply.

"Assertive," Scarlett declares. "I like it!"

Lionel sniffs.

"A cheese that stands up for itself," Scarlett continues, raising her voice for the benefit of the opposite side of the street and nearby mountains. "Take note, Lionel."

Lionel is folding his yellow slicker into a neat rectangle. He's about to attempt the impossible, namely returning a hooded, sleeved, plasticky item to its original doll-sized pouch.

Rosemary frowns. "Scarlett," she says in a tone as ominous as the clouds.

"Lionel can stick up for himself, dear," Scarlett snips. "Or will he scamper off again in a pout? Like the other ni—"

Lionel is zipping the slicker into the pouch. Another unlikely feat has just occurred, although I'm not sure why. Scarlett appears to have rendered herself wordless. Her mouth hangs open, but her face is frozen.

Time for me to step in. "Let's enjoy some Munster!" I announce. "We're a little early, so we can explore the front of the shop before our private sampling and lunch."

I open the door wide. No further enticements are needed. Scarlett loops her arm through Rosemary's and tugs her inside. I've seen more delicate maneuvers in Jordi's rugby matches.

"More apologies," Benji whispers as he passes. He mimes slugging a drink. "Negronis bring out Scarlett's outspoken streak. Gin! We forgot—gin affects her like chardonnay!"

"I hear that!" Scarlett calls from within.

Benji shudders. "Gives her vampire hearing."

I refuse to let this get me down. Raindrops the size of grapes splat on the sidewalk. For now, we're safe in a boutique of cheese and the Silver Spinners are under my watch.

Right after I check my messages, that is.

My phone buzzed several times as we were leaving Kaysersberg. I'm popular today. Usually, I can go for weeks without voicemail on my personal line.

Nadiya trots inside, shaking off rain. I tell her I'll be right there, then step under an awning and brace myself for more messages from the unknown caller.

There are three voicemail messages, all from Chief Annette Dubois.

I take a deep breath, summon the good luck of storks, and play back the earliest one.

The message is all of three words. "*Tu avais raison.*"

You were right. I was right! That cart—the vintage handcart by the wineshop—was my tipoff to the chief. The cart wasn't out when Keiko brought me to the courtyard around midnight, looking for a corpse. I assumed it was brought inside when the shop closed. However, it was there after hours last night, filled to the brim with potted geraniums. Geraniums that could be easily moved to another doorstep or flowerbox if someone needed to cart away a large, dead weight.

I replay the message because it's nice to have affirmation once in a while, even if Annette Dubois does sound like her favorite cheese has taken on ammonia overtones.

I press the second message. In snappish tones, Chief Dubois informs me that she will need to speak with all my riders, *immédiatement*.

Immediately? About a cart? A cart I helpfully tipped her off about? I've already missed her "immediately." She left that message over an hour ago.

I press the third message, left four minutes after message two: "Deliver Lionel Lloyd and Rosemary Perch to me right now." There's a pause. I wait for the chief to stick to her five-second message trend, but there's more. "And tell Jacques Laurent to never hang up on me again!"

There's a smacking sound then, like she's thumped her cell phone to give it that old-fashioned slam-the-handset emphasis. The message ends.

I stare into the rumbling sky and ponder the messages.

It's good news about the cart, but why does she need to see my riders, especially Lionel and Rosemary? And what does she mean about Laurent hanging up? He called her? I check my phone again to make sure he hasn't called or texted me. Nothing, but then I haven't responded to his text.

I tap out: **You called Annette?**

Yes, I've cowardly avoided his "what's wrong" question, but seemingly he's called Chief Dubois, and I'd like to know what was said.

As for her messages . . . If I call her back, she'd surely order me to return, and what would I say? No, sorry, we have a curated lunch of cheese to enjoy?

The sky cracks and rumbles. Lightning flashes. I cringe and hurry inside. I can't—won't—expose my riders to a dangerous storm. I've given the chief a clue, and we've already told her all we know. I slip my phone into my pocket with only an ounce of guilt. She could have said please and *merci*.

A dozen cheeses later, I am no longer worried about Chief Dubois, the storm, or even the anonymous texts.

"Cheese is like life," the cheesemonger, Frederic, is telling us. He's a philosopher in a white chef's jacket, topped with a canvas apron. "Both are to be enjoyed, to be savored."

"To be gobbled up with reckless abandon," Benji chuckles, to which the elder Silver Spinners clink glasses of Gewürztraminer and slice into the most aged, most oozing, and smelliest Munster of the lot.

"It's not bad," says Lionel, sampling a slice as thin as skin. "If one ignores the beastly smell."

"There's a fine analogy for life too!" declares Maurice. "To ignoring beastly stinks!"

More clinking of glasses. The elder Spinners stretch to reach Rosemary's glass. She eventually gives in and raises hers toward the ceiling as thunder booms.

"That calls for another bottle," Scarlett declares as potato fritters, charcuterie, tomatoes draped in vinegar, and layered terrines are once again passed around the table. Lionel perked up when the terrines came out. It seems he's a huge fan of organ meats. Meats which, for the record, made Scarlett shudder. I wanted to point that out to her. *See? Lionel's not boring. He has quiet pleasures. Photography, terrines, and Rose Petal Shortbreads.* She was busy flirting with the cheesemonger, though, and I wasn't foolish enough to mess with her in her spikey gin mood.

"Life is most beautiful when you have friends," Frederic waxes, gazing into Scarlett's pulsating eyes. "Life is to be shared with friends, like cheese. Those who share fine cheese will have many, many friends."

We toast to that.

I snap a shot of the cheese board and catch myself thinking that this would be perfect to text to Laurent. Except, he hasn't responded to my previous text. My mind churns. What did he and the chief talk about? Just how well do they know each other?

Thankfully, Frederic interrupts my thoughts with his most philosophical proclamation yet. He holds up a pyramidal lump of goat cheese, mottled with blue-gray mold. "It is not beauty that matters. It is the emotional impact. This is true of humanity and *fromage*, my friends."

Oh, he's good, and La Grande Boutique de la Fromage is certainly having an emotional impact on me. I love this place. I could spend the entire tour here, safe and sheltered from murder, lost loves, and personal conflicts.

Alas, as in life, all good cheeses must come to an end. We finish our meal with a palate-cleansing salad—topped with more cheese and a "delicate" cheese mousse drizzled in forest honey.

I can't very well call Chief Dubois back now. There's no way I could "immediately" cycle anywhere after that feast. Luckily, our afternoon plans include waddling off lunch—because a gentle stroll will surely negate the cheese, honey, and meats—and then a leisurely ride back to the inn. Jordi will be on hand to offer van rides in case anyone wants.

I'm savoring a tiny cup of espresso when the cowbells on the front door clang. Voices burble through from the front of the shop. *Someone eager for cheese,* my cheese-coma brain interprets. *Really eager. Like they're demanding cheese* . . . The words fail to coalesce into anything other than high emotion.

Footsteps stomp our way.

Frederic downs his espresso in a gulp as his young assistant pokes her head around the door. He'd left her in charge of the counter and register. "We are not yet finished, Coco," he says. "Soon, then the next group can come in."

Soon? No, I'm never leaving! I sip a minuscule drop of espresso.

Coco opens her mouth. When no words come out, she flings the door wide, and I can see back into the shop, to the glass cases, the towers of jarred honey, the antique equipment, and the faded photos on the wall. All the way through to the shop window and outside to the flashing lights of a police vehicle. At the center of the shop, Annette Dubois frowns down an innocent platter of spice breads as if she might arrest them.

She sees me, looks as happy as a crocodile spotting the Easter bunny, and strides our way.

If my wishes had their way, the door would slam shut and lock.

It doesn't. "Madame Greene," the chief says. "What a fine place to dine. Your innkeeper gave me your itinerary, but you are who I thank the most. You have confirmed my theories." She smiles around the table, stopping at the youngest couple. "Rosemary Perch, Lionel Lloyd, I require your presence at my station for further questioning." She points her smile at me again. "Immediately."

I think of my "helpful" tip and the anonymous message. *Remain silent*. I dearly wish I had.

CHAPTER 18

Tour-guide tidbit: Have you noticed the witches in the souvenir shops? These trinkets reflect a dark past. Witch hunts fueled fear and superstition across this region in the sixteenth and seventeenth centuries. Thousands of people—many of them women—were falsely accused.

"I'm calling my lawyer," Maurice declares. He sets down his espresso cup with a rattle and pats the zipper pocket in his cycling jersey as if it might hide a Rolodex.

"Our *solicitor*," Benji corrects. "Call Helena in London. She's the mean one."

"I'm mean and I'm right here," Scarlett says, pushing back her chair. "Let go of my goddaughter."

Chief Dubois doesn't exactly have Rosemary in her clutches. Her hand hovers just above Rosemary's shoulder, but it's enough to render Rosemary immobile.

"Here now," says Lionel, with all the teeth of a teddy bear.

The cheesemonger has taken on the hue of a fresh chèvre—pale with hints of gray. "Is there a problem?" he asks.

Oh, there are problems.

The chief pronounces in extra-loud French that, yes, Monsieur, new evidence has come to light in a "serious incident of deliberate killing" and that she must speak to those "directly involved."

The cheesemonger steps back.

"New evidence?" Scarlett repeats in translation. "What new evidence?"

This breaks Rosemary's freeze. "What did you find?" she asks hopefully. "Do you know what happened?"

The chief steps back, dips her head, and waves a palm as if inviting Rosemary to fall down a rabbit hole. "This is what I must speak with you about, Madame Perch. You and your gentleman friend? You will assist me in my inquiries?"

That's what they always say to suspects on Law and Order*!*

"Of course!" Rosemary springs up, bundling her jacket and bag.

Scarlett steps between her goddaughter and the door. "You don't have to go anywhere except with us," she says. "That officer cannot compel you. Rosemary, I *know* these things."

"She does," Benji affirms. "Oh, she really does." He lowers his voice. "That time in Tunis . . . Thank goodness Helena stepped in then. Maurice, have you found her number?"

Maurice is poking at his phone, glasses tipped precariously at the crooked tip of his nose.

I decide that Tunis is something else I don't want to know about and that Chief Dubois shouldn't know either.

"But I *want* to help," Rosemary says, stepping around her godmother. "I *will* help. Lionel, come along."

"Lionel, you're not doing Rosemary any favors," Scarlett warns. "Show some backbone."

Brave in the face of a gin-stoked godmother, Lionel loops his arm through Rosemary's. Scarlett swings her glare to me. I push back my seat, all my cheese bliss melted away.

"I'm coming too," I announce. I catch Nadiya's eye.

She nods briskly. "Jordi will be here. We will have the van."

Meaning Jordi can transport Lionel and Rosemary's bikes. Nadiya can handle the other Spinners, whether they want to cycle back or get a lift.

"You're not their *avocate*," Chief Dubois interrupts my mental sorting.

No, I'm not their lawyer. "I'm their guide," I say firmly. And I know the non-legal advice I'll be giving them in the police car. *Keep quiet.*

An hour and approximately fourteen minutes later, Lionel, Rosemary, and I sit in an interview room with a dungeon-decor vibe. The floors are stained cement, the wooden chairs are nubby-backed torture devices, and the scrolled window bars look hand-forged. Beyond the dusty windows, green hills beckon. The view is nice but somehow worse than a blank wall or a fetid dumpster because it flaunts where we *could* be. We could be rolling through sun-dappled oak forests, sweet wind whistling through our helmets.

At the moment, I'm not staring wistfully into the trees. I'm shooting Rosemary my most pointed look. A look of daggers and reason. A look that silently screams, *Please, please be quiet* and *remember what you promised!*

Rosemary ignores the look. She disregards my subsequent throat clearing and follow-up series of sharp coughs. For goodness' sake, I sound like I'm coming down with a minor plague and she doesn't even glance my way.

Lionel, dear man, pushes the water pitcher toward me. The water kicks up little waves as the pitcher bumps across the tabletop. The wood is etched with a dictionary's worth of multilingual epithets and a few jagged hearts struck through with arrows and initials. Some people will destructively profess their love anywhere. Bathroom stalls. The tender skin of poplar trees. Padlocks threatening the structural integrity of historic Parisian bridges. Police interview rooms. It seems like courting doom to me.

Also courting doom? Rosemary, the woman who, in the back of a police vehicle, had solemnly agreed to my plan to "listen but say nothing."

"Yes, that is most definitely a Rose Petal shortbread," Rosemary is saying, to my glancing, coughing dismay. "See the little fragment of an '*R*' on that corner? And the scallops on the edges? The crumbliness, that's my family's secret recipe."

"Wonderful," Chief Dubois says encouragingly. "You're being very helpful."

Too helpful. But then, I suppose the origin of the cookies can be confirmed in other ways. If this were *CSI: Most Beautiful French Village*, a scientist with glamorous hair would have already analyzed the cookie crumbs. There would be three-dimensional laser modeling and isotopic analysis and date stamping by the age of the butter.

But who needs fancy butter-analysis technology when Rosemary and now Lionel are dishing up answers? The chief opens the evidence bag at Lionel's request and holds it under his nose. Lionel leans in, nose up, eyes half closed, sniffing like a wine connoisseur. He even waves his hand over the opening, breathing in the waft of crumbs.

"Fine English butter and rose petal water," he declares. "Perfect for afternoon tea or enjoyed with English bubbly."

The chief has a translator in the room, a young woman who was at the reception desk doing her nails in candy-apple red when we arrived. She sits just behind the chief, like I've seen translators do at the UN. She could be a pro. She gets every word, although she adds a judgmental sniff at "English bubbly."

The chief sniffs in agreement. "So, for my records, you both confirm that these fragments are Rose Petal Shortbread?"

They do.

"They sound delicious," the chief says. "Do you have any of these internationally renowned cookies that I could try?"

Rosemary and Lionel practically leap for the handlebar bags they've carried along like purses. Before I can stop them, they each offer up single-serving packets. The chief snags them both, but I doubt it's because she's hungry.

"*Très utile,*" she says. Very helpful. "I shall save them for later."

She slips the packets into separate evidence bags and murmurs instructions for the translator to label them by name.

Come on! I want to huff. I aim this sentiment toward Rosemary and Lionel. *Come on, be careful and wary!*

"Would you like a shortbread, Sadie?" Rosemary asks.

Why not? I might as well get a cookie out of this misadventure. I open the packet and savor the buttery shortbread. Nice. Just the right amount of rose. I see why they're popular.

"I'll help you dispose of that." Annette Dubois swipes my wrapper.

"Oh, come on," I do say now. "You can't think I had anything to do with this."

She shrugs. "Elimination prints."

Which I would have given if she'd politely asked. "Where did you find those cookie crumbs?" I ask, although I'm afraid I know.

The chief's smug smile affirms my theory. "The same place I found the blood droplets."

She found them in the cart. The blood-speckled vintage handcart that I so helpfully pointed out.

"They're just cookies," I protest, dusting crumbs from my fingers.

"Not 'just,' " says Lionel. "World-famous, beloved shortbreads made with a secret family recipe."

I reroute my argument. "Exactly! Rose Petal cookies are very popular and available in many shops and countries. Right, Lionel?" If he wants to talk, now would be the time.

"Why, yes," he agrees. "We distribute to discerning specialty shops in France, mostly metro Paris. Also, Belgium, duty-free airport shops in Barcelona and Florence, a half-dozen tea shops in Sweden, vending machines in Amster—"

"Internationally adored," I summarize with a beaming smile I have trouble holding. "Plus, the streets are teeming with British tourists and other travelers who could have picked up these delightful cookies on their journeys."

"How many routinely carry them around in their bicycling bags?" the chief asks, sharing a smirk with her translator. "How many of these tourists did the deceased marry?"

Actually, that's a good point. Edwin/Eddie could have left a string of wronged women across Europe. But I do know of one common-law wife with access to shortbreads.

"Shortbread makes a wonderful gift," I say. "Lionel kindly sent some sample packets to our innkeeper, Gabi Morel, over the summer."

I wriggle in my chair, both because the carved wooden back is biting into my vertebrae and because I feel icky about pointing to Gabi.

Rosemary's brow crinkles. She takes out another shortbread packet. The packaging resists until she rips it apart with a frustrated huff. Crumbs scatter. Her hands tremble. Lionel reaches for them, but she yanks them away.

The chief smiles like a lioness might look upon a lame gazelle. "Madame Perch, tell me again, when did you last see your husband?"

"See him?" Rosemary asks, fingers tightening on an unfortunate shortbread.

"Before he was discovered dead," the chief clarifies. "When did you last see him alive?"

"I last saw Edwin fifteen years, four months, and three days ago," Rosemary says crisply.

Lionel looks at his watch, as if about to add the hours and minutes. I shake my head and mime shushing.

Chief Dubois nods to the translator, who produces a manila folder. "Madame Perch, you were in the village the night your husband was killed," she states.

"No!" I blurt, since Rosemary is preoccupied dusting up crumbs of shattered shortbread.

The chief removes a photo and slides it across the scarred table. It's the kind of photo I'd see on the news back in Chicago: *Police ask for help identifying this blurry blob under a baseball cap, photographed at an overhead angle in the dark at five-pixel resolution.*

This is a blurry blob among half-timbered homes and cobblestones. A good lawyer—say, the vicious Helena—could easily argue the person is unidentifiable. I'm about to say just that, but Rosemary is already answering.

Like the picture, she's drained of all color. "Yes, that's me."

She studies the marred table. "I was out for a walk. No reason. I was just—"

"Leaving," I interrupt. "We're leaving. We've answered enough questions and it's certainly no crime to stroll around a village. A very beautiful village, very peaceful after dark."

I push back my chair, praying the chief will allow my bluff.

The translator looks from the blurry figure to Rosemary and back. Chief Dubois gently taps the photo.

Rosemary and Lionel remain solidly seated. I reiterate that we really should go.

Lionel stiffens in his seat. "Rosemary was only in the village because she was looking for me. I went out first that night. She came to find me."

"And why were you out?" the chief asks mildly.

"Needed air." Lionel manages to make the two words sound evasive.

Rosemary grips his hand. "My godmother was atrociously rude to Lionel. I learned of her behavior and went seeking Lionel to apologize."

"Ah," says the chief.

I can guess the scenario her suspicious mind is weaving because I'm thinking it too. An angry current boyfriend stomps off and runs into his beloved's long-missing husband. Fearful that the ex will throw a wrench in his romantic hopes, the current beau lashes out.

But this is Lionel. He wouldn't erupt in violence.

Rosemary grips his hand. "Lionel and I found each other by the historic tower. We can vouch for each other."

"Aw," says the translator. "That is sweet."

"*Romantique,*" the chief agrees. "Everything is easier when you are a couple."

Like murder, I guess she's thinking. *Like hefting a body into a cart.*

Lionel opens another packet of cookies and offers Rosemary one.

Like sharing cookies and leaving their crumbs as evidence.

CHAPTER 19

Tour-guide tidbit: If you think Riquewihr seems like a fairy tale, you're not alone. Riquewihr and neighboring villages likely inspired the backdrop for Disney's *Beauty and the Beast*. The tale has a long French connection. The original story, *La Belle et la Bête*, was published by French novelist Gabrielle-Suzanne Barbot de Villeneuve in 1740. Remarkably for an early fairy tale, it had a happy ending too.

We're leaving. I feel like pinching myself. I do pinch my palm, a reminder to stay on guard.

"I'll be in touch," Chief Dubois says, holding open the door to the interview room.

I bet she'll be in touch. Cats let mice scurry off so they can prolong the joy of the hunt.

"Let me see you out," the chief says pleasantly.

Rosemary is thanking her. Rosemary is way too kind for her own good. Lionel is offering to bring by a complimentary tin of Rose Petal Shortbreads.

"Better not," Chief Dubois says, rubbing her flat belly. "Some might construe that as criminal bribery of a law enforcement officer."

I know one such construer. She's leading us back down

the cement-block hallway to a lobby in clashing tiles of mint and olive green set against dishwater gray walls and flickering fluorescent lights. The judging criteria for Most Beautiful Villages of France must not include their police stations. This, I base on anecdotal evidence. I've been in how many stations in seriously beautiful French villages now? Three? Four? Five, if I count meeting Laurent for lunch dates. Any way I count it, they've all been aggressively ugly, as if done up by design-school criminals.

Our translator has gone ahead and is already back at the reception desk, filing a nail to a perfect tip.

"Unlock?" she asks her boss as we approach.

"Wide open," Chief Dubois says, waving to the double glass doors as if we're the lucky contestants of a game show, the kind my mom used to watch where you could win a full dinette set or a sectional sofa larger than your living room.

There's a click. The receptionist must have a remote. Our prize isn't a sofa or an all-expenses trip to Disneyland Paris. We step outside, and my eyes dazzle with flashes before I fully register the mini-pack of reporters waiting on the steps. They call my name. They bellow Rosemary's. Lionel steps gallantly in front of his girlfriend, then stops to rummage in the handlebar bag that doubles as a fanny pack. The doors click behind us.

Lionel's fanny-pack rummage has the reporters shrinking back, allowing me to get a head count of them. Four. Just four, but four too many. When they see Lionel produce nothing more dangerous or exciting than another zippered pouch, they start yelling again. Voices bounce off the cobbles and stucco in English and French and a smattering of German.

There are the expected questions. *Rosemary, Lionel, did you kill Edwin Perch? Did you know he was hiding here?*

Reasonable, given the circumstances. I can't fault them.

But then there are the questions that they can't expect anyone will answer. Questions yelled solely so they can write headlines such as BIKE GUIDE REFUSES TO ANSWER WHEN ASKED IF CYCLING TOURS ARE CURSED. WIDOW DENIES KILLING HUSBAND TWICE.

With a snap of his wrist, Lionel unleashes the yellow rain slicker he'd so carefully repacked earlier. He drapes it over Rosemary's shoulders, shields her face with the hood, and takes her arm. Together, they walk down the steps and turn left in the direction of the main avenue.

The reporters crowd after them like bees on sangria.

"I'll answer your questions!" I call out, before my feet and self-preservation instincts can coordinate and run the other way.

The scrum turns to me, and I know how deer in headlights feel. Questions fly around me. *Do I realize it's been only two months since murders struck my tour? Have I considered exorcisms? How can I call e-bike riding cycling?* I could issue a righteous speech about that last question. I hold back and keep my response easily quotable. "E-bikes allow cycling access to riders of all ages and abilities."

None of the reporters write this down. That's okay. Out of the corner of my eye, I see that Rosemary and Lionel have turned out of sight. Now I have to get away somehow. I could retreat to the police station, but there was that telltale click after we left. I'm betting the door is locked. Photos of me tugging on a barred police station door could be more embarrassing than my current position, standing awkwardly halfway down stone steps in padded bike shorts. My hair is likely helmet-smooshed, my cheeks flaring from the situation and the sun. I summon my best tour-guide stance, straighten my shoulders, and assume what I hope is an appropriately sorrowful expression. I *am* sorry, so it's hardly an act.

"My guests and I are saddened by the unfortunate events," I say, sticking to English. No way I'll risk French grammatical errors in print. "We're assisting the police and are grateful that they are investigating all angles, including—" I stop myself.

Dare I mention the art thefts? There is a criminal prowling around. One who brazenly struck in daylight next door to Eddie's home. A likely suspect, to my mind. Plus, I'm pretty sure Annette Dubois tipped off this reporter flash mob.

My hesitation has had a dramatic-pause effect. The reporters are leaning in, keen to hear my big reveal.

I take a deep breath before continuing my statement. "The police are investigating all angles, including any connection to the ongoing case of major art theft, a crime that began long before my guests arrived to tour this beautiful region."

With that, I make my way down the stairs, inwardly repeating the advice given to hikers faced with bears. *Do not run. That will only provoke them. Do not look them in the eye.*

Unlike with bears, however, I turn my back to the reporters. I only risk a glance when I hear thudding and knocking. They're clustered at the police station door. One—the flashbulb-happy photographer—is yanking on it. Yep, it was locked.

While they're occupied, I turn and set off at speed-walking pace. I've accelerated to a fleeing jog when a hand reaches out and grabs me.

The only reason I don't scream is that he's caught me mid-inhale. And because he looks so pleased and guilty at the same time.

And because he's here? Wait, am I imagining this? Is this some kind of mirage sparked by overindulgence in Munster, wine, and stress? His grip is firm. That seems real enough. His linen shirt is rumpled over crinkled cargo shorts. I've never seen so many wrinkles on Jacques Laurent.

"What are you doing here?" I demand. This isn't the most welcoming thing I could have uttered, but, really, how is he here? *Why* is he here? Shouldn't he be on an Alp somewhere?

Jacques Laurent grins and leans in. For a second, I close my eyes, anticipating a kiss. I open them when his warmth and cologne brush by. I yank my eyelids open and see he's looking over my shoulder, around the corner.

"We shouldn't stay here," he says. "If Annette keeps those reporters out, they'll come looking for you again. You gave them quite an interview."

I'm stalled, goggling at him. He's here. I have more questions than the reporters. He saw that crash equivalent of a press conference? He's on a first-name basis with Annette Dubois?

"What are you doing here?" I repeat, this time with more marvel than shock. "Shouldn't you be training in forests or mountains or alpine patisseries?"

He smiles. "*Bonjour* to you too, Sadie." He places his hands on my shoulders and launches *bisous*, kisses that miss the air and brush my cheeks. "The training was done. I have vacation days. I was going to visit a friend in Chamonix and mountain bike, but then I heard—" He holds up an index finger and cocks his head, ear toward the station. We both listen hard to a silence that makes me uneasy. Either the reporters have gotten inside or . . . I picture them tiptoeing down the lane, fingers to their lips, ready to leap around the corner and jump me.

"I assume you know every twist and turn of this town already?" Laurent asks, his voice low as a whisper.

"Hardly." But I know enough. I can guess where he'd like to go too. I start walking that way, fast. We'll turn a corner and another, then dogleg right, past a fountain and a sign in the shape of a gingerbread man, a bite taken out of his grinning head.

When we're almost there, I ask, as if just remembering, "Where would you like to go?"

He hedges. "I shouldn't take you from your work . . ."

As if a murder investigation and reporters haven't already derailed my work. And does he really think I'm letting him get away without explanations?

We round the elbow corner. The bistro I'm aiming for is tucked away from the main tourist drag and hopefully the reporter trail too. It even has the perfect name, L'Échappée Belle, which suggests a pleasant getaway or a narrow escape.

"Will this do?" I ask.

Laurent stops to breathe in savory delights. A rustic sign hangs above a door carved in woodland scenes and arched like the entry to a hobbit's home. The windows are divided into diamond panes and decorated in a profusion of geraniums.

"How'd you know?" he asks. "I'm starving."

Before I can answer that he's not that hard to deduce—he's *always* up for a good meal—he slips an arm through mine and answers his own question. "You have the intuition of a detective, that's how. I should warn you, though. You're toying with trouble with Annette."

"So I've been told. Is that why you're here?" I ask, as he hefts open the door. "Because of Annette Dubois?"

"In a manner of speaking."

A hostess with two thick blond braids and a full-length ruffled apron greets us. I request a seat in the garden, and she winks like I've uttered a secret code. We weave through rustic rooms with age-darkened beams and deep-set windows that hold back the summer heat. The hostess opens a nondescript door, and we step into the secret garden.

"Beautiful," Laurent says. A tall stone wall and the half-timbered sides of neighboring buildings enclose the space.

A wisteria drips flowers that look and smell of candied grapes from an overhead trellis. A real grape vine as thick as my arm climbs the timbers. Laurent's appreciative gaze lands on me, lingering so long my cheeks warm. When we're seated, I hide my blush behind the wood-encased menu.

Not that I could eat anything after my earlier cheese feast. Especially not with anxiety knots tightening in my stomach. The implications of what I've just done are settling in like five pounds of Munster. I have pointed headline-hungry reporters to the case Annette Dubois failed to solve, her great embarrassment, the case that has her determined to redeem herself with a high-profile arrest. *Great job,* I tell myself. *Smooth move, Sadie. Why not find a hornets' nest and poke it? No, better yet, why not shake said hornets into my bike helmet and ride into a thorny shrub?*

I bite back a groan. Laurent studies the menu like a jeweler presented with a treasure chest of gems.

When a waiter glides over, I ask for a glass of Riesling. Laurent interrogates the waiter about sausage origins. They move onto grape varietals and vineyard weather conditions in the year 2018. Knowing this could take a while, I risk gauche dining behavior and text Nadiya and Lionel to check that everyone is okay.

Laurent settles on a half-bottle of 2019 Gewürztraminer. "And the baeckeoffe, *s'il vous plaît.*"

Baeckeoffe would be the clay vat of many meats, potatoes, onions, and a savory broth simmered with Riesling. He *is* hungry. He sets down the menu and switches to the Oxford English instilled by his British father and several formative years in British boarding school. "I can't say I've suffered your recent hardships, but the culinary conditions of that barracks were horrendous."

"You're a survivor," I joke.

He nods seriously and smooths a white cloth napkin

over his rumpled shorts. His dark hair is as neat as ever, close-clipped at the side but long enough for waves on the top. His five-o'clock shadow looks to be several days old and is hiding an angry scratch that runs from his right ear and down his cheek.

"You hurt yourself." I point to his cheek.

"Tree branch," he says and touches his forehead. "You did too."

My bump has turned into an ugly rough scuff. "Ceiling beam. They're dangerous around here."

"Many things are. You and your group are in serious trouble."

He didn't have to leave the Alps to tell me that. The waiter drops off our wine with a flourish. Laurent immediately studies his half-bottle's label like there will be a pop quiz.

"You know . . ." I say, after giving him a minute or two to read. "I'm delighted to see you, but there is this newfangled technology called telephoning and texting."

He puts down the bottle. Dew races down the sides in rivulets. "You didn't receive texts saying I was coming?"

I shake my head.

"Not mine, exactly," he amends, running a hand over his chin stubble. "I had some phone troubles so I had a friend text you to let you know I was on my way. Did I mistake your number? Did his messages not come through? There was poor reception in the mountains, but he was hiking into a town this morning so the messages should have reached you."

Ohhh . . . Oh! I take out my phone and show him the anonymous texts. "I kept these as evidence in case the killer was warning me off."

He reads, then winces. "First, well done preserving evidence. And, ah, that phone trouble I mentioned? I dropped my phone. Down a cliff. A very high, rocky cliff. It's gone.

I asked my friend Freddo to text you. I told him that you are American but to go ahead and explain in French, that you would understand."

Freddo, apparently, thought comprehension of French would be impossible for an American. That's one mystery solved and good news too. *The killer isn't coming for me!* I'm celebrating with a sweet sip of Riesling when my logic lobe crashes the party. I shouldn't assume. All I know is that the killer didn't send those texts.

"I hope you're not offended that I'm here," Laurent says, as the waiter drops off a basket of baguette rounds and herbed butter. "I know you can take care of yourself."

Offended? I could pretend to be. I can hold my own, I might protest. However, right now, I want all the help I can get. Especially if it comes with eyes that could turn *fromage*—and my knees—into melty fondue.

Cyclist's Log

Monday evening, princess bed, Inn of the Three Storks

You know what's better than a snapshot of two wine glasses clinking? Better than crystal lit by the late afternoon sun, with amethyst grapes and an earthenware casserole dish, steam mingling with the summer heat? Dew on the water carafe. Swifts darting overhead. A handsome man smiling across a café table.

Yeah, you know what's better than a photo, Diary. Reality!

I'll admit, I keep pinching myself that Laurent is actually here. What a surprise! I'm glad I didn't kick him. He later said I should have. I should lash out at anyone who grabs me. I should scream and jab fingers in their eyes. Good policy, I agreed, but only after I make sure they're not his eyes and shins.

We lingered for two hours in our secret garden. I wasn't shirking my duties, I promise. Nadiya had cycled back with the elder Spinners. They'd worn out their batter-

ies—of bikes and bodies—and were napping at the inn. Lionel texted back and reported he and Rosemary were also exhausted and in for a lie-down. No doubt. Confessing to opportunities to commit murder must be tiring!

Sorry, that sounded snarky, but really, those two practically served themselves up as prime suspects.

Laurent confessed that his phone disaster has far greater costs than buying a replacement. He'd been talking to Annette when it happened, hiking up a trail in the rain, gripping the phone too hard. His foot had slipped and the phone was gone, bouncing off rocks to a shattering death. Annette interpreted those last crashing moments as Laurent—Jacques—aggressively hanging up on her. Laurent has witnesses who could back up his story, but she won't be swayed. Once Annette latches onto a theory, he said, she won't let go. That gave me a chill, even sharing a table with Laurent's vat of bubbling casserole.

There is one happy point about the dead phone. Laurent remembered my number! To prove it, he punched it into the temporary phone he'd picked up at a train station. I'm the first number in its contacts.

I know Laurent's number, of course. No disrespect to Wordle or crossword puzzles, but memorizing phone numbers is a more practical mental workout. I also memorize license plates and the longitude-latitude co-ordinates of my favorite bakeries.

Laurent said he only remembers a few numbers, those of important people. Let me tell you, I was feeling pretty special until he added that during my previous tour troubles, he'd pulled phone records of suspects and mine kept showing up. Again, if this were a romance novel, our meeting would not have been the classic cute kind.

I'm low on Annette's suspect list, according to Laurent, but I'm more worried for Rosemary and Lionel. Here are some words Laurent used to describe Annette Dubois: in-tense, focused, driven, tenacious, and ruthless. (I could have guessed those.) Also: former girlfriend, which I'd pretty much guessed from all her first-name drops. They dated for several years in college and then during a police training course.

Several years and cadet training sound

like a pretty serious relationship. I didn't ask why they broke up, and he didn't offer.

Talk of relationships got us onto Gabi and her Eddie. Laurent couldn't believe that Gabi had never probed into Eddie's past. How did she fail to do a simple Google search?

I know how. She simply didn't. She was happy with their relationship as it was, in the present.

Laurent granted that he could see that personally. I should hope so! I've never pried into his past, online or otherwise. Laurent knows about my ex, Al, but dear Al also found his way into the June events. Murder investigations can also tell you a lot about a person. Laurent can be assured that I don't have skeletons in my background, like a criminal record or going missing off the Cornish coast. And I know he'll go above and beyond to come to my aid. To get here, for instance, he took a train across Switzerland. Hardly a scenic hardship, but the point is, he crossed another country to be with me.

Laurent wants to talk to the investigators who handled Edwin Perch's missing-person case. First, he has to approach Annette about assisting, officially or off the books. He walked me back to the inn after his "light" late lunch. He was going to call Annette and ask if they could talk.

I haven't heard from him since. It's nearly eleven, so I doubt I will tonight. Here's a coincidence: He's staying at the hostel where the cat took me. I told him about the tasty—

CHAPTER 20

Tour-guide tidbit: Are you a night owl? If you return in early autumn, you could join in a nighttime harvest. Some winegrowers harvest in the cool hours from sundown to dawn. Cooler grapes are firmer to handle and slower to prematurely ferment.

I freeze, pencil pressed to my journal page. Goosebumps rise on my bare legs. I'm in my nighttime comfy clothes—drawstring shorts and a silly-long T-shirt advertising an anchovy festival. Laurent won the shirt at a carnival stand. He's a deadeye shot at suction-cup darts.

I listen to a breeze whisper through the shutters. I heard that . . . Didn't I? A crash, followed by a guttural outburst.

Is one of my riders hurt? Is there an intruder?

I slip from the bed, slide into sandals, and tiptoe to the door. The hinges groan, mocking my attempt at stealth as I peek into the hallway. It's empty except for the sound of heavy footsteps on the back stairs. They seem to be going down. *I hope they're not coming my way!*

My riders have rooms on the second floor. They'd take the main stairs with the burled-wood banister, the faded oriental carpet, and more of Gabi's disapproving ancestors watching from the walls.

I grab my phone and scan the room for a weapon. Anything can be a weapon. I know this from logic but also from perkily paranoid clickbait articles titled things like "Ten Accessories You *Literally* Can't Live Without." I lack pepper spray, hot sauce, a whistle, the ability to whistle loudly, hair spray, a nail file, and/or a really big multi-faceted diamond ring. If I had mile-high stilettos, they'd be the death of me first.

My eyes light on my keychain, half hidden by a map on the dresser. *Ah-ha!* I haven't been carrying it here because the keys fit locks in Sans-Souci, but they and the emergency corkscrew could be last-ditch weapons. With a key extending from my fist, I approach the back stairs. A motion-sensing light flicks on. A glow beyond the turn in the landing confirms someone has been down before me.

I hesitate, questioning my next move. I could call the police. And report what? That I was scared by a bump in the night? That one of my riders took the back stairs when nicer stairs are available? Chief Dubois would love that.

I could text Laurent . . .

I could also determine if there's truly a threat. Sticking to the less creaky edges of the steps, I make my way down. I hold my breath at the twist in the stairs and again as the steps narrow and steepen before plunging out to the dark corridor. At the main hallway, I turn on my cell phone's flashlight, which manages to be blindingly bright yet reaches only an inch from my hand. I switch it back off. I don't need to light myself up as a target.

A single lamp glows at the end of the hallway. Its beam casts shadows, creating the illusion of grasping branches. I gulp back a gasp. One of those shadows is moving! Down by the breakfast room, a formless figure reaches for a portrait.

The art thief!

Without daring to breathe, I retreat into the nearest

room, the library, where I'd left Lionel resting his eyes after the discovery of Eddie/Edwin. My phone screen seems as bright as a lighthouse when I tap it on and text for help.

Laurent could be asleep. He could have his new temporary phone off. I don't dare call 112. I'd have to speak to the emergency services operator, and even a whisper would be too loud. Every sound seems amplified in the dark, including the muffled footsteps plodding my way to the tune of a low, off-key whistle. My heart pounds so hard, I'm sure the thief can hear it.

Just then, my phone pings like a quarter-ton church bell. I fumble to silence it, but the sound can't be taken back. The whistling has stopped. The footsteps are rapid now, shuffling like the scuttles and skittles of a horror film monster. A door slams somewhere in the maze of the old inn.

I tally my options.

1. Hide in the library. A library is always a good option!
2. Run back to my room. Another fine idea.
3. Follow the intruder. A very, very unappealing choice. Foolish. Foolhardy. Way down and off the bottom of any sensible list.

Except this could be my chance to clear Rosemary and Lionel, to free us all from this case, to provide closure for the widows. I rush to the side hallway in time to see the shadow—now rectangular with the stolen painting—duck into a room.

But which room? Farther down the corridor, I find two doors. One leads to a half-bath. It's no larger than a coat closet and empty except for stacks of paper products, cleaning supplies, and a rust-stained pedestal sink.

The thief must have picked door number two. I swing it open with one hand, my corkscrew raised in the other.

With my phone's flashlight, I illuminate a closet, mostly empty except for a vacuum cleaner and stand-up fan. I shine my light into the corners, expecting any moment to see eyes flashing back. Nothing.

Now more frustrated than afraid, I reach inside and pull a cord to switch on an overhead light bulb. Yep, just an empty closet with scuffed paneling and hints of musty vacuum cleaner and mothballs. I'm about to implement option four—barricade myself in the breakfast room and raid the shortbread tin while I wait for Laurent—when I detect an odd scent amidst the mothball camphor. Fresh air.

I know I'll regret this if the thief sneaks up behind me and shuts me in—or worse. I step in the closet anyway and press at the paneling. Pushing does nothing, but sliding does. A panel stutters aside, revealing a stone landing. To my left, steps lead down into darkness.

Nope! I draw the line at a creepy basement!

To my right, a door waggles as if beckoning me out and into the night. I'm well aware that my reaction to this should also be *no way*! I step to the landing, fast as if I'm barefoot on hot coals, push through the door, and burst outside.

I'm in Gabi's pretty garden. Of course I am. Did I think I was going to enter another realm? I don't see anyone, but I hear that whistle again. It appears to be coming from around the corner, from the patio outside the breakfast room. Maybe the thief is also in the mood for cookies. The wind kicks up. The door slams behind me. I fail to stifle a yelp, but that's not the sound that curdles the night.

The scream freezes my veins. A woman's scream. A male voice yells, followed by a crash of metal. The spooky cellar is looking more and more appealing. I firm up my white-knuckle grip on the corkscrew and run.

* * *

"Attacked! Attacked in my own home!" Pépère brandishes a metal watering can, the source of the clanking. "Get back! Be gone, thief!"

"On my Rupy's grave!" Scarlett wears a satin gown, creamy white and glowing in the moonlight, cinched at the waist like an old-Hollywood starlet. She spots me and points to Pépère. "Sadie! Thank goodness you're here. This little old gnome man scared me half to death and back again!" She repeats this in French.

"Gnome," Pépère cackles in delight.

Scarlett smooths her immaculate hair. "About turned my hair white."

"Gutted to inform you, Scarlett, it's too late for your hair." Keiko appears in the doorframe. She raises a hand to cover a yawn.

Pépère gasps and waes the watering can again.

I see why. Keiko's other hand grips a knife.

"Kei-Kei, what are you doing?" Scarlett chides. "That's the fruit saber. Put that down. You're scaring this little old honey."

"Little old honey?" Keiko says dryly. "I thought *he* was terrifying *you*."

Scarlett tuts that he's clearly harmless. She doesn't translate this for Pépère, who's still brandishing the watering can.

Keiko stretches her shoulders, her fists raised and back, including the one holding the knife.

When someone is holding a knife that size, the blade is pretty much all you see. Thus, it's taken me a moment to register Keiko's attire. She's in cycling shorts and her windbreaker. She hasn't been out riding in the dark again, has she?

"Everyone, stay where you are!"

I just about jump out of my skin. Pépère curses.

"Ma'am, put down the knife." Laurent's voice is calm but deadly serious. He's in cargo shorts and a form-fitting black T-shirt, as if his recent training had included a summertime beach invasion. He's also slightly out of breath. Did he run here? He doesn't have a car. I quizzed him about his transportation choices. After the train ride here, he'd taken a taxi to town.

"Ohhh . . ." Scarlett coos. Accentuated by shadows, her lashes resemble butterflies about to take flight. "Who do we have here?"

Laurent frowns. "Where is the thief?"

"There!" Pépère declares, waving the watering can at all of us. "These *touristes* have stolen my family home."

I step forward, holding up my palm. "Laurent, I'm so, so sorry. There's been a misunderstanding." I gesture to the grumbling gnome. "This gentleman is the innkeeper's grandfather. This is his house. I thought . . ." I switch to apologetic French aimed at Pépère, explaining that I thought he was the art thief.

"*Pfft!*" Pépère cradles his portrait. "There is an art thief, but it is not me."

Keiko yawns again. "I'm going to bed."

Good! Bed is good. "Sorry we woke you," I say.

She shrugs. "I was thinking of going for a ride, but clearly there are still too many people up and making noise. Scarlett?" She raises an eyebrow at her friend. "Are you going back upstairs too?"

"I'll stay and assist the law," Scarlett says, back to fluttering at Laurent. "Sadie, darling, you didn't tell me you had a handsome policeman in your pocket. Where's he been all this time?"

Laurent is on his new phone. He's speaking low, but I overhear the key words. *Fausse alerte.* False alarm. He holds the phone away from his ear as Annette Dubois has what I guess are choice words about me.

"We've had to deal with an extremely hostile policewoman," Scarlett practically bellows. She must recognize the griping voice on the other line. She's beginning to translate "hostile policewoman" into even louder French when Laurent issues an urgent "Annette, *désolé*, I must go," and jabs at his screen.

Did he just hang up on Annette Dubois again? She's going to be livid, mostly at me.

"Let's get you home, Monsieur," Laurent says to Pépère and offers to carry the painting. "Who is this?"

Pépère's grandmother, it turns out. "Fought the Germans with her bare hands and a cabbage, she did! You know, there are mysteries in these lands, young man. Under our feet!"

Laurent, bless him, asks to hear all about them.

I fall back with Scarlett, who takes the opportunity to suggestively elbow me. I try to wheel her back to the more immediate point. "You heard a crash?" I'll have to go back and investigate what fell.

"I did," she says primly. "Not all seniors are deaf, Sadie, darling."

"I didn't mean—"

She cuts me off with a friendly slap. "I'm joking, dear. My Rupy couldn't hear a fire alarm until I bullied him into getting hearing aids. I shouldn't have. I could say anything around him before." She tuts. "Those days are over, sadly."

This evening, I entered dark stairways, hallways, and secret doors, following what I believed was a dangerous criminal. Why not add another bold and ill-advised choice?

"Sir Rupert . . ." I say. "He's, ah . . ."

"Burning up in penance for his lust," Scarlett says with a grin and a twinkle.

He's alive. He must be! She couldn't be getting so much enjoyment out of this otherwise, right?

Before I can pose further questions for Scarlett's enjoyment, Gabi bursts outside.

"Pépère!" she cries. "Not again! Were you up in the village? Next door? Not bothering our guests?"

"Who is bothering whom?" Pépère asks.

Laurent produces his gendarme ID card from one of his many cargo pockets. "A misunderstanding, Madame," he says. "We are sorry to disturb you."

Gabi raises an eyebrow to me.

"Pépère was, ah . . . visiting the inn," I say. "I couldn't tell who it was in the dark. I saw someone removing a painting and thought it was the art thief. Detective Laurent came by as a friend."

"There's been a thief in the house, all right," Pépère declares.

His granddaughter makes soothing sounds. "Come in, everyone. Have some tea, won't you?"

"Delighted to," says Scarlett, stepping past us.

"It's late," I protest, mindful of the actual time and Mom's rules of don't-be-a-bother. "We shouldn't bother you."

Gabi is saying she'd welcome the company. "I couldn't sleep."

"I hear you. I've slept like a gnat since my fifties," Scarlett says. "Smallest sound wakes me and that's it, I'm up for hours."

I look to Laurent. He smiles and raises his eyebrows and shoulders in a why-not gesture.

"Monsieur," he says to Pépère, when we're all in the kitchen and Gabi has turned on the electric kettle. "Why did you fear for your painting tonight?"

"I read the news on Facebook," the old man says proudly. "There's word that the art thief is still around and killing folks too. It doesn't make sense, but what does on Facebook?"

Gabi sets out packages of tea: chamomile, licorice, linden, and caramel. When we've chosen, she fills our mismatched porcelain cups.

"Regrettably, the thief has not yet been caught," Laurent says, dipping a linden sachet, perfumed like summer. "And we do not know who is responsible for the murder."

In the soft, anxious clatter of teacups and spoons, I almost miss Pépère's mutter.

"Thought the thief was taken care of."

I glance at Laurent. His raised eyebrow tells me he's heard. Did Pépère think Eddie was the thief? And if Pépère had thought that, would he have tried to stop him? Maybe I actually was following after a killer tonight.

Pépère is sipping caramel tea with surprising delicacy. I'm thinking he looks innocent enough when he slaps the table, startling everyone except Laurent.

"I'm off to bed," Pépère declares. "I have things to do tomorrow. I'm not on vacation like the rest of you. I think I'll do some digging."

Gabi kisses him on both cheeks. "You *do* have things to do tomorrow, but not digging. You're going to the bank in Strasbourg with me, remember? We'll get a late lunch at your favorite restaurant afterward for *lewerknepfle*."

Poached liver dumplings. I've yet to try those. I'll try any dish once, but I'm pretty sure I'd prefer *tarte flambeé*.

Laurent is getting the details of the dish and the restaurant.

I finish my tea and push back my seat. Scarlett is already up and perusing the room. She's studied the portrait of disapproving grandma and a collection of alpine-themed ceramic objects: a white cow with a yoke of flowers, a colorful clog, a gnome who looks like a jollier Pépère. She moves on and looks a little too interested in a brass bar cart of dark-glassed bottles.

"Scarlett and I have a full day too," I say. "We should get our sleep. We have a cookie tour."

"Subtle," Scarlett says. "Yes, Mother, I'm off to bed."

"Sounds sweet," Gabi says, lips pressed in an attempt at a smile.

Guilt sours the soothing taste of chamomile. I shouldn't have flaunted our touristy fun. Scarlett slips from my grip and grabs Laurent by the arm. She's flirtatiously "allowing" him to escort her back to the inn.

I linger to thank Gabi for the tea. We apologize simultaneously for the Pépère misunderstanding, and Gabi again wishes me happy cookie adventures.

"It's a good idea to do something nice," she says solemnly, as we step out into the garden. Constellations twinkle overhead, brighter than I'd ever see back in suburban Illinois. Insects turn off their tunes as Laurent and Scarlett pass by, resuming in waves. Gabi is saying that she hopes Rosemary enjoys the cookie demonstrations. "Rosemary must be doubly disorientated, to be facing such a shock and to be far from home."

Gabi's a saint. Such empathy for her fellow widow. But then, if anyone would understand, she would. I remember my vow to Rosemary, made right before she volunteered too much information to the police.

"Rosemary was wondering about Eddie's official documents," I say. "His ID, birth records . . . Do you happen to have them?"

I expect her to say that the police have those too.

She's shaking her head. "No. The police asked, but I have not yet found them. Eddie did not like paperwork or keeping it organized. It'll be here somewhere . . ." She looks vaguely around as if official documents might appear amidst the knickknacks.

I wish her a good evening and good luck at the bank and step back out into the night. Crossing the garden, I spot Laurent and his yellow cruiser bike.

"I almost had to call you for help," Laurent whispers.

I raise an eyebrow, but I can guess why. He confirms my deduction. Scarlett had tried to lure him upstairs.

"She asked if I liked older ladies," Laurent says, gripping the bike's handles. The bike has tassels—lemon-yellow tassels! How adorable! There's also a wicker basket with a metal ring that could hold a baguette.

"Cute bike," I say, unable to stifle a grin.

Laurent pats the handlebars. "A beauty, isn't she? I 'commandeered' her from a woman at a bar. Your text scared me. Did you not receive my reply, begging you to stay back?"

I can honestly say I didn't have time to read that text.

"Because you were busy following a burglar," Laurent says. "A burglar you thought could also be a murderer."

I give my best couldn't-be-helped French shrug. "Turns out I was wrong," I say, then add, "maybe."

Laurent looks grim. "The old man? You suspect him?"

"Suspect everyone, isn't that what you say? He didn't like Eddie, and he carries around shovels and hefty walking sticks. Does Annette know what the murder weapon was yet?"

He shakes his head. "As-yet-unidentified blunt-force object, likely wooden."

"That narrows it down," I say, meaning just the opposite.

"Quite," Laurent says dryly. He smiles at me. "I'm glad you're safe."

"I'm glad you are," I tease. "You know, Scarlett was probably trying to set you up with her goddaughter."

"Rosemary? The primary murder suspect?" Laurent hefts the yellow bike in a tight turn. "Dating a killer is frowned on in my line of work." Muscles ripple in his forearms. The bike must be old-fashioned heavy metal.

"Ah, well, Rosemary's already seeing someone," I tell him.

"So I've heard. The other murder suspect. They sound like a good match. She's likely out of my reach then." He leans over and brushes my lips with a kiss. "Good thing I have my heart set elsewhere."

CHAPTER 21

Tuesday:
It's Christmas in August—let's bake *bredels*! The term "bredel" encompasses a variety of cookies with tasty histories dating back to the Middle Ages, when monks and nuns prepared these special Christmastime treats. Treasured recipes include local ingredients such as honey, nuts, and spices.

The breakfast room is surprisingly quiet when I arrive at eight, having boldly set my alarm to sleep in until 7:45. Keiko is serenely segmenting a grapefruit. Lionel and Rosemary are studying a fold-out map. Maurice and Benji are reading the classifieds and sports sections of the local paper, respectively. Sections I haven't seen them read previously.

"*Coucou*, Sadie," Benji trills. "Top of the morning to you." Paper crinkles as he re-crosses his legs.

I tilt my head and spot a corner of newsprint poking from beneath his underside.

He sees me looking and shakes his head. In case I don't get the message, he adds a cautionary waggling finger.

I agree. I don't want to see the day's headlines. Except, I'm also sickeningly drawn in like a rubbernecker gawking at a highway accident. Will the front page show Lionel, shielding widow Rosemary under his rain jacket? All three of us, squinting at the daylight as we step out of the police station? Me, taunting the woman who could arrest us all?

"Tractor for sale," Maurice reads out loud, gazing low through his spectacles. "Grape crusher, never used. Must be a sad story behind that."

"Herd dog competition this weekend," Benji reads from his section. "Paragliding camp. Not for me, paragliding."

"Mmmm . . ." Maurice sounds interested. "Skydiving is the true thrill. Paragliding, you merely run off a slope. Will we still be here on the camp days? We could all give it a try."

I picture us on our bikes, rolling into the sky. I'm with Benji. That's not for me.

"You don't run anymore, darling," Benji says. "Besides, look what happened last time you got adventurous."

Lionel clears his throat in disapproval. Yeah, Maurice's last "adventure" broke open a barrel and a murder investigation.

I help myself to coffee and plunge into small talk. "Did everyone get a good night's sleep?"

"After all the screaming?" Keiko asks with a sigh.

"Screaming?" Benji asks with a titillated gasp. "What did we miss?"

"How *did* you sleep through such noise?" Keiko asks.

"We weren't asleep." Benji's eyes sparkle with mischief.

"We were up in the village until the wee hours," Maurice reports. "When on the continent, we keep Barcelona hours."

"We saw our Chief Annette letting her hair down," Benji reports. "She was out at a bar with a serious man—seriously handsome. Maurice and I waved, and she didn't even wave back. I'm beginning to think she doesn't like us." He faux pouts.

I make sure I'm not doing the same. That serious man would have been Laurent. I'm glad they were out. My text didn't wake him, and he'd gotten information including a vague description of the murder weapon. Plus, if he and Chief Dubois are getting along, he has a better chance of talking her down from any rash arrests of my riders.

Unless he looked serious because she was convincing him of their guilt.

My thoughts are interrupted by the sound of elephants approaching. *Clomp*, *clomp*, *clomp* down the stairs. *Thud*, *thump*, *scrape* along the hallway. Maurice and Benji drop their papers and leap up.

My eyes tug to the headline on Benji's abandoned seat: PORTRAIT OF A KILLER? BIKE GUIDE CLAIMS WIDOW IS FRAMED! There's a half-folded photo showing me, index finger raised like some spandex-clad Sherlock.

That's not *too* bad, I think. I don't look awful, and the art-thief allusion is rather clever. Then I imagine Annette's reaction and correct my assessment: It's bad. Very bad.

So is the scene taking shape at the door. Scarlett limps to the threshold. "My hip!" she declares, leaning on twin walking sticks. Like Pépère's, the sticks are sapling thick and carved in swirls following the grain of the wood.

Scarlett rolls her eyes so dramatically, she almost tips over. "Heaven help me! At this rate, I'll be joining Rupy in the overheated beyond."

"A gurney!" Benji cries. "Get this woman a gurney. No, a chariot!"

Maurice offers a "good spinal cracking."

Rosemary jumps up to flutter at her godmother's side. I'm doing the same. Together, we're like those helpers in curling competitions, brushing the path of an oncoming force. Even Keiko joins in the slow-motion shuffle to the breakfast table.

Only Lionel remains seated, meticulously buttering a chunk of baguette.

Scarlett bats off our ministrations and eases into the nearest chair with a groan. "My hip senses any cooldown in the weather," she says. "I do apologize, Sadie, I will not be cycling today."

I launch a blizzard of queries: Does she need pain medication, a doctor, a physical therapist, a massage therapist, a pharmacy?

"I'll take a massage," Benji says, raising his hand. He's back in his seat and crinkling the headlines.

Scarlett forcefully resists all. "I will rest in a lounge chair in the garden. I'll read and nap. You all can bring me back cookies."

"I'll stay with you," offers Rosemary, the group member most interested in cookies and for whom I specifically arranged the cookie-making workshop. But, even cookies won't redeem this tragic tour for Rosemary, so I don't protest.

Scarlett does, bellowing a refusal so forceful that Rosemary rears back. Scarlett softens her tone. "Rosemary, dear, I want you to investigate French cookies. Be free! Have fun! Stay out of sight of that sour Chief Dubois." She snaps her fingers. "Sadie! I've just had a brilliant idea!"

As she says this, Nadiya comes in, holding a thermos. She catches my eye and puts a finger to her lips before filling the thermos with fresh coffee. I deduce that Jordi's magic coffee sludge is powering up ants or wilting flowers in the garden.

Scarlett carries on. "Sadie, call up your hunky policeman friend right now. Tell him he can have my bike and go along on the tour today to protect my goddaughter."

"Hunky policeman?" Nadiya tightens the thermos lid and grins. "Detective Laurent? He is no longer camping?"

"He rode in like a knight on a golden bike," Scarlett says. "Very chivalrous. A man of *action*, you can tell." She says this to Lionel, who actively ignores her, studying the map.

"Laurent has vacation days after his training exercises," I tell Nadiya casually, as if it's no big deal for a man to cross Switzerland for me.

"*Ahh* . . ." In that single drawn-out sound, Nadiya suggests I've just explained the universe, the heart, and everything. "He uses vacation days for you? Where was his vacation to be? Home, with that mother you do not like?"

It's not that I dislike Madame Laurent, owner of the Hôtel Topaze, a seaside boutique hotel that I book for many tour groups. She, however, seemingly despises me. This despite all the best efforts, smiles, and hotel-lodger income I throw her way. I dodge that issue and tell Nadiya that Laurent gave up mountain biking with a buddy in the Alps.

Nadiya touches her heart. "You are more desirable than an Alp, Sadie. An Alp!"

Or I attract more murder, Laurent's professional pursuit.

Nadiya, Scarlett, and Benji share knowing nods. Keiko mutters that romance is overhyped.

"Then, it's settled. The handsome detective must ride with you," Scarlett says. "Personal police protection—if he can keep up with the Silver Spinners!"

Around the suggestive cooing and chuckles, I politely decline on Laurent's behalf. We don't need police protection to bake cookies. At least, I hope we don't. I still wonder about Lionel getting shoved off the road on the way to the castle. At the time, I didn't know that Lionel had been anywhere near the scene of the corpse and thus might be an unwitting witness.

"I could stay with you, Scarlett," I offer. "Nadiya can guide the group and translate."

Scarlett finger-wags an admonishment. "Absolutely not. I am *not* an invalid. My hip requires peace and rest, and that's what it shall get. Don't make an old lady dwell on her ailments, Sadie."

"Silver Spinner motto," says Benji. "No organ recitals."

I must betray my confusion. Organ recitals? Plus, didn't they have another motto? Pedal to the end? Ride until they die? Maybe I like this one better, whatever it means.

"Organ recitals: yammering on about our ailments like a bunch of *old* people," Benji tuts. "We shan't behave like that. *No* to organ recitals!"

"That rule does not apply to musical organs and my upcoming Wagner festival," Keiko says. "You'll all be there, I'm sure."

"If my hip allows," Scarlett says and reaches for a croissant.

Keiko mutters what sounds like *You don't fool me.*

I sip my coffee and attempt to focus on a very good croissant, easily an 8.5 out of 10 on my rigorous scale. My mind keeps veering back to Scarlett. It's not that I *don't* believe her. I would never discount another's pain, and so much pain is invisible.

On the other hand . . .

Pointed looks shoot around the table. A wink from Scarlett. A nod from Maurice. Rolling eyes from Keiko. Then, there's Benji, dabbing his napkin at lips that—since I've been at the breakfast table—have touched neither food nor drink. Is he covering a grin?

I recall my lessons learned on this tour. Most important for the moment: Don't trust Scarlett. Don't let the Spinners out of my sight.

Both will be difficult if I leave Scarlett on her own. But

not impossible. I join the circle of knowing smiles. They might be cooking up a plan, but I have one too.

"She will not break through my defenses." Jordi flexes his biceps, animating tattoos of a cross, a rugby ball, and a Catalan flag. We stand by the Oui Cycle van, which is parked by the inn, angled to occupy most of the driveway. When Jordi sets up his lawn chair, he'll have a clear view of anyone (as in Scarlett) trying to leave the property.

"Just watch out for Scarlett," I say. "She might need, ah . . . assistance."

"She might be up to something," Nadiya translates. "All of them, they are sneaky."

Jordi cracks his knuckles. "Like I said, she will not escape me."

"Do not tackle the elderly lady," Nadiya clarifies, to my hearty agreement.

Jordi scoffs. "As if I would tackle *that* lady. She would hurt me. I see it in her eyes and in how she handles those sticks."

Scarlett has hobbled out to supervise the cycling preparations. Apparently, Greta, the breakfast assistant, carves the walking sticks. When delivering a bowl of hard-boiled eggs to the breakfast table, Greta told us her sticks were useful for walking. "And for fending off large beasts, like wild boars in chestnut forests."

Scarlett is waving one close to Keiko's nose. Keiko doesn't flinch. I think of Keiko, ready to set out for another midnight ride last night. She has no fear. I'm not sure if that's good or bad.

"Call me if anything happens," I stress to Jordi. "Anything at all. If it's really serious, call Laurent."

"*Pah!* I will not need the *police*, especially him. Always meddling." Jordi is flexing again. Biceps, pecs, even his buzz-cut skull.

I get it, he and the police have bad feelings about each other. His issue with Laurent seems more personal, although I've never figured out what it is.

Nadiya kisses him. "We will bring you cookies."

Jordi blushes, all bluster and huff gone. Aw . . . I can only hope my day will be half as sweet.

We roll into the town of Sélestat a little over an hour later. Because we have time before our cookie demonstration, I stop in front of the Tour des Sorcieres, the Witches' Tower, and encourage the group to hydrate. I'm waiting on Keiko as well. She's been drifting off the back, engrossed in her music. A few times, I caught her waving a finger as if conducting.

"Discover the enchantment," Lionel reads out from his phone as the others gaze up at the thirteenth-century tower, four-sided and topped in a stork's nest. Lionel is a quick draw on Google this morning.

"Defensive structure," he sums up in a tone that suggests that's all there is to say. He returns the phone to its handlebar holster.

"Remember how we talked about witch trials yesterday?" I ask.

Rosemary snorts. "Yes!"

Keiko has rolled up but hasn't removed her earphones. I let that go and wave my palm in front of the tower. "It's believed that accused witches were held here before going to trial." I hope the Spinners will humor me by allowing a dash of tour guiding, especially if it's somber.

Lionel snaps some photos with his big camera. The others obligingly look and murmur.

After the tower, I detour to point out the Humanist Library, which we'll visit after cookies and lunch. "The library dates to fourteen fifty, ah . . ." All of a sudden, dates escape me. Panic rises as if my brake lines have just failed.

Recalling dates is more than my job. It's a point of personal pride.

"Fourteen fifty-two," supplies Maurice. "The library, one of Europe's oldest, holds over four hundred fifty manuscripts and five hundred fifty incunabula, the latter referring to books printed before 1501, representing the infancy of printing technology. Scarlett adores my talk on typeface mimicking medieval calligraphy. Pity she won't be here to shush me."

Okay, okay, I get it. They've heard it all before, they know it all, and now I've unleashed Maurice's professing. He's talking sheepskin bindings and stitching.

Rosemary is closest to me. She smiles and whispers, "Don't worry. He won't know a blessed thing about baking."

She's right about that. L'Atelier des Bredle, the Cookie Workshop, is a wonderland, redolent with the scents of holiday baking: cinnamon, sugar, ginger, and cloves. Antique tins, molds, and cutters decorate the walls, and a jolly woman named Émilie will be our baking guide.

Lionel presents Émilie with a tin of Rose Petal Shortbreads. I snap photos of their smiling exchange of cookie tins. Rosemary is in her element, especially when we get our hands in flour and sugar. We make star-shaped cookies from almond flour, icing them with a sweet meringue. We move on to spicey gingerbreads with a kick of black pepper and soft sugar cookies decorated in gemlike candied fruits. We take silly pictures of our hairnets and aprons, and Émilie's enthusiasm needs no translation, even as she sifts among English, French, German, and what I guess is an Alsatian dialect.

Benji and Maurice are charmingly hapless and fully admit it. Lionel is a measurement pro, which doesn't surprise me. I could forget my troubles amidst this sugary bliss.

A tray of chubby gingerbread men has just gone into the oven when Nadiya nods toward my flour-dusted front.

"You pinged," she says.

Our aprons provide more full-body coverage than most hospital gowns. I struggle to access my thigh pocket.

Nadiya pings too. She's quicker, and we tap on our screens simultaneously.

"More gingerbreads coming out!" Rosemary announces as an oven timer chimes.

"*Lebkuchen*," our rosy-cheeked teacher trills, naming the cookies.

Benji is singing "Jingle Bells." Keiko is humming along.

"Police," Nadiya and I say as one, each turning our screens for the other to see.

Jordi has written the same message to both of us. Police raid! Scarlett arrested. What do I do?

I look to Nadiya. She shakes her head. I gaze around the kitchen. Cookies gleaming with sugar crystals rest on trays. Maurice and Benji are high-fiving in oven mitts. Keiko is sneaking an almond star. Lionel is photographing Rosemary holding a tray and beaming.

I can't answer Jordi's question. I turn it on myself: *What do* I *do?*

CHAPTER 22

Tour-guide tidbit: We're rolling across the footsteps of giants. According to legend, the town of Sélestat was founded by the benevolent giant Sletto and his canine companion Argos. The two mythical beings symbolize kindness, strength, and loyalty and are still honored today in tales and festivals.

In a movie, I'd have to beg the rideshare driver to floor it. I'd be forced to confess that I'm a cyclist in desperate need for dinosaur-bones horsepower. In reality, I'm bracing for impact as a souped-up Renault surges back toward Riquewihr and our inn. The car goes airborne over a traffic hump. Appropriately, my driver's name is Serge. He's steering with two fingers while wildly gesticulating out the window with his other hand.

"Tourists!" he splutters, after I admit I'm a tour guide. "They invade us in summer, at the harvest, and at Christmas, *ooh là là*, let me tell you about Christmas! Tourists go mad for Christmas. If I want a pork knuckle—a simple knuckle—at the Christmas markets, I must fight through hundreds, thousands!"

Serge's grumbles batter my ears. Summer scents assault my nostrils. I detect flowers, earth, the musk of grapes, and the diesel exhaust of the cargo van Serge has just passed one-handed.

"I understand," I say. Empathize, listen, repeat concerns. These are essential skills of the tour guide. "Overtourism is a difficult issue in the south of France where I live too."

"The south?" Serge commandeers the left lane for no other reason than he appears to relish danger. A tractor pulls in from a farm road. I wince down to my toes. Serge sways right with a laconic twist of his wrist. He and the tractor driver wave, and he turns back to me. "You live in the south? Where?"

"Near Perpignan," I say, naming the nearest city.

"And you wear a cycling costume?" Serge stares deeply into the rearview mirror. "Ah-ha! You are the famous cyclist, *non*? Yes, yes, you are! I saw reports of your press conference yesterday. *Brava!* That will show the police. They know nothing!"

That will show me to mess with the press. I thank Serge if only to get him looking at the road again. A vintage Citroën chugs toward us, hugging the center line. The entire rural lane is barely wider than a one-way alley back in Illinois. I'm wishing I'd cycled. Sure, it would have taken longer, but I'd be in control. I'd reach Riquewihr alive!

"*Très chanceux!*" Serge proclaims.

Very fortunate would be missing the Citroën. I suck in my sides, as if that will help.

Serge and the other driver speed by so close, they could give each other air kisses.

"*Oui*, scary times," Serge says. "I have been thinking about the crimes, this mystery of yours." He swivels to look me directly in the eye. "I have a theory."

Here's another thing I've learned about murder investigations: everyone has a theory. I suppose it's the same for other professions. Like dermatologists and screenwriters must forever hear about suspicious moles or script ideas.

"Oh?" I ask, unclenching as we're slowed by a Dutch camper van as large as a barge.

Serge curses. Twitches to the left suggest he's about to pass by forging a lane through a vineyard.

"Let's take our time," I say. "I want to hear your theory."

Serge eases off a little, though we're practically camped on the RV's bumper. "Well, it is probably obvious to someone as experienced as yourself," Serge says, suddenly modest.

I place internal bets. Who will he name? Rosemary? Gabi? The most unlikely Chou Chou?

"All of them!" Serge announces, throwing up both hands as if he's scored a goal.

"All of them?" I repeat.

"All of your guests. They discover the traitorous missing husband in France. They plot their deadly revenge. They hire you as their guide. That is the key, you, Madame, the cyclist with the most murders in France. No one will be surprised when a man falls dead."

The camper has turned on its right blinker but appears to be lumbering left.

"Think about it . . ." Serge taps his forehead.

I am. It's absurd. Ridiculous! Insulting, even.

"It is like the story by Agatha Christie," Serge says. "What is it called? There was a movie. Everyone gets together and—" He mimes a blow to the head, a knife to the neck, vigorous stabbing. "Am I right?"

No, of course he's not right!

Yet, I hear Benji, chuckling that they picked me as their guide for excitement, saying they never thought they'd *get their own murder*. And then this morning . . . I'll bet my beloved bicycle that they planned whatever Scarlett stayed back to undertake.

What did she do? In my haste to get back to the inn, I

neglected to ask Jordi a key question. *The* key question: Why was Scarlett arrested?

I lean forward so sharply, my seatbelt snaps me to a stop.

"Serge," I say. "Can we speed up?"

Serge shifts like a Formula One driver, plants both hands on the wheel, and punches the gas.

Laurent is leaning against the back panel doors of the Oui Cycle van as Serge skids in with a squeal of brakes.

I hop out and attempt to overtip Serge.

"*Non, non,* I will accept only your autograph." He produces a notepad. "And also, your mention of my name and full credit when I turn out to be right. Here, take my card so you can recite my phone number and social media handles."

From the corner of my eye, I see Laurent's lip quirk.

Serge hands me a pen. I'd rather give him ten Euros, twenty Euros, more!

Reluctantly, I sign. Serge snaps a selfie of us in which I likely look stunned. His phone rings. He answers and is speeding off a moment later.

"What's his theory?" Laurent asks.

I'm about to say *You don't want to know,* but it's more that I don't want him to know. I trust Laurent. I don't necessarily trust the company he keeps. Farther up the drive, Chief Dubois stands with Scarlett and Pierre-Luc. Jordi is off to one side, desolately watching Chou Chou dig the trench of Pépère's dreams.

"It's nothing," I say, which only makes Laurent look more interested. I switch to the current crime. "What happened? What did Scarlett do?"

"You're not insisting on her innocence?" He chuckles.

"No comment."

"Good policy. Your guest, the Lady Crabtree-Thorne,

was discovered in the act of burglary. Breaking and entering. Annette is . . . Let's just say she's not happy."

I'm not either. But wait, I am! Laurent made no mention of murder or bodily injury.

He's describing the events leading up to the emergency call. "A Monsieur Pierre-Luc Bauman from the estate next door arrived to return a shovel. While approaching the home, he heard noises from inside. Knowing the owners were out, he called the police."

"Like a responsible citizen." Chief Dubois strides down the drive. "Jacques and I were together, so we immediately sped here and caught the perpetrator in the act."

For the record, she emphasized "together" and "Jacques."

She's smiling, a rather terrifying look on her. She's also wearing red lipstick that I don't recall from our previous meetings. "The property owner is returning to press charges against the burglar and her lookout man. You hire criminals?"

A tour guide's most valuable tool is getting along with just about everyone. With effort equivalent to cycling the highest Alp, I ignore her jibe about Jordi's minor record (okay, major—he hacked several international conglomerates).

"Scarlett was visiting the main house?" I ask, all innocence. "I don't see the problem. We are guests here."

"*Highly* paying guests." Scarlett joins us, beckoning Pierre-Luc to follow. "Not that I mind paying. Use it or lose it to the grave, I always told my Rupy, and he believes that now. That's *Sir Rupert* to our lawyers."

"Sadie," Pierre-Luc says, pressing his palms into a pleading gesture. "Forgive me. With the thefts and Eddie . . . I confess, I overreacted. Had I known it was my friend, Madame Scarlett, I would have invited her over for tea or wine."

"You're a doll, Pierre," Scarlett says, "I'll forgive you if you offer me some of that award-winning Riesling of yours."

"You did the right thing, Monsieur," Laurent says. "We discourage the public from putting themselves in danger." He shoots a wry smile my way.

Believe me, I'd be happy to avoid danger.

Scarlett is saying she's glad Pierre-Luc called the police. "I wanted to, but I couldn't. That's why I went over to Gabi's in the first place. I lost my phone. I must have left it last night. While I was searching for it, I found a clue. *The clue!* Sadie, wait until you hear. I found—"

"You broke into a private residence," Chief Dubois interrupts. "That is a serious crime." Her smile could freeze the Mediterranean. The look reminds me of someone . . .

Oh my gosh! The realization hits like a slap with a frozen fish. Annette Dubois's icy disdain reminds me of Laurent's mother!

I'm sure I look appropriately horrified.

Pleased, Chief Dubois continues. "Scarlett Crabtree-Thorne, by her own admission, was in the European Union at the time of our third reported art theft. A still life." The chief goes into too much detail about the painting: a bunch of grapes and a Delft-style vase. She talks of its eighteenth-century origin, dodgy provenance in the early 1900s, and an incredible auction price and competitive bidding in the early 2000s.

She's showing off, but what I hear are cautionary tales. Cautions about provenance, underinsuring, and overbidding. Also, about obsession, by collectors and also by Annette Dubois with the art-theft case. But most of all, it's a caution to me as a tour guide. Thank goodness the Silver Spinners cut off my lengthy memorized speeches. I would have bored them silly.

Scarlett bats her eyes between Pierre-Luc and Laurent. "Well, there you have it, gentlemen. I'm innocent. I have no interest in still lifes. I'm a woman of *action*."

"Madame, you are thrilling," Pierre-Luc says.

Scarlett titters.

The chief turns her frown on me. "As you so helpfully suggested, Madame Greene, the art thefts could be connected to the murder of Monsieur Eddie Ainsworth, also known as Edwin Perch."

"Yes, but not—" *Not by my riders,* I start to say.

Scarlett interrupts. "I was in Spain, not up here stealing lifeless painted fruit. You can check with my masseuse and my credit card bill. Now, let's get to the good part. *My* clue! Sadie, *you'll* appreciate this: His bags were packed! Edwin was either running away again or our sweet little innkeeper had had enough of him. Bless her heart, Gabi had every reason to be furious."

"As did you, *Lady* Crabtree-Thorne," Chief Dubois points out. "As did your entire group."

"Quite so," Scarlett says agreeably.

I think of Serge and his wild theory that they all did it. How happy he'd be. A lot happier than me.

We're still gathered around the Oui Cycle van when Gabi peels in at a speed to rival Serge's. Her curls fly wild from her tangled bun. Her grandfather is snoozing in the passenger's seat.

"There's been a robbery?" She jumps from her cheery yellow hatchback.

Scarlett waggles her fingers in greeting. "Only a petite misunderstanding, dear."

"A criminal act," the chief counters.

"My grave mortification," Pierre-Luc says. He explains with profuse apologies. "I am retreating to my home in chagrin. Will anyone join me for a bolstering beverage?"

Laurent accepts. He's heard about Pierre-Luc's wines, he says. I want to believe that he plans on subtly interrogating Pierre-Luc about his neighbors. Or he'll simply be enjoying a tasting flight while I fend off his grouchy ex-girlfriend.

Jordi looks ready to race them to the tasting room, but Chief Dubois orders him to come with us. Jordi watches Laurent and Pierre-Luc go with the expression of Chou Chou denied a treat.

Gabi exhales deeply. "I'd like coffee. Shall we go to the inn?"

I recognize her brittle brightness as the taut tones of a hospitality professional about to snap. She settles her grandfather in the garden with Chou Chou and a bag of cheese puffs they can share.

"Pépère is not good company today," Gabi says. "First, he was grumpy with the bank manager. Then he complains all the way home because he will miss his favorite chicken livers."

Scarlett offers to buy them a liver feast, but I doubt that's Gabi's main concern.

I urge Gabi to sit, then volunteer to make the espressos. Chief Dubois requests tea. I wonder if she's just being contrary. In any case, I'm glad. She's given me a chance to show off my small clue. As the electric teakettle hisses to a boil, I present the chief with the Rose Petal Shortbreads tin of mismatched teabags.

"Oh!" Gabi says, drawing a sharp breath. "Is that still here?"

"Oh," Chief Dubois says, lacing the sound with suspicion.

Gabi stares at the tin. "Usually, I do not come here for tea."

"Or check your cabinets?" the chief says, and I'm glad she asked the question I was biting back.

"Greta demands to handle the breakfast and beverage

supplies," Gabi says, reaching for the tin and brushing her fingers over the embossed rose on the lid. "Friends gave us this when Eddie and I were first together. Eddie said I should bring it over here to the inn. He had no taste for English things."

She turns a sad smile to me. "Yesterday, when you visited my kitchen and spoke of shortbreads, I recalled that moment, but I did not wish to offend Rosemary by saying so. Although, it strengthens my point, does it not? Our man, he had no memory of England."

"Or just the opposite," says Scarlett darkly. "I bet that man knew exactly what those cookies represented. His guilt!"

Chief Dubois has been listening intently while dunking a sachet of licorice-mint tea. "Like you knew you were guilty of trespass and breaking and entering, Madame Crabtree-Thorne?"

Scarlett tunes her drawl to honey sweet. "Heaven's no. I misplaced my phone last night, Chief Dubois. What with all the excitement and yelling, I got confused. Age! I do get befuddled."

Right. Sure she does.

Chief Dubois is rolling her eyes so I don't have to.

Scarlett gushes on, patting her veritably heaving bosom. "We had a prowler in our inn. Officer Laurent could tell you how terrified I was. He escorted me safely back. Sadie, you have a chivalrous one there."

"I was with Jacques Laurent when we got the call," Chief Dubois says dryly. "The elderly gentleman whom you accuse could hardly burgle his own property. You, however, Madame. You contend you lost a phone, so you break into a private home?"

Scarlett clarifies that she stepped in. "A window was open, one of the great big ones that go practically to the ground. All I did was unlatch the hook and walk in. French windows are so inviting."

Gabi smiles tightly. I bet she'll be locking her windows until we're gone.

"And why weren't you cycling, Madame?" Chief Dubois asks.

"My hip." Scarlett pats her right hip.

I could swear she was favoring the left one this morning. Not that it matters. I've known all along that the hip was a ruse.

"Which is why I needed my phone," Scarlett says. "I was all alone here with my bad hip. What if I'd fallen?"

"Yet there was a capable young man from your tour company, strangely positioned in a garden chair in the driveway," the chief points out, dipping her chin toward Jordi. "You didn't think he could help?"

Jordi rubs at his rugby tattoo like it's a worry bead.

"Young Jordi was sleeping so peacefully on a lounge chair," Scarlett says. "I didn't want to wake him."

"I was blocking the driveway with my chair and body," Jordi says to me. "No one could have gotten past me."

"For assistance," I hurry to add. "He was ready and waiting to assist."

"Sure, yeah, to assist," Jordi repeats. "I'm sorry I fell asleep, boss. It's the fresh air. I sleep too well out of doors."

Scarlett huffs. "You're all forgetting the important part. Two suitcases were stuffed with men's clothes. All tossed in, squished asunder! Now, did you do that, Gabi, dear, or was Edwin about to leg it when he found out we were coming? I wouldn't blame him. If the Silver Spinners had caught him, well, you can just imagine!"

Her ominous tone helps our imaginations along.

Scarlett barrels on. "You were at the bank this morning, Gabi? Did your *Eddie* drain your accounts, like Edwin did to my Rosemary? Good luck finding the money. And by *good luck,* I mean, you might as well give up. We never found Rosemary's."

Gabi looks away. Tears flow and she swipes at her cheeks. "I packed those suitcases the other night. I couldn't bear to see his clothes in the closet, hanging like empty shells. They made me too sad."

The chief asks to see the suitcases. "But after you finish your coffee, Gabi. Take your time. You have had an upsetting morning."

Scarlett leans in, her words tickling my ear. "Crocodile tears. I know 'em when I see 'em, believe you me."

I do believe her. She wouldn't have to demonstrate. Of course, she does. Scarlett raises a napkin and yawns behind it—the kind of teeth-bared yawn hippos make before engulfing a river raft. A single tear seeps from her eye.

She swipes at it dramatically. "Oh, Gabi, darlin'," she sniffles. "I'm so sorry. I'm a silly old woman, too dependent on her phone."

Chief Dubois is unmoved by Scarlett's performance. "Had you and your phone been to that room last night, Madame?"

Scarlett wipes at her mascara. "I get lost from time to time." She reaches over and squeezes my hand. Rings bite at my knuckles.

"She does," I confirm, and Scarlett's grip loosens. "This entire group, they can get lost anywhere."

Especially when they do it on purpose!

CHAPTER 23

Tour-guide tidbit: Local lore says that Alsatian glassblowers were the first in France to produce glass baubles for Christmas trees. The idea sparked in 1858 when a drought devastated orchards and the traditional tree decoration: apples. Beautiful ideas can arise from terrible circumstances.

"Sadie, petal, we knew if we told you, you would have been *practical.*" Benji stretches across our dinner table, dodging candles and carafes. He refills my wine glass before I can cover the rim.

Practical. The word feels like a *there-there-dear* condescending pat on the head, a kind put-down akin to being crowned Miss Congeniality or Miss Smiles-at-Everything or Most Predictable. That last one would be me, a title granted by my high school class. *If they could only see me now . . .*

Or maybe they have if they follow lurid English tabloids. Back in June, headlines of my previous tour horrors reached suburban Illinois, to the immense embarrassment of my mother. The Oui Cycle Facebook account gained over a thousand followers. I also received "friend" requests from old acquaintances who probably couldn't place my face if I ever showed up at a school reunion. *How predictable!*

Wine glasses and bottles clink and stretch before me. I sip the wine, a floral pinot noir, and decide I can loosen my guide-on-duty alcohol restrictions. We're at a nice restaurant in Riquewihr. The blackened beams are wavy with the marks of hand-hewing. The plaster is painted the red of old wine. All surfaces save the linen-draped tables and stone-tiled floors are covered in antique tools. Really quite deadly tools, I think, gazing around.

The rest of my group returned to the inn right on schedule just before five. Nadiya had put them through their paces. They had enjoyed their freshly baked cookies, then lunch, followed by an appreciative tour of the Humanist Library. They had stopped at two fountains, five of Sélestat's thirty-five listed historic buildings, three monuments, and a gorgeous vista.

"Miss Nadiya leads with a firm hand," Maurice had said appreciatively when they rolled up, making me think I've been too nice and lenient. I insisted that Nadiya take the night off. She and Jordi were going to swing by Sélestat to retrieve my abandoned bike and have a romantic dinner, my treat.

After fussing over Scarlett and her "troubles," my riders retired for naps and woke refreshed. We walked to the village for dinner, making small talk about the obvious beauty: *What a lovely garden, just look at that rose!* However, at the restaurant, the conversation soon shifted to Scarlett's "explorations."

"I got lucky," Scarlett says, with hitherto unseen modesty. "I picked the winning straw."

I nearly choke on my *amuse bouche,* a tart tablespoon of grape gazpacho. "You drew straws to see who would break in?" My voice rises. I remember we're in public. The table of four closest to us is speaking Swedish, or maybe

Finnish. Danish? In any case, odds are they also speak fluent English. I lower my voice. "You planned this?"

The elder Spinners clearly see this as a rhetorical question. They smile indulgently, except for Keiko.

"*I* didn't play draw straws," Keiko says.

"That's only because you were in the shower when we did it," Scarlett says. "But you *are* playing, Kei-Kei. You made the first move by finding Edwin's body. Now we just need to reignite that auditory memory of yours." She sloshes more wine into Keiko's glass.

"Rosemary and I were not informed," Lionel says stiffly.

Scarlett rolls her eyes. "Well, of course not. You would have fretted, Lionel. Worse, you would have grassed us to Sadie."

"Grassed?" Rosemary says. "Really, Scarlett."

Her godmother reaches over and pats her hand. "Snitched? Ratted us out? Informed the higher authorities? In any case, sweetest, we didn't want to worry you on cookie day. Did you have a good time?"

Rosemary mutters that she did—until she found out what her godmother had done.

"But that wasn't until you got back here," Scarlett says. "What you didn't know didn't hurt you."

She pauses to bat her eyes at a good-looking waiter who swoops in to supply dinner knives with serrated blades suitable for battle.

"It all turned out perfectly fine," Scarlett continues, picking up her knife and inspecting its gleaming teeth. "Better than fine. We provided the police with a valuable clue."

"Muddying the suspect waters," says Maurice, looking over his spectacles. "Admirable work, Scarlett. Rosemary, Lionel, you're swimming in a more populated suspect pool now. Downright cloudy."

"Murky," Benji intones. "But clear to me. I always said

it was the wife. Ow! Maurice, you kicked me! I meant the *current* wife. Ouch!"

When our main plates arrive, talk turns to pleasant topics of cookies and ancient books. Rosemary picks at her local trout in cream, capers, and a touch of the ubiquitous sauerkraut. Something isn't sitting well, as she makes clear when she starts back up on Scarlett. "I wish you hadn't interfered, Scarlett," she says.

I do too, in theory. However, her discovery of the packed suitcases seems important. Who packs away their loved one's clothes mere days after his death? Unless he wasn't so beloved? Unless Eddie did that packing—planning to run off again—and Gabi caught him out?

"Interfering is in my nature," Scarlett says.

"Yes, well, quite," Rosemary says dryly. "But to break into a widow's home! Scarlett, you could have been arrested. And poor Gabi."

She frowns, and I wonder if she's questioning Scarlett's actions or Gabi's.

"*You* didn't discard Edwin's clothes for years," Lionel murmurs, above a clink of the knife and fork he's wielding to expertly dissect his trout.

"Not for *my* lack of trying," Scarlett says, waving a forkful of steak. She's gone for a classic dish of steak *frites*. Excitement, she informed the handsome waiter, gives her an appetite. "As for the chief arresting *me*, let her try!"

I could point out that Chief Dubois would have happily done more than try. She was ready to arrest Scarlett and Jordi as her accomplice. Gabi insisted she wouldn't press charges. When the chief threatened to arrest Scarlett anyway, Gabi declared that inn guests had the run of the property.

"Suspicious all around, if you ask me," says Benji. "Those suitcases are fishy, for sure. But so is Gabi. She's being too nice to you, Scarlett. I wouldn't have been, if I'd caught you snooping in my closets. Did our poor Gabi buy into your weeping old lady act?"

Scarlett dabs her red-painted lips. "I expect so. People are blinded by advanced age. They think perfectly capable adults degrade to infancy." Her *there-there* look to me suggests I'd been blinded too.

"I *did* suspect you were up to something," I say, well aware that I'm being goaded into this admission. "That's why I left Jordi parked in the driveway, to keep an eye out."

"Leaving a mere lad to watch over Scarlett?" Maurice asks, chuckling.

"If you'd left your handsome detective, I might have been distracted in my mission," Scarlett says. "Where is our Detective Laurent?"

"Out with a friend," I say, aiming for a tone as cool as the perfectly chilled Riesling making its way around the table.

Only, she's no friend to me. Laurent is having dinner with Annette Dubois.

After our last scoops of apple tarts à la mode, I expect the Spinners to scatter—off to explore, to hunt down nightcaps, to get into more trouble.

Keiko is the first to yawn. Yawns, as everyone knows, are more catching than earworm songs. Pretty soon, we're all declaring that we'd like an early night and are walking back to the inn under dusky purple skies.

A motion light flicks on as we near the inn. Gabi's house is already slumbering, the windows dark. I note that the lower windows—those I can see, at least—are closed.

My riders bid me goodnight. I linger downstairs, listening to their paths in footsteps on floorboards and doors softly closing.

Do I trust them? No. How could I? I could sit up and lurk in the darkened library like the mother of a truant teenager, ready to catch them slipping out.

Another yawn grips me. Exhaustion, more from stress than cycling, tugs at my limbs. Rationalizations propel me up each step of the back stairs to my attic suite.

They're adults. They're paying guests. I can't lock them in. I'll leave the shutters open to hear any devious giggles, any breaking and entering. I'll just read a little, under the covers. I'll just close my eyes for a second.

My Kindle screen has gone dark and fallen to my chest when the buzz of a text jerks me from sleep.

Laurent: hope I'm not waking you. I see your light?

I blink, disoriented. He sees my light? Where is he? Not in the room. The beams reach to the floor, angled like lodgepole pines. I'd left on a bedside lamp, part of my fib that I'd read for a moment, then update my journal. The bulb casts a yellow glow, pressing against the dark. What time is it? One, I guess. Two, three, the depths of morning?

I squint at the tiny clock in the phone's upper corner. Barely eleven? We got back just after ten.

I text back: **I'm awake.**

I add a smiling emoji. It's no longer a fib. I am wide awake now. Why is it that the very best sleep is always interrupted? But I'm glad to hear from Laurent, and if he can see me, then I have two guesses about where he is. One: In the drive, like an old-fashioned suitor, doing the digital equivalent of tossing pebbles at my window? Two: The cool-kids hangout spot at Pierre-Luc's château? I'd bet on option two.

His next text confirms I'm right. An impromptu salon is in full swing. He asks if I'd like to join them.

I'm grateful he's not here to read my internal conflict. On the one hand, I'm in my lovely bed. The sheets are soft, and that sleep was so sweet. On the other hand, a gathering at the château with a man who crossed mountains and another country to support me?

No contest. I hop out of bed and text that I'll be right over.

It's not until I'm dressed and tiptoeing down the back stairs that two counterpoints join my list. One: Am I being too eager? Relationship "experts" would probably say I should pretend to have plans for the next week, if not month.

But that's not me. Seize the moment—that's the spirit of travel and my new life in France.

Point two, however, has me hesitating as I step into the garden. Do I dare leave the Silver Spinners unattended? Dewy air cools my skin. I stop and look back at the inn. I left my attic lamp on to make it appear as if I'm in and watchful. All the other windows are dark. The Silver Spinners have had their adventures for the day. I can have mine. Besides, I'll be right next door.

I cut across the garden, through the poodle-pruned trees, and am met by two grinning males. Laurent and Chou Chou wait by the burbling fountain in the drive's circular turnaround.

"That was quick," Laurent says.

My mind flicks back to the relationship experts of French magazines, not to mention the style consultants. I've looped my hair up in a loose ponytail and tugged on my go-to non-cycling outfit, the tiered skirt in dusky lavender and a white V-neck T-shirt.

"You look lovely," Laurent says, bending to kiss my cheeks.

Chou Chou breaks the moment with a soulful whine. "And you both look handsome," I say, patting the grinning dog. Chou Chou sports a paisley bandana. Laurent is in his linen—again perfectly pressed—and slim jeans. A medley of music, laughter, and chatter filters through the open doors.

"You're already hanging out with the hippest people in town," I say.

"Because you paved the way," he says. "I bumped into Pierre-Luc up in town after dinner. He invited me over and encouraged me to call you. Your riders are in for the night?"

He laughs when I groan my true feelings. *Oh, I hope so.*

A half hour later, I'm sipping surprisingly delicious sparkling water scented with hops, an offering from a craft brewer who lives just across the border in Germany. Among the guests are vintners and brewers, a sculptor, a metalsmith, and a watercolor artist I've already met.

I'm a bit nervous when Céline makes a beeline across the room to speak with me. "You told Annette," she says, her mouth firming to a grim straight line.

"I'm sorry, I—"

Céline raises a flute of wine, bubbles dancing up through the pale liquid. "*Tchin-tchin!* Cheers! I haven't had such fun in ages! Annette needed my information so she had to be *nice* to me. You could tell it was killing her."

We're standing by an interior stone wall, where her gorgeous watercolors hang as if floating. Laurent has been drawn into a conversation about politics. He can have that. It's too pretty a night to debate pensions and Brexit.

The same could be said about talk of murder. I ask anyway. "That night you saw Eddie. Did he have anything with him?"

"Like the killer?" Céline beams and sways. She's had more than one glass of bubbly, I guess. "*Everyone's* been asking me that now. Pierre-Luc told me I should be careful, that the killer *always* goes after key witnesses."

I admit that I was thinking more about luggage. "Did he have a suitcase with him?" A flashback strikes: high school, my French teacher making us form sentences around luggage. How boring, I'd thought at the time. Who goes around France incessantly talking about suitcases? Me, that's who.

For most of my tours, we stay in different lodgings every night, and luggage is a main concern of my days. "But," I hurry to add, "*was* there someone with him?"

Céline tilts her head, as if to tip out a memory. She's in a belted jumpsuit, white but splattered with so much paint it must be intentional.

"No obvious killer," she says thoughtfully. "I was the only one around. As for baggages . . ."

I wait.

"*Non,*" she says. "I don't remember a bag. But he was hurrying. That's why he did not stop and compliment me. Do you think he knew his ex-wife and friends were in town? Was he running, hiding?"

If he was running, wouldn't he go farther away than the village? Why did he stay? Where did he hide?

Céline drifts off to talk to another painter. The music shifts to a clubby beat that reminds me of the fateful sports-car crashing into the barrel. Outside, Chou Chou barks in four bass woofs.

"Sadie." Pierre-Luc weaves through his guests and swings me into air kisses that leave me dizzy. "You are too kind to take time from your riders."

"You're too kind to invite me," I counter. "My riders are asleep, so I could slip out."

He raises an eyebrow. "Asleep? Then who just rode by on electric bikes?" Chou Chou saunters in and pants up at me. "You saw, didn't you, Chou Chou? You raised the alarm. Good boy."

Naughty, Silver Spinners!

I excuse myself and wriggle into Laurent's small group, where an artist is discussing oil pigments.

Laurent excuses himself, backing away. "*Ouf,*" he says when we're out of earshot. "You saved me. I enjoy obscure topics, but I was about to fake a crisis to get away from the pigments."

He frowns, reading my face. "Is there a problem?"

"I don't know yet. Probably not." But this time I won't wait to find out. I explain that the Spinners are loose on the town. Laurent volunteers to come with me.

"No, please, you stay here," I say. "Enjoy. They could have just gone out for a nightcap, in which case, I'll be right back."

"I'll be waiting," he says, squeezing my hand. "I'll be ready to help."

I run across the lawn, Chou Chou bounding and leaping at my side. "Go home," I urge. "Go back to your party."

He has a giddy grin. I'm his party. A whistle slices the night. Chou Chou's ears shoot back.

"Go!" I tell him. "Don't get in trouble because of me."

He turns and runs back. I wish I could follow him, back to the laughter and flickering candlelight, where I can see Laurent and Pierre-Luc in silhouette by the fountain. Instead, I rush to the inn to retrieve my bike. I'll have to pedal hard. The Silver Spinners have a head start and I know how quickly they can disappear.

CHAPTER 24

Tour-guide tidbit: One of the oldest single-day cycling races is the Paris-Roubaix, infamous for its bumpy cobblestones. If you go for a ride on cobbles, remember to keep a firm grip, consistent pace, and steady focus.

I don't find Maurice so much as I run into him. I'm zipping around a corner when he rolls around the same curve from the opposite direction.

"Har!" he cries, raising a fist from his handlebars.

I shriek. A small shriek, but it must carry because somewhere in the darkness, a yelp and urgent bell-ringing sound in return. The bells approach at a frantic pace. Maurice and I press ourselves and our bikes against a wall to avoid a collision with Benji.

"Shhh!" Maurice urges, as Benji skids to a halt.

As ringing vibrations settle from my eardrums, I note my guests' attire. Both men wear black from their helmets to their cycling tights to the black socks wedged in Benji's leather sandals. Maurice's helmet is the same color as always, a classy matte black with a single glossy stripe. Benji's, however, used to be white with red and blue racing stripes.

"Is that electrical tape on your helmet?" I ask.

Benji pats his head. "Gaffer's tape. Is that the same

thing in American?" His hand moves to thump his heart. "You two scared me half to death! Maurice, peach blossom, I heard your scream and was certain you were engaged in mortal combat! Sadie, what are you doing out here?"

What am I doing out here? I mentally repeat the question, first with indignation, then with true querulousness: What am I doing? I should be back at Pierre-Luc's sipping bubbles by candlelight, sitting with Laurent by a fountain, our eyes to the stars.

These are my guests, I remind myself. Guests aren't always right, but I need to make sure they're okay.

"I came to see what *you* are doing," I say. "You were seen riding by the château."

"Snitches," Benji mutters, swiveling to scowl into puddles of shadows.

"We're out for a ride," Maurice says stubbornly. "We're fully fledged adults, Sadie. Twice as seasoned as yourself and allowed to stay up past our bedtime. You can't give us a curfew."

No, I can't, but it is my job to keep them safe. I try another tactic. Namely, sympathy. "I left a soiree at a château because I was worried about you."

Benji gives a clap of delight. "*Oooh* . . . sneaking out yourself, were you? Good girl! Are the handsome boys there? Your detective and the dashing vintner?"

They are, I confirm. "And I told Detective Laurent I'd be right back, but I can't leave because, honestly, I don't believe you."

Maurice smiles. "Forthright," he says. "I like that. Fine, Sadie, if you really must know, we're engaged in a little memory exercise. We're jogging Keiko's subconscious. Dark territory, the subconscious. Freud said . . ."

My subconscious blocks out thoughts of Freud.

Benji pouts dramatically, apparently mirroring me. "Don't

look so glum, Sadie, dearest. Are you upset we didn't invite you? You weren't there when Edwin's body showed itself to Keiko the first time. Although . . . Now you're here, we can recreate the whole scene!"

The beeps of incoming texts interrupt Benji's hand-clasping glee and Maurice's guttural pronunciation of some twenty-syllable term in German, presumably Freud's doing.

"Positions!" Maurice declares, reading a text. "Keiko is about to ride. Scarlett is at the north gate. Lionel and Rosemary are recreating their lovers' search for each other."

"Sweet!" declares Benji. "Let's hope Lionel ups the romance this time. Second chances!"

They adjust their helmets, flex fingers, and roll shoulders.

"Wait a minute," I say. "I get how Keiko might jolt her subconscious, but what are the rest of you doing?"

Identical looks of *there-there* pat my head.

"Rosemary and Lionel were here that night," Benji says. "They might have seen something they don't realize too."

"The subconscious," Maurice intones.

"Never know what it's up to," Benji agrees. "Also, Scarlett insisted. She's a wee bit upset at our Lionel for luring Rosemary out that night and making her a suspect. Of course, if our darling Scarlett hadn't berated the dear boy, he wouldn't have stomped off for a midnight walk."

"She's mad at herself, but the subconscious deflects," Maurice muses.

Their phones ding again.

Benji sucks in a breath. "Scarlett knows we're talking about her! Must go, Sadie. Sorry!"

"But what is your role?" I ask, as they settle in on their saddles.

"We're here for protection," Maurice says.

Benji flips off his handlebar lamp. "We're more than that. We're playing the killer! Isn't that thrilling? We keep out of sight, but Keiko will sense we're around, just like the killer must have been."

Footsteps make us all freeze. Someone inhales sharply. Maybe that's me. Maybe it's all of us.

A young couple steps around the corner, the man's arm draped over the woman's shoulders. She's dipping as if he's leaning too heavily.

"*Bonsoir,*" Benji says cheerily.

The woman does an abrupt 270-degree turn and tugs her beau down the nearest lane.

"Cute couple," Benji says. "Shy."

"Let's ride," Maurice declares. "Sadie, are you joining us? The only rule: Keep away from the death-scene courtyard. That's Keiko's to recreate."

"I'll catch up," I tell them. I need to make a call first.

"Reenacting?" Laurent booms the word so loudly I hold the phone from my ear. He's speaking over the club music, chatter, and laughter, I tell myself. Okay, he's also appalled, and rightfully so.

"Jogging Keiko's memory," I try to explain. "The subconscious. Something about Freud?"

"Let me talk to them. Any of them." His words come out as an order. I'm pretty sure it's not me he wants to order around.

A cricket chirps, close but hidden. I sigh. "I wish I could. They've ridden off. It's okay. I'll stay up in the village until they're done. I'll text when we're on our way back, if it's not too late."

I hear a blur of words, like he's covered the phone to talk with someone. I look around. I walked my bike to a lamplit corner to make the call. Beside me, a Christmas shop is painted in almost the same lavender as my skirt. Its shutters resemble gingerbread biscuits painted in drops of red and white icing. The village is quiet under a muffle of low-hanging clouds.

When Laurent comes back on, I startle.

"I'll be there," he says. "Wait for me by the main gates? Ten minutes, tops. I'm borrowing a bike."

Jacques Laurent is a man of his word and even speedier than his promise. Nine minutes later, he's rolling up to the gates on a thin-framed racing bike.

"This place is almost prettier at night," he says, gazing up the avenue of ancient half-timbered structures.

"One of France's most beautiful villages." I wave toward the scene, which, at the moment, seems more like an ominous fairy tale than a Disney fantasy. The clouds smudge out the roof peaks and chimney pots. I imagine witches looking down. Or, more correctly, the roving spirits of those unjustly accused women.

Laurent dismounts the tall bike he's borrowed from Pierre-Luc. By tacit agreement, we push our bikes up the main cobblestoned avenue.

"So, which way did they go?" Laurent asks.

"Every which way," I say. "Keiko is reenacting her ride. Lionel and Rosemary are acting out their search for each other."

"And the rest?" Laurent asks, mirroring my questions.

"They're backup and a presence," I say, leaving off how they're the presence of the killer. "Maurice was on about Freud and buried memories."

Laurent scoffs. "I'll give them this: I've never heard of a bicycling crime reenactment. But with Freud? Do they know he loathed bicycles?"

"Really?" Freud had a low opinion of women, too. I knew I wasn't a fan! "Would you mind if I borrowed your tidbits about Freud and bikes?" I ask. "I'd like to tell Maurice. I bet he doesn't know, and usually he knows everything."

"Be my guest. I can't see myself having the opportunity to share that again anytime soon."

A giggle filters down a narrow alley. A rattle of wheels, like bones. I shiver despite the muggy summer night.

"Your riders are trying to help," Laurent says. "I see this in many investigations. Maybe not to such an active, invasive extreme, but people *want* to help. They want to be involved. They often cause more trouble."

Tell me about it.

"They have created more doubt," I say, as we pause in front of a bakery with a window display of ceramic kugelhopf molds in shiny earthtone glazes. "You have to admit, Eddie's packed suitcases are odd. As much as I like her, Gabi has a huge motive. She might have found out who Eddie was or that he was about to leave her. Or she didn't know, but she figured out he was spending all her money. Besides, you've seen her kitchen?"

Laurent's head tips in confusion.

"She's no minimalist," I explain. "She has mementos and lovely collections of knickknacks. Every wall is covered in family portraits. She's sentimental, is what I'm saying. I can't believe she'd pack up her partner's things hours after his suspicious death. Unless she wanted him gone, that is."

"People deal with tragedy in unexpected ways," Laurent says carefully, "But you're right about the money motive. Annette told me that your inn is having financial troubles. It's gotten around town that Gabi has applied for a loan." He waits a beat and adds, "In her name only."

Only her name because she didn't want Eddie on the loan? Or did he—or both of them—fear his ID wouldn't be up to snuff? I ask Laurent, but he won't speculate.

I will. "Eddie was a gambler. That probably didn't help their financial situation or her trust in him."

"High stakes games?" Laurent asks. We're walking toward Dolder Tower, its top muffled in the mist.

"Poker with the château set," I say. "He won Chou Chou, actually. Well, kind of—he gave up winnings and still had to pay extra."

Laurent snorts. "Now I do question his financial reasoning. That dog attempted to steal my shoe earlier—the shoe was still on my foot."

We gaze up at the tower, solid enough to withstand armies, time, and a pedigreed chewer. It's peaceful. Companiable. Romantic . . . Laurent has turned his gaze from the architecture to me. He's smiling, eyes crinkled, the same melt-chocolate look he had at the station before we parted in Sans-Souci, right before that kiss—

I'm sure I have a goofy smile. I don't care. We're leaning in when—

The scream makes us both jump.

Laurent thrusts a hand to his hip, but he has no weapon. He whips around. The scream—female, desperate—echoes around the maze of lanes.

"That came from behind us," Laurent says, staring as if he can see through the walls of old stone and timber. "The west? Southwest?"

I don't know the cardinal directions, but I'm afraid I can guess. "The courtyard? Keiko was supposed to end up there."

We leap on our bikes and ride, my teeth chattering from more than the cobblestones.

CHAPTER 25

Tour-guide tidbit: When cycling at night, play it safe with front and rear lights, reflective strips, and bright clothing. Always let someone know where you're going, and stick to well-lit routes.

Laurent speeds ahead. I'll admit, I'm a little vexed. Not because he's left me behind in a dark village with a killer on the loose and those screams still echoing in my eardrums. The first scream was bad. The second was all too clearly a cry for help—literally, "Help," wailed in English, leaving me with no doubt my riders are in trouble.

No, I'm vexed because *Does Laurent know where he's going?*

As I think this, I almost miss a turn. I redirect and find myself at the confluence of passageways, the spot where I stopped the other night, having momentarily lost Keiko.

I'm not alone tonight. Scarlett is already there, eyes flashing like the silver in her hair. "Did you hear that?" she demands.

How could I not? "I'm heading for the courtyard," I say, pointing down the dark lane to the left. "Laurent was with me. He's going that way too."

"Which way? I'm all turned around."

Scarlett's bike is aimed the right way. I point to the dogleg lane. She whirls past me, her bike wheezing ahead at highest power. I'm on her wheel, ready to squeeze the brakes, but I'm not prepared for what I see.

A figure sprawls across the cobbles, dark hair with a silver shimmer covering a delicate face. Keiko. Her bike lies a few feet away, the front wheel up to the sky, unmoving. Faint music escapes from an earbud lying feet away from her outstretched hand. The sound is tinny and old-fashioned, as if broadcasting in from a distant time.

Laurent kneels beside Keiko and presses fingers to her neck. He wasn't the first one here. Rosemary scrabbles backward on the cobbles. Her hands are smeared with dust and—

My stomach turns. Is that blood? Shards of smashed terra-cotta litter the pavement.

"Kei-Kei!" Scarlett throws aside her bike and rushes to her friend.

"Rosemary?" A man's voice calls out from somewhere in the dark. "Rosemary, where are you?"

Lionel. It's impossible to tell where he is. He could be right around the corner or his cries amplified through the twisty lanes.

Rosemary scrambles to her feet. "Lionel? Lionel, we're here!"

There's a crash and the ding of a bike bell hitting stones. I hear great gulps of panting before Lionel rushes in and wraps Rosemary in a protective hug. In the distance, another bike bell rings frantically, someone yells "shut up" in French, shutters bang, and more footsteps pound our way.

Laurent orders everyone back. He looks to me. "Call an ambulance and the police."

My phone is already ringing in to 112.

"I lost you again," Lionel says, holding Rosemary close.

"What were you doing here? This isn't the way you came that night. Is it?"

"I found her," Rosemary says tremulously, her eyes glued to Keiko. Laurent has brushed Keiko's hair aside. Her bangs stick to her forehead and a nasty gash.

"She's breathing," Laurent says.

Rosemary inhales. "Oh, thank goodness. I tried to help."

In my ear, a bored voice on the phone wishes me good evening. "What is your emergency, Madame?"

"*Un accident,*" I say, my mind stumbling over the easy French. My grammar is fine. It's the words that aren't right. This was no accident.

"You said this was an *accident.*" Chief Dubois, vocabulary police, scowls at me.

I hold up my hands. Come on, I was under pressure, and I'd correctly asked for medics. They're attending to Keiko, still prone on the cobbles.

Scarlett flutters like an anxious butterfly around the periphery. "She's groaning!" Scarlett crows. "She's okay! Kei-Kei, we're here!"

All the Spinners have found their way to the courtyard, the last being Benji, who took a wrong turn.

"She's wincing! Kei-Kei, wake up!" Scarlett claps and ignores an EMT's suggestion that loud noises aren't ideal for patients with a severe concussion.

Four medics have arrived, two on call and two others who happened to be in the area. The biggest—the bravest—places two hands on Scarlett's shoulders and presses her back toward the cluster of Silver Spinners. An ambulance waits down on the road, as close as it can get. Its blue lights flicker against the clouds like wavering ghosts.

"We don't know what happened yet," Laurent reminds

his ex. "When our victim regains full consciousness, hopefully, she can tell us."

What wicked irony. This misguided exercise was supposed to jog Keiko's memory.

"We know what you saw, *Jacques*," Chief Dubois says, proving that even in a crisis she'll take time to needle me. "You were the first to witness the victim and perpetrator."

She's speaking rapid French. My inner translator strains to keep up, mainly because her vocabulary isn't right. "Victim" is correct, although I'd prefer "hard-headed survivor." But "perpetrator?" Besides Laurent, only Rosemary was here. *Rosemary isn't the perpetrator . . .*

Rosemary stands with the others by the wineshop. The antique cart is again absent, probably in police custody for its blood stains and incriminating cookie crumbs, key bits of evidence that the chief is now outlining in slow, pedantic French. In the background, Scarlett is translating for the others.

"When Jacques Laurent—a gendarme officer—entered the courtyard, he witnessed one Rosemary Perch removing a bicycle from the stricken victim."

Scarlett raises her hand. "*Ah, excusez-moi, non.* Rosemary was trying to help. She thought Keiko had suffered a cycling accident."

"I did," Rosemary stresses. "I thought she'd fallen. Bicycles can be *very* dangerous." She narrows her eyes at me.

Take away murder and the worst afflictions my tour guests have suffered include a brush with poison ivy, a tumble into a ditch, and a run-in with a wild boar. Oh, and Lionel was run off the road, and Maurice nearly killed himself on a penny farthing . . .

I stop listing.

"Certain tours are dangerous, yes," the chief agrees, pleased with this petty zinger. "In this case, initial examination suggests that a potted geranium was bashed onto the victim's head with force." She waves to the shards of terra cotta.

The Silver Spinners grimace and gasp.

"Would you like to hear my theory?" the chief asks, not waiting for an answer.

"A widow discovers she is not actually a widow." Chief Dubois raises her index finger, suggesting we're in for a lengthy tally, which usually I adore. I shift from foot to foot, anxious for action. I want to accompany Keiko. I want to pester the EMTs and make them tell me that she'll be okay.

The EMTs place a stretcher on the ground beside Keiko. They start a count. *Un, deux, trois . . .* With a collective heave, they shift her over and raise the stretcher. Metal legs unfold and click into place. I wince at the thought of those small, hard wheels bumping over the cobblestones.

"I should go with Keiko," I say, interrupting the chief, who's saying something rude about bitter, desperate widows. "Someone she knows should be with her."

"I'm her best friend!" Scarlett says. "I'll go."

"We should both go." I step forward. The stretcher is rattling away.

"*Non,*" Chief Dubois says. "I will arrest anyone who leaves as obstructive."

The elder Spinners huddle, whispers hissing from their little circle. I hear the name Helena, the vicious solicitor.

The chief raises a second finger. "As I was saying, the abandoned wife follows or lures her wayward husband to this spot in the dead of night."

The stretcher has rolled out of sight, but the staccato symphony rattles back to us, discordant in offbeat percussion and the angry squeak of wheels.

"She kills him," Chief Dubois declares, jarring me back. "Voilà! It is the perfect crime. She will hide the body. If he is never found, it will look like once again, he has run away from his family and responsibilities."

"He'd do that," Scarlett mutters. "He did it once."

"Cad!" Benji agrees.

The chief dips her head in a little bow. "Yes. The killer—alone or with a conspirator—hefts the body to the wooden cart of the wineshop. But then, she hears someone coming. A witness—our current victim. The killer hides herself and the body, but later, she must fear that the witness will remember something that will give her away. All of you, you are determined to make your friend Keiko recall a clue." She smiles, awaiting what? Applause? Wails of guilt?

"That doesn't make any sense," Maurice says.

"Absurd," Lionel agrees, bundling Rosemary closer.

"*Non?*" Chief Dubois says, as if innocently querulous.

"It's ridiculous," declares Scarlett. "If Rosemary was the killer—which, Rosemary, dear, you're decidedly *not*—then she'd know she had nothing to fear from Keiko."

The chief raises an eyebrow.

"Kei-Kei is my best friend," Scarlett repeats with emotion. "She'd never hurt *my* goddaughter!"

"Silver Spinners motto," Benji says.

I wish I was standing close to him. I have a feeling I want to slap a hand over his mouth.

"True friends help friends bury the bodies," Benji says. He winks at me. "Scarlett has that on a refrigerator magnet."

"That magnet was a gift from Kei-Kei," Scarlett says, patting her heart. "She gave it to me after Rupy departed for the fiery realm. Remember?"

If they're aiming to confuse the police, they've succeeded. Chief Dubois looks like she could arrest everyone for the crime of irritating her. Laurent's brow wrinkles.

I hold up my hand. "Let's wait and see what Keiko has to say when she's better."

The blue lights flicker against the clouds. The siren moans

into a wail. A dog howls in chorus, and voices and laughter burble nearer. A festively tipsy group rounds the corner.

"Pierre-Luc!" Scarlett cries, recognizing the leader of the bacchanal. "The most awful thing has happened!"

"Madame," he says, halting his group with an upraised hand, Céline and a good half of the salon party strain for a view.

"Nothingness," whispers the female artist keen on oil pigments. "They stare at nothing but the broken shards."

"Was there another murder?" Céline gasps. "*Mon Dieu!* We are witnesses to yet another crime!"

Laurent crosses the courtyard to confer and keep them away from the broken shards. Crime techs are on their way to examine the scene.

The chief firms her shoulders, as if emboldened by the crowd. Her words reach my ears as a blur. *Madame Perch, vous êtes en état d'arrestation.*

Madame Perch, you are in a state of arrest. My shocked mind spins around the grammar.

"Arrest? No!" Scarlett and Lionel blurt simultaneously.

"You cannot arrest my goddaughter." Scarlett steps protectively in front of Rosemary. "Her lawyer is on the way at this very moment."

"As soon as she can get a flight, or perhaps the Chunnel is faster . . ." Maurice mutters. "She'll send a colleague from Paris in the morning."

Chief Dubois smiles mildly as she approaches my group. "As your legal advisors will know, I am permitted to hold the suspect for twenty-four hours. Madame Perch, you have rights. You have the right to remain silent."

The crowd is growing, not only from Pierre-Luc's party, but also in locals and tourists and a too-avid cell-phone photographer. What's surreal to me is the silence. Everyone from the partiers to the old stone homes seem to be holding their breath.

"You may—" Chief Dubois continues, her voice pitched to an emotionless monotone.

"It wasn't Rosemary. I did it!" Lionel steps out from the Silver Spinners. "I killed Edwin Perch. *J'ai assassinate . . . ?* Oh, however you say it. I bashed him on the head. I wanted him dead and gone for good."

A collective gasp siphons air from the square. The chief repeats Lionel's words in French, frowning as if she can't believe her own translation. "And the assault tonight, on Keiko Andersson?"

"Had to be done," Lionel says ambiguously.

The chief shakes off her frown. "Works for me." She re-aims her recitation of rights at Lionel. A parade worthy of the Pied Piper follows her and Lionel down to a waiting police car.

I stay behind with Laurent.

"Lionel is Bea's favorite nephew," I tell him. "He's sweet. He's kind. He didn't particularly want to come cycling. He couldn't have done it."

Laurent makes soothing but noncommittal sounds.

"He confessed." Someone else has stayed behind too. Gabi steps from the shadows alongside the pizzeria. "He *said* he killed my Eddie. Yet still you do not believe?"

I switch to pleading. "He confessed for love, misguided love to help Rosemary."

"Is that so?" Gabi's glassy eyes harden to icy. "Why, then? Because he thinks Rosemary did it? The woman who pretended to weep with me in my kitchen, she killed my Eddie?"

"There are other suspects," I say, then realize I'm making this argument to my main prime suspect. I bite back questions, such as, Where has she been all evening?

"I am sorry," Gabi says. "I am sorry for you, Sadie. We are both in hospitality. I understand that this is hard for you, however . . ."

I brace for impact, like I'm back in Serge's surging Renault.

"You may stay through tonight, obviously," Gabi is saying, "but tomorrow, I will need you and your group to find other accommodation. You understand."

There are worse things to worry about, I tell myself, as she strides off into the darkness. Murder, arrest, severe concussion . . .

But to add finding new lodging? In prime vacation season?

Laurent loops his arm around my shoulders and squeezes. I let my head drop into his shoulder. Just for a moment, I can allow myself to wallow.

"Any room at your hostel?" I ask. He smells of sunshine and cedar cologne and lemony almond soap, different from his usual.

"I got the last dorm bed. It's better than the military barracks but only because of the outstanding food. I can ask Céline if anything is opening up."

Scarlett, in a dorm? I groan.

"After the crime techs arrive, I'll go to the station," Laurent says.

"Thanks." I force myself to part from the hug. That frees me up to follow the ambulance to the hospital. Now all I need is to find a ride—that and to find the real killer.

Cyclist's Log

Wednesday, deep early morning, Hôpital Pasteur, Colmar

Journals are for recording new experiences, right? Here's one I never wanted and hope to never repeat: It's 2:30 in the morning and I'm still at the hospital in Colmar. I'm in Keiko's room. The nurses are waking her up every half hour, encouraging her to speak (curse, more like it) and shining a bright light in her eyes (to more cursing).

I called Nadiya earlier to tell her what happened. She and Jordi were tucked in their tent, all nice and cozy. Jordi tried to comfort me. He's suffered oodles of concussions, from rugby tackles to cycling accidents to getting bonked in the head with an oversized wooden clog. I was too tired to ask about the clog. He says the waking up is standard treatment, which is why he avoids treatment whenever possible. Not exactly comforting, except that he is still alive and highly functional.

Keiko will be too. She has to be!

She regained consciousness on the way to the hospital, thank goodness! She's still confused, though. She doesn't remember what happened. She was riding and then pain and everything went blank. I'm not pressing her. I just want to be here.

Although I might get kicked out soon. A new night nurse is coming on shift soon. I've been warned she won't let me stay. It might be a relief, honestly. This place is as grim as, well, a hospital, and I'd like to grab some last few minutes in my princess bed.

Speaking of our imminent eviction, there is a positive. Not in terms of lodging. I still haven't found anything for the days we need, even doubling up Scarlett and Keiko and with me sleeping somewhere else. The van?

But the positive: I've been searching private rentals—Air BnB, Abritel, even leboncoin, which is kind of like a French Craigslist and isn't optimal. Some of the rentals offered there require you to bring your own sheets and towels. No way am I going shopping for linens.

Sorry. I'm tired and veering off course. So,

during this search, I came across a great listing: central village, four bedrooms, luxury kitchen, linens provided (Egyptian cotton!), wine cooler, washer/dryer, gorgeous beams, top floor, and oh my goodness, the views! I couldn't help myself. I looked at all the photos, and guess where it is? Those views look out over a crime-scene courtyard!

It's no big surprise to find a rental near that courtyard. Half the apartments around—maybe more—are probably gobbled up as short-term rentals. This is what's interesting, though: the latest renters gave that lovely place a two-star review. They said that someone had left a rucksack filled with men's clothing and photos of women and kids under the bed. They were creeped out. They were two women, traveling alone, and felt like some guy was going to come back and burst in on them. At the very least, they questioned the thoroughness of the cleaning.

Men's clothing. A rucksack. An apartment right above where Eddie was killed and where his body temporarily disappeared.

Did I just find where Eddie was staying?

I'm sure Annette Dubois will be <u>*thrilled*</u>

with my clue. That was sarcasm, Diary, but you know that. Will it matter if Lionel sticks to his confession?

Squeaky footsteps are coming toward me. I bet that's the night-nurse replacement. I better get out before I'm evicted from the hospital too.

STAGE 3: Secrets of Alsace

CHAPTER 26

Tour-guide tidbit: August is a hot month for travel. Sixty to seventy percent of French workers take vacations in August and millions of foreign tourists arrive for visits. If you're among them, make sure to claim your reservations early.

"She's mad at us?" Scarlett huffs. Morning sun flashes on her magenta highlights. She, Maurice, and Benji have settled in their usual seats for breakfast. Other seats are conspicuously empty. "Why on France's green hills would Kei-Kei be mad at *us*?"

It's 8:35 a.m. and I'm operating on less than four hours of sleep. Approximately. For once, I refuse to make a more precise calculation. The meager hours and minutes would be too grim. Ignorance isn't bliss, but it also isn't as painful as the truth right now.

Which is also why I really, *really* don't want to spell out Keiko's anger to Scarlett. Keiko isn't mad at "us." Not all of us, I hope. Before breakfast, I called the hospital to check on Keiko and was patched through to the impatient patient herself. Keiko was particularly fuming about Scarlett. Scarlett had bullied her into the reenactment ride, Keiko claimed, thus setting her up as a target. Keiko sounded a lot more awake and forceful. That was good. Not so good? She had choice words about nurses, cycling vacations, her friends, and beautiful villages of France. I chalked those up to her head injury and all the overnight proof-of-life prodding.

"Concussions," I say now, aiming to soothe her friends. "Concussions muddle the mind. The doctors say Keiko needs rest and quiet most of all. She's still experiencing some blurred vision and vertigo. They want to monitor her at the hospital for a full twenty-four hours, at least."

"But the ambulance hauled her away after midnight." Benji checks his watch. "Does that mean they'll kick her out on the deadly idyllic streets in the middle of the night?" His slow headshake suggests he's already mourning Keiko's impending fate.

"No, I'm sure they won't." I offer a hopefully comforting anecdote about French hospital care. On one of my first tours, a rider from Ohio was stricken by back spasms—from a long-ago horseback-riding incident, I hasten to add, nothing cycling related.

"The hospital sent an ambulance to pick her up," I say. "By the time she got to the ER, she felt okay, but they kept her overnight anyway. She feasted on beef bourguignon and watched movies. The hospital sent her back in a private taxi."

All of that cost her less than a fancy restaurant meal. I follow her social media. Whenever she gets back twinges, she'll joke about booking a room at her hospital "spa," with some follow-up bicycling.

"Keiko wants us to pedal on," I say. So . . . this is a bit of a fib. Her exact words were "You go on without me because I'll eat my bike seat before I roll another foot on your death tour!" *Concussions! They can truly alter a person's personality!*

"But how can we go on without Kei-Kei?" Scarlett says.

She looks to the empty seat, where just the other morning Keiko sat sourly disemboweling her grapefruit, grumpy at her friends' dismissal of a dead body.

"How do you go on without Sir Rupert?" Benji counters, reaching for the coffee carafe. A papery crinkling comes from his seat. I guess he's hiding the front page again. I'm glad for it. *I will not look!*

Scarlett smiles and reaches for a croissant. "Dear, dear, forsaken Rupy. I do endure, don't I?"

A pointed throat-clearing interrupts their giggles. Rosemary stands at the threshold in a floral sundress that brings out the red in her eyes. "How can we go on without Lionel? Shouldn't we be asking that too?"

"Sweetheart!" Scarlett leaps up to wrap her goddaughter in a hug.

Maurice and Benji shove every breakfast goodie toward the seat that Scarlett is pulling out, the one I think of as Keiko's. Even with the four of us stress-eating, there's a lot of breakfast left. The bread baskets offer baguettes, *pains au chocolat*, croissants, and braided brioche topped with snow-ball sugar. The serving tray holds miniature jars of jams and Nutella. There's freshly squeezed orange juice, the almost-empty coffee, and—now being supplied by Maurice—a flask filled with I-don't-want-to-know-what. There is also a single grapefruit that no one has touched.

Rosemary resists all offerings but coffee.

We're going to need more coffee. Buckets of it. We'll have to stop somewhere. I don't dare ask our breakfast hostess, Greta, although she's still banging around in the kitchen. Since nothing on the table required cooking, I assume she's clanging pot lids to make a point.

I was first to the breakfast room this morning. Greta emerged and slammed down the offerings as if they were surrogates for us. She thumped glassware. She dropped silverware in a violent clatter. And her big move? She absconded with the Nespresso machine, coffee pods, and both Rose Petal Shortbreads tins and made sure I noticed. Harsh!

But I get it. She sees one of us as a confessed killer. Also, she had to chase reporters away with her walking stick at dawn. She'd demonstrated the latter by thrusting a baguette like a sword.

I owe her big-time for the reporter shooing. Helpfully, she told me the gift she'd like in return.

"You shall be leaving immediately after breakfast," Greta said, sloshing down a carafe of juice. Her tone implied "good riddance" as subtly as a neon sign. "I will not see you again."

Scarlett drawls into my musings. "You should be proud of Lionel, dear," she's telling Rosemary. She drops a sugar cube in her goddaughter's coffee. "He's proven himself a man of decisive action, regardless of his actual actions."

Rosemary grabs a spoon and fishes out the dissolving cube. "I *am* proud of Lionel. What do you mean, his 'actual' action?"

"Well, did he kill Edwin or not?" Scarlett says, face smooth with innocence or cosmetic magic. "He did stomp off, awfully angry that night. I do doubt he'd attack Kei-Kei, but desperate love is unpredictable."

"You'd know about that," Maurice comments, turning to the classifieds.

Rosemary gawps in stunned silence.

"You're right, Rosie, dear," Scarlett says. She holds up a manicured finger. "We shouldn't say anything aloud with that Greta woman rampaging around the kitchen like a forest troll."

Metal clashes like cymbals.

"Blink once if he did it, twice if no," Scarlett says.

Rosemary covers her face in her hands. Her hair flops over like a curtain. "Stop!" The word comes out muffled.

She flings back her hands and repeats. "Scarlett, stop! Of course, Lionel didn't kill anyone. He can't kill a mouse. Literally, he can't. We had a wee mouse in the shortbread storeroom. He caught it in a box and drove it to the countryside. The man's a sweet fool to confess."

"Lucky for you he did," Scarlett says, patting Rosemary's hand. "That awful police chief would have arrested you. Very noble of our Lionel. I'll admit, I underestimated him. I expect Helena will have some less pleasant words regarding his confession, but she's a lawyer—she navigates truth and lies. Lionel will be fine, one way or the other."

"One way or the other?" Rosemary repeats. "He's *innocent*, Scarlett. That dear, innocent man is in prison because of me. You all may continue your *cycling*, but I will not be riding. I will be staying near Lionel." She sits back in her chair, arms folded across her chest, lips pressed in a pout that quivers with determination or imminent tears.

"Now, sweetest, don't be silly," Scarlett tuts. "What would you have us do? Camp out in front of the police station?"

"That would do," Rosemary says, pushing aside her coffee. "We'll demand proper action be taken."

"Action by all those reporters and ghoulish tourists who'll want to take our photo?" Scarlett tuts. "In that case, I have a nice new lipstick you should try, dear. You're looking pale."

Rosemary has gone paler than baguette innards.

"I'll wait here for Helena, then," Rosemary says, setting down her cup with a decisive clink. "I'll be close by in case Lionel needs me."

I was going to break this gently. The opening Rosemary has given me is more like a chasm. "Well, um . . ." I say, tiptoeing to the edge. All eyes turn to me.

"Gabi is dealing with a lot," I say by way of massive understatement. "She, ah—"

"Yes?" Scarlett prods.

"I know!" Benji raises his hand. "I know what's going on! Gabi is kicking us to the curb." He reads my expression and delights. "I'm right, aren't I? Oh, I'm good at this detecting business."

"Gabi asked that we pack up, yes," I confirm.

Scarlett huffs. "This is because I discovered she packed up Edwin, isn't it? She could have sent him packing in more ways than one, you know. Where was she last night? Did I see her in the crowd of rubberneckers? I did! Hard to miss that red hair."

I nod but stick to our immediate challenge. "We can pack after breakfast. There are many lovely lodgings in town."

Benji tuts. "This is why I advocated for a point-to-point tour. We can't get kicked out if we only stay one night at each stop."

"We could . . ." Maurice gazes over his glasses. "We have been. Remember Sardinia?"

"That was fun," Benji says. "That yacht we sneaked onto was divine!"

"Fine," says Scarlett, as if we have a choice. "As long as it's someplace *nice*. Make sure to get a suite for Keiko, preferably a two-bedroom suite. I'll be watching over her. A bath with jets would be nice. And make sure it's historic, of course."

"Of course," I say. "There are loads of great alternatives." *All of them already booked.*

I help myself to a sugared brioche and remind myself of another positive: I may have nothing firm on lodging, but I do have that clue, and Laurent is already looking into it.

An hour later, I have failed to grant Greta's wish to never see us again.

"Why are you still here? You cannot stand there with

your baggage." Greta points one of her carved walking sticks at the small mountain of luggage assembled at the top of the drive.

"We'll be leaving as soon as possible," I say, to Greta's mutters of *not soon enough*. "My van driver is stuck behind a broken-down tractor."

Jordi called from the road a few minutes earlier to report that he was penned in between a tractor and a Swedish camper. There was no turning around to detour unless he took out some grand cru grape vines. I told him not to worry. Worrying about unfixable problems does no one any good.

On the other hand, worrying about a large woman with a very large stick is entirely reasonable.

"You will leave," Greta repeats. "Or I will call the police." She brightens. "No, I will call the reporters. They will delight to take your photographs."

"Okay, okay." Her smile is even scarier than her stick. "I'll remove the suitcases," I say.

"*Et les vélos.*"

"And the bicycles," I agree. "And us."

My riders are in the garden. *Relax, that's your only job for now,* I'd told them. I'd also claimed that I had only a few small details to sort out. Ha! A few? I have no hotel, a rider is in police custody, another rider is in the hospital, my van is stuck in traffic, and there's no one to help me move the luggage and bikes. I look around. There is a flowerbed of daisies I could throw myself into and hide from reality.

"Get to it," Greta snaps.

I'm hefting the heaviest suitcase—Scarlett's—when I hear my name called. Moments later, a furry tank storms through the daisies.

Chou Chou plants dirty, daisy-petalled paws on my chest.

"You're not leaving us?" Pierre-Luc rounds the flower bed.

"We all agreed it's best if we find new accommodations," I say. "To give Gabi some space."

He nods solemnly and murmurs about *difficult times.* "But you are going to a hotel nearby?" He dips his chin toward the luggage.

"For now, I'm just taking these down to the road to wait for my van," I say. There's a smacking sound behind me. I glance back. Greta is slapping the stick to her palm like a mob enforcer.

"Ah . . ." Pierre-Luc says knowingly. He aims a cheery *bonjour* at Greta, who grunts and turns her heel back to the inn.

Pierre-Luc smiles. "If you like, you may wait at my place. Let me get my utility vehicle and my vineyard helper. We will carry your luggage over."

I murmur token *I couldn't bother yous* and hearty *mercis.* This is a much better plan than hiding in a bed of daisies. Better for the daisies too, as Chou Chou is busily uprooting them.

"It is no problem," Pierre-Luc says. He shakes his head. "I feel for your group. It has to be a shock to know that one of their own is a coldhearted killer."

And just like that, my relief is as crushed as the daisies.

CHAPTER 27

Wednesday:
Today's the day! Let's ride among the cabbages and learn about the art of sauerkraut!
Revised itinerary: Colmar, here we come!

A good guide knows when to detour and not only to dodge roadblocks. A guide needs to read her audience. The star of my itinerary today was cabbage. I know, I know . . . I hear the groans of those picturing watery coleslaw or sad casseroles. I get it. Throughout my childhood and probably to this day, my mother had gone on "wonder soup" diets. *Eat as much delicious cabbage soup as you like!* And Mom wonders why I'm borderline obsessed with patisseries.

Cabbage's dour reputation is exactly why I'm excited about today's tour. My itinerary is a lesson in never underestimating the quiet and overlooked. The humble cabbage traces the history of the continent. Armies from the Far East carried wooden barrels of pickled cabbage along on their invasions in the fifth century. The Germans perfected salt brining in the sixteenth century. Alsatians honed recipes that became symbols of French pride. Alsatian choucroute is another culinary gem enjoying protected geographical status.

There's even a brotherhood of sauerkraut, the Confrérie de la Choucroute. A brotherhood! Sisters are included too, as I understand it. The higher-ups of the organization hold glorious titles such as Grand Choucroutier and Grand Garnisseur—the grand preparers of the sauerkraut and its garnishes. *Imagine!* If I ever move to this region, I'd strive to become a member.

My itinerary doesn't stop by any old cabbage patch, either. No, no, I would have us shuttling by the Oui Cycle van to the self-declared capital of sauerkraut, a village with kraut in its name—Krautergersheim. Once there, we would take to our bikes and roll through fields of cabbages, soaking in the scents, visiting a grower of giant cabbages (how dear to my Midwestern giant-vegetable-competitions heart), then spinning on to a nearby town to enjoy a sauerkraut-preparation demonstration. From there, we'd head to a lunchtime feast of award-winning choucroute delicacies. In essence, today *could* offer a finely tuned sauerkraut extravaganza.

"Or we can reroute to Colmar today," I say to the too-small group gathered in Pierre-Luc's salon. Pierre-Luc has stepped out to direct a delivery van to a proper parking spot. Not blocking the bicycle parking space, *non, non, non, Monsieur!* Monsieur at the wheel is looking dramatically aggrieved, a feeling to which I can relate.

I remember to smile and continue with the alternative choice for today. "We could *try* to visit Keiko while we're there, although she's said she's refusing visits. *Maybe* I can change our lunch reservation, and we could, um, walk around the city and possibly rent some rowboats or—"

"That's the one!" Scarlett interrupts. "Colmar. That's what I choose."

Maurice and Benji murmur in agreement. *Fine by them.*

An exquisitely curated cabbage tour versus random mulling around, possible boats, and likely refusal from a hospital. I know what I'd pick, but then I also understand that friendship is priceless.

"Great!" I say, already rationalizing the decision. This is for the best. The sooner Keiko and Scarlett make up, the better for everyone. Keiko needs to see how much her friends care. Besides, we'd be delayed if Jordi is still stuck in traffic. This will give him time to stash our luggage—somewhere. Plus, we're tired. Cabbages deserve full mental and emotional attention.

I step outside with my phone, dodging the delivery guy, who's dramatically grunting as he hefts a box of what appears to be corks. How heavy can corks be? Chou Chou joins me.

"Who should I call first?" I ask him. *First, give a dog a treat,* his toothy grin suggests. He adds his trio of treat woofs. I ruffle his ears. "I don't have anything."

Chou Chou turns and trots off. I'm giving him credit for an outstanding doggy vocabulary when I hear Benji calling his name and offering up Rose Petal shortbreads.

I return to my quandary. Should I call the sauerkraut company first to gush apologies and beg for a rain check? The lunch reservation? I'm going to get a reputation as a chronic reservation shirker. Who am I kidding? I have a much worse reputation as a two-wheeling crime spree. When Benji stood from the breakfast table, I saw the headline he'd been hiding: LES TERREURS CYCLISTES. The cyclist terrors? Talk about overdramatic.

My finger is hovering over Jordi's profile pic—buzzed-cut and grinning, rugby ball pressed to his cheek—when I hear the familiar friendly beep of the Oui Cycle van. The van, a 1980s-vintage Peugeot, always makes me smile, with its cute round headlamps, mirrors that protrude like ears, and two-toned paint: rusty red on the bottom, cream on top. A compact trailer for carrying bikes and luggage rattles at the back. Nadiya's arm hangs out the passenger's window, gently surfing on the summer air. On a crest, she raises a wave.

"We make it," she says with a heavy exhale, as they pull up beside me. "I thought we would be stuck forever. The Swedes, they started a campfire on the pavement and were cooking sausages."

"*Très bon,*" says Jordi. "Delicious sausages. We got a second campfire breakfast. What could be better?"

"Coffee?" I suggest to Nadiya, who's looking like a lot of things could be better, a look I understand.

"Please!" she says, not hiding her desperation, as Jordi has hopped out to open the trailer.

"*Ah, bonjour.*" Pierre-Luc strolls out with warm greetings to Nadiya. "How lovely to see you. How good you made it." His expression turns regretful. "I apologize, but would you mind moving the van to the other side of the fountain?"

Jordi has come around and is handling the luggage like it's an all-you-can-lift challenge. He has two suitcases in hand and two pressed under his arms. It's completely unnecessary, except for his clear delight in the feat.

"Move the van?" he says, and grins at the sign designating bike parking only. "Sorry, didn't realize you were serious."

"As serious as my plumbing problems," Pierre-Luc says grimly and gestures vaguely toward the ground beyond our bikes. "I'm having sinkage in my foundations and old clay pipes. I can't be responsible for collapsing the family pile of stones."

Nor can I. Thankfully, Jordi is already in the driver's seat and Nadiya is sensibly moving two suitcases toward the trailer. I nod in empathy to Pierre-Luc and think, *Château owners, they're just like us.*

"I had a blocked drainpipe in my bike barn," I say. "The biggest challenge was getting a plumber out to fix it."

He puffs his cheeks. "*Oui.* To find a plumber working in August, *c'est impossible.*"

"Anything's possible," I say supportively, hoping that's true for my sake too.

Out on the road, it feels odd to have such a small group. Nadiya leads, followed by Scarlett, Benji, Maurice, and me bringing up the rear. Rosemary insisted on staying near Lionel. Pierre-Luc offered his salon with its entertainments of books, magazines, and music.

"Hide from Gabi, if you see her," Scarlett warned before we left.

And from her grandfather, I thought but didn't say with Pierre-Luc in the room. I don't want to be responsible for crashing neighborly relations too. *Unless one of them is a killer.*

My mind spins on murderous motives on the ten-mile ride to Colmar. I snap back to work mode when Scarlett veers off the road to a fruit stand, where we buy jewel-like green grapes. "The English are obsessed with grapes at hospitals," Scarlett opines. "I told Rupy, buy a vineyard so I can keep you well stocked."

At a bakery—a random bakery unknown to my pre-tour pastry research—we stop for a box of assorted cookies. I get a croissant and am pleased when it earns a 9.5 score by my criteria of golden, shattery, buttery goodness. Then, on a whim, I detour us to a Fnac—a French chain that reminds me of a cross between Barnes & Noble and Best Buy. We buy Keiko earmuff-like headphones, a *Good Food* magazine, and a box set of Agatha Christies EN ANGLAIS ORIGINAL—IN THEIR ORIGINAL ENGLISH—according to a sticker on the front of the box.

We pull up to the hospital with bags swinging from our handlebars.

"No bike racks," observes Nadiya at the cement and glass entry. "I will stay outside." She seems more than happy to, and I don't blame her.

The exterior isn't the hospital's only unwelcoming feature. At the reception desk, a nurse in smiley-face scrubs has no smiles for us.

"*Non, impossible,*" she snaps to my formal and gushing request to see Keiko "just for a minute."

"But we come bearing gifts!" Scarlett protests. "We're her family. Brothers, sister, and niece."

The nurse looks unconvinced and rightfully so.

"Please . . ." Benji pleads.

"We won't leave," Scarlett threatens.

"One of you, only," the nurse finally agrees, probably to get rid of us.

"Give her our love," Benji calls after Scarlett, who designates herself as our representative.

"Remind her of the Spinners' motto," Maurice adds. "All for one, one for all!"

Scarlett's departing form salutes.

They're really a sweet group of friends. I could get a little misty-eyed, thinking of all the travels they've had together. They truly are like siblings.

"They're up to something," Nadiya intones, when I escape the somehow chilled yet stuffily stifling lobby to wait with her and the bikes.

Nadiya is rarely wrong, but to my happy surprise, the Silver Spinners behave like perfect tourers for the rest of the morning. We admire the old quarter of Colmar, with its colorful homes set against the River Lauch. We snag seats on a flat-bottomed boat tour. No one goes missing. No one goes snooping. There are no reenactments, unless they're of appreciative tour guests. I even get to share some of my memorized facts.

It's not all rosy. Our troubles grumble at the back of my mind. Keiko's injuries. Lionel's confession. Rosemary's double anguish of a husband dead and a boyfriend in jail. Our current state of no place to stay. I left Jordi in charge of the lodging problem, thinking he might find an option I missed. I call him when we're about to start back for Riquewihr.

"All settled," he says, when I dare ask about lodging. "I have identified the perfect place. A place *des plus extraordinaires*."

Okay . . . I'm in for a most extraordinary place. I ask for important details like cost, location, amenities, and whether they serve breakfast.

"All will be a surprise!" Jordi declares.

I'm a planner. I'm not big on surprises. However, I was happily surprised when Laurent showed up, and Jordi sounds so delighted. I let him have this secret.

When we roll into Riquewihr, I kick myself. I should have asked Jordi for the address. My riders have just had a full day, and I have nowhere for them to rest their legs.

"Don't worry, Sadie," says Maurice. "We will take ourselves to the nearest bistro and enjoy a restorative beverage."

"Perrier menthe for me," says Scarlett. "I'm in a minty mood."

"A Campari spritz for me," says Benji.

"Nice glass of Riesling," says Maurice. "Text us when we're ready to check in."

They leave in a little line, politely walking their bikes.

Nadiya has been checking her texts. "Jordi is at Pierre-Luc's," she reports. "Rosemary is there too."

Perfect, I allow myself to think. Jordi can reveal his surprise. I'll confirm rates and rooms at our new place and then collect Rosemary and the others.

"Something is still up," Nadiya says darkly. "They are too good today. I do not believe it."

And yet they didn't get lost or sneak into the hospital or stow away on a boat to Germany.

"Maybe they're behaving for our sake?" I suggest. "Maybe they feel bad about what's happened to Keiko and Lionel?"

Nadiya scoffs. "Jordi, too, he is too happy with his surprise. I do not trust any of this."

I cling to the day's good fortune. "We have bigger problems than people being too well-behaved and happy."

"Perhaps," Nadiya says. She swings a leg over her bike. "Perhaps not."

We ride to Pierre-Luc's and park at the sculpturesque bike rack. Jordi greets us, bubbling with enthusiasm for his chosen lodgings. The beds, they are so airy. The view, amazing. The ambience, truly outstanding and one of a kind.

"Where is it?" Nadiya demands.

"A stunning panorama of nature," Jordi continues. "Peaceful yet filled with music."

Nadiya folds her arms.

"You know how I told you my friend, the goat farmer, has the equipment for glamping?" Jordi says.

"Glamping?" Nadiya demands, as my stomach plummets. "What is this, glamping?"

"Glamorous camping," I explain, as Jordi gushes about amenities such as therapeutic goat-petting and practically unlimited *fromage de chèvre.*

"Everyone adores camping!" Jordi declares. "Glamping takes camping to another level of delight. Nadiya thought she would miss beds and walls, but now she experiences the relaxation, the calm, the beauty."

Ah, true love. Nadiya is biting her lip.

To me, Jordi shrugs his broad shoulders. "There was nothing else available that is so glamorous and affordable. I think your Silver Spinners will adore it. They like adventure."

My phone buzzes, saving me from comment, though he is right about the Silver Spinners and adventure. Distracted by thoughts of glamping, I answer before registering that the caller is a local number I don't recognize. "*Bonjour*, Sadie Greene, Oui Cycle, where we—"

I'm cut off by a veritable punch of French. "Did you know about this?"

I recognize the voice and the oh-so-polite (not!) manners of Chief Annette Dubois.

"Chief Dubois," I say brightly. Rosemary has drifted over from Pierre-Luc's salon, pale as a ghost shut up for winter. She mouths what I guess is "Lionel?"

I raise a just-a-moment finger. "Know about what?" I ask. "My riders and I have just returned to town after a day's excursion. Keeping out of your way, letting you do your work. Did you check out that vacation rental with the left luggage?"

Her huff is so loud, I swear I feel it through the line.

"*Oui*. You were right. The victim stayed there."

I wait for a "*merci*" or a "good job."

"Did you know they were plotting this?" she repeats.

Rosemary, Jordi, and Nadiya are hovering close. Good thing, because I feel like I'm going to need the support. "Plotting what?" I ask, while assuring myself that "plotting" has many positive connotations. Plotting a fun surprise. Plotting a joyful itinerary.

"Plotting to confess." The chief pauses.

"Confess?"

She huffs. "You don't know everything, I see. Three of your riders have marched into my station. Each one of them claims that they and they alone are the killer of Edwin Perch."

"But—" I'm protesting to a dead line. The chief has hung up.

"I knew it!" Nadiya crows. "I am not bragging, but I said they are too good to be true. That is always the case."

"You were right," I tell Nadiya, because it's always nice to hear those words. I should have listened to her, and, by now, I should know that troubles can always get worse.

CHAPTER 28

Wednesday:
"Give me your tired, your poor, your huddled masses yearning to breathe free . . ." These lines, from Emma Lazarus's sonnet, "The New Colossus," are famously inscribed on the Statue of Liberty in New York Harbor. Lady Liberty has Alsatian roots. Her sculptor, Auguste Bartholdi, was born right down the road in Colmar.

Two pigeons frenetically peck crumbs on the steps to the police station. A chartreuse haze of freshly sprayed graffiti mars the station's brass nameplate. Laurent stands by the doors in knee-length cargo shorts and impossibly crisp linen. He looks like a man on vacation, except for his expression.

"How was Colmar?" he asks, which I appreciate. It's nice that he cares about my work. Plus, I get to pedal through the day again. What clues did I miss?

"Colmar was beautiful," I say, which is like declaring that water is wet or croissants are delicious, an obvious, undeniable fact. I extol the scenery, the history, Little Venice, the ancient houses, the pretzels and the bakeries, and our delicious spontaneous lunch of wood-fired *tarte flambée*.

"Yeasted dough or a true flatbread?" Laurent the gourmand inquires.

"Cracker crisp. Probably no yeast involved." As a Chicago girl, I'll always appreciate some puffy crust, but I'll take a crispy *flambée* any day.

"No signs of trouble when you were out and about?" Laurent asks.

"The Bartholdi Museum was closed for a plumbing leak," I say, clinging to normal tour-guide setbacks for a day. "Do you know Bartholdi? He's the sculptor who designed the Statue of Liberty. Also, only one of us was allowed to visit Keiko in the hospital, but we took gifts, and I think she and Scarlett patched up their friend feud. So . . ."

I trail off, thinking of Scarlett's report after departing the hospital. She complimented the food: *Doesn't look half bad*. She reported that Keiko still seemed muddled: *Poor dear.* She informed Maurice and Benji that she'd promised they'd all attend Keiko's Wagner events forevermore.

Kill me now, Benji had groaned.

I frown, recalling what Scarlett said as we got back on our bikes. *Kei-Kei says she's with us in spirit.* I took that to mean she was cycling with us in spirit, but did Keiko give her blessing to this absurd plot? We'd pedaled off to another rousing cry of "All for one, one for all." Do they see themselves as the Three Musketeers of confession?

I rub my temples.

Laurent raises inquiring eyebrows.

"They were so well behaved," I say, pinching the bridge of my nose. Unless they'd been plotting in plain sight. I fast-forward my mental replay. After lunch, we'd snagged the last five seats on a flat-bottom boat, paddled gondolier-style by an expert guide. Nadiya and I took the two seats directly behind the guide, who did an amazingly smooth job of rowing and reciting landmarks. A group of Austrians filled the two bench rows behind us. The elder Spinners squished together on the back bench, shoulders pressed. Each time I looked back, they appeared to be gazing at the scenery, lips murmuring—about the relaxing, floating scene, I'd told myself. About the lush greenery, the gardens, the history . . . *About their foolhardy plan,* I bet!

I sigh so loudly the pigeons scatter. Then I register the pouncing blur of calico fur and realize that this bit of chaos wasn't entirely my fault. My feline guide from the other day misses the birds by meters. I bend and cluck my tongue to her. She approaches but drops to the pavement to roll a few feet from my hand. *What a tease!*

"What are the Spinners saying?" I ask Laurent, watching the cat's cute performance. She's exposing her belly fluff and kneading the air.

When I glance back, he's watching the cat fondly. And me too? He smiles wryly, draws a notebook from a handy cargo pocket, and turns to a page.

"Lady Scarlett says she has 'wanted to smack Edwin Perch upside the head since precisely two minutes upon first meeting him.' Quite specific, that."

I ponder the specificity. A "good" liar will veer away from details that might betray the fib. On the other hand, details can make a lie *seem* believable, and it's hard, if not impossible, to disprove a feeling.

Laurent continues. "Lady Crabtree-Thorne further claims she hasn't slept solidly since age fifty-one and a half. Awake and restless, she went out for a walk at precisely 11:13—"

Now that could be tested.

"She happened across Edwin in the courtyard. The shock shook her so vigorously that she 'let loose and smacked him a good one—a bit too good.' She further said that if her dear Rupy were with us, he'd confirm that she reacts violently to surprises."

Down the way, the pigeons have landed again and are squabbling over a potato chip. The cat watches them intently, her tail swishing like a fluffy dustmop. I think of the courtyard crime scene at midnight. The cobblestones had been clear of a body and everything else. Had someone swept up? What kind of killer totes around a broom? Could that have been the blunt object that killed Edwin Perch?

"What does Scarlett say she smacked him with?" I ask.

"Good question," Laurent says. "The lady declined to answer. Again, I quote, 'You police can do *some* work on your own without relying on elderly women and bicycle guides to solve your crimes for you.' "

I bet Annette responded well to that. Laurent is saying that Scarlett's borrowed walking sticks have been taken into evidence.

"But there are more possible weapons now," he says. "The crime techs are busy. You're to thank for that. That rental apartment you identified is a big find. You should be pleased."

I am pleased. I allow myself a moment of satisfaction.

Laurent continues with the confessions. "Mr. Maurice Guidry contends that he was also out for a stroll when he recognized Edwin Perch and attempted to 'take him into custody so that he might explain himself to his first and legal wife.' Edwin Perch then lunged at Mr. Guidry, whose military training kicked in."

The calico rolls onto her feet and waddles over to Laurent.

I'll admit, I feel a bit dissed. I had been actively courting her attention, but then, I do understand the attraction.

Laurent reaches to pet her under her chin. She fawns shamelessly. "Mr. Guidry then had many things to say about the history of boxing and Scottish stick fighting. You can imagine."

Oh, I can.

Laurent continues. "Apparently, a single shove by Mr. Guidry caused Mr. Perch to fall back and hit his head. Mr. Guidry says his lawyer will argue self-defense in an unfair fight."

"Unfair because Maurice is two decades older?" I ask.

Laurent grins. "Ah, no, because the cowardly Mr. Perch was so easily overcome. Mr. Guidry then shared many opinions about a man who would desert his family."

"Any explanations for why he then hid Edwin's body in a wine barrel?"

"Yes, in fact. He didn't want to ruin your cycling tour."

If only . . . "And Benji?" I ask, already imagining how Benji might spin the tale. I'm betting on something elaborate, a plot from a Golden Age mystery involving a poisonous Amazonian tree frog and darts.

Laurent snorts softly. The little cat purrs louder. "Mr. Benjamin Patel claims he cannot recall what happened, only that he found himself above the deceased and, out of shock, concealed the body. He says he is in a deep state of fugue."

"Oh, please!" At this, the cat toddles over to rub my ankles. I squat down to pet her. "Can you believe any of that, Miss Minou?" I ask in singsong tones.

"No," answers Laurent bluntly. "But Annette is considering charges."

My groan is interrupted by a clacking of heels. A woman approaches with a stride reminiscent of a racehorse held back from full gallop. Dark curls are piled in a bun. Ringlets frame a face that Scarlett would call dewy, as in actively dripping sweat. I'd put her in her forties, although maybe her professional aura has skewed my calculations. She wears a navy sheath dress and a summer-unsuitable blazer that gives me flashbacks to my cubicle days. That is, if my stuffy office jackets and slacks had been bespoke tailored. Her shoes look like they pinch, and her briefcase is polished leather. I guess she's not here to admire the architecture and pickled cabbage.

"Helena?" I ask, rising. The calico throws back her ears in offense and waddles off to bother the pigeons.

The woman who neither confirms nor denies she's Helena comes to an abrupt stop and runs steely eyes over my spandex attire. "Sadie Greene," she replies, not a question. "I've had five hours on trains—plenty of time to read about you."

The good, the bad, the tabloid torrid? There's no telling from Helena's face, which is somehow blankly unreadable yet ferocious.

"Oh," I say. "That's ah . . ." Probably not nice.

"Right," says Helena crisply. "Where are my clients?"

I point to the police station. "Still inside. There are four of them in there now."

Laurent introduces himself and offers to escort her. "Your colleague from Paris is already with them."

Helena is aware of the colleague and the number of clients. She turns down an escort. "Thanks all the same. I'll be jolly on my own." She and her serious jacket stride up the steps, looking anything but jolly.

At the double doors, she turns back. "Ms. Greene? Can you chase me down a room for the night? A bed-and-breakfast? An auberge? Nothing too touristy or twee. My assistant is on holiday."

Making me her new assistant? If she can get the Silver

Spinners out of this mess, I'll chase down all the non-twee hotels she wants (although I'm not entirely sure where the twee cutoff lies). "I'll find you something nice," I promise brightly. If all else fails, I can share my glamping tent.

Can you call it tailing if your tail is in front of you? The cat trots in and out of sight ahead of us, leading the way to the notorious courtyard. I'd asked Laurent if I could see Eddie's rented apartment in person. He'd agreed to take me.

"We won't be able to go inside," he warns again as we wind down a meandering lane. "I went in earlier when Annette doubted you were right."

We dodge a clump of laughing tourists, and he adds, "I could have told her you were correct. Actually, I did tell her. That made her more determined to prove me wrong."

To prove *me* wrong and make sure Laurent knew it, more likely.

"That's okay," I say. "I've already toured the inside via online listing photos." Our internet age really is a wonder for armchair travelers and real estate snoops. Not as much for residents of vacation destinations seeking places to live. A shocking number of homes and apartments in this ancient village have been turned over to short-term rentals.

We pass a home with ivy covering the timber bones. Lace curtains and periwinkle window trim suggest a grandmotherly resident baking up gingerbread. I know from my searches that the building is divided into three vacation rentals, totally renovated to include modern appliances, "smart" everything from the TV to the toilet, and prices so eye-watering, I was relieved for my bank account to find it fully booked.

Eddie had found a pretty good deal: king-sized bed, separate kitchen, lounge, ideal location in the medieval core, right above a wineshop. "How do you access the apartment?" I ask. "Surely visitors don't go through the wine-shop?"

"Now that would be a deal," Laurent says. "Nice shop, that. But, no, these old buildings have all kinds of odd connections and corridors. There is an interior stairway between the wine and antique shops. It goes up to two apartments. The one over the antiques shop is owned by an extended family who don't rent it out. It was unoccupied."

"Didn't the police question nearby residents and visitors?" I ask. "No one heard or saw anything?"

Laurent shrugs. "They've tried to contact folks, but there's a lot of turnover in the summer. A tourist reported hearing noises outside that night but didn't think anything of it. A local said she heard bicyclists rolling around at all hours. She acknowledged that perhaps she'd heard a cart too, but she hadn't looked outside. She assumed she knew who was responsible."

"Tourists," I say with a sigh. "We get all the blame." Rightfully so, in some cases. I turn the subject back to the mysterious Eddie. "Which of his names did he use to rent the apartment?"

Neither, according to Laurent. "He was Mr. Smith who paid cash through an app. The owner doesn't live here. She never sees her guests. The cleaner claims she left the rucksack under the bed on purpose, thinking it belonged there. She probably just missed it. She said the apartment barely needed any cleaning when she went in."

Because the killer scrubbed it clean? The cat slips under a garden fence before the left turn to the infamous courtyard. Smart girl. Scared girl? She was running away that night when Keiko first swerved to avoid her. I wish she could tell us what she saw.

When we reach the courtyard, my gaze lifts to the pretty

balcony above the wineshop. I'd recognize it from the listing photos, even without the men in puffy Tyvek suits inspecting the geraniums for evidence. Deputy Allard and his notebook step from the ground-level door between the wine and antique shops. He greets Laurent with respect bordering on a stand-at-attention salute. He gushes at me like I'm his new best friend.

"Madame Greene," Deputy Allard says. "Your tours are most extraordinary. Until now, I had no opportunity to work such serious crimes. Murder. Assault. Breaking and entering. Major theft. A cold case from England?" He looks as if he might kiss his fingertips in delicious delight. At least I'm making someone happy.

"Have you ever aided the Brigade de Recherches de la Gendarmerie, Deputy Allard?" Laurent asks.

That big name? That's Laurent's serious-crimes unit. The gendarmes are a national force. Laurent works out of the unit for the Department of the Pyrénées-Orientales. He has no standing here, as I understand it. But he only asked Allard a question. He didn't claim to be officially on the case.

Allard clutches his notepad to his heaving chest. "Never," he breathes. "But it is my great desire to do so."

Laurent jerks his chin toward the balcony, where a tech is now smooshing the geraniums to reach the antique vineyard implements decorating the upper story. "Find anything interesting up there?"

Allard snaps the notebook open. "I am not qualified to judge. However, I have made a *pointage* so that I may contemplate in my off-duty hours."

A *pointage*. A tally! Allard *is* my new best friend! He lists off items of clothing that sound like a beach vacation: swimming trunks, sandals, light shirts, chinos, shorts, no socks.

"A diamond ring," Allard says in the same tone as he's just listed a summer-weight suit jacket. "That was in a clear bag hidden within the lining of the trekking sort of sack. A very big diamond. Also in the hidden location, a necklace, possibly of many emeralds. A gold ring. Another gold ring. Cufflinks, very nice, probably many diamonds. Cash in a yet-uncounted amount but quite substantial. A notebook containing addresses, telephone numbers, and possible passwords and account numbers. The notebook also contained a photograph of a young dog and a photograph of two blond boys, also young. Several photographs of women. In addition, found separately under the bed, a toiletry kit containing sunscreen, a razor, a—"

"One moment," I interrupt. "Sorry, but the photographs? Have you identified those?"

Allard looks to Laurent, who raises an eyebrow. "Tentatively?" asks Laurent.

"Tentatively," repeats the deputy, scratching at his peach-fuzz sideburns. "The women I identify as Madame Gabi Morel and Madame Rosemary Perch, when younger. The dog appears to be an immature Bouvier de Flandres, the same breed as the large dog living next door to the victim. The dog has a record of digging vines and is known to the police."

I smile, imagining Chou Chou's mug shot. I picture his triangle ears perked, dirt dusting his wooly muzzle, his expression gleefully unrepentant.

Allard is saying, "The children resemble those left by Edwin Perch in England. I say this most unofficially. I only know their photographs from the internet. However, I searched many sites. Too many. It is an intriguing case."

For a moment, Allard and I are nodding at each other. He, approving of me bringing this crime buffet to his village. Me, glad to hear that professional detectives go Google diving too.

Then the sad reality sinks in. A photo of two boys, now grown men too busy to take time off to fly to France. Two women who might never have known where he'd gone. The dog he loved.

I consider the other items. What people pack for a trip can reveal a lot: their aspirations, their ability to plan ahead, their willingness to fling off work and the mundane and have fun. Eddie's clothing sounds like that of a carefree guy going away for a long weekend. In the stashed cash, jewelry, and photos, however, he seems like a man on the run. Then why didn't he leave? Was he watching, waiting to see if the Silver Spinners truly were here by coincidence?

"He knew his previous identity," I say, gazing at Eddie's last hideaway. "He didn't have amnesia." A door opens again. A crime tech steps out for a smoke. Before the door closes, I get a peek at a broad wood-paneled lobby, stairs leading up, and what look like more vineyard tools lining the walls. No wonder the techs are busy.

"Seems likely," Laurent says. "Who else knew who he was? That's the key question."

Deputy Allard raises an eager hand. "Four suspects in custody allege they recognized him and killed him. I have made another list." He turns back several pages.

Those four confessed murderers seemed truly shocked to see Edwin Perch emerge from a broken barrel. I'm about to tell Deputy Allard that he can't believe any of them, but this is probably not the best argument for their innocence.

Allard is reading from his questionable transcription of Scarlett's statement. "She says she will 'smack up and down his head'? I find this baffling. Does it mean she—"

He's interrupted by Laurent's phone ringing. Laurent answers. The voice on the other end is female and terse.

"*Oui, oui,*" Laurent says, his face hardening as he listens. "We'll be right there. Can you tell me—" He slips the phone back in his pocket. "We're needed back at the station," he says, already striding that way.

I thank the thrilled deputy and jog to catch up. "What's happened?"

"A development," he says. "I don't know what kind. Annette hung up on me. Just like old times, but she didn't sound happy, which could mean good news for you."

CHAPTER 29

Tour-guide tidbit: Alsace is known for its cows' milk cheeses, but goat cheeses are popular too. Goat cheeses shine in salads, tarts, and quiches, and pair beautifully with local Rieslings and Gewürztraminers.

"That worked out well." Scarlett steps from the police station, raising her face to the soft evening skies.

"Indeed!" Benji agrees. "Those little finger sandwiches they fed us were surprisingly yummy too. Good butter. Butter makes all the difference."

No argument there. I would dispute Scarlett's "worked out well," but I'm busy holding my tongue.

Maurice agrees that the sandwiches were a lovely snack. "But the atmosphere was quite unpleasant."

That's what jails are like, I want to yell.

"Institutional dungeon decor," says Benji. "They could step it up with a fresh coat of paint." He turns to Helena, who's slipping out of her lawyerly suit jacket. "You, Helena, darling, went above and beyond, as always."

"Worth your hourly rate of gold," Maurice says.

I remind myself of the positives. Three of my guests are out of jail. They've enjoyed a free, catered meal. Thank goodness for that because we've missed another reservation!

And . . . they're giggling. They're happy. That's good, even if I'd like to scream with exasperation.

I allow myself a sigh and some honesty. "What did you think you were doing?"

"Fine question," agrees Helena, letting down her curls and fluffing.

"You all could have been arrested," I continue.

"Still could be," Helena says pleasantly.

"You'd save us, Helena," Scarlett says. "Just like you did this afternoon, you brilliant woman, you."

"Paperwork saved you for now," Helena says. "That policewoman doesn't have time to write a bunch of fiction from unreliable narrators."

The Spinners chuckle.

"We're nothing if not unreliable," Scarlett says.

Benji chuckles. "That's our new motto!"

I give thanks for paperwork. From Laurent, I know that French crime reports are akin to novellas. All that work—the details, the theories, the clues and evidence and rationales for arrest—is then turned in to prosecutors who decide whether to investigate further. The investigation is out of the detective's hands then, out of their control.

"The chief doesn't want to be made a fool—again," Helena is saying. "She's not happy with this lot."

I almost wish Annette Dubois had come outside instead of inviting Laurent to her office to debrief. We might have shared a moment. I'm not happy with this lot either.

"But what about Lionel?" I ask Helena. "You couldn't get him released? He's okay?"

"He's fine!" Scarlett declares. "Lionel's proven that he's tougher than he seems. He'll carry on for love."

"First come first serve," Helena says, addressing my question. "The chief viewed this recent mass confession as a ploy. She's sticking with Lionel as her suspect." She snaps open her satchel, draws out a paper, and hands it to me.

At first, I think she's torn a page from a tourism brochure. Does she want me to guide her somewhere too? She points to a photo in the upper corner, a classic glitzy party shot of good-looking women in strappy dresses and men in open jackets, no ties.

I squint. Then I see it. The elder Spinners hover at my shoulder, and one by one, they do too.

"Edwin!" Scarlett declares. "He's a bit blurry, which is exactly how I remember him."

"The Perch himself," Benji murmurs. "Mingling at the periphery."

"This is a photocopy of a page from a tourism magazine," Helena says. "One of the publications the tourism office mailed to Lionel when he was over-preparing for your trip. He *says* he never noticed Edwin in it."

"I did immediately," Scarlett says. "We all did!"

Helena gives her a withering look. "Don't make my job harder with lies, Lady Crabtree-Thorne. You did your part. Your outrageous confessions have momentarily muddled the case."

The Spinners murmur approvingly and congratulate each other on good work. Helena reports that she and her French colleague will meet with a judge tomorrow and argue that Lionel should not be kept in custody.

"Lionel would need someone responsible to vouch that they will keep him out of trouble," Helena continues. "A relative?"

His closest relatives are happily, obliviously cruising halfway around the world. "A guide?" I ask.

Helena smiles. "You, Ms. Greene? I enjoy a challenge,

but even I would be hard-pressed to argue that your tours stay out of trouble."

Low blow, I think. But then, I can't make that argument either.

A half hour later, my little group plus Helena sit on a low stone wall, swinging their feet and enjoying ice cream cones covered in colorful sprinkles.

"Back home," Benji says rather wistfully, "I'd order hundreds-and-thousands as my sprinkles."

In England, he explains to me, tiny decorative sugar balls go by the name hundreds-and-thousands. How delightful! On a normal tour, that new knowledge would be a highlight of my nightly journal.

As it is, hundreds and thousands seem like the number of troubles on this tour. I call in backup, namely Jordi and Nadiya.

"We'll meet you at the medieval gates," I tell Nadiya. "We'll get everyone and the bikes in the van, collect Rosemary, and then if anyone wants, we can pick up camping snacks on the way to the farm."

Glamping with goats is seeming better and better. The farm is several miles out of town, so no easy midnight spins into trouble. In my revised dreams for tonight, we'll relax by a crackling campfire and get to bed early.

"Almost to you," Nadiya says at the same moment I spot the van rumbling down the road like a happy bug.

I relay the plan to my riders. "Helena, I've booked you a lovely room right here in the village. It's easy walking distance to everything." *Like the police station.*

"Helena's coming with us to the château," Scarlett declares, sliding off the wall. Her cone is dripping. A sprinkle slips down a little pistachio-flavored river.

"Oh, well, okay, but we can't stay long," I say, making sure to add a smile.

"Nonsense!" Scarlett counters. "We can't snatch Rosemary and run off. How rude! Come along, Helena. You enjoy art. You'll *love* this place and Pierre-Luc. He's single, quite a catch . . ."

Helena offers me a shrug that says *What can I do?*

If a high-priced power lawyer can't fend off Scarlett, what chance do I have? But now I have a new manners quandary: Will Pierre-Luc welcome three confessed murderers?

"You did what?" Rosemary is aghast. She's in a full-length rubber apron, as is Pierre-Luc. We found them back in his wine-bottling area. Rosemary was affixing labels to long-necked green-glass bottles. Before she spotted us, she seemed contentedly distracted by the task. Her expression morphed from oh-so-hopeful to crumpled and crushed as she watched us file in, one by one. Me, Scarlett, Helena, Maurice, Benji, Jordi, Nadiya, and Chou Chou, trotting from front to end like a herd dog. No Lionel.

Scarlett waited until we were back in the tasting room area to fill her goddaughter in on their exploits.

Rosemary's "You did what?" is repeated by Pierre-Luc as if in simultaneous translation. He chuckles, produces wineglasses, and pops a cork.

"Why on earth?" demands Rosemary.

"Isn't it obvious?" says Scarlett. "I should think you'd be happy, Rosemary, dear. You get more and more like your mother every day. Too practical."

"It is not obvious," Rosemary says, accepting a glass from Pierre-Luc. "Such behavior is far from ordinary."

"Never said we were ordinary," Benji says, as Maurice sniffs his glass and murmurs of hints of flowers, the A39 highway in Cornwall, and linzer torte.

"*Obviously,*" drawls Scarlett. "We're helping your Lionel, dear. Chief Dubois strikes me as stubborn."

Maurice and Benji share a look. "Pot calls kettle . . ." Maurice says.

"If that police chief is fixated on heroic but foolish Lionel," Scarlett continues, "she won't consider other options. We wanted to open her mind to alternate possibilities." She raises her glass to me. "As the best cycle touring does."

In other circumstances, I'd find that affirming.

Pierre-Luc is nodding solemnly. "Rosemary was telling me about Lionel. He does not seem like a man who would kill."

"Anyone can kill," Helena says. She's been pacing the room like an art-appreciating predator. "It's the ones you don't expect that scare me."

I know too well about that. I glance at my riders. Rosemary gazes into her wine. The others are toasting. Their hands show their age, and their hair is dashed with white. As killers, no one would see them coming, especially if they made obviously false confessions.

Cyclist's Log

Thursday, 12:05 a.m., La Ferme des Chèvres Rêveuses—The Farm of the Dreaming Goats

The goats bleat softly. They aren't dreaming yet, and neither am I. The other tents have gone dark. I hope that means everyone else is asleep. I have to say, my group took the "glamping" in stride.

As I should have known, they've glamped before at places that put the glamour in camping. They enjoyed king-sized beds and spa services at a safari park in Botswana, tree houses in an ancient redwood forest, and yurts at an outdoor opera gathering in Mongolia. Reminiscing about Mongolia prompted them to call Keiko. She was still feeling fuzzy-headed, but insisted she didn't see or hear anything that could identify her attacker. She had been listening to music full blast, she said.

When Scarlett chided her for not paying attenion, Keiko snapped back. "You said to recreate the night I found him!"

It was good to hear Keiko feisty again. Her outburst let loose a secret too.

Previously, Keiko hadn't admitted that she'd been listening to Wagner at highest volume. So much for her musician's subconscious recalling auditory clues.

We ended up staying at Pierre-Luc's for several hours. Keiko would have enjoyed the gathering. Two guitarists showed up and played amazing acoustic renditions of Bach. I sound like I'm someone who can identify acoustic Bach, don't I? Benji filled me in.

Céline popped in to drop by more paintings. Pierre-Luc had some blank spots in the tasting room, and he hung them immediately. Céline was thrilled to see "all the murder suspects" and again bemoaned that she'd failed to help poor, poor Eddie. To save him, of course, but also because he owed her money for a painting.

Benji and Maurice have their eye on one of her paintings. They and Pierre-Luc stood before it, admiring the glow and vibrance of the landscape. Maurice and Benji will acquire it before they leave town, they promised. They will have it as their own! Unless they end up in the slammer, they laughed.

Céline encouraged the purchase, slammer

or not. "I will give you a discount. You are notoire."

Benji delighted in being "notorious." He suggested adding it to their group name, the Notorious Silver Spinners.

Céline had offered me an even bigger discount. Does that mean I'm more notorious?

Toward the end of the evening, I had a minor panic. I thought I'd lost Benji and Maurice. Benji went looking for one of Pierre-Luc's eight bathrooms. Eight, and Benji took over a half hour to find one? Maurice went in search of Benji. When he didn't return for ages, I went looking. I took along Jordi and his muscles as backup.

Jordi was as jumpy as a mouse, imagining murderers around every corner. We eventually heard their voices. They were outside by the property line talking to Pépère.

Pépère was grumpy. Gabi had forbidden him to visit the château because we were there. He'd laughed at that. "You don't look dangerous to me. I've fought off worse!"

"You never know." Benji had laughed. As for his lengthy trip to the loo, he'd gotten turned around in the hallways. He blamed his brain fugue. He and Maurice were ogling the art, more likely.

"We were talking about Eddie," Maurice told me.

Benji winked, in case I didn't get that they were sleuthing and egging on Pépère.

Pépère launched a rant about cuckoos in his nest. Which reminds me, remember how he confused me with talk of salads? Well, I googled: Raconter des salades translates to "talk of salads," meaning "to tell tall tales."

Did Pépère know that Eddie was all tall tales? I was ready to join Maurice and Benji in asking more, but Gabi came out to call to her granddad. Her glare was my cue to hustle Maurice and Benji away. Since I was at it, I gathered up everyone and headed for the goat farm.

Jordi's right. It's pleasant here. The goats are like kids playing Marco Polo in a pool. A call here, a call there, distant and close. My bed is a double-decker air mattress. The tent has screen flaps on top, and I can see the stars and rustling trees. It's hardly glamorous, but it's better than a sleeping bag on the ground. Way better than a budget hotel by the highway.

My riders will have stories, that's for sure. That time we confessed to murder, had ice cream, and slept under the stars with a hundred and fifteen goats.

I hope Lionel can see the stars. I hope he knows we're all working to get him out. I wish he could hear the goats and Rosemary breathing beside him.

CHAPTER 30

Tour-guide tidbit: Want to get back to the land on vacation? The network Bienvenue à la Ferme connects farmers with visitors seeking rural experiences in France. Pick grapes, make cheese, or simply enjoy the fresh countryside air.

The aroma of coffee seeps into my stress dream, but the dream won't release its grip. I'm at an airport, and there's trouble with my luggage. Clothes have spewed out, yet my suitcase is mummified shut in tape. The last boarding call is sounding, and I'm frozen in place. The worst thing about these nightmares is that they nudge too close to reality. Other people's stress dreams come with clear tipoffs. Like, would you really be back in high school, about to attend prom in the buff?

The coffee smells acrid. It's burning! My dream skips a frame. *I'm on my bike, speeding down a mountain, brakes smoking, precipices on either side!*

There are bells. Chiming, chiming . . . A baby cries. No, screams. Wait, is that a . . . ?

A goat. I fuzzily remember where I am. The farm. The canvas tent with the view of the sky. The surprisingly nice pillows. I clutch one like a life raft offering a few more precious moments of sleep. The move causes my inflatable bed to list and roll as if we're out to sea. I don't so much fall out as ooze to the ground, pillow to my chest, my hip smacking on a rock.

I roll onto my back and pry open my eyes to blue-gray dawn.

I could crawl back onto my air-raft bed, but a songbird is whistling loudly just outside my tent. Only, it's not a bird. I lift the edge of the privacy curtains and peer through the screen. The warbler has rugby tattoos on his biceps, a buzzcut, and abysmal campfire coffee-making skills.

I tug on shorts and a T-shirt. Jordi greets me with a beaming smile.

"A paradise," he declares, hands sweeping as far as his muscular shoulders allow.

My hip aches from the wake-up call on that rock, but he's right about the scenery. We arrived after dark last night, so I could only make out forms: a stone farmhouse and barn, resting against dark pillows of forest. The goats like ghosts huddled against the barn, the soft clonk of alpine bells.

Now I take in the whole scene. The farm is tucked in the foothills, trees to the west, a pasture nibbled down to a lawn by the herd. The goats are white with busily flicking tails. The young males waggle impressive goatees and clack horns languidly.

"Glorious," I agree. Also glorious: the amenities include a barn with private outdoor showers and—better yet—indoor plumbing. Camping has already shown me something about myself. I do appreciate basic amenities. When I return, Jordi hands me an enameled mug, speckled like an exotic blue egg.

"Nadiya adores camping," he says. "The farm life suits her."

Is Nadiya that skilled an actress? Maybe she's having a

better time than she's let on to me. I thank Jordi for the coffee, which, outdoors in the cool, green freshness, doesn't seem so bad.

Jordi recites goat facts, which stops my mind from circling my troubles. The goats are Saanens, a Swiss breed, known here in France as Chèvre de Gessenay.

"They have an elegant build," Jordi says. "They only see certain colors. Pastel blues and yellows."

I let my eyes droop and try to imagine their world.

"They prance," Jordi adds, tattoos dancing as he hefts a cast-iron skillet over his campfire coals. "That is how my friend Guy came to be a glamping entrepreneur. He had dreams of making the best goat circus in France."

"We're in goat-circus tents?" I have to smile. There's a fun first for my books.

"Exclusive," Jordi intones. "Very rare."

"Exhausting." Nadiya crawls from their tent, rubbing tired eyes. "All night, worse than ever—goats, goats, goats, and their stomping feet everywhere."

Jordi greets her with kisses and coffee. She smiles at the kisses and pours half the coffee onto a shrub when Jordi turns away to tend the fire. "You did not hear the noises, Sadie? Around two in the morning, I think. Jordi, you slept like the log. Like the log being attacked by chainsaws."

"All this fresh air," Jordi says blissfully.

I guess I slept more soundly than I thought.

"I could feel their feet, vibrating," Nadiya grumbles. "Like they are outside our tent, breathing and stomping." With resignation and a wince, she sips her remaining coffee.

Rosemary emerges from the next tent with a rose-decorated toiletry bag in hand. She waves to us on her way to the showers. Scarlett is next, resplendent in full makeup and a red satin dressing gown.

"I slept better than I have in ages out here in the wild," Scarlett says. She accepts coffee with a "Thank you, darling," and a "Well! That's strong enough to rouse my Rupy!" She looks around. I wonder if she's seeking somewhere to dispose of the bitter brew or looking for a backup giggle from Benji.

"The boys are sleeping in?" Scarlett asks.

The boys, Maurice and Benji, chose the tent farthest from the goats. Their tent has thick blue and white stripes, like a beach hut in Breton. Or at a goat circus. Now I can't get the image of acrobatic goats out of my head.

"Must be," I say, but worry nibbles. "Maybe someone should check on them?"

I've knocked on guests' doors before. I've never gone knocking on a tent, and they're not technically late for anything.

"I'll check on my way to the facilities," Scarlett volunteers. She tightens her sash. The goats and I watch her go. The goats, with their slightly alien eyes, peering to the side. Me, with a trepidation that turns to a drumbeat when Scarlett raises the pitch of her greetings.

"Boys, yoo-hoo! Rise and shine, sleepyheads. Maurice? Benji? That's odd . . ."

Nadiya and I hustle to join her. She's raised the entry flaps to reveal a king-sized bed, inflated to a height well above my knees. An empty bed.

"Must be in the shower," Scarlett says.

We'd hear that. We'd see feet. Rosemary's are visible in the farthest curtained stall.

Nadiya jogs down to the barn. I tell myself happy stories. Maurice and Benji have gone for a ride to see the sunrise. They've cycled to a bakery and will return shortly with bags of fresh croissants and brioche to share.

Nadiya yells back. "Their bikes are gone!"

My stories stand. Except my mind is replaying Nadiya's account of disrupted sleep, and my gut is telling me something is wrong.

"You're camping?" Laurent takes in the farm with a twinkle of amusement. The goats are farther afield, dotting the pasture like distant daisies. Rosemary, Scarlett, and I met Laurent and his driver at the barn.

"I thought you said you'd found somewhere posh?" Laurent's attempt to hide a smile is so poor that I suspect he's not trying at all.

"We're glamping," I say in what I hope is a breezy, I-glamp-everyday tone. "That's glamorous camping."

"Ah, so it is." Laurent rubs his chin stubble. His hand hides his lips, but the smile fans his eyes.

"*Ah* . . ." This "ah" is heavy with suspicion. In a case of just-my-luck, Laurent called a rideshare and was paired up with Serge.

"Yes, yes, my theory comes terribly true," Serge continues. His dark hair is rumpled, his shirt is unbuttoned to mid-chest, and when he's upwind, cigarette smoke and cologne assault my nose. This might be the tail end of Serge's night, but he's clearly energized. He practically bounces in white leather sneakers with haphazard red stitching. "As soon as I realized I was driving an officer of the gendarmerie, I knew I would be taking him urgently to you, Madame Greene. There will be trouble, I thought. Yes, the plot unfolds."

"No trouble," I say, a clear lie, now being refuted by Scarlett.

Still in her red satin gown, Scarlett throws herself at Laurent. He holds her up, while Rosemary tries unsuccessfully to peel her godmother away.

"Officer, my friends are missing!" Scarlett cries.

"They have not sneaked away to commit more foul deeds?" Serge asks.

More just-my-luck: Serge speaks English.

Scarlett gasps. "Well, I never! Who are you?"

"Serge," says Serge. "I know who you are, Madame. Yes, I do."

"Would you like coffee, Serge?" I ask, waving to Jordi's smoky campfire. This diverts Serge. He's already declared that he will wait around in case Laurent needs a ride back—and because he wants in on the action, I'm sure.

"Benji and Maurice have turned off their phones," Scarlett tells Laurent. "Or someone turned them off. Benji never shuts down his phone. Maurice is the same, although you won't get him to admit it." She's chattery with nerves.

"Did anyone hear them leave?" Laurent asks.

I tell him about Nadiya's unsettled dream of footsteps outside her tent. I then admit that we've waited almost an hour, telling ourselves they'd gone on a sunrise ride. We'd picked at Jordi's campfire breakfast: incinerated bacon, eggs over-singed, and extra-burned coffee. Scarlett had held forth on what romantics Benji and Maurice are. They adore a sunrise.

"Something's terribly wrong!" she repeats now.

We're standing by the goat barn. From here, I can see the unpaved road winding out into a dappled beech forest. By daylight, it's a tempting path for cycling. At night, it would have been pitch dark under the trees. What were they thinking?

Laurent had been inspecting the barn's stonework. He fixes Scarlett in an assessing gaze. "You didn't plan this, Madame? Another ploy? I must note, as a group, you've already broken into a private residence, recreated a murder scene with unpleasant consequences, and confessed to murder."

Rosemary murmurs about the godmother who cried wolf.

Scarlett flicks her hand. "Yes, but those were all *my* ideas, Officer. I don't need to be right, you see. I leap in and then assess the depth of the water. Why do you think I've been married four times?" She adds a murmured "rest their souls" and again looks sadly around for Benji.

"So, the other Silver Spinners do not share your reckless approach?" Laurent asks, sounding slightly—and rightfully—incredulous.

"My lusty approach," Scarlett corrects. "Maurice needs to know everything and then some before he makes a move. He doesn't want anyone to know that. He scurries around in secret, like a squirrel gathering treasures of information so he can trot them out later. Sadie, did you think he goes around knowing all those tedious dates of battles and treaties and castles and what have you? He's been afraid you'll introduce a topic he's not completely up on. Competitive old fool . . ." She says the last fondly.

I'd feel affirmed, except her concern is catching. I doubt Maurice and Benji cycled off into the night to investigate cabbages and show me up on sauerkraut.

Laurent says the right things: Let's not jump to conclusions. They haven't been gone long. We don't know anything yet.

"Exactly!" Scarlett cries. "We have no idea where they are!"

We might, though. Something must have sparked their secret mission. "Who did they talk to last night at Pierre-Luc's?" I ask, to Laurent's gratifying affirmation. "Anyone who might have sparked an idea, a theory?"

"Oh, those two . . . They talked art, art, art," Scarlett

says dismissively. "That Céline girl caught their interest. Pretty paintings. Pretty girl, too, but she's too thirsty for attention and accolades, if you ask me."

I note a smile wisp across Rosemary's face. It withers when she says, "Céline spoke with me about Edwin. Eddie, she called him. He was a different man, wasn't he? Céline says he and Pierre-Luc went to all the gallery openings and soirees—soirees!" She shakes her head at the word. "Céline said she hadn't seen him around as much lately, at the salons and wine tastings. She thought Gabi had tamped down his fun. Gabi was unhappy when he was happy, Céline said. I wonder if Edwin thought that of me . . ."

Rosemary sighs and continues. "Life can't all be fun. We can't all bicycle and tour for a living."

I bite my lip as she talks on about the responsibilities of raising kids and running a shortbread factory. True, but are we not on the same cycling tour of crime? My job is not all easy pedaling.

Scarlett tsks. "Clearly, Edwin needed more tamping down. Long overdue, I'd say."

I steer the conversation back to Maurice and Benji. "They spoke with Pépère too." I tell Laurent about finding them out in the garden after they'd supposedly gotten lost in the château. "They had Pépère grumbling about Eddie. I think Pépère knew Eddie was a fraud." I repeat Pépère's French proclamation about salads.

Laurent understands without any Google-assisted translation.

"That settles it," Scarlett declares. "They must have gone back to the inn or Gabi's house. Where's your driver, Officer? We'll tear that property apart!"

I let Laurent do this tamping down. He soothes with a dash of authority. "We cannot intrude on an official investigation, Madame. In fact, I should probably alert the local authorities that two individuals released from police custody on the condition they not leave the jurisdiction are unaccounted for and—"

"Fine!" Scarlett interrupts. "What would you have us do, then, Officer?"

I have the answer for that. "You and Rosemary stay here in case they return." I turn to Laurent. "There's surely no crime in dropping by Gabi's and Pierre-Luc's to chat."

CHAPTER 31

Thursday:
Shall we try for cabbages today?

Serge skids to a stop in front of Pierre-Luc's remaining barrels. "Of course, this is where we are. You suspect they return to the scene of the crime," he says with delight.

Laurent had kept him talking about the French football league on the terrifying ride back to Riquewihr. The chances of Montpellier making the finals were discussed as Serge passed three campers in a row on twisty roads. The storied history of the Saint-Étienne team was detailed as Serge swerved around an obstacle course of cabbages, presumably fallen from a farmer's cart.

Cabbages! The very vegetable my riders should be admiring today. It seemed like a sign from the universe—or a taunt.

"Exactly. We must suspect everyone," Laurent says, handing Serge some cash and his business card, the latter in case Serge spots two older male cyclists on e-bikes.

Serge peels off with high hopes.

I gaze out over the miles and miles of undulating vineyards, now threaded with a plume of Serge's dust. There are so many places Maurice and Benji could be. So many more that they aren't.

Laurent reads my thoughts. "Small increments, that's how you find missing persons. Think of it as pedaling up a mountain."

We agree that he'll visit Gabi. I'm obviously not her favorite tour guide. I, meanwhile, will drop by Maurice and Benji's next-to-the-last-known location. Chou Chou greets me and bounds ahead as my guide. Pierre-Luc sits in his sunny salon, fulfilling my image of a château denizen at his leisurely breakfast. The double doors are open to the summer morning. A *cafetière* is plunged to a thick layer of coffee grounds. A baguette is missing a hunk. He's engrossed in paperwork.

He rises when he sees me. "Sadie, but what is wrong?"

Are troubles written on my face, or does my mere arrival signal new disaster? I remember Céline and her offer to give me a hefty notoriety discount.

"You are on foot!" Pierre-Luc continues. "Have you had an accident?" His gaze travels from my still-scuffed forehead to my dog-slobbered feet.

"Oh, no, I'm okay." This makes me smile. My missing bike was his concern. I am notorious for cycling.

Pierre-Luc clears an upholstered club chair and urges me to sit. "Something is wrong," he persists. "You are not with your riders?"

I sit, dodging Chou Chou's kisses. So much for stalling with small talk. Pierre-Luc has given me the perfect opening. "Maurice and Benji went missing last night."

"Missing? But . . ." He frowns. "They did not leave here with you? I was occupied, I'm sorry to say. I did not notice."

I admit to losing them in the night. "But maybe they went for a pleasure ride and lost track of time? They didn't happen to stop by here, did they?"

Man and dog scan the room as if two cyclists might pop out from behind a stack of books. Pierre-Luc exhales, ruffling his lips. "Chou Chou and I went for our morning walk earlier. We inspected the vines. We are only back for half an hour or so." He gestures toward the breakfast. "You are welcome to look around." He grins. "Would they be like Madame Scarlett and, ah, how did she put it? Invite herself in?"

I'm glad he brought that up. "They might."

He's offering to help me search when his phone rings. "Apologies. I must answer this. Supplier problems. Do you want to look? You may go on your own. Actually, no, it is safer if you take Chou Chou. Look anywhere but at messes. I am a bachelor, as you know."

A bachelor with impeccable taste and, I'd bet, a cleaner. My guide dog and I stroll down hallways that could double as art galleries. We peek in tidy rooms until I feel like a voyeur. Once or twice, I call Maurice and Benji's names. My voice comes out hushed in the regal house. Chou Chou has no such reverence. We're upstairs—where I only glance into a room with an unmade bed—when Chou Chou trots to an open window to bark. Laurent stands with Gabi in her pretty garden. She looks toward the château. I draw back from the window.

"They're not here, are they?" I say to Chou Chou, as we make our way down marble stairs. "You'd tell me."

When we return to the salon, Pierre-Luc is gone. Chou Chou lopes to the winery side, where we find Pierre-Luc staring at a wall, hands on his hips, scowling as if he's critiquing a perplexing work of art. That stare, however, is aimed at a blank spot.

"Have I gone mad?" Pierre-Luc scrapes a hand through his hair.

"I might not be the best judge of that." I join him to gaze at the un-adorned square of stones, like we're in a modern art gallery, contemplating a great work of nothingness.

"I placed Céline's painting here last night," Pierre-Luc says. "The painting of poppies and vineyards and the light that was both hopeful and tragic. Did she sell it? *Non*, I would know . . . There were no prospective buyers last night except your friends." The scowl turns to me. "Maurice and Benji, they said they wanted it. Did you hear them say that?"

I did. I replay their words with growing dread. *We will acquire it before we leave town! We will have it as our own.*

It was Laurent who made the call, and I knew what to expect. Chief Dubois would not be happy. Indeed, stepping from her official vehicle after the three-minute drive from the station, she berated me for losing track of "international criminals," for failing to call her immediately upon learning of their "absconding behavior," and for claiming that glamping is possible among goats.

I should have anticipated her more unpleasant reaction: delight. Her eyes, gazing upon Pierre-Luc's art-absent stones, might have been enjoying a private viewing of the *Mona Lisa*. She shared her thrill with Laurent ("Jacques," as she gushed), her "dear and victimized friend" Pierre-Luc, the hassled Helena (although Helena must be anticipating many more billable hours), and me.

"I felt it," Chief Dubois says again. "I felt this case was coming together."

She felt it because four out of six members of my tour walked up and confessed! I'd taken that as evidence of their innocence and general foolhardiness. They're making it really hard to prove that belief.

Chief Dubois snaps her fingers at Deputy Allard, who's

also been contemplating the bare wall. "Recite the relevant pages, deputy."

He opens his notebook, clears his throat, and reads in a monotone: "If I went missing, I would go bigger than Cornwall in spring." Deputy Allard breaks character. "That was said by Monsieur Benjamin Patel. He then said he would take a boat to the Amazon and pretend to be eaten by fishes. Something about chums? Friends, perhaps? I did not understand. His partner, Monsieur Maurice Guidry, then said, 'What about me?' They agree to go missing together. To Dordogne or Ibiza or Thailand, preferably the north of Thailand for the noodles."

"There you have it," Chief Dubois says.

"We don't know why they're missing," Helena says, to which I vigorously agree. "They could be having brunch. They are big fans of brunch."

"Or they're lost," I chime in. "They tend to get lost. They're elderly and frail and Benji is experiencing a fugue." I've just proven they're not hiding within hearing distance. They'd jump out and accuse me of agism if they heard that. I continue. "They're at-risk. Does France have an alert system for at-risk missing persons?"

"Fear not," Chief Dubois says brightly. "I'll be looking for them. I have alerted my colleagues throughout the department. Jacques, you'll accompany me to the gendarmerie to coordinate the search?"

Laurent parts himself from the wine bottles. "We'll find them, Sadie," he says.

"We will," promises the chief. "And when we do, they will not be allowed to flee again."

CHAPTER 32

Tour-guide true crime: On May 20, 2010, a lone thief nicknamed "Spiderman" broke into the Museum of Modern Art in Paris and sliced five paintings from their frames. The works were valued at over one-hundred-million dollars. Later, a co-conspirator confessed to an even more horrifying crime. He claimed to have destroyed the stolen paintings to hide evidence of the theft. Skeptics hope that he was lying. They contend that he was a true lover of art and would not have harmed such beauty.

"What has happened now? Did they find your missing men?" Gabi sinks into the patio chair beside me.

I'm sitting in the shade of an arching linden, watching a crime-scene tech dust Pierre-Luc's walls like an overambitious maid. What does the tech expect to find? To lift a painting, all one would have to do was grasp and, well, lift.

"Pierre-Luc is missing a painting," I say, avoiding more negative words like theft and crime. "One of Céline's."

Gabi's red curls bounce chaotically at her shoulders. Her floral sundress is so bright, it's returned some color to her cheeks. She gestures to the police vehicle and crime-tech van parked in the bike-parking-only spot. "So many police rush here for a *missing* painting? Céline's painting? Are they sure she didn't steal it herself for the attention?"

Now there's a theory. I raise an eyebrow.

Gabi responds with a one-shoulder shrug, nonchalant about her uncharitable, but perhaps brutally truthful, suggestion.

"They think Maurice and Benji took it," I admit.

She smiles ruefully. "Your riders are implicated in all manner of crimes. Do you believe their stories? There is one I find particularly difficult. Did they truly arrive here by chance? Here to this village, to my inn, because of a brochure in Rosemary's closet?"

It's my turn to shrug. "If that's true, then it was Edwin who ordered away for the brochure. Rosemary said that Edwin collected all sorts of tourism literature. Maybe he planned to leave?"

"Like he planned to run away from me?" Gabi asks bitterly. "I heard about the jewelry and money the police found in his get-away bag. That watch he was wearing when we found him, that was my father's. A Rolex. I kept it in my safe."

She's hit the angry stage of grief, unless she was mad way before Eddie's death. I decide there's no better time to ask. "Céline was here last night," I say gently. "She said you'd kicked Eddie out before. Is that why his bags were packed, Gabi?"

Gabi drums fingers on her armrest. The chairs are minimalist rockers in pretty Provençal blue. They'd be perfect for sipping morning espressos, listening to the birds and burbling fountain.

"Céline exaggerates," Gabi says, not answering my question. "She is a fantasist. It is what makes her paintings so eye-catching. Eddie and I had our disputes. Any couple does. Keeping an inn, it can be very stressful. You are always on call."

Same with tour guiding.

She's saying that Eddie disliked anything unpleasant. "He took himself off if we squabbled or if he found guests disagreeable. He stayed with friends, having his fun. Sometimes, I wished he would stay gone. He always came back."

Chou Chou comes over and she ruffles his chin. "Like you. You run off but always return, and that is good."

"What did you squabble about?" I ask.

She snorts. "Can you not guess? Once again, I am on my way to the bank in Strasbourg. It is my fault, I suppose. I do not like finances, so I let Eddie handle them. I knew he took a little allowance for himself. I did not know how much, though I should have. He wanted a life we could not afford."

She rises abruptly. "I should go. I mourn Eddie, of course I do. However, as always, I must sort out his mess."

I hold Chou Chou around his wooly chest so he won't follow her. Also, for comfort.

Annette Dubois has every officer in the region searching for Maurice and Benji, but Gabi had a way better motive to lash out and kill Eddie, whether she knew of his past or not. What if dear Lionel confessed to cover for the wrong woman? What if they all did?

I sit and think until the crime tech leaves and I hear Pierre-Luc calling his dog.

"Sadie, you are still here," he says. "Did I see Gabi? You are friends again?"

I'm not sure about friends. Fellow beleaguered hospitality professionals? A widow and her confidant? A killer taunting her very amateur detective? Or a nice woman fooled by love? Maybe she's all of those.

"She's off to the bank again," I tell Pierre-Luc. "Eddie left her with some money problems."

"*Mais oui,*" Pierre-Luc says, ruffling his lips. "Eddie was not the best with money."

"You knew?" I ask.

A shrug. "I spotted him a few hundred once in a while. If I'm honest, probably several thousand over the years. I would have given more, he was my friend, but I cannot afford much."

My eyebrows rise rudely on their own. I can't stop them.

He laughs. "Do you know the old saying: How do you make a million in wineries?"

I don't. "But if it applies to cycle touring, I'd sure like to know."

This laugh is rueful. "Start with two million. Or more. Start with ten million, a fortune. Your money will sieve away. Add in a massive family home to upkeep, and I am lucky to keep Chou Chou in his gourmet croquettes."

Even dog kibble sounds more glamorous in French, I catch myself thinking.

Pierre-Luc smooths his rumpled chinos. "Speaking of business, I must go. There is a meeting of the local *vignerons*. You may stay, of course. You could entertain Chou Chou."

He apologizes to his dog, who is not invited to the winemakers' meeting. "You must stay here. You know why." He whispers an explanation to me. "Cats. Two cats live at the hosting location. Chou Chou likes cats too much. He will shower them with loving kisses."

Chou Chou pants at this happy thought.

I'm saying I'll be going too when my phone buzzes with a text. Pierre-Luc's rings simultaneously.

"Annette," he says, as I say, "Laurent."

The message is the same. Two bikes have been found. Two new-model e-bikes with Oui Cycle of Sans-Souci-sur-Mer etched in a small oval plate attached to their frames.

"Where?" I hear Pierre-Luc asking, as my phone buzzes in a text with the answer: the train station in Colmar.

Pierre-Luc looks grim when he hangs up. He lures Chou Chou into the tasting room and locks the door. "Your riders are on the run," he says, shaking his head in apparent disbelief. "With Céline's painting? I always told her she would make it big."

Pierre-Luc offers me a ride. His meeting is in Colmar, where the bikes have been found. There's no use in me going there. The police will confiscate my bikes as evidence. As for Maurice and Benji . . . They're likely long gone. From Colmar, one can catch a high-speed train to Strasbourg or Paris. And from there? Anywhere. Buses, planes, trains, or hire cars could take them out of the country or down to the Dordogne, one of Benji's locales for his imagined new life.

Or they could hop a local line and hide out in a pretty village right next door. They could be brunching in Colmar. They could be anywhere!

I don't know where I should be. I decline Pierre-Luc's gracious offer to stay, try to block out Chou Chou's whimpers at a window, and set out on foot, feeling lost and aimless without my bike. On two wheels, at least I could pedal away the stress, powering up hills until my legs and lungs ached.

Why would Benji and Maurice steal Céline's painting? It was priced at just under €2,300, around $2,500. My budget would require roof-tile repairs before art indulgence, but if Maurice and Benji could induce a high-priced lawyer to cross the English Channel, they could easily afford the painting. Would any painting be worth making themselves obvious suspects in theft and murder?

On autopilot, I head for the village. Some people swear by retail therapy. I say croissants are the cure for just about anything. I'm almost to the medieval gates when I hear footsteps behind me. Lots of feet and heavy panting. I turn moments before Chou Chou lunges. His paws go to my shoulders.

A passing group of Spanish-speaking tourists snap our photo. I imagine the picture: Chou Chou's arms on my shoulders like we're dancing. It's the kind of romantic image that graces touristy placemats, the laminated kind with collaged photos of regional landmarks, baby animals, and folk dancers, splattered with big red hearts. I'm removing Chou Chou's paws when the tour group moves on and reveals a more worrisome photographer. A balding man in khakis with a long-lens camera is striding toward the car park.

"Paparazzi!" I whisper to Chou Chou, whose ears perk. Paparazzi is an exaggeration. I recognize the man as one of the reporters from the police steps. I'm pretty sure he's local, charged with covering public meetings, fetes, rogue llamas, and rare outbursts of crime associated with cycle tours.

"Be discreet," I whisper to the grinning dog. As if power walking through a village with a wooly mammoth at my side is discreet. How did Chou Chou escape? Did he squeeze through an open window? Break the latch to make his own opening? However he did it, I'm happy to have a companion. We'll get bakery treats, then I'll take him home.

We're weaving down a back alley when I spot another furry friend. The calico leaps down from a patio wall when she sees me. Mid-leap, she registers my companion.

Fur rises on her back. Her tail poofs. Chou Chou gives a delighted single bark, almost a boyish yip. A friendly yip, I think. An I-want-to-smother-you-in-slobbery-kisses yip.

The cat is having none of it. As soon as her claws touch the cobblestones, she scrabbles off with a hiss. Chou Chou gives chase, with me racing behind them. I must catch Chou Chou. I will not add harassment of a soon-to-be-mother cat to the list of disturbances linked to my tour.

"Chou Chou!" I call. He yips again, the sound sharp against the close façades. The cat streaks around a corner, and—*great, just great*—we're headed back to the scene of the crime. As I think this, a scream echoes down the lane. I round a corner to find a woman cradling a mini-poodle, its teeth bared. Chou Chou gazes adoringly at the snarling dog.

"Control your dog!" the woman huffs.

"Sorry. Very sorry, Madame." I grab Chou Chou's collar. She stomps off. Chou Chou radiates heat under his collar. He tugs me around the courtyard enthusiastically, giving the pizzeria and wineshop thorough sniffs. When he looks up again, he whines and yelps in the direction the cat fled. *Come back and play!*

His yelp rings in my ears, but it's déjà vu that has me off balance.

"Say that again?" I ask Chou Chou. "Where's your friend? Where's the pretty *minou*?" He sits and whines, pouty.

I don't need him to bark again. I hear the pitch in my memory. That night—the night Keiko led me through the village in the dark—her ears were filled with Wagner. Despite her friends' best misguided efforts, she couldn't recall any audio clue. But I can. I'd heard the single sharp bark of a dog. I'd also imagined myself riding back in time, as if I could practically hear the scrape of wooden carts over cobbles. Maybe I did hear a cart, an antique loaded down with a body.

"Were you here?" I ask Chou Chou. His tongue lops out. He's looking around the courtyard for more fun. "Did you follow your next-door dad? Did you chase the cat?"

He could have slipped out on his own.

Or he could have come with Pierre-Luc. But Pierre-Luc was Eddie's friend. Am I reading too much into the bark of a dog at midnight?

CHAPTER 33

Tour-guide tidbit: Did you know, France was the first country to create an official dog registration system? In 1885, the Société Centrale Canine was established to maintain records of dog breeds and promote responsible breeding practices.

By the time Chou Chou and I return to the château, I am both sweatier and more uncertain than when I set out.

Chou Chou has no hesitation. He bounds up his drive and disappears around the back of the stately home. I follow, rounding the wing where just last night, Benji and Maurice riled up Pépere about Eddie.

Chou Chou woofs twice, back to his baritone.

"Ahoy!" responds a voice and the equally gravelly sound of digging.

Just the man I want to talk to. "*Bonjour*," I call to Pépère. I up my greeting to a yell when he fails to hear me the first time.

He frowns a greeting and touches his ear. The shrill screech of his hearing aid deepens his frown and my hesitation.

"What are you digging for?" I ask.

He scoffs. "You'd like to know, wouldn't you?"

I would, but there's something else I want to know more. "Can you hear Chou Chou from your house?" I ask. "When he barks, I mean?"

Another snort. He's looking particularly gnomish in green coveralls and a beret. He aims a sharp-bladed shovel at the ground and grunts with the effort. "You think I'm deaf?" He winces as the shovel clangs against rock.

"No, no," I soothe. "I was asking because I'm sure you can hear Chou Chou. He can be, ah . . . vocal."

"Nuisance, that's what he is. That's why we get along." The old man grins and hands Chou Chou something from his many pockets.

The treat is inhaled immediately, but I recognize the wrapper of a Rose Petal shortbread.

"He likes those cookies," I say. "Do you?"

Thwack! Pépère aims the shovel again. He adjusts his cap and gives me that impish grin. "*Aucun rapport avec la choucroute?*"

I roll the words around in my head, first in French, then in English. *No relation to sauerkraut?* Then I grin back. I came across this idiom during my cabbage research. It's the French equivalent of *What's that have to do with the price of tea?*

"No reason," I say.

At that, Pépère declares he can't stand shortbreads. "Too sweet. That's why the beast here gets them." Man and dog grin.

I try again. "Do you remember if Chou Chou barked the night Eddie's body was found in the village?" I remind him of the date, day of the week, and approximate time.

Pépère mutters about cabbages and continues to hack at the stubbly grass. Pierre-Luc's would-be lawn looks like the victim of an unfocused groundhog. Little holes everywhere. "*Pourquoi?*" he eventually asks.

Why indeed? Because Pierre-Luc said he was awoken by Chou Chou's bark around the time Keiko returned to wake me.

"I thought that if anyone would hear, it would be you," I say. *Unless he removes those hearing aids for the night.* I wonder if there's a French saying for barking up the wrong tree.

"*Bof,*" he says with exaggerated indifference.

I'm beginning to regret that I raced over here. I should have gone for a restorative, mind-focusing croissant.

"Heard you last night, didn't I?" Pépère addresses the dog. "Your *ouaf, ouaf.*" He ruffles Chou Chou's head.

"What time was that?" I ask, expecting a belligerent shrug.

I get the shrug, but also precision. "Three twenty-five. I wake twice in the night. That's how we're made to sleep, that's how our ancestors did it in the medieval times. I'm early to bed and up around midnight. I walk about to the village or get some exercise with the old shovel. Then back to sleep and up again with the birds."

He resumes digging.

"Did you see anyone else out here last night?" I ask.

He cackles. "Who would I see? The thief?" He gives the earth a mighty whack at the thought.

I back up, leaving him to his shovelings, tallying what I've learned. Pépère is strong. He's up and about at night. He has no fondness for art thieves or his unofficial son-in-law. Chou Chou barked around half-past three. Maurice and Benji may have left the goat farm around half-past two. They could have cycled here, gathered their courage—their foolhardiness—and then broken in. Did they break back out?

When I reach the front of the grand manor, I stop by the burbling fountain and dial Laurent's number. He won't laugh that I'm pondering dog barks, will he? His line rings—

once, twice . . . Pépère's shovel thunks and scrapes in the background, but there's another sound too, a pounding, closer but muffled.

Laurent's voicemail kicks in. "It's Sadie," I say, distracted by the sound. "Call me when you get this?"

The banging isn't reverberation from Pépère's shovel. I press an ear to the glass doors of the tasting room. I do the same at the salon and windows in between. *It's like it's coming from below* . . . Feeling rather foolish and hoping no one's looking, I kneel down and put my ear to the ground. *Thunk, thunk, clank*. The notorious plumbing?

I scramble up and jog around the back. Pépère and Chou Chou are sharing another packet of Rose Petal shortbreads. Pépère tosses his cookie to the dog. I could care less that he's fibbed about his sweet tooth.

"How did Chou Chou get out?" I ask. I hold up a preemptive hand. "I know, what's that have to do with the price of cabbages?"

Pépère laughs at that. "He asked, so I let him out. Spare key's under that rock. Or is it that one? One of those . . . I put it back somewhere." He points to a patch of large river rocks ringing a copper drainpipe. "Country folk. We're too trusting. Except for me!" He waves the shovel.

"Is there a basement here?" I ask.

The smile widens, creasing his wrinkles. "A basement? *Oui, Madame*. And tunnels! *Ooh là là*, the tunnels. Have I not told you?"

I know I could seriously regret this. Pépère is a prime suspect, to my mind. He's also handily pre-armed with that shovel.

"Can you show me?" I ask.

Here are some questions I've never faced as a guide or, for that matter, ever: Should I call the police while I'm actively breaking into a château? Is it okay to break in if my riders might be inside and in danger? Is it really breaking and entering if I walk in with the resident dog and next-door neighbor who knows where Pierre-Luc keeps his spare key? Pépère did not, however, remember where he'd re-stashed the key after freeing Chou Chou. In the long minutes we spent looking under rocks, I hoped Laurent would call and talk me down.

He didn't. I dial his number again as Pépère thumps down the hallway. He's left the shovel behind and replaced it with one of Greta's hefty walking sticks. A small forest of them stood in an umbrella rack by the backdoor.

This time, I pay more attention to the paintings on Pierre-Luc's walls. They're landscapes and still lifes, the type of art that was stolen. But a lot of people like landscapes and still lifes, I assure myself.

When Laurent's line goes to voicemail, I leave another message. "I'm at Pierre-Luc's. Call me when you can?" Best not to record that I'm breaking and entering.

"Lost," Pépère mutters and reverses course. A few wrong turns and grumbles later, we're in what appears to be an old kitchen. There's a long porcelain sink and an inglenook fireplace blackened from centuries of fires and roasts.

"*Et voilà!*" Pépère swings open a slender door I'd have taken for the entrance to a pantry or broom closet. Narrow steps disappear into darkness. Pépère waves his stick. "Madame, you go first."

That's my cue. My cue to say no way! I will *not* traipse into dark cellars making banging sounds.

Frantic banging sounds. Someone-could-be-in-dire-trouble banging sounds.

"Hello?" I yell toward the abyss. "Maurice? Benji?"

Chou Chou responds in happy barks. Chills rise up my neck. Two barks. Greta said that Chou Chou has special barks for individuals and situations. I've heard him bark twice. That's how he greets his favorite person.

I whip around, ready to chide my overactive imagination. *Silly me! Imagining sounds, picturing—*

I was picturing Pierre-Luc, but he's no figment of my imagination. He stands at the door to the kitchen, his face flushed, his hair mussed. He holds a rifle. I hadn't pictured that.

"I wish you hadn't done this, Sadie," he says.

That makes two of us.

CHAPTER 34

Thursday:
Free time ideas: Why not take a spin and count castles? Just remember, there may be more to châteaux than you see in the sky. Some include underground passageways added as escape routes, storage areas, and defensive features. Keep your eyes on the ground for secrets!

Pierre-Luc makes Pépère leave his walking stick behind. Handily, there's a railing to the underground domain. If insurance adjustors stop by, they'll be pleased with this safety feature. They won't approve of Pierre-Luc's hunting rifle, nudging my back when I fail to keep up with Pépère's sprightly descent.

Back in the kitchen, Pierre-Luc told us that his "old man" left him the gun. "Never had a use for it. I find no enjoyment in blasting pheasants or wild boar. Or people."

I hope he won't use it now, but I don't like the route we're taking.

"You're supposed to be in Colmar," I say, extending a foot down into the darkness. The stairs seem uneven, but that could be my wobbly nerves. "Didn't you have a meeting?" With every step, the air feels cooler, older, like it's been trapped for centuries. Up in the kitchen, Chou Chou has given up whining at the closed door.

A soft chuckle from behind me. "We were having a fascinating discussion on biodynamic techniques when my security system alerted me to intruders on my property."

"Invaders!" Pépère declares.

"Yes, a digger in my back garden," Pierre-Luc says. "That did not concern me as much as a nosy cycling guide. I decided I should leave my meeting early. I'm glad I did and that I installed motion-detecting cameras above all of my entrances. One can't be too careful these days."

"With that art thief in the area?" I ask, allowing sarcasm into my tone. A spiderweb brushes my cheek. I fight a serious freak-out urge on multiple fronts.

Another chuckle. "Ah, yes, because of the art thief. That is exactly why I require security."

Because he's the art thief! The gun nudges me, which I take as confirmation of my silent deduction.

Pépère has reached the base, a pool of darkness. Pierre-Luc motions us to step back. He tugs a string, and a single bulb illuminates the shadows. I make out bike wheels and frames. If I had a cellar, I'd keep bikes in it. In my dreams, the basement would also have a wall of wine racks filled with dusty bottled treasures, like I see at the dim reaches of the illumination. In my nightmares, there would be a door to a tunnel with a low arched ceiling in stone and crumbling plaster.

Pierre-Luc directs us down such a passageway, griping about the grit underfoot.

"Those police," he says. "They shouldn't have parked where they did, but what could I say? I really must reroute the drive or reinforce these basements. I can't very well hire the average handyman or gardener, though, can I? Would cost a fortune, too . . ."

Ah, the trouble of finding handymen. I can relate! Keeping tunnels and crimes secret? Not so much.

The tunnel leads to two more doors, each solid wood with too many locks to be protecting jars of sauerkraut and jam.

"Do not try anything," Pierre-Luc says, rattling keys as he approaches a door. Locks clonk and creak. A scuffling sound comes from within, too big to be scurrying mice.

"Time to join your friends," Pierre-Luc says. To his credit, he sounds half-hearted, almost weary about imprisoning us in his basement dungeon.

"No friends of mine," Pépère grumbles.

"Wait," I say, desperately stalling for time. Time for Laurent to listen to my messages and, what? Race over here to find no one home but Chou Chou, who's probably wandered off to chew on a chair leg? "Why did you kill Eddie? He was your friend."

"My friend?" Pierre-Luc scoffs. "A friend would not betray in such a way."

Good friends don't kill each other, either.

"Eddie betrayed *you*?" I ask Pierre-Luc. *Keep him talking*. "Rosemary and Gabi would understand that."

Both men huff indignantly.

"He used us," Pierre-Luc says. "All of us," he says, generously including Pépère. "He wanted the lifestyle without any of the work. Sadie, you work hard for your passion. You would not have put up with him."

Yet more commonalities, except for me never killing anyone.

"You even lent him money," I say.

"Lent?" Pierre-Luc spits the word. "*Le chantage.*" When he guesses this is vocabulary I haven't learned in school or everyday life, he helpfully translates. "In English, you say 'blackmail'? Eddie discovered my passion, my collecting."

"You like art," I say. "That's a worthy passion."

He sniffs. "Yes, why shouldn't I have beauty? How is my approach different from that of a wealthy man who buys more than he needs and hides it away, unloved? Or museums with troves never allowed to be seen?"

In a way, I get his point. "So Eddie blackmailed you," I say, prompting him. I might as well have the satisfaction of knowing what happened.

"He wanted *my* money to hide his troubles." Pierre-Luc's voice rises, echoing on the stones. "His gambling losses, his secret."

"He told you his secret?" I ask. "About changing his identity?" That clears up one mystery. Eddie didn't have amnesia.

Pierre-Luc scoffs. "*Oui,* he bragged. He knew I could tell no one. He had luck more than cleverness. Luck no one saw him leave his things on that beach and run away. Luck that he had a common face that went unrecognized."

"Why?" I ask. "Why didn't he just get a divorce?" I really want to know. The next room has gone silent. Benji and Maurice must be listening hard too.

Pierre-Luc sounds disgusted. "He wanted a clean break, a fresh start. He wanted to be someone else. He could not be that as boring Edwin Perch. He rationalized that his wife had her shortbread business, that she cashed in his life insurance, that his sons have grown up to be fine men. Now that I have met Rosemary, I say this even more strenuously: he was a coward! You know what is most offensive?"

Murder?

Pierre-Luc continues. "Eddie said that he and I were similar. We are cunning, he said. Men of action. Men who take control of our paths. Ridiculous!"

Pépère snorts. "I knew he was trouble. I sniffed out his type."

Pierre-Luc is back to himself. "I host artists. I promote art. I am a champion of art."

"May we see your collection?" I ask. I sense a hard "no" but barrel on anyway. "As a tour guide, I'd really love to see something so special, so rare. Right, Pépère?"

"Treasures," the old man says with a gnomish twinkle. "I've been looking for treasures my whole life. Only found that one Napoleonic coin."

Pierre-Luc shrugs. "Why not? Why not see something beautiful before, well . . ."

I shiver. Pépère elbows me and nods.

"Was Edwin—Eddie—going to run away again?" I ask. "He had cash and jewelry with him."

Pierre-Luc scoffs and stretches his hand into the darkness above a sagging beam. I shudder, imagining spiders. He jangles a rusty ring of keys. "Eddie thought he'd been found out by his wife and her friends. He was frantic. I told him it is time for you to leave. Leave before Gabi kicks you out. He wanted a new life anyway. An easy life in the sun, maybe Provence or Spain . . . He 'asked' me for money. I was compelled to give it to him, but then I took him to the station, telling myself we were done."

"But he came back," I say.

"He came back," Pierre-Luc repeats darkly. "He said he needed more. I could sell a painting, he said. Or two or three or more paintings. I would never have been free of him!"

Pépère elbows my ribs, sharper this time, and winks.

"Surprised you pulled it off," Pépère says. "Surprised you didn't get caught stealing those paintings."

"That was easy enough," Pierre-Luc says. "I'm invited many places. I merely invite myself back. I have found my talent, my passion. Do you know, a few of my 'sources' haven't even noticed their masterpieces are missing? That is the real crime."

Pépère addresses me. "Don't let him fool you. He doesn't have a *talent*. Not like his father. That man knew how to win. He won the bike races. Won all the wine awards. A real treasure, he was. A winner."

I wince. Berating a proud criminal holding a gun is not the strategy I'd choose.

"Bet you didn't steal anything that good," Pépère continues with his signature cackle. "Is that why you hide your collection down here in the dust. Can't be worth much. Look at the state of that rusty old lock."

This elicits a soft snort from Pierre-Luc. "You're fooled and foolish, I see," he says, inserting a key. The lock groans. Hinges whine. Lights flick on and I gasp.

Far from a dusty root cellar, the space is gorgeous. Museum-style lamps illuminate gilt-framed paintings. Armchairs with fine leather cushions are positioned to gaze at luminous landscapes, still lifes, and a knight fighting a dragon. Pierre-Luc "stole" his own dragon painting! That's one way to throw off any suspicion.

"Paintings of grapes," Pépère scoffs, nudging me again. "Boring! What's that one? A vase? I could paint a vase."

"That one?" Pierre-Luc says. "Why that is a—"

With a grunt, Pépère shoves him. Pierre-Luc stumbles inside. Cackling, Pépère slams the door, which would be a great idea except we don't have the keys to secure the locks. We press ourselves to the door. Pierre-Luc is strong and shoving. Our feet are slipping, and Pierre-Luc still has the gun. He could shoot a hole right through that door. And us.

I shoot a desperate glance at Pépère. He's grinning wildly. "Go," he croaks. "Run."

Pépère can't hold the door alone, but hopefully, it'll take Pierre-Luc a few seconds to realize that.

I run. Dust falls like gritty snow as I dash through the tunnel. A door bangs. A rough, old voice yells. Footsteps pound after me. I take the stairs two at a time and burst into the kitchen, where Chou Chou is napping in the hearth. He runs to me, giddy. I push past his leaping paws and rush for the hallway. Chou Chou doesn't follow. He barks twice. Fear urges me on.

Behind me, I can hear Pierre-Luc scolding his dog.

"Get away, Chou Chou. This is no game!"

It's not. Pierre-Luc's footsteps pound closer, closer . . .

I'm too scared to remember directions. When I spot the front entry, my heart leaps. I've made it! My palms slap against the massive door, but when I twist the knob, it won't budge. A deadbolt, missing its key, holds the door firm.

"Sadie!" Pierre-Luc bellows. "Stop!"

Which way to the salon, the back door? Then I remember Scarlett's approach to "visiting." If she can break in through a window, I can break out by one. I fumble to unhook an old-fashioned latch and swing the window in toward me. There's no screen, thank goodness, and the shutters are open to a beautiful sight.

A Renault with a throaty muffler speeds up the drive and swings into the no-parking zone. Laurent leaps out. I climb through the window and sprint for him. From the driver's seat, Serge gives me two thumbs up.

"It's Pierre-Luc! He has a gun!" I cry. "Take cover!"

Laurent throws himself in front of me. *Reckless man!* Serge revs the engine, as if he's ready to run my attacker over.

"No bullets," a leaden voice says behind me. Pierre-Luc drops the rifle and jerks his chin at Serge. "You shouldn't park there."

CHAPTER 35

Thursday:
Cycling burns a lot of energy! Let's enjoy some well-earned rest and recovery time.

Later that evening, we sit in Gabi's kitchen. Her distant relative glares from her frame on the mantel, but the table is filled with the smiles of friends reunited.

Keiko sips restorative mineral water, which Scarlett keeps topping up. The doctors okayed Keiko's release. Her vertigo and wooziness are mostly gone. Memories of her whack on the head have completely fled, which seems like a good thing to me. Why remember a desperate art "collector" aiming a potted plant at your skull?

Lionel has been released too. He and Rosemary remind me of a three-legged race modified for dining. They're pressed side by side, inner hands linked, outer hands raising glasses. It hasn't been all hugs and kisses. Rosemary met Lionel at the police station and promptly chewed him out for thinking she could be a murderer.

"But you can be *anything* you set your mind to," Lionel had said. "You're the most talented and focused woman I've ever met."

Smooth, Lionel. Fast thinking. Even Scarlett agreed.

To my right, Pépère sneaks treats to Chou Chou: bites of crispy *tarte flambée* crust and salty-sweet cured ham wrapped around cubes of melon. To soothe the dog's guilt at ratting out his killer dad, Pépère says. Chou Chou's love of cats triggered my memory of his bark at the scene of a crime.

At the end of the table, Jordi and Nadiya toast to life and a gift from Gabi. Gabi is gifting them a posh room at the inn tonight. Jordi admitted that he would enjoy someone else's breakfast cooking.

And then, the kings of the table, tellers of the greatest adventure the Silver Spinners have had yet: Maurice and Benji.

"I could still throttle them," I whisper to Laurent, who sits to my other side. "So reckless!"

He raises an eyebrow and refills my wine before passing the bottle to Serge. The group awarded Serge honorary Silver Spinner status for speeding Laurent to the scene and for rushing to the basement to free Maurice and Benji, following the sound of Pépère's bellows. On his way, Serge found the rusty ring of keys that Pierre-Luc had dropped in his panic to stop me.

"We were chained in the dungeons!" Benji recounts, thrilled. "That château looks nice, but the foundations are rotten!" This is about the dozenth retelling, not that I'm counting. If you get imprisoned in a dungeon while cycle touring and snooping for stolen art, you can retell the story all you want.

"Once we'd twisted around to loosen our chains, we banged on the piping," Maurice says. "You have keen ears, Sadie." He raises his glass to me. "Smart thinking! Bold to race into danger."

The soft snort beside me suggests that Laurent thinks otherwise. As he well knows, I did call him twice. He'd been in a meeting with Annette and the departmental bigwigs. Annette had been laying out her case for Maurice and Benji being part of an international gang of elderly art thieves, who—during said nefarious robberies—had identified Eddie Ainsworth as Edwin Perch and devised a plot to kill him, each confessing to throw suspicion off the others.

Upon getting my messages, Laurent called me back repeatedly. When I didn't answer, he summoned Serge, who'd been driving around Colmar hoping to find Maurice and Benji.

Scarlett tuts. "What about our all-for-one motto, boys? Why didn't you tell the rest of us what you were up to, *mmmm*?"

Maurice looks appropriately contrite.

Benji waves a toothpick of cantaloupe and ham. "Yes, we know, we were naughty, but we needed to be sure."

Scarlett catches my eye. I raise my glass a twitch, acknowledging that she was right. Benji had indeed gone snooping in the château the night before, when he was supposedly looking for the loo. Behind Pierre-Luc's bedroom door, he'd spotted a painting that he and Maurice were 95.5 percent sure was one of the stolen works.

They're again recounting their ride from the goat farm.

"We kept our lights off the entire way," Benji says. "It was thrilling!"

That's not the part that boggles my mind. "You thought you could break into not only his house but also his *bedroom*? With him and his dog inside?"

"Maurice is a Marine," Benji coos, patting his partner's hand. "Besides, we unlatched his back window before we left the party last night."

"Premeditated crime," Laurent murmurs.

"Absolutely!" Benji agrees.

"But his bedroom," I persist. "You must have been pretty sure he was a sound sleeper."

Simultaneously, Laurent and Maurice correct me. Pierre-Luc was out for the night.

"We heard him making plans to stay with Céline, the hungry artist," Maurice explains. "It was our one opportunity. We thought, Why not?"

"Or . . ." Laurent says. "Why not call your friendly gendarme?"

This earns him a group *pah!* Even Chou Chou joins in. Laurent feigns insult.

"We would have been fine except for those pesky security cameras," Benji says. Alerted by his security system, Pierre-Luc had fled Céline's loft and raced home to catch the snoops in the act. If need be, Céline would have been his alibi. She was already prepared to cover for him the night he'd slipped from his own party and whapped Keiko on the head. Like Eddie, Céline had seen Pierre-Luc's home and lifestyle and assumed he was her key to the good life.

"The police!" Scarlett scoffs. "Calling the police would have tipped Pierre-Luc off. Roll boldly, that's the Silver Spinners' motto."

I turn to Laurent. "Has Pierre-Luc said anything more?"

Laurent raises a shoulder, as if it's heavy with the weight of the world and criminals."He is adamant that he didn't *want* to kill Eddie. Like Pierre-Luc told you, Sadie, he was scared he'd never be rid of his former friend."

Rosemary shakes her head. "Everyone thought I did it for the opposite reason—because Edwin left me."

Gabi admits that she thought that.

Rosemary waves off her fellow widow's apology. "I suspected the same of you, Gabi."

Laurent nods. "Eddie caught his mate Pierre-Luc lifting a painting on one of their outings, some big house where the owner apparently failed to appreciate the family art hoard. Eddie saw a chance to share his secret, to 'unburden' himself to his pal. Maybe to brag. But, as time went on, he saw a way to pay off debts without going to the bank, which would have been risky, given his background."

I think of something Céline had said. She hadn't seen Eddie around as much. Blackmail will break up a friendship.

Lionel squeezes Rosemary's hand. "You're finally free of him."

Lionel really did make a good suspect, I think. They all did.

Serge leans back in his seat, seemingly to stretch. He catches my eye and waggles his brows. Guessing he's thinking the same thing, I smile and shake my head no. He makes a *shhh* gesture, as if we're in on a secret.

Laurent leans back too, but he's deep into his story. "Pierre-Luc took Eddie to the train station, praying he'd never see him again. Then, Eddie returned. I think Eddie wanted to see if he had been recognized by anyone from his past life. Down deep, I think he wanted to stay."

He pauses and looks around the table. "Did any of you know he was here?"

The Silver Spinners shake their heads in unified denial.

"If we'd known . . . ," Maurice says ominously.

"Indeed!" Scarlett proclaims, miming throttling again.

"I truly did find that brochure in my spare room," says Rosemary. "I didn't think anything of it, really. Edwin would send away for brochures. He was a dreamer."

"Schemer," Benji mutters.

Laurent continues. "Eddie summoned Pierre-Luc to the vacation apartment he'd rented. Eddie proposed to go to Pierre-Luc's and pick out a painting to sell. It was almost midnight. No one would see them. Pierre-Luc was enraged. He grabbed an antique hammer from the wall of the rental, stormed after his former friend, and . . ."

Even Scarlett shivers at the thought. She recovers quickly. "Pierre-Luc hid the body in his own wine barrel? That's either incredibly brave or foolish."

Laurent smiles. "In a way, it was the perfect hiding place. It would have been easy to roll the cart downhill from the crime scene and not far to push on to the safety of his own barrel. A barrel, I'll note, that no one had cracked open for at least four decades."

"My bad," murmurs Maurice.

"Your good," Benji counters.

Laurent continues. "Pierre-Luc wouldn't say, but I imagine that barrel was a temporary holding place until he could find a better solution. His most important goal was hiding the body. If the corpse was never found, it would look like Edwin had run away again. There wouldn't even be a murder investigation, merely more mystery surrounding a disappearing man. It was Pierre-Luc's bad luck that you chose to visit him that morning."

Scarlett tuts. "I was drawn to him. I am drawn to dangerous men, what can I say?"

"Like your Sir Rupert, breaker of hearts." Benji chuckles.

"To Rupy." Scarlett raises a glass. "Gone to a better place!"

Okay, I have to ask. "Sir Rupert," I say. "Where is he?"

Looks flash around the table, sly and twinkling.

Scarlett deftly changes the subject to murder. "Pierre-Luc's first problem was when our Keiko sleep-cycled into his crime." She squeezes her friend's hand.

Keiko yanks it away. "I was not asleep. I *like* to cycle at night." She looks around, defying anyone to question this. "I was listening to Wagner. It was blissful. Then that cat ran in front of me and I had to swerve in a different direction. I didn't see or hear whatever he thought I did."

"Chou Chou," I say, and the dog's ears point. He's staying with Gabi until a better home can be found. "He was with Pierre-Luc. He has a certain yip just for cats. I heard it later that night." Chou Chou's stubby tail wags.

Laurent rubs his chin pensively, imagining the scene. "Pierre-Luc didn't have time to hide Eddie's body when he heard you coming, Keiko. He hid himself and Chou Chou in the rental apartment. When you cycled off, he saw his chance. He emptied the cart of flowerpots and hauled in the body. He said he'd made it across the courtyard when he heard cyclists returning. He'd left the door to the rental unlocked. He managed to haul the cart and Chou Chou back inside just in time."

I shudder. What would have happened if Keiko or I had taken a different turn?

"So Pierre-Luc left the shortbread crumbs to set us up?" Lionel asks. "Devious!"

Laurent shakes his head. "Those crumbs apparently came from the victim's own pockets. He had access to travel packets both at the inn and his home."

Rosemary touches her heart. "He took them for his travels. He did feel fondly for my shortbreads."

Lionel harumphs. "He ran away from all that was good in his life and let fine shortbread crumble in his pocket."

Rosemary squeezes his hand.

Keiko touches her bandaged head. "Meanwhile, I missed all the clues and ended up with stitches." She raises her glass to me. "Good show, Sadie. For the record, I wouldn't have gone near that basement."

I admit that I was about to retreat and run for help. "If Laurent and Serge hadn't shown up, Pierre-Luc would have caught me and then . . ."

"Then we would have broken out and all rescued each other," Maurice says.

"Any moment, surely," Benji says with a strained chuckle. "We would have Houdini-ed those chains."

But the group isn't laughing this time.

"The police thought you boys had run off," Scarlett says, breaking the somber mood. "Pierre-Luc left your bikes at the train station and pretended you'd stolen that painting. You would have forever been infamous criminals on the run."

"Might have been a good way to go out," Maurice says. "We'd have a legacy."

"We should buy that painting," Benji says. "I wonder if Céline will still offer a discount? She needs new patrons."

Keiko rolls her eyes, then holds her head. "Paintings. Why would Pierre-Luc risk so much for old paint on canvas?"

Serge, who has been listening with interest, chimes in. "I know why. I know his type. He has a rich-man's attitude, but he is not so rich, so he takes what he wants."

"He was obsessed," Scarlett muses. "It happens to the best of us. Like you and that opera, Kei-Kei."

Keiko seizes the moment and reminds her friends that they owe her big-time. "You can help me with the stage props and refreshments."

"Take me back to the dungeon!" Benji groans.

More wine is passed. We skip a main meal and roll straight to the cheese course and dessert.

"Here's the most important question," Scarlett says. She holds a dramatic pause. I try to guess the most pressing mystery. *What will happen to Chou Chou? Will Gabi find the money Eddie hid away? What did Pierre-Luc plan to do with four hostages?* I shudder again.

"Tomorrow," Scarlett says, startling me from thoughts of tunnels, cold as graves. "Where do we cycle tomorrow, Sadie? Spontaneity is well and good, but our itinerary is a wreck."

All eyes fall on me.

I pause, but only to match Scarlett's suspense. I know exactly where we'll go.

"Cabbage," I announce. "Tomorrow is our promised tour of sauerkraut."

Laughter and clinking glasses tell me we're finally in for some fun.

Cyclist's Log

Home sweet, leaky-roofed home! I'm so glad to be back in Sans-Souci! The Silver Spinners headed back to England yesterday. It was a tour they'll never forget, they assured me at the Strasbourg station. Helena was traveling with them. If they got into trouble on the train, at least they had legal representation.

We arrived at the station early, so you know what? I gave them my talk about the station's history and architecture. Ha! Even Maurice politely listened.

As the train doors were sliding shut, Scarlett called out: "Let's do it again!"

No, thank you!

No, that's not true. I'd love to see them again. If I do, I'll watch them every second!

Bea and Bernard will return home in a few days. Lionel finally told them what happened, but I think he must have left out a few arrests and assaults.

Alsace sounds exciting, Bea texted me.

That's for sure. Laurent and Helena convinced Chief Dubois to drop all charges against my riders. The Silver Spinners bordered on ungrateful—as if they actually wanted records for false confessions, trespass, and hindering police investigations. In exchange, Annette gets the full glory for cracking not one but two major cases. She'll be moving up the ranks.

Annette loves a win, regardless of whether she's right, Laurent said. That's the main reason they're not still together. Again, he didn't elaborate, and I didn't press.

How about more good news?

Chou Chou is living on the goat farm. He adores goats. Better yet, they love him back. Jordi is envious. The dog will live in paradise, he said.

Yes, paradise is in the eye of the beholder. Which brings me to Sir Rupert, AKA "Dear, dear Rupy, gone to the fires below." He's alive! Sir Rupert Thorne is on holiday. Specifically, at a posh villa somewhere on the Costa del Sol in southern Spain. He lies on a beach all day and roasts! Like beef, Benji told me with a just-between-us conspiratorial giggle. A proper Sunday roast.

Scarlett cannot abide by lying around in the heat, so they take separate holidays. "Their little secret for not killing each other. Yet." Again, Benji's words.

And now, my favorite: I'm planning a vacation for two. Laurent and I will return to Riquewihr in the fall. We're thinking late September or early October, when the vineyards will be golden. Woodsmoke in the air, mulled wine, cool weather for enjoying sauerkraut casseroles and baked goods . . .

Won't that be lovely?

I hope so. Pedal away from regrets is still a fine motto, but pedal toward joy is even better. I want happy memories to override the bad.

If it works out, we might come home with more than memories. Mamma Calico had her kittens! Gabi has taken in Mamma and promises to hold a kitten for Laurent and me. I know—co-parenting a kitten is a huge relationship step, way bigger than camping. But not as big as murder investigations, and surely loads more fun. Bea and Bernard will help. They're right next door to me and have a senior Siamese who adores little ones.

There are two tabbies, an orange-and-cream, and a tiny calico girl. I have my eye on the calico.

You know how calicos are, Keiko told me that night in the courtyard missing its corpse. Yep, I sure do. Calicos are excellent guides to solving crimes.

Recipe

Sadie's *tarte flambée*

*T*ARTE FLAMBÉE*, or* **flammekueche,** *is a traditional dish from Alsace, similar to a thin-crust pizza and topped with* **crème fraîche,** *onions, and lardons or bacon. If you're dining in Alsace, the dough may be cracker-crisp and made with no yeast. Sadie, however, enjoys a puffier pizza-style crust. She also can't resist adding cheese. For a tasty vegetarian version replace the lardons with mushrooms.*

Ingredients:

For the dough:

- 2 cups all-purpose flour
- ⅔ cup warm water
- 1 tablespoon olive oil
- 1 teaspoon kosher salt
- 1 teaspoon sugar
- ½ teaspoon dry yeast

For the topping:

- ¾ cup *crème fraîche* (see note below)
- 1 large white or yellow onion, thinly sliced
- Approximately 7 oz. lardons or bacon, diced or cut into small strips
- Salt and pepper to taste
- A pinch of nutmeg (optional but tasty)
- ¼–½ cup grated Gruyère cheese, other pizza cheese, or

rounds of goat cheese (optional, although Sadie would say there's no question and she would probably add even more)
- Fresh chives, parsley, or basil for garnish (optional)

Instructions:

1. Prepare the dough:

In a largish bowl, mix the flour, salt, and sugar. Dissolve the yeast in warm water and let sit for a few minutes until bubbly.

Add the yeast mixture and the olive oil to the dry ingredients. Mix until a dough forms.

Knead the dough on a floured surface for about 7–10 minutes, until smooth and elastic. You can also knead in a food processor or mixer, according to their dough instructions.

Place the dough in a lightly oiled bowl, cover with a damp cloth or plastic wrap, and let rise in a warm spot until doubled. A microwave with a mug of steaming hot water inside makes a great proofing box.

2. Prepare the toppings:

Slice the onion as thinly as possible.

In a skillet, cook the lardons or bacon until crispy. Drain on paper towels.

Add the *crème fraîche* to a mixing bowl. Season with salt, pepper, and a pinch of nutmeg, if desired. Stir in the onions.

3. Assemble the *tarte flambée*:

Preheat your oven to its highest setting (around 500°F if possible). If you have a pizza stone, place it in the oven to heat up for at least half an hour.

Stretch the dough very thinly on a floured surface.

Transfer the dough to a pizza peel (if using a pizza stone) or to your pizza pan.
Spread the *crème fraîche* and onion mixture evenly over the dough, leaving a small border around the edges.
Scatter the cooked lardons or bacon on top.
Add cheese if using.

4. Bake:
Bake in the preheated oven for 10–15 minutes, or until the crust is golden and crispy and the onions and cheese are lightly browned.
If using a pizza stone, your *tarte flambée* may cook faster, so keep an eye on it.

5. Serve:
Remove from the oven, garnish with herbs if desired, and serve immediately. *Bon appétit!*

Note: If you can't find crème fraîche, sour cream (regular or full-fat) will work in a pinch. With a bit of googling, you could also experiment with making your own crème fraîche with the simple ingredients of cream, buttermilk, and time.

Acknowledgments

What fun I've had rolling through France with Sadie and her crew! This series began with real-life cycle touring. My editor, Wendy McCurdy, was pedaling through the green hills of Vermont when the idea for rolling mysteries sparked. She and the leader of her tour, Bill Reuther, began hatching plots, and I'm honored that Wendy invited me to come along on the fictional adventure.

Though I've yet to experience one of Bill's Discovery Bicycle Tours firsthand, I've had the pleasure of riding along vicariously. Bill has called me from the road to share his expertise and tales that feel plucked from fiction. Thank you, Bill! Some of those stories are destined to appear in the third book's bachelorette shenanigans.

Heartfelt thanks to my incredible agent, Christina Hogrebe. Thank you for connecting me with Wendy and the amazing team at Kensington. What a ride we've been on through cozy mysteries, from a Santa Fe café, to a bookmobile in Georgia and a bookshop in the Colorado mountains, and now spinning through France.

Speaking of France, I owe so much to my Franco-American family. To my husband, Eric: thank you for our travels and for the study-abroad chaperoning trip that opened my eyes to the potential terrors (and joys!) of tour guiding. To my wonderful parents-in-law: your dual-nationality love story is a constant source of inspiration.

All my love to my side of the family too. I'm beyond lucky to have parents and aunts who cheer on my storytelling. Special thanks to Jane and Carol for their eagle-eyed proofreading and plot suggestions. Any lingering mistakes are, of course, my own. I hope I've caught them all this time—missing a big one is a former copy editor's greatest agony!

I don't know if I would have dared to publish—or known where to begin—without Sisters in Crime. I'm especially grateful to my local Colorado chapter and friends I've made through our shared love of mysteries. I deeply miss Laura DiSilverio and our plotting teas and talks. We lost a brilliant writer and a cherished soul far too soon.

Most of all, thank you to readers, librarians, booksellers, and fellow bibliophiles. There are countless books to read and places to travel, both on pages and in life. I'm honored and humbled that you've chosen to ride along on Sadie's tours.

Don't miss the next head-spinning Cyclist's Guide mystery,

A CYCLIST'S GUIDE TO POPPIES & PREDICAMENTS

by Ann Claire

Springtime in Provence brings flower-filled meadows, sun-drenched coastlines—and a bachelorette cycling tour that guide Sadie Greene hopes to pull off without a hitch. However, the ride takes a deadly detour when a killer crashes the party.

Sadie Greene has broken her streak—her crime streak, that is. For months, her bicycle tours through France have been blissfully uneventful, marred only by the occasional punctured tire or crushed croissant. Thus, when Sadie takes on a last-minute booking for a bridal party, she expects love, laughter, and champagne toasts. But more than prewedding jitters come along for the ride.

A bossy bride, rowdy party games, and a tagalong stranger threaten to turn Sadie's carefully planned itinerary into a tour de farce. She can shift gears to keep the bride happy, but she can't please everyone. A road rager targets the group. So does a killer. To add to Sadie's horror, the murder victim is found wearing the bride's tiara.

While the police dig into the victim's past, Sadie suspects a deadly case of mistaken identity. Fearing the real target may still be on her tour, Sadie once again says "I do" to a murder investigation. As her suspect list spins out of control, Sadie uncovers secrets and motives that could shatter the bridal party. Love, life, and liberty are on the line as Sadie races to unmask a killer before the wedding turns into a wake.